DIVICA
STORMBORN CHRONICLES
II

STORMVEIL

STARR Z. DAVIES

First published in the United States in 2025 by Character Assassin Books an imprint of Starr Z Davies, 1328 Lynn Avenue Altoona, WI 54720 USA. Email: starr@starrzdavies.com

Cover illustration and title page art by Kateryna Vitkovskaya
Cover design and typography by Starr Z Davies/Character Assassin Books
Book layout and design by Starr Z Davies & Atticus software
Maps, glyphs, and illustrations relating to maps by Starr Z Davies & Inkarnate software
Character art by TL Combs, Mu'sab, Fondly Framed.
Chapter header and section break illustration by Therena Carlin

www.starrzdavies.com

BOOKS BY STARR Z. DAVIES

<u>Divica Stormborn Chronicles</u>

Stormvalor

Stormveil

Stormcrown

<u>Divica War of Two Crowns</u>

Volume 1: Darkness Falls

<u>Powers Series</u>

Ordinary

Unique

(extra)ordinary

Superior

<u>Powers Origins</u>

Miller: Origin

Enid: Origin

Celeste: Origin

<u>Powers Legacy</u>

Powers Legacy: The Prequel

Desolation

Infiltration

Insurrection

Invasion

<u>Fractured Empire Saga</u>

Daughter of the Yellow Dragon

Lords of the Black Banner

Mother of the Blue Wolf

Empress of the Jade Realm

Prosperous Eternity

<u>Stand-Alone Stories</u>

Stones: A Steampunk Short Story

For Von—

Who showed us that belief is not the absence of struggle, but the courage to keep shining

through it.

This story carries a piece of you in every heartbeat.

Your courage lives here, between every word.

May your light keep guiding us home.

LUTHIA
RUINS OF KRUC
PAL KA'IKO
GALAN BLUFFS
SABAK DUNES
GOKA'ATUN
ULA'AN UUL
N
W
E
S

VARYOVA ICE CAP
RIDGEBACK ICE MOUNTAINS
MURANDY HILLS
ELYSIA
BLEAKBURN
ELPISIO
VOROVESTI
MORDELIC
CLIFFS OF HOPE
GREAT RIVER
STORMVALOR
CROWTOWN
LEMHELLER GAP
UMBR
DEADWOOD
PORT VERIX
MT. FJAROE
BARDEN
NOVAVITO
SEORAS PLAINS
ARITH MOUNTAINS
OSHON
ARITHIA
LAGO
ISLES OF STORM
CAVERN OF LOST SOULS
DIVICA

<h1 style="text-align:center">Contents</h1>

Trigger Warnings

He comes with the fury of the gods
and calls forth the storm
to strike down the blackened hearts of men,
and a storm is coming.

CHAPTER 1

Solfia's Prophecy

Approximately 1000 Years Ago

Blood dripped from several cuts on Solfia's face as she bowed her head and blinked away the stars from the Black Guard's punch straight to her jaw. She coughed up blood, the metallic tang coating her tongue. Her knees ached as she kneeled on the hard marble tiles of the Vorovesti throne room. The invisible bonds pulling her arms behind her back made her shoulders scream, but no physical pain came close to the agony and grief tearing through her heart.

Tiberis, the light of her life, the reason her heart beat, lay dead in a pool of his own blood a handful of steps away from where she kneeled. His sightless blue eyes faced away from Solfia, mercifully. She wasn't sure she could stand seeing his dead eyes. Solfia squeezed her eyes closed, trying to convince herself that he only slumbered. That he would wake soon despite the quick, deep slice through his throat, and bring vengeance down on his brother's head. That he would *smile* like all the light in the world belonged to him and him alone. It was a beautiful, pointless fantasy.

A cold, powerful hand grasped Solfia's chin, and her eyes snapped open as she was forced to gaze up and meet Narcisse's hard, depthless black eyes. Such eyes could only be a curse from the gods. A curse this vile man deserved.

Blood filled Solfia's mouth.

"You will join your husband soon enough, outlander," Narcisse said. His voice remained as devoid of emotion and life as his unnaturally black eyes. "But not until I've taken what doesn't belong to you."

Solfia spit blood at him. It joined the blood already covering his marred armor. Tiberis's blood. Before she had time to burrow further into her grief, blinding pain hammered into her chest, knocking the breath from her lungs and once more darkening her vision.

Narcisse's grip shifted to her golden-red hair, and it was all that kept her from falling over onto the floor when his boot connected with her ribs. She was fairly certain they were nearly all broken, just like her arm had been when the Black Guards had captured her and forced her into this position. Just like her heart.

Tears burned in Solfia's eyes, and she blinked furiously to push them back. Narcisse was a monster, the most despicable sort of villain to have walked this world. He had taken everything from her. She would not give him her tears, too.

As her vision cleared once more, Solfia's gaze fell on the bodies beside her in the throne room. Queen Vanna, her sister-wife—the noble Tiberis chose as his queen because she was the only one who treated Solfia with kindness—stared lifeless at the bloodied sacred pond lining the center of the room. Solfia had loved her nearly as much as she had loved Tiberis. It was hard not to. Vanna was kind and passionate with those dear to her heart, and wickedly fierce to those who threatened her family and her people. Solfia adored the fire that burned in Vanna's spirit. Even in death, Vanna looked as defiant as she had been in life. That defiance cost her life, as it soon would cost Solfia her own.

Beside Vanna, King Tiberis remained with his back to Solfia. His final moments had been those of utter suffering. Suffering Vanna and Solfia had shared with him. Narcisse's Black Guards had marched both of Tiberis and Vanna's sons into the throne room and made them watch as Narcisse killed the boys slowly and painfully while Tiberis begged him for mercy. Vanna cursed him with every breath from her lungs. Solfia fought against the invisible hold over her magic, aching for just a sliver of it to stop Narcisse from hurting those boys.

Purging the corrupted Vorovesti line, Narcisse had called it. As if Narcisse were the only pure one in the family.

"You don't have to give it willingly, outlander," Narcisse said coldly as he yanked her head back, towering over her. "But I hear it's much more painful if you fight back."

A coil of darkness and light wrapped around Solfia, like mist and sunshine, storms and calm waters. Solfia couldn't explain the sensation any other way as it tightened around her. She gritted her teeth as it reached into her, pulling at the very essence of her power.

Solfia couldn't imagine a pain worse than the loss of her entire world. How wrong she had been. How terribly, completely *wrong*.

Agony wrenched at every part of her body—worse than the broken ribs and shattered soul. Solfia screamed as her magic fought to stay within her, clawing at her nerves to hold on. Narcisse grinned as her magic surged and twisted, pushing outward... toward him. But no matter how hard she tried, not a trace of her magic answered to her control.

Solfia's body shuddered, rendered immobile by some invisible force. The power within her, that deep well she had used against Narcisse countless times in battle, the magic that had decimated thousands of his men with a single blow, slowly slid away.

Narcisse dropped to his knees in front of Solfia as he pulled her magic into himself, far too close to her for Solfia's comfort. A moan of ecstasy slid past his lips in a way Solfia was certain no woman had ever made him feel. His grip on her hair tightened, pulling at the roots. But the pain of his grip was nothing compared to the agony of her magic yanking free of her body.

An apparition of fire and desire and sin stalked around the two of them, her seductive hips swaying with each step. Fire licked up the skirt of her red dress making it appear as if it were made of flame. Her red hair shifted and flowed like molten lava.

"Good," Fiara cooed, her voice as seductive as the rest of her. "She resists, but she is no match for you, Narcisse. Not with the power of the gods flowing through you." The Goddess of Fire and Vanity slid around his shoulder, her manicured fingers brushing intimately, possessively over his shoulder.

Solfia screamed again as he pulled harder at her magic, extracting it so slowly the pain grew increasingly excruciating with each passing second. Weakness crept in as the magic that had once bolstered her strength began to fade.

What fools they had all been. The War of Two Crowns had not been about crowns at all. It has been about power, control, revenge against the gods themselves. At some point, Goddess Fiara had seduced Narcisse. They hadn't only fought for control over every human kingdom and the extermination of the elves, but for all magic in every form. From humans, to the elves, to the gods themselves.

Narcisse had killed all the other gods and stolen their power, guided by the hand of Fiara herself.

Once the gods fell, dragons fell with them, linked to the divine power. Mortals never had a chance against Narcisse after that. His dark army swept across the continent, subjugating those who bent the knee to him, killing those who refused, stealing the magic from all who possessed it. When the Kruos elves fell, the Luthian elves fled like cowards, vanishing from the world and leaving the humans to Narcisse's cruel whims. Only Tiberis and Quade remained to stand against him.

Today, King Tiberis and his entire court fell.

Tomorrow, Narcisse would hunt down King Quade.

Solfia gritted her teeth against the force leeching the life from her veins.

Narcisse's lips parted and his hand slid to the back of her neck, leaning almost intimately close in a way that repulsed her. Solfia tried pulling away as his grip slackened, but he tightened it quickly, grasping her hair, her neck, in his iron fist once more. Solfia whimpered. His touch was nothing like his brother's. Tiberis had a firm but gentle hand. Narcisse was unyielding and unforgiving.

"I will have it all, outlander," Narcisse crooned, his voice bleeding with pleasure, breath rolling over her face. Solfia wanted to refuse, to recoil, to tell him that he would *not* have it all, but she was utterly helpless to stop him. How could a mortal fight the power of six gods in one body?

"Nearly there, my love," Fiara sang in his ear as her fingers slid through his snow-white hair.

Narcisse's eyes rolled back in his head as he shuddered. He collapsed against Solfia, pressing his forehead into her shoulder, his other arm snaking around her back as if he wanted to hug her closer, pull her into him. He didn't release his grip. If anything, it tightened. Solfia groaned in pain as his nails dug into the skin between her shoulder blades, drawing blood. Nothing about Narcisse in this moment made Solfia believe him weakened though. No, he held her so tightly against him she was certain he believed he could absorb her body and soul into his own. His hot breath rolled across her shoulder and down her chest.

A flash of power rushed through Solfia, like a lifeline reaching out to give her a second chance to fight back—like the gods acted through him, blessing her in these final moments with one last act of defiance. Most of her magic was gone. Only a trickle remained. But that gods-given lifeline provided her complete control of her magic.

Solfia pressed her lips close to Narcisse's ear as she wrapped her words in all that remained of her magic, binding them to him.

Fiara gasped as she sensed something had changed. "Narcisse!"

But the warning came too late. Solfia murmured the prophecy that would condemn Narcisse, a promise that all he had achieved would be undone.

"Bloodlines thought buried shall stir once more,When the half-breed heir reclaims their throne,Eyes of light shall pierce through darkness,Eyes of storms shall breech walls of stone.The mighty shall falter, false thrones shall fall,And justice shall rise with the blood of kings,Bearing the weight of ages, to shatter your reign,A legacy restored, for the rightful shall justice bring.And then the storm will come for you."

Her eyes burned with power as she spoke the final word pointedly directed at Narcisse, to be clear that her words were meant for him and him alone. A magical backlash pushed the two apart. The invisible magical bonds holding Solfia's arms vanished as they both crashed onto their backs.

Fiara roared in rage as the last dregs of magic were stolen from their grasp.

Narcisse lay on his side, glaring at Solfia. His nostrils flared.

Solfia's entire body had been weakened by the loss of her magic and that final blast. But the sacrifice had been worthwhile. She could only assume that flash of power had been a gift from one of the goddesses—perhaps Solisina or Astra—like a final chance to strike out against the man who had stolen their power and killed them.

Narcisse seemed to come to the same conclusion. Rage turned his normally pale face red. In a heartbeat, Narcisse kneeled over Solfia, a knife to her throat, drawing a bead of blood.

"Where is he?" Narcisse growled.

Solfia blinked slowly. She would die either way. But her last act would be that of courage, of defiance. Then she could join her husband and sister-wife in the afterlife.

Narcisse's black eyes burned with stormy fury. "*Where is your son?*" he roared, spittle flying from his mouth.

Solfia closed her eyes and pictured her beautiful son's face as she knew it—not as it had been changed by the protective charm she had placed over him. His hair like molten gold. His eyes shining like brilliant sapphires. *Live well, my lovely.*

"Beyond your grasp."

Narcisse screamed in a frenzy and thrust the knife into Solfia's throat.

But when her eyes opened, she didn't see his anger. Instead, Tiberis—her beautiful Tiberis—reached out to her. Vanna stood at his other shoulder.

She had done all she could do.

Solfia slid her hand into that of her husband, the light of her life, her heart and soul.

Chapter 2

The Princess & The Savage

The booted footsteps of her assigned Black Guards followed Aslyn Kiernan along the streets of Lemheller Gap in the very early hours of the evening. She wondered if they could hear the rapid beat of her heart increasing with each step toward Bloodstone Manor. If so, they would be on high alert, making the trap they were about to fall into even more dangerous for both her and the shadows waiting for them.

A week ago, she had convinced Marek to allow her freedom to venture into the city. He, in turn, had convinced his father, who only agreed if his hand-selected Black Guards escorted Aslyn any time she left the manor grounds. Even on the manor grounds, she detected them watching her every move. Only behind the closed doors of her bedroom did she have any sense of peace—assuming Marek didn't drop in for a visit.

Aslyn turned the corner, the guards following a few steps behind. Their presence was even more cloying than Elisio had been in Stormvalor, perhaps because she had trusted Elisio on some level. Aslyn had never loved him, but she cared for him. The Black Guards, however, reported to Marek's father and obeyed his orders above any other, except the emperor.

It hadn't occurred to her until a week after leaving Stormvalor that she had no idea what happened to Elisio after dismissing him from her service. Was he part of the massacre in the royal suite? Despite the wound his betrayal of her trust had created in her heart, Aslyn hadn't wished ill on him. He had just needed him to understand that things had changed, that they both had duties, that his judgment was clouded by his desires. She hadn't taken the time to really look through the victims in the suite with everything else happening. Did he die defending her mother? Guilt gnawed at her every time she considered his demise. *I hope he isn't dead*.

The people of Lemheller Gap were sharp-tongued and crass in ways that often infuriated Aslyn. Their markets were sparse, and the few times she had purchased from a vendor, they had inspected her coins as if suspecting they were counterfeit. No one bothered giving her thanks. They simply pushed her purchase into her hands and turned their attention to the next buyer or eyed her Black Guards anxiously.

Most of the buildings and homes were built of spruce trees harvested from the Umbr Mountains towering over the city. Each building rose two or three stories above street level, compressed thin and tall. Aslyn eyed some homes butted up close to each other. The upper floors extended beyond the main level, supported by thick spruce timbers. Some homes appeared slightly off balance. Builders created roofs out of carved slate from the mountains. She found each of them ugly, like a sloppy child's version of a home.

Aslyn reached the narrow street that would serve as a shortcut back to Bloodstone Manor. Little light from the over case sky illuminated this street at any time of day, shadowed by the tall homes and the mountains beyond the city.

As she turned to venture along the shadowed street, a heavy hand fell on her shoulder, pulling Aslyn back.

Furious that he dared to lay a hand on her, Aslyn jerked away and rounded on the Black Guard. "Touch me like that again, and I will see that Lord Bloodstone hears how you manhandled me. This is a shortcut back to the manor, and I have no intention of arriving late for dinner."

His black eyes tilted toward her own, not showing regret or fear. In fact, Aslyn couldn't sense any emotion in him at all. Meanwhile, her own heart thundered in her chest.

Then his gaze darted toward the narrow street, searching for signs of danger.

Aslyn held her breath, worried about what he would find. The seconds ticked by painfully slow. The manor was still several blocks away, but this alley-like road would cut across a few of those blocks, shortening the trip back to the manor by at least fifteen minutes.

At last, he dropped his hand and stepped back. It required every ounce of willpower for Aslyn not to puff out a breath of relief.

Aslyn focused on putting one confident step in front of another despite the way her body trembled. Could they see or sense her limbs shaking? *Seven Gods help us,* Aslyn prayed to the lost gods. *If this goes sideways, I'm a dead woman.*

Since leaving Stormvalor, Blackblade had always been somewhere nearby, hiding in shadows like a silent guardian. He had managed to sneak into her room in Bloodstone Manor four times to speak with her. Those were the only times they had spoken, and always with clipped words. Blackblade was not the same man as Zayne—in body, yes, but not in soul—and the transformation infuriated Aslyn. Lies and deception would do that to a person. Still, they both had their own objectives, and for the moment they aligned...

... Find out what the emperor was up to before it was too late to stop him. It was for this reason they planned this trap—or more specifically, Blackblade planned it. She needed a way into the imperial palace. He needed one of the Black Guards alive.

Three more steps with the Black Guards following close on her heels.

Why did I ever agree to this?

Five more steps. Aslyn sensed his presence. She still didn't understand how she knew when Zayne was near.

No, not Zayne, Aslyn, she chided herself. Zayne was a false name, a fraud, a fake by the name of Blackblade. He had lied to her for so long, manipulated her, betrayed her trust in nearly every way she could imagine.

For some reason, Blackblade had given her a blood oath. So far, he had kept to that oath, keeping her from harm from the shadows, but Aslyn wasn't certain she could ever trust him again. Not fully.

Ten more steps. Aslyn could now point directly to where Blackblade hid in the shadows of a stack of barrels. Her fingers subtly slid along the handle of the knife he had given her back in Stormvalor. According to Blackblade, it contained a sedative. All she had to do was cut the skin and it would work quickly.

Blackblade had instructed where to aim with her knife the moment she had the opportunity so that she would not strike armor but instead pierce skin. She resented taking orders from him. But if anyone would know where a Black Guard's armor was weakest, it would be the famous shadow assassin. *"Don't kill him,"* Blackblade had ordered. As if she would.

The street was eerily silent, save for the faint click of Aslyn's measured footsteps against the cobblestones, followed by the thump of Black Guard boots. Aslyn's airy gray and red dress swished around her legs with each step.

Four Black Guards flanked her like ominous black forms of lethal grace. Their armored bodies moved with precision; the faint clink of their gear drowned in the oppressive quiet. Why was this street abandoned?

The narrow street darkened with each step, save for occasional bursts of light between houses that illuminated the red on her dress. She paused and tilted her face toward the sky, wishing she could enjoy warmth on her face. The Black Guards paused in unison, their hands resting on their weapons.

The first strike came as a whisper of air. A knife, forged of darkness and steel, hurtled through the shadows and embedded itself into the cobblestone between two of the guards. The sound was sharp, deliberate. A challenge. Aslyn nearly scoffed at Blackblade's arrogance. He was *warning* them? Taunting them? What a fool!

Blackblade emerged from the shadows, his form melding with the dimness as his twin black knives reflected no light. He was a wraith, more a presence than a man. Even expecting his appearance, Aslyn gasped in alarm, her pulse quickening in fear. He wouldn't hurt her. Not if he intended to keep his oath.

Without hesitation, the first guard surged forward, sword slicing through the air. Blackblade slipped to the side with liquid grace, one of his knives catching the guard's blade and redirecting it into a spruce wall where it embedded in the wood. The assassin spun, his other knife carving through the guard's armor with a chilling efficiency. The guard released his sword and staggered back, silent even in death, before crumpling to the ground.

The second and third guards attacked in unison, their movements calculated and swift. One guard's blade sang as it sliced through the air toward Blackblade's neck. The other guard drove low to cut off his retreat. Aslyn pressed a hand to her throat to fight off the fear that Blackblade was about to take a lethal blow. Instead, shadows surged at Blackblade's command, forming a veil that swallowed him whole. Their weapons met only air and they stumbled a step.

Aslyn recalled her sword fight with Blackblade in Stormvalor. She had met him swing for swing. But the wraith before her now was *not* the same man. The man in Stormvalor had been holding back. Blackblade was a deadly force of shadows even the Black Guards couldn't match. *Maybe he really wasn't trying to hurt me in Stormvalor*, she realized.

The fourth guard marched straight for Aslyn. Her heart beat so wildly she could feel it all the way up her throat. He grabbed her arm and pulled her toward the mouth of the narrow street, leaving the other guards to deal with Blackblade.

Aslyn stumbled along, her fingers fumbling over her knife as she watched over her shoulder.

The two guards engaged in a deadly dance of weapons with the shadow assassin. Every time Aslyn was certain Blackblade would take a blow, he became a wraith once more, appearing behind them.

One of Blackblade's knives raked across the second guard's back, finding a vulnerable seam in the armor, while another knife deflected the third guard's strike with a clash that echoed down the street. The second guard collapsed, immobilized by the strike to his spine. The third guard spun to face Blackblade, who danced away from the second guard's gloved hands as he reached to unbalance Blackblade's feet.

Aslyn's final guard yanked her up the street without glancing back to see how his brethren fared against the assassin. Watching Blackblade over her shoulder, she stumbled and nearly fell a few times, only to be hauled roughly back to her feet by the unbreakable grasp on her arm.

This last duel was savage. The remaining guard's movements were ferocious, each swing of his blade aimed with deadly precision. Blackblade met every strike, his knives moving in a dance of deflection and counterattack. Shadows rippled around him, tendrils lashing out to unbalance his opponent. The guard fought valiantly, his silence an unyielding defiance, but Blackblade's speed and mastery were unrelenting. A feint with one knife led to the other plunging into the guard's chest through a gap in the armor. As the man fell, Blackblade finished with a spin, plunging a knife into the second guard's neck to be sure he was dead.

The third guard fell, his sword clattering to the ground, leaving Blackblade amidst the carnage, his breath steady and calm.

The clatter finally caught the attention of Aslyn's guard. He let go, spinning to find out what caused the noise, probably hoping to find Blackblade on the ground.

Instead, Blackblade vanished in a puff of shadows, emerging only a few steps away in an obvious challenge to the sole survivor.

Her guard took a step toward the Blackblade.

Aslyn's panic made her move, knowing her window of opportunity closed. She had been so mesmerized by the fight he had forgotten her only task. She palmed her knife as the guard lifted his arm to draw his sword. Her heart thundered in her ears, reminding her that death loomed near.

Before she could chicken out, Aslyn sliced upward into the fourth guard's armpit where no armor protected his skin. He didn't make a sound. Not as she cut him. Not as his sword fell from his fingers. Not as he fell face-first to the ground.

Aslyn stared at the blood on the knife, praying she hadn't killed him. She'd never taken a life before. Blackblade promised that move would only render the guard unconscious. But could she trust him?

"It's alright, Aslyn," Blackblade said gently.

Aslyn jumped, startled from her own thoughts, to find Blackblade in front of her. His gloved hand fell over her wrist, easing the knife down to her side.

"He's not dead," Blackblade reassured her.

Aslyn's gaze slipped from his to the guard she had cut. Sure enough, his chest rose and fell with steady breaths, eyes closed.

"Are they all...?" Aslyn eyed the guards.

"They deserved their deaths."

Aslyn scoffed. "No one deserves death."

"No one?" Blackblade didn't lower his hood, but Aslyn could see clearly enough inside to notice his brows rising in surprise. "These men have killed innocent people in the name of the Imperial Seat. For all you know, they could have been responsible for what happened to your mother and guards in Stormvalor."

Aslyn flinched. She hated that Blackblade was right and certainly would never give him the satisfaction of hearing her say it. "What gives you the right to make that decision?"

Blackblade turned from her, yanking the helmet off the unconscious guard. The man's skin was sickly pale, his hair limp and thinning.

"He can't return," she said, realizing that the guard could give away what she had done, who she worked with. "If he does…"

"Don't worry. He won't."

Aslyn didn't wish this guard ill. He simply followed his orders. But if he returned and informed Lord Bloodstone that she had conspired against these guards, and continued conspiring against him, Lord Bloodstone would not be forgiving. He would hurt her, perhaps torture her. He wouldn't kill her, not if he wanted his son to marry her. But there were a lot of ways he could teach her a brutal lesson without killing her, and everything she had worked so hard for—everything she had sacrificed for it—would be destroyed.

"You need to kill him." She wrang her hands to fight off the tremble.

"Look who's suddenly not opposed to killing when it benefits her," Blackblade grumbled as he crouched and searched the guard's pockets.

Aslyn didn't understand why Blackblade wanted to do this. He insisted he needed one guard alive, and that she would be unharmed—which physically she was.

"What is your plan, Blackblade?" Aslyn demanded. "I won't be your pawn."

"That's rich from you." He rose slowly, peering at her like a deadly predator. "Your time is running out."

Aslyn shuddered. She was well aware of that. Marek reminded her several times a day. Aslyn had hoped for more answers this past month, but the Bloodstone family had kept her under such close watch she hadn't learned much about the emperor's plans at all.

"I'm working on it," she said sharply.

"Right." Blackblade strolled toward Aslyn. Despite herself, Aslyn stumbled away from him until her back was against the wall of a home. "Meanwhile, I intend to get some answers *for* you. But that requires one of them alive and a Black Guard uniform."

Blackblade towered over her, his stone-gray eyes drilling into her.

Aslyn lifted her chin defiantly. "Can't you just sneak in? Sneaking is the only thing you seem proficient at. That and killing."

Blackblade's jaw twitched. He reached a hand up and Aslyn tensed as it slid into her hair. She could knee him in the groin. That would teach him for touching her.

A pin fell from her styled hair, making part of it fall.

"What do you think you're doing?" Aslyn hissed, hating how her stomach churned at his touch.

His steely eyes shifted to her shoulder, then his hand followed suit. "If you return in the same state you left, they will never believe you." He ripped her long chiffon sleeve clean off her dress in one smooth motion. "There needs to be some sign of a struggle." He tossed the sleeve.

Aslyn froze in place, unable to think clearly with him so close to her.

"Turn around, Sol'ami," Blackblade commanded, but the words were so soft, and far too friendly.

Aslyn blinked in alarm. "What?" She hated when he called her that, and hated even more that she still had no idea what it meant. The nickname felt far too intimate, a remnant of his lies and betrayal. She wanted to scrub that nickname from existence.

He seized her shoulders and spun her around, pressing her chest against the wall of the spruce log home with one hand. His breath rolled down her shoulder-blade.

"Get off of me, savage," Aslyn snapped.

"Calm down," he grumbled.

A moment later, she heard a rip and felt a draft in her skirt. Aslyn prepared to unload a string of curses at him when his hands released and his body heat vanished.

Aslyn spun, ready to slap him, but Blackblade crouched several feet away over the bodies, moving them into different positions. Setting the stage, she realized. She inspected her skirt. The tear had been placed well enough not to be indecent, but enough to be clearly visible.

"Why the back of the skirt?" she asked.

"Well, you would be running away, wouldn't you?" Blackblade said as he worked. "A rip on the front of the skirt might be suspicious."

She peered down the front of her dress. Dirt stained the dress from when he had pressed her to the wall. She certainly looked like someone had assaulted her.

"They will double my guard for this," Aslyn muttered as she fingered the ripped material.

"Good." Blackblade didn't bother glancing in her direction as he worked. "Maybe it will be a fair fight then."

"Arrogant asshole," Aslyn muttered under her breath.

He froze just long enough for Aslyn to know her words struck true. Good. He deserved it. "Better run along, *princess*. Before anyone sees you loitering with a savage."

Aslyn gritted her teeth to bite back a retort, pulling her heels off so she could run. "Better make yourself scarce then, because I fully intend to make a scene."

"I would expect no less from you."

Aslyn couldn't stop herself. She whipped a heel at him. He repelled it with shadows, not even moving a muscle in his body.

I hate you so much!

Then she dropped the second shoe, scrubbed her hands in her hair to make it a further mess, pivoted, and sprinted out of the side street, summoning all the panic she could muster.

But the tears that streaked down her face were far too real.

The moment Aslyn vanished from the street, Bast Blackblade dropped the shadows he had used beside a set of stairs leading up to the front door of one of the homes. A handful of bodies appeared—all men who had threatened Aslyn's safety by tracking her movements outside the manor or trying to hire men to kidnap her. Every coin intended to harm her ended up in Bast's pocket as he took the job.

And every man who hired him ended up dead to ensure they didn't hire anyone else when he "failed" the job.

Savage.

Bast clenched his jaw in irritation as he pulled one of the bodies into position. That woman knew exactly how to get under his skin. He had taken dark pleasure in ruining her hair and her dress, even if his reasoning remained sound.

She has no idea the lengths I've gone to protect her, he thought bitterly as he arranged another body.

True to her word, she burst from the narrow street with her skirt hiked up, making a ruckus. He would only have moments to finish this and vanish before more Black Guards arrived on the scene.

Even from over a block away, he could hear her cry for help as he arranged the final body into position beneath one guard, positioning their weapons in a dual-death position.

That she was worried about her dress and her guards clarified just how skewed her priorities were. Not that Bast would expect any less from a royal of any court. Aslyn acted like the entitled princess she was, condemning him for being judge and executioner only moments before doing the exact same thing—but demanding it of him.

A muscle in his jaw twitched.

Bast gritted his teeth as he hoisted the final guard up over his shoulder. The shadows sang to him as he pulled at their magic, wrapping them around him. Then he ducked cautiously out of the narrow street and followed his predetermined path to the abandoned house he had selected for this interrogation.

If Aslyn had any idea what Bast intended to do to get this guard to talk, her delicate sensibilities would be personally affronted and she would likely faint. He couldn't help smirking as he imagined exactly that, watching her fall to the ground in shock. But as he realized there was still every opportunity for her to screw this up, his smirk faded.

She had better not fuck up her story, he thought as he slipped around another corner when a pair of guards appeared.

CHAPTER 3

Put on a Good Show

The stone walls and thick iron gates of Bloodstone Manor rose before Aslyn as she stumbled toward it. Tears streaked her face, and she felt the blood on the soles of her feet from where they had cut open on the cobblestone streets of Lemheller Gap.

The manor house sat on a small hill deep in the gap, near the valley entrance to the Umbr Mountains where the Citadel nestled in a cradle of jagged peaks and the Imperial Castle sat overlooking everything. Because of Lord Bloodstone's position in the Imperial Court, the manor was the largest building in the city as well, spanning several blocks of sprawling land. Guards endlessly walked the walls and guarded the entrances.

Aslyn stumbled. toward the main gate. The moment she saw the two guards on duty, Aslyn let out a cry of relief.

"Help!" she called to them, her voice hoarse from screaming through the city streets.

A guard rushed forward, recognizing her after a moment. The second startled, straightening his spin and calling for the gates to open.

Aslyn fell into the outstretched arms of the first guard, a sobbing mess. "Marek," she cried into the guard's shoulder. "I need him. Please."

The guard escorted Aslyn through the iron gates and she leaned heavily on him. "Marek!" she called, her voice breaking over his name.

Kaiti was the first to appear at the doors, and her eyes widened at the sight of Aslyn as the guard guided her through the trimmed hedges. Pebbles from the gravel path embedded in Aslyn's bare and bleeding feet and she cried out.

Marek burst from the door a moment later, racing toward Aslyn. "What in the name of the Seven Gods happened?" he barked at the guard escorting her. "Where are her guards?"

The man fumbled over his words, stepping back as Marek scooped Aslyn into his arms and marched into the manor.

Aslyn buried her face in his shoulder, clinging to him. All of this was for show. If she didn't sell this well enough, it would all be for nothing. The trembling in her body was very real, though, and the blood and pain in her feet was as well.

A gasp told Aslyn that Marek's mother was nearby. "Set her on the chaise," Lady Bloodstone commanded.

Marek eased Aslyn down and she clung to him like she was afraid of letting go. He stroked her hair and kissed her head, then used his free hand to pry her hands from his neck. Aslyn blinked back tears and swallowed, taking in the sitting room from where she now lay on the chaise lounge. It was the only truly bright room in the entire manor, and Lady Bloodstone's favorite place to entertain.

And Aslyn was getting blood on Lady Bloodstone's favorite white and red chaise.

Marek kneeled before her, anger and worry creasing his face. Lady Bloodstone lingered a few feet away, giving Kaiti quick orders to gather healing supplies and the healer. In moments, Aslyn's maid vanished.

Marek's focus remained singularly on Aslyn. "What happened?"

"The guards and I were headed back from the seamstress," Aslyn said, her voice breaking over each word. "A group of men attacked us in a narrow street. They... they..." Aslyn closed her eyes tight and choked back a sob.

"It's alright dear," Lady Bloodstone said gently. "Take your time. You're safe now."

Safe. Aslyn was far from safe within these walls, but she wouldn't insult her hostess.

"And the guards?" Marek asked.

Aslyn shook her head. "I don't know. I think..." She opened her eyes slowly, sorrow creasing her features. "It all happened so fast. One of them grabbed at me and... I was able to break free and run. The last thing I saw was one of the guards falling and another giving chase to one of the attackers who escaped."

Marek's jaw twitched as anger burned in his dark eyes. "Ruffians outmatched your Black Guards?"

It only took a moment for Aslyn to realize why Marek didn't buy her story. He thought it was Aethan coming to rescue her. But why would she run if it were him? Surely Marek wasn't dumb enough to think she would come back here when Aethan was an option.

Aethan isn't coming. Not if he keeps his promise to me.

"Marek, give the poor woman space to breathe," Lady Bloodstone said, easing her son back with a touch on his shoulder. "She's been through quite enough already."

Marek grimaced but rose to his feet and took a step back.

Lord Bloodstone stormed into the sitting room, his very presence casting a dark pall on the bright white walls. His furious gaze landed on Aslyn, taking in her state in an instant.

"What's all this about?" Lord Bloodstone asked gruffly.

Thankfully, Lady Bloodstone eased some of Aslyn's burden by regaling what they had learned of the tale so far.

Marek stepped toward his father and lowered his voice, whispering, "He's here."

Lord Bloodstone grunted and rolled his eyes. "Don't be daft, Marek. If Starkling was here, your precious bride wouldn't be. I'm certain she would have abandoned you for him in a heartbeat."

Marek flinched. "Who else could outmatch four Black Guards?" he asked, stepping out of the way as his father pushed on toward Aslyn.

Everything inside of Aslyn recoiled as Lord Bloodstone drew near. Marek, she could control. Lady Bloodstone was proper but timid. But Lord Bloodstone carried a darkness that terrified Aslyn.

He sat on the edge of the chaise, once more studying her from head to toe, searching for any sign of deception. Aslyn grudgingly admitted Blackblade had been right to tear and stain her dress. Not that she would ever say as much to him.

Lord Bloodstone ran his fingers along the ripped edge where her sleeve had been attached. The warmth from his hand sent a shiver down her spin. Aslyn flinched, but thankfully he thought it was because of the assault.

"My men will need detailed descriptions," Lord Bloodstone said, his cold gaze snapping to meet her eyes.

"I... I was so scared. I don't think... I didn't get a good enough look." Seven Gods, let him buy that, because Aslyn knew only what Blackblade told her to say. "One had long dark hair. I think. And... and..."

Somehow, Aslyn conjured more tears.

"Darling, you're scaring the poor woman even worse," Lady Bloodstone said, but her words were guarded, as if afraid of his reaction.

Aslyn suspected their marriage was less than amicable. Lady Bloodstone had never said anything negative about her husband, but the few times they had talked since Aslyn's arrival, Lady Bloodstone's praise of her husband had sounded false. Aslyn suspected he punished his wife behind closed doors if she stepped out of line. Like he probably thought she did with that one statement. Would he punish her for it later?

"At least tell me how many men attacked," Lord Bloodstone pressed, shooting an angry glare at his wife.

She shrank back. Yes. Aslyn was certain Lady Bloodstone would suffer the consequences later, and she wanted to help the woman somehow. Lady Bloodstone had only shown Aslyn kindness.

"My Lord!" A guard rushed into the room, bowing just inside the door. "The Black Guard found the bodies."

For several excruciatingly long seconds, Lord Bloodstone stared at Aslyn, waiting for her to give some sign of deception. Aslyn bit her lip and averted her gaze, allowing tears to slip down her cheeks.

Finally, Lord Bloodstone surged to his feet and marched toward the door. "See that she is healed and cleaned up by the time I return. Marek, with me."

Marek didn't hesitate to obey, but when he reached the door into the hallway, he paused and studied Aslyn. She hugged her arms over her chest, unable to meet his gaze. Out of vulnerability, as far as he would be concerned.

And as they left the manor, Aslyn wondered if she had baited a trap unknowingly. Was this what Blackblade had hoped for? To lure the Imperial Military Advisor and his heir into a trap, to their deaths? She couldn't say she would miss either man.

Aslyn allowed Kaiti to tuck her into bed for "rest" once the healing had been completed and she had cleaned herself up. No one had required her presence at dinner, instead sending it up to her room. When she asked about Marek after dinner, a servant stated the lords had not returned to the manor yet.

Worry gnawed at Aslyn's gut. It wasn't Marek's life she worried over though. If Blackblade assassinated the two men, Aslyn would be left sitting here in the Bloodstone manor without knowing a thing. Was that his plan? Did he think her safer here? With or without Lord Bloodstone, Aslyn would never be safe in Lemheller Gap.

What she truly wanted was a trip to the emperor's castle. Not that she had been given any opportunity. She had even asked if she could go to visit Prince Valen and his bride but had been denied. Aslyn hoped Sybil fared well in that palace alone. More than once, Aslyn had stared out her bedroom window toward the castle and its many spires high in the Umbr Mountains, imagining that she could see Aethan's sister on a balcony watching her. Foolish, of course, but a nice little fantasy to help ease her burdened mind either way.

A bedside lamp glowed softly beside Aslyn's massive four-post bed. Black and crimson embroidered curtains hung from each post. She could pull them closed for privacy, but the one time she had tried that, the close quarters made her uncomfortable.

Most of the room was bathed in rich shades of red. Tapestries of the forests of the Umbr Mountains adorned the walls. Her windows only opened enough to allow a breeze in, and there was no balcony by which to escape. Once, Aslyn had tried to squeeze through the narrow window opening and nearly broke it off the hinge. She still didn't understand how Blackblade had slipped in through those windows.

Though given every amenity she could ever want, including a private bath and massive closet, Aslyn remained a prisoner. Would today's excursion condemn her to the house once more?

Kaiti had closed the bedroom door an hour after dinner, leaving Aslyn utterly alone in her room for what felt like hours.

Finally, the door to the main sitting room connecting her room to Marek's closed with a thud. That could only be Marek. A moment later, she heard his voice, muffled by her closed door.

Aslyn's heart leaped into her throat as the door opened and Marek strode in, a Black Guard on his heels. She pulled her blanket up tighter around her shoulders, her back against the headboard.

"As you can see, she's perfectly safe," Marek said, waving a hand toward Aslyn even as he marched to her bed.

The guard's mask was down, blocking his face completely from sight. He was like black stone in her bedroom doorway. Despite his covered face, she could feel his eyes on her, examining her.

Marek settled on the edge of the bed and the guard stiffened, his hand falling to his sword.

Aslyn's heartbeat kicked up. A guard wouldn't act that way. They never showed outward signs of emotion, and certainly not against a member of this household.

Blackblade? Could it be him, wearing the armor of one of the men he killed?

"You may leave now, guardsman," Marek said harshly. But he studied Aslyn with a hunger she had managed to keep at bay shining in his dark eyes.

The guard must have sensed it, too, because he hesitated.

Marek stroked Aslyn's cheek. She flinched.

The guard's hold on his sword tightened.

Aslyn cleared her throat and peered past Marek at the guard. "Thank you for giving me a chance to escape, but I'm perfectly safe now."

Marek half turned to give the guard a quizzical look, not understanding why the man had not left them alone yet.

Get out of here before you blow the whole plan, Aslyn thought, giving a subtle shift of her chin toward the exit while Marek's wasn't looking.

The guard bowed and left them alone, but he didn't close the door behind him. Aslyn wondered if Blackblade would linger outside the door in the shadows to listen to them talk.

When Aslyn returned her attention to her captor, Marek had shifted closer.

"My patience wears thin, Aslyn," Marek said. His voice was low, like his warning had been intended as a seductive call. Instead, it gave Aslyn chills. He tucked hair behind her ear, then slid his fingers into her hair, leaning closer. "Two days." His breath rolled across her face. Aslyn struggled not to flinch away. "And if I find out you and Starkling are conspiring under my nose, I'll have the guards rack him and make him watch my patience vanish."

Aslyn leaned back, smacking her head against the headboard. "First of all, I agreed to revisit the issue. I never agreed to give in."

Marek's fingers tightened painfully in Aslyn's hair. Instead of yelping in pain, she scowled at him.

"Secondly, I came here voluntarily with you," Aslyn said smoothly. "Or did you forget how I rejected him and turned away from him in that hallway in Stormvalor?"

A shadow of doubt flashed in Marek's dark eyes. While Marek was no idiot, he wasn't always the smartest in the room either, which made it easier for Aslyn to manipulate him to match her own needs. She reached up, seizing this moment of doubt, teasing her fingers along his jaw, then pulling his face toward hers.

Marek closed his eyes, ready for the kiss. But Aslyn's lips landed softly on his cheek instead. Before he could respond, she whispered in his ear, "I just need time, Marek."

He yanked at her hair and Aslyn yelped despite her attempts to remain composed. "So you keep saying, but you haven't given me any hope that the end of this waiting is coming any time soon. I might have to take matters into my own hands." Marek pressed his face closer to her neck.

Aslyn wanted to push him off, but she walked a tenuous line. He had to be handled gently. So as his lips brushed her neck, Aslyn didn't pull away. When his teeth scraped her skin possessively, Aslyn whimpered. Though it had been a whimper of fear, he had taken it as a positive sign. Marek eased back, releasing her hair and grabbing her jaw instead.

Aslyn knew what would come next and that she had two choices. Resist and leave a clear sign that she was no longer interested, or give him a sample of what he wanted. And she had but moments to decide.

Marek's kiss was hungry, but Aslyn allowed it, just this once, to ease some of his doubts. As his tongue became more insisted, Aslyn sighed against his lips and gently broke the kiss, placing her hands against his chest. She eased him back and, thankfully, he relented.

But the hunger in his eyes had grown more intense. Months ago, when she thought he was a different person, a sensitive person, that look in his eyes would have made her knees weak for all the right reasons. Now that she knew his true, dark nature and saw the ugliness inside of him, it made her gut churn in fear.

Aslyn ran her teeth over her lips like she was trying to pull his kiss in and savor it when really she just wanted to scrape it off her skin. His hooded gaze watched with wanting intent.

"It won't be long, Marek," Aslyn whispered. "I promise."

And it wouldn't be long. With or without the information she came searching for, Aslyn would leave Lemheller Gap soon. Because if she didn't, Marek wouldn't wait any longer and she knew it. That promise was empty, but he didn't seem to know it. Marek didn't even consider that she would break her promise because of her honor. But when it came to men like him, her honor be damned.

"I've been dreaming about it," she admitted. And it wasn't a lie, though it wasn't with him. Aslyn dreamed of that one glorious night she shared with Aethan often.

"Really?"

Aslyn nodded. "But when I'm awake, I worry so much about my father and his safety that... It gets in the way."

Marek smirked devilishly. "I'm more than happy to provide a distraction."

Aslyn giggled. "No. Not yet." She ran a hand along his collar, smoothing it out. "Please, just be patient a little bit longer. That's all I ask."

The dangerous, predatory look in his eyes vanished, replaced by genuine affection. "I just find you so irresistible. But I'll do my best. For a little bit longer."

Then he kissed her forehead and left her to rest, closing the bedroom door on his way out.

Aslyn held her breath, listening to Marek's heavy steps across their connected sitting room. A moment later, she heard the thump of his bedroom door closing. She heaved out a sigh, gaze darting to the deep shadows in the corner of her room.

"I know you're there," she said, though in truth Aslyn only suspected Blackblade lingered nearby.

"You're playing a deadly game, princess," Blackblade said, his voice soft, coming from every shadow in the room.

Aslyn's gaze darted to the closed door, worried Marek could hear them.

"Relax," Blackblade said, easing out of the shadows in the Black Guard armor. "I can use my shadows to hinder sound. He can't hear a thing."

Aslyn found it unnerving to listen to him in that armor. She couldn't remember a single time she heard any of the Black Guard make a sound—beyond their heavy footsteps.

Blackblade pulled the face guard up so Aslyn could see his face.

"Did you get the information you needed?" Aslyn asked.

Blackblade grimaced. "Did you know the Black Guard have no vocal cords? I went through a lot of trouble and he didn't make a sound. And their blood isn't... like ours."

What did that mean? "I've seen it. Their blood is red like anyone else."

"I always suspected something but never had a chance to examine one of them so closely before," Blackblade said. His stone-gray eyes shifted around the room at everything except for Aslyn. Why wouldn't he look at her? "Anyway, they aren't just men the emperor selects. Either they are something else entirely, or they are changed to be something else."

Aslyn wondered why the emperor would use such creatures as his chosen guards, but she supposed men who couldn't share his secrets were more useful.

"Lord Bloodstone and your boyfriend had a bit of an argument when they got back to the manor," Blackblade said. "It was impressive, actually, watching Marek barely keep himself from throttling his father. He has more self-control than I gave him credit for."

Boyfriend... Aslyn's nose wrinkled at the notion of Marek as her boyfriend. No, he was a tool to use. Nothing more.

"Lord Bloodstone thinks the attack targeted you, and that another attack could come," Blackblade said evenly. "He is moving you to the palace."

Aslyn's heart stopped. "The imperial palace?"

"It's what you wanted, isn't it?" Blackblade didn't move out of the corner. The shadows continued to mask most of him, making him appear almost wraithlike in the corner of her room. "Marek wasn't happy. Especially since it will mean he sees less of you. You're welcome, by the way."

"For what?" Aslyn snapped.

"I'm the reason you will get farther from Marek and closer to your answers. So you're welcome."

Aslyn growled in rage at his obstinance, searching for something, anything, to throw at him.

Blackblade chuckled. "No shoes handy, princess?"

"You're insufferable."

He smirked. "And yet you suffer me."

Those five words only stoked her anger.

"Why haven't you compared those letters?" he asked. Blackblade flipped the face guard down and once more the shadows enveloped him completely.

Aslyn's throat tightened. Blackblade had slipped two letters into her possession in Stormvalor. One from her brother, another sent to Blackblade that he claimed was also from her brother. Somehow, he knew she hadn't taken them from their hiding place in her pack. Aslyn dealt with so much since that day, she hadn't the heart to see if he had been correct. Confirming Blackblade's claim that her brother was somehow behind their family misfortune made her body tremble and her heart crack in fear.

"Why are you still here?" she hissed.

"Compare the letters, Aslyn." The cool confidence in Blackblade's voice sent a shudder down her spine.

"I gave you what you were after," Aslyn snapped. "I don't understand why you linger here. Take the necklace to your buyer and leave me in peace."

Silence.

Was he even there to hear her?

Good riddance, she thought as she settled back in bed once more.

And at her feet, Aslyn noticed the two letters waiting. Aslyn snatched them and stuffed them under her pillow. She would read them when she was damn well ready to read them. Not at his command.

Chapter 4

Bay of Shimmering Sapphire

Aethan Starkling's hands tightened around the rail at the ship's prow. A warm ocean breeze ruffled his pale blonde hair. An endless expanse of gently rolling waves stretched into the horizon on the port side of the ship. But that wasn't where his attention fixed.

Slowly, the lead ship upon which Aethan stood turned toward starboard, headed for the distant docks nestled in a bay of shimmering sapphire. Breakwater rip-rap embraced the massive Arithian harbor and beaches to prevent erosion or danger from high tidal waves.

The city of Arithia rose in intricate, beautiful levels of white stone cradled by a backdrop of the lush green Aryth Mountains. Domed buildings and peaked spires sparkled as overcast light shone off the golden tiles atop them. High above, the Novavito palace towered like a guardian over the rest of the city. Even from a distance, Aethan could see the dam that controlled the flow of water from the Great River through the city itself. The river pulsed like a vein through the heart of

Arithia. Cascading waterfalls flowed in almost purposeful patterns from high in the mountains, down past the palace, and into the many fountains of the city below.

While Aethan loved Mordelic, his own homeland capital, he had to admit that Arithia was just as beautiful in a very different way. Mordelic's walls and primary buildings were composed of onyx marbled with veins of silver and gold. Arithia's entire city seemed composed of brilliant white marble capped in domes of gold.

One day soon, this would be his home. He would become responsible for its people and its protection, supporting their future queen. That thought should have lifted Aethan's heart with hope, but instead it made his gut churn.

Aslyn had gone with Marek back to Lemheller Gap. He had only received one brief message from her since. A reminder to stay the course. She had a plan. Not that he knew what that plan was. All he knew was that he had promised to get her father back and she held him to that promise. Aethan would do his best, but every day brought a fresh wave of torment knowing that she was in Marek's clutches. What would he do to her? What had he *already* done to her?

The captain's falcon flew in from the city. Aethan tracked the falcon as it headed straight for the stern where the captain guided the ship, then tucked its wings and landed on the captain's shoulder.

Aethan pried his fingers from the rail, only then realizing how tightly he'd been holding on as his joints ached with the movement. Flexing his stiff hands, he descended the creaking wooden steps, crossed the main deck, and climbed back up to where the captain was finishing the message.

Captain Barrow was in his mid-forties, with weathered features and peppered hair. King Orrin had selected Captain Barrow because he was the best in the fleet and could command as many as twenty ships with little need for help. The king hadn't given Aethan twenty ships for this rescue mission—only five. But five should be enough for the task. While King Orrin put his nephew in command, Captain Barrow was the one who controlled those five ships.

Without comment, the captain handed the note to Aethan, who read it quickly as the captain spoke. "Prince Dorin expected us. Not sure if your princess sent word ahead somehow. He'll have men waiting for you and your guard at the dock."

Aethan nodded and tucked the note into his pocket. "I suppose I should gather my things then."

When he reached the narrow hallway leading to his quarters below deck, Aethan was greeted by a flurry of motion as his friends prepared to disembark as well. He couldn't fault their eagerness. They had been on this ship for nearly three weeks, only making landfall to stop in Lago so Weylen could report to the king of Oshon, his liege lord.

Aethan nodded to Von as he slipped past and ducked into his quarters. During the journey, Von had spoken endlessly with Gorim—and sometimes with Aethan and his other companions—about the legend of the Cavern of Lost Souls deep in the Isles of Storm. Legend claimed that the gods stored a great power in the cavern, and that one day their chosen Champion would pierce the stormveil, enter the cavern, and obtain the power in the name of right and light. But the way Von spoke of it made the legend sound more like a prophecy. He tried to ignore it, for the most part.

Because of how many men were aboard the ship, many of them had to double up on quarters. Aethan's space remained his own. Or it had, until one of Captain Barrow's men uncovered a young stowaway a few days into the trip.

Aethan had been furious that Roric had the audacity to undermine his orders, but some part of him had been secretly happy to see the boy. With nowhere else to put him, the captain had insisted Roric share quarters with Aethan. But only after Roric had been forced to spend a day in the brig for his crime, and then he was forced to work off his occupancy by swabbing the decks every day.

Now, Roric shouldered two large packs when Aethan entered. "All packed and ready, sire."

"I would say it might be safer for you to remain on the ship," Aethan said as he reached for the suit jacket he had discarded earlier in the day. "But something tells me you wouldn't listen."

"I go where you go, sire," Roric said, raising his chin proudly.

Aethan inwardly sighed. He expected as much. At least Roric had proven himself to be an adept spy in Stormvalor. That might come in handy to help Aethan dissect Arithian court intrigue during his brief stay.

He strapped on his sword belt, noting the way Roric eyed the blue-hilted weapon with awe. The boy had endless questions about the sword. Questions Aethan was unprepared or unequipped to answer. So much about the sword remained a mystery.

Aethan had discovered it in the Shrine of Justis, God of War. The weapon sat atop an altar, untouched for hundreds of years—perhaps longer—as if waiting for someone.

For him.

He recalled the way it had called out to him, pulling him closer until he wrapped his hand around the sapphire blue leather hilt. The way it had fit into his hand as if made for him. How it hummed and sang and whispered in response to his touch and movements.

The blade showed no signs of age, and the edge remained razor sharp. The sapphire stones on the pommel and cross guard sparkled as if powered by some inner light.

Aethan hadn't told his father. He hadn't shown him the blade either. Aethan didn't know why he hadn't told his father. Perhaps, deep down, he feared his father would reprimand him for venturing into the tomb again and stealing an ancient relic, then demand it be returned to its rightful place. But the sword had called to him. It *chose* him, and he felt bonded to it in a way his father would never be able to understand.

Whenever anyone asked about the new sword, Aethan simply stated it had been a gift. Most left it alone and accepted his statement. Only Roric persisted with his questions, though Von and Gorim had given curious glances. Thankfully, they never asked for more details.

By the time Aethan returned to the main deck, the ship had sailed past the breakwater and eased toward the harbor. The rest of his companions waited.

Six of his fellow competitors had accompanied Aethan on this mission. Kern and Weylen, from Oshon, were both expert archers. Gorim and Von, from Elpisio, were excellent with hand-to-hand combat. Cormic and Cavis were twins who hailed from Novavito. They were both good fighters, and Cavis's skill with a sword was exceptional. Of course, for the two of them, this was a homecoming, and joining a mission to rescue their own king had required no coercing from Aethan.

It hurt Aethan when Trystain had declined. They were brothers through thick and thin. Or they had been. But when Prince Valen stole Sybil away from Trystain, something about Trystain had changed. Aethan hoped his friend just needed time to process what had happened and find a new path for himself. For all Trystain's insistence that he was fine, Aethan could see the hurt his best friend had tried to hide beneath normal banter.

Since leaving Vorovesti's military port, Cavis had spent a little time coaching Aethan on what he knew of Novavito politics. Not that Aethan's own education lacked, but getting insider information on specific people would likely prove helpful in the days to come. Cavis had a lot to say about Prince Dorin, Aslyn's brother. And the warnings about Ambassador Umbogo would not go unheard. Not that Aethen would ever underestimate an ambassador—and he knew why Aslyn feared Umbogo. She thought he was after her hand in marriage, which put Aethan in a dangerous position the moment he stepped foot in the city.

"Are you ready for this?" Cavis asked when Aethan joined them.

"Do I have a choice?" Aethan teased, though a hint of seriousness bled through. He couldn't go on a mission to rescue the Novavito king without touching base with the Arithian court. Even with Aslyn's blessing.

"I guess not," Cavis said.

Aethan glanced at the others gathered around him as the gangway was situated for them to disembark. "The invitation to the palace extends to only myself and my squire," he told them. "Cormic and Cavis will see you in reputable establishments close to the palace. Don't wander. If I need you, I will send word through the brothers or Roric. Otherwise, enjoy yourselves. Just remember that we are here for a reason. Let's not insult our hosts during our stay."

They nodded and grumbled in agreement, accepting him in the leadership position without any arguments. Was that because of his connection to Aslyn and the Vorovesti king?

Aethan's gaze swept the bustling harbor, landing on the royal coach waiting nearby, a footman ready to assist.

The others descended the gangway first, marching and lining the path to the coach like they were his personal guards. It felt strange having these men do that. They were his friends. His equals.

Roric made himself nearly invisible as he trailed behind Aethan with the packs. As the footman opened the carriage door, another appeared to take the packs from

Roric. With a last glance at his friends, Aethan boarded the carriage and began the journey through the streets of Arithia to the palace.

"I assume I don't need to tell you what to do once we're settled," Aethan said to Roric as he stared out the side window, watching the bustling streets of Arithia.

"No, sire," Roric said.

"Do your best to avoid Ambassador Umbogo during our stay," Aethan instructed. "And if he corners you, tell him nothing, promise him nothing. Ambassadors can be tricky, and from what Aslyn has said, Umbogo is no exception. Make no mistake. We may be welcomed into the palace, but we are entering a foreign court. Be on guard."

Roric scratched his chin thoughtfully, then sighed. "I thought you were engaged to their princess. Shouldn't that offer us protection?"

Aethan wished it were so easy, but even though he and Aslyn had agreed to the marriage, her mother was murdered before signing an agreement. And she died while visiting the city his family controlled. Aethan wasn't sure how that would go over with Prince Dorin.

"Just be on guard."

They fell into tense silence as the carriage drew closer to the palace. Another would follow with Cormic and Cavis soon, bringing the remains of Queen Giata home. They had no choice but to burn her body before leaving Vorovesti. The bloating of her corpse and the scent of death would have been overpowering on a ship for weeks—not to mention the potential illness such a thing could wreak havoc on a confined ship.

Aslyn hadn't instructed Aethan to bring her mother home, but he knew it was what she would have wanted. He had to be very careful about not accepting any form of responsibility for what happened to the queen. Especially if Umbogo lingered nearby.

At a glance, Arithia appeared a rich city vibrant with life and wealth. But the closer Aethan watched through the carriage window, the more he saw the tell-tale signs of decay and poverty found everywhere in the realm. The wealthy moved through the streets with servants trailing carts and goods, while people watched each other warily. Houses showed cracks, dirty awnings, and shuttered windows.

Beggars waited in the shadows, emerging only when guards were gone. Even the food on display was far from quality.

All in all, it reminded Aethan of Mordelic—except something festered in the heart of Arithia. Was this all because their king was missing and the heir to the throne had not yet returned? What would Aslyn do if she knew the state her people were in? Would she abandon her mission and return home? Did her brother not know how to rule as steward until one of them returned?

The carriage wound its way up the streets hugging the side of the mountain, slowing only for sharp turns. When they at last reached the courtyard and stopped, Aethan ran his fingers through his hair and adjusted his jacket to be sure he was presentable. Nervous tension writhed in his gut. The door opened.

Aethan drew in a breath to steady his nerves, then released it slowly before stepping out.

The warm summer air in Arithia was more stifling than the summers in Mordelic and he regretted the heavy material of his jacket the moment the thick heat beat down on him.

A tall, thin man in his middle years waited to greet Aethan atop the palace steps. Aethan straightened his coat and marched confidently forward.

"Lord Aethan Starkling," the man said, bowing just deeply enough to be deferential, "We are surprised by your arrival but pleased to host you all the same."

Host? Aethan resisted the temptation to glance toward the city. They were not playing host. He would be King Consort soon enough, and only Aslyn would have power beyond his own. When he finished the rescue mission, he would do what he could to help restore balance in this city for her and her father, at their will. But as far as Aethan was concerned, this would be home. For now, he would play their political games.

"I hope it isn't too much of an imposition," Aethan said. He kept his back straight and chin proud as his father taught him, resting a hand non-threateningly on his sword.

"No, of course not," the man said swiftly. "I am Javon Nadier, King Novin's royal accountant and personal assistant."

Aethan vaguely recalled Aslyn mentioning this man once. He nodded politely. "Pleasure. If you don't mind, my squire would like to get my things settled into my room. Once I've had a chance to clean up, I would like to speak with Prince Dorin."

"As you wish," Javon said, motioning them inside.

He led Aethan left, and up a set of wide, winding stairs to the third floor of the palace, watching Aethan from the corner of his eye all the way as he shared pieces of history about priceless pieces of art as they passed. Aethan took it all in politely, but he spent most of his life in a palace. If Javon hoped to impress Aethan, he would be disappointed.

At last, they stopped inside a large sitting room adorned with colorful tapestries and sheer curtained windows that fluttered in the breeze. Aethan could hear one of the many waterfalls somewhere in the distance.

"Please get cleaned up and make yourself comfortable," Javon said from the doorway. "His Majesty would be honored to host you over dinner."

"Thank you, Javon," Aethan said politely.

Javon bowed and slipped out the door, holding the handle to pull it closed behind him. But he paused, glancing at Aethan. "Do you know when we might see the princess? Her brother is quite worried."

Aethan had to fight to keep his face neutral. "I will speak with him about it over dinner."

Javon murmured subserviently before closing the door.

Roric had already vanished deeper into the suite. Aethan could hear the water running.

How could he possibly explain what happened to Aslyn to her own brother when he did not himself understand? Aethan scrubbed his hands over his face nervously, then heaved out another deep sigh and ran his fingers through his hair.

This would be a very long evening.

Prince Gannon sat back in his seat at the council table, fingers hanging casually over the dragon claw end of the chair arm. The fingers of his other hand flipped a coin across his knuckles, and he leaned weight against his elbow. Outwardly, the Vorovesti Crown Prince appeared unbothered by the argument around him. Inwardly, he fumed just as surely as his father, though not as vocally.

Ambassador Zambul and King Orrin stood on opposite ends of the table. Where Zambul remained calm and collected, Gannon's father pressed his knuckles against the table, leaning forward with a menace that would send any sane man running for his life. Understandably, the other lords around the table sat in silence, their faces varying shades of white. None dared interrupt their king. But no one ever claimed Zambul a coward.

"Hundreds of people died in the Stormvalor attack," King Orrin shouted. "Including the Novavito queen! And under the protection of my *kingdom*. All accounts point to that cheating bastard, Marek Bloodstone and his disgraceful companion Bryse."

Zambul quirked an eyebrow, his voice as cold and collected as ever. "Are you accusing the Stormvalor Champion of killing the Novavito Queen?"

"I am demanding answers from the emperor!" the king roared.

All six lords around the table flinched back, averting their gazes anywhere but their king or the ambassador. One man, Lord Cyrus, dared a glance in Gannon's direction. Something like disgust crossed his features. It was fleeting, but Gannon noticed it all the same. Did Lord Cyrus assume Gannon was an entitled prince? *Good*, Gannon thought. *Let him make his assumptions. Until I know who we can trust, they cannot know the game I'm playing.*

Gannon intended to slowly draw out any hidden spies for the Imperial Seat. The best way for him to do that was to allow these men to think of him as the dutiful, entitled prince. They would underestimate him, let their guard down, make a mistake with him. Then he would find those truly loyal to Vorovesti first. Because the end of the Imperial rule was coming. Gannon could feel it as surely as he felt the wind in his hair—a minor disturbance, easily missed when one wasn't paying attention.

But Gannon was paying attention.

Zambul hissed. The sound made bumps rise across Gannon's arms. "The emperor answers to no one, ruler or refuse. His rule and his actions are absolute and above reproach."

Gannon raised a brow as his father growled at the ambassador. Oh, he was so close to losing control.

"The people are not *refuse*," King Orrin argued. "That Umbrian swine bought off the officials to steal the title from the rightful winner, then used forbidden magic to attack any who stood in his way. His actions resulted in the death of dozens of my soldiers, the injury and near murder of Lord Lux Starkling, and the deaths of visitors and natives throughout the city. He will answer for his crimes!"

Zambul folded his hands behind his back and straightened, raising his chin. "By rightful winner, you assume your nephew. You would have the champion revoke his title so you can give it to your own kin? And if you have evidence that the title was bought off, perhaps you should have Lord Starkling inspect his officials more thoroughly. Had they any integrity, surely they would not have been bought. As far as the accusations that Marek Bloodstone used forbidden magic, your evidence is what? The word of a young man and his friends who were angry because they thought Marek stole the title from him?"

Gannon snorted, drawing all eyes to him. He flipped the coin and caught it between two fingers. "According to Imperial Law, any noble house may raise dispute against another as long as they have witnesses and or evidence against the accused." Gannon slowly raised his gaze from the gold coin, meeting Zambul's black eyes with his own sea-greens. He waved his hand almost absently toward Lord Cyrus. "Would you so discredit the merit of Lord Cyrus' own son, or that of men from four of the five kingdoms?"

Zambul opened his mouth to respond, no doubt with some cold, intelligent comment. Gannon cut him off. "By law, we are well within our right to levy accusations against Marek Bloodstone and his house. Unless you stand in the way of the emperor's laws?"

Zambul's jaw snapped shut. For the first time, his expression darkened dangerously. "I uphold the emperor's laws—"

"To the letter," Gannon finished for him, using words he heard the ambassador throw about at least a dozen times a day for years.

Some shift of pattern rippled up along the gray bands on the ambassador's black robes. Magic. It had to be. Yet no one else seemed to notice except Gannon. It happened quickly.

"My son is right, Zambul," King Orrin said sharply. "Marek Bloodstone's actions could result in a war between Novavito and Vorovesti should Aethan's mission fail. If the Novavito royals determine Vorovesti's men were at fault for the death of their queen, they will be well within their right to retaliate."

"And who do you propose was responsible, if not the Starkling guards?" Zambul asked.

King Orrin glanced at his son. Gannon knew what that look meant. They had discussed it at length while alone, as well as with Aethan and Lux Starkling. Only Black Guards could be responsible for such a butchery. The problem, it seemed, was that no one could determine the motivation behind it, nor how to prove it. And to levy such accusations against the emperor himself was as good as death.

Not true, Gannon reminded himself. Aethan and his father both stated they believed the attack was the Bloodstone's way of keeping Queen Giata from signing a marriage contact with Lux Starkling, thus leaving Marek open to pursuing Princess Aslyn further... And discrediting Aethan's claim of betrothal to the princess. Only the king or queen could sign that agreement. One was dead. The other missing. *Convenient, but Aethan will find King Novin Kiernan.*

"Lord Bloodstone and his son and their dark magic," King Orrin said at last.

No one breathed as they waited, stunned by the accusation against the Bloodstones.

Zambul broke the silence, his voice quiet yet just as dangerous as a razor-sharp blade. "Am I to understand that the kingdom of Vorovesti accuses the emperor's military advisor and his son of sedition?"

King Orrin responded just as quiet and dangerous, unafraid of the danger of his next statement. "Yes. Under Imperial Law, we demand an investigation by High Council."

Gannon's stomach twisted. He knew this was coming. He and his father had discussed it backward and forward. But now that the words were out of the king's mouth, Gannon couldn't help wondering if they made a terrible mistake. It had been obvious to Aethan and several others that the Imperial Heir had something to do with the death of the Novavito queen and her guards, as well as the shadow demons Marek summoned that day.

If the High Council, men and women from each of the five kingdoms selected to investigate the incident and reach a verdict, found the Bloodstone's guilty, the trail would likely lead straight to the Imperial Seat. And then what?

Gannon watched his father from the corner of his eye as he resumed flipping the coin between his fingers. He knew the answer, but his job at this moment was to give off the appearance of disinterest and complete lack of worry regarding the results.

Because if the path led to the Imperial Seat, there would be only one result. It would be the first time since the War of Two Crowns nearly a thousand years ago that the realm would see anything like it on this scale.

War.

Chapter 5

A Clever Plot

Aethan waited near the doors out to the garden veranda where he would meet Aslyn's younger brother over an informal dinner. Hushed, urgent voices beyond the glass doors left Aethan with a clear sense of tension and foreboding. He peered through the closed stained-glass doors at the distorted forms of two people at a table on the veranda.

His escort, Javon Nadier, rapped once firmly on the door to announce their presence, which Aethan had wished he hadn't done as the voices fell utterly silent. He had been close to catching some sense of their urgent discussion before Javon silenced them.

After a command from the other side, Javon opened the door wide and stepped through, giving Aethan a full view of the stunning landscape. A riot of colorful flowers bloomed all around the garden space, framing the white metal table with its swirling patterns, curving legs, and matching chairs. Willow trees bowed and swayed on the warm summer breeze, ushering the scent of jasmine and roses his way. The smell made his heart ache. Aslyn smelled like jasmine and roses.

"Your Majesty, Lord Aethan Starkling," Javon said as he motioned Aethan through the door.

Only one of the two men at the table rose for him, offering a politely deferential bow. Aethan instantly recognized the black uniform and depthless eyes as an ambassador. He studied every inch of Aethan with scrutiny and jealousy. This could be no other than Umbogo, the ambassador who coveted what Aethan now had—Aslyn's hand in marriage. He couldn't be more than a few years older than Aethan.

The second was younger, perhaps eighteen, with features that instantly reminded Aethan of Aslyn, though he lacked her brilliant amber eyes. His clothing was finely made and lightweight, but something about the way he wore it made him seem casual and carefree. The jacket was unbuttoned completely and wide open. The white shirt beneath bore wrinkles and bunched around the waist, with two of the top buttons undone.

Dorin's brown eyes took Aethan in swiftly and his brows lifted ever so slightly as the corner of his mouth curled upward. "Please, Aethan—can I call you Aethan?"

Aethan gave a nod and Dorin breezed on.

"Join us for dinner." Dorin motioned to a vacant seat. One of four.

"It's a pleasure to meet the brother Aslyn told me so much about," Aethan said as he crossed the veranda. He released the bottom button of his light jacket as he settled in his chair, though for much different reasons than Dorin's completely undone appearance. Lux Starkling would have torn Aethan to shreds if he hosted *anyone* over dinner in such a state.

"A pleasure indeed," Dorin said. "I certainly see why my sister was taken with you."

Javon made a noise in the back of his throat that made Dorin grimace.

Aethan shifted slightly in his chair, uncomfortable with the comment. Aslyn had hinted that her brother had preferences their father had disapproved of. The way Dorin eyed him made Aethan feel awkward, and he did his best to mask the discomfort. Dorin could do what he wished with anyone else he desired and Aethan couldn't care less. But he didn't want to be the recipient of that interest. If it persisted, Aethan would say something. For now, he let it go.

The advisor settled into the fourth chair to Aethan's left, leaving Umbogo to the right and Dorin directly across from him.

Dinner smelled delicious, but almost anything would be better than what Aethan had been forced to eat for weeks at sea. Slices of roasted bird with baked potato wedges and steamed seasoned vegetables decorated a platter in the center of the table. A decanter of iced water and another of white wine also waited. Dorin didn't hesitate to pour a glass of wine, then held it out to Aethan.

"I hear a toast may soon be in order," Dorin said as Aethan graciously accepted the drink.

Javon and Umbogo waited for the prince to help himself to the food first, then for Aethan, as etiquette would require. Royals first, then guests, then aids.

"Yes, well, it took us both by surprise," Aethan admitted. He had to be careful how much he said about the situation around the ambassador. They played vicious games with words and knowledge. "The first time we met, she all but called me presumptuous." He wouldn't dare tell them the truth about how he actually met Aslyn in a hallway where she pretended to be a commoner.

Dorin chuckled. "Yes, that sounds like my sister."

"Were you?" Umbogo asked, expertly carving through his meat with a knife.

Aethan thought back to their conversation at the mixer and a warm smile curled the corners of his mouth. "Maybe a little," he admitted before taking a drink of wine. The flavor burst across his tastebuds in a way that only Murandy Hills wine could. "But the more time I spent with Aslyn, the more she wormed her way into my heart."

"His Majesty has been gracious enough to welcome you into his home, but you arrived without his sister," Umbogo asked bluntly. "What should we make of this?"

Aethan hesitated, glancing around the table at the three men studying him with varying levels of interest. Finally, he said, "I had hoped to speak with Prince Dorin alone about the rest."

Dorin's expression didn't shift. Javon scowled at Aethan's response.

But Umbogo would not be deterred. "With the rest of the royal family missing and rebels threatening the throne, you will have to forgive us if we are unwilling to leave anyone alone with the prince." He rested an elbow on the table and pointed his knife at Aethan in a way that would appear non-threatening were Aethan not aware of the tension in the man's demeanor.

But Aethan didn't flinch.

"We received a message directly from the Imperial Seat not long before you arrived," Umbogo pressed on. "He is worried about the security of the Kiernan royal family."

Aethan nearly scoffed. The Imperial Prince Valen hadn't seemed terribly worried about Aslyn's security in Stormvalor.

"Come down now, Umbogo," Dorin said, sounding bored by the threat in the ambassador's tone. "Can we not enjoy dinner first?"

Aethan set down his silverware and rested his forearms on the table. "Have I done something wrong? If so, I assure you it was unintentional."

"Was it?" Umbogo asked.

Dorin heaved a dramatic sigh and set his own silverware down. The glare he shot the ambassador made Aethan's skin crawl, but not nearly as much as the way Umbogo dipped his head in shame. How did the prince get an ambassador to show such humiliation?

Aethan waited patiently, but his stomach became a nest of nerves, every one of them warning him to prepare for a fight.

At last, Dorin brushed his hands over the napkin in his lap and met Aethan's gaze. "We have some... reservations toward your intentions."

Aethan didn't flinch. "Such as?" What had he done wrong?

"Firstly, we've been informed that, while Aslyn had initially accepted your proposal, she turned her back on you and left with Marek Bloodstone," Dorin said evenly.

This time Aethan did flinch. He would never forget the look in Aslyn's eyes the moment before she turned away from him. It haunted him. But he had been certain her words were a code. He was doing as she expected him to do. Except, he couldn't admit as much. At least, not in front of the emperor's ambassador. Which was why he wanted to explain himself to Dorin alone.

"She has been there nearly a month now," Dorin continued, "getting to know the Bloodstone family. According to the emperor, she intends to marry *him*. Not you."

Aethan fumbled for something to say. He should have been prepared for this, but he had expected Aslyn would at least send word to her brother before his arrival.

"What's more distressing is news of my mother's death at the hands of Black-blade," Dorin continued.

Blackblade? They thought the shadow assassin was responsible for what happened in that royal suite? If so, Blackblade was more butcher than assassin.

"I don't believe Blackblade was in Stormvalor," Aethan said. Though he had to admit he was unsure, even if he was fairly certain what happened in the royal suite was not Blackblade's doing.

"But my mother *is* dead, along with all of her guards, in a city where primary military control belongs to *your* family," Dorin said, but the words sounded more like a question.

"Are you accusing me of something, Prince Dorin?" Aethan asked sharply. He hated how swiftly he shifted to a defensive tone. That wouldn't help matters and he knew it.

"No," Dorin said at last.

Aethan relaxed slightly, but then he noticed the gleam in Umbogo's eyes and his fingers brushed the knife beside his plate. "But *he* is?" Aethan asked, nodding toward the ambassador.

"You misunderstand, Aethan," Dorin said, sounding bored by all of this. "Or perhaps it isn't misunderstanding as much as willful ignorance."

"Excuse me?" Aethan hissed.

"Upon investigation, my father's financial officer discovered something quite troubling," Dorin continued as if he hadn't just insulted his guest. "The rebels who struck our palace weeks ago were well-financed. Javon followed the trail of money."

Leave, Aethan. Now. But morbid curiosity froze him to his seat.

"It led Javon to an account covertly linked to the Starkling family name," Dorin said. "The same account that funded the assassination of Lord Corinth months ago."

"That's preposterous," Aethan retorted. Who was Lord Corinth?

"Is it? I've reviewed the documents myself," Dorin continued.

Aethan shifted in his seat, closing his hand around the knife beside his plate. Someone set him up. Was it Marek's family setting him up to take the fall so Aslyn could never marry him? With Aethan out of the picture, Aslyn would have to choose between Marek, Zayne, and Umbogo. He didn't know where Zayne was anymore. The man had vanished the same day Aslyn left Stormvalor.

"It took me a little while to put all the pieces together, but it's pretty clear to me now," Dorin said, and that boredom in his eyes vanished, replaced by a fox. "All of this ties back to the throne. Your family wanted you crowned alongside my sister so badly you took up the services of the assassin, Blackblade. Corinth was just a test. Once that test was completed, you funded his next venture. After you secured my sister's hand in marriage, Blackblade would take out the entire royal guard as well as my mother, ensuring Aslyn depended on you utterly in the hours following the end of the tournament. But her marriage wouldn't be enough as long as my father still sat on the throne, which was why you funded the rebels in Arithia. They would only close the trap once you had my sister right where you wanted her."

Aethan's head spun. None of this was true, nor did it make any sense. "I only heard about the rebels after the fact, when your sister came to me."

"For help," Dorin interrupted.

"No." Aethan's temper rose and it took intense willpower to keep it in check. "She came to me and told me she loved me, but she also told me that to save her father, she would have to choose Marek because she needed ships to mount a rescue."

"Ships you now have waiting just beyond our breakwater," Javon pointed out.

"Well, yes, but I brought those ships to rescue your father," Aethan said quickly, leaning forward and pressing urgency toward Dorin. He needed the prince to believe him. "Why would I rescue a man I am allegedly responsible for kidnapping?"

Dorin raised his brows in amusement. "Seriously?"

"Yes!"

"You know exactly where my father is, and once you bring him back home, you look like the hero!" Dorin smacked a hand against the tabletop. "Why wouldn't my sister want to marry the man who brought her father home?"

"This is madness," Aethan muttered. Heat and rage crackled beneath his skin like a warning that a storm was coming. Clouds slid across the gray sky, masking the sun and casting gloom over everything. A gloom that matched his foul mood.

Umbogo noticed something. He glanced up at the sky, frowning at the sudden storm clouds. His gaze then flicked to Aethan, black eyes wide. *Why is he staring like that?*

"So it would seem on the surface," Dorin agreed. "But both Umbogo and Javon have uncovered evidence."

"Fabricated!" Aethan snapped. "Whether by them or someone else, it doesn't matter. None of this is true."

"They're called facts for a reason," Dorin said.

"Let me play along with this delusion for a moment," Aethan said sharply. "If what you say is true, I stand to gain nothing without the formal contract, which was never completed before everything went sideways in Stormvalor. My agreement with your sister was spoken and personal. But without that contract, I hold nothing here in Arithia."

Dorin shook his head sadly. "But how can I ignore what has happened right under my nose since you arrived in my palace?"

"*Your* palace?" Aethan hissed. This was bad. So bad. They were accusing him of treason against the Novavito crown, a sentence punishable by death.

Dorin ignored him, nodding once past Aethan's shoulder.

Aethan twisted in his seat as he heard the scuffling of feet resisting each step. A muffled sound of protest came from behind Roric's gag as the guards dragged him onto the veranda.

"He's a child," Aethan said, his heart aching as he noted the defiance and rage in Roric's eyes. "He has nothing to do with any of this."

"He's your spy," Umbogo snapped. "The guards caught him eavesdropping in places he didn't belong."

Why did Roric have to insist on joining this mission? Guilt gnawed at Aethan's stomach as he watched the guards holding the boy. Aethan tensed his hold on the knife, calculating the number of steps between him and the guards, as well as his odds of freeing the boy and escaping alive. It didn't look good. If he tried to fight, it would likely only make him look guilty of the treason they accused him of.

Dorin stood and started toward the exit. Aethan was nearly out of time.

"Cavis and Cormic!" Aethan exclaimed, thinking quickly. Dorin paused, turning back with his arms crossed. "Your father selected them himself. He trusted them enough to represent him and his throne in the tournament. If you don't believe me, speak with them. They are here in Arithia, likely back home. They saw Aslyn and me together. They trust me, but their loyalty is first and foremost to the Novavito Crown. They will be character witnesses to discredit all this lunacy. Someone has set me up."

Aethan held his breath as Dorin considered his plea. Every second that passed grew more agonizing. Roric stopped struggling, watching Aethan and Dorin with wide, desperate eyes.

Dorin ran his fingers through his dark hair, further enhancing his disheveled appearance. The near collapse of his family clearly placed a great burden on the prince's shoulders. A burden that wore on him. And these men around Dorin had to be making some play against the throne. If they weren't in on it, Aethan would swallow his sword. Umbogo, for certain, had a lot to lose if Aethan married Aslyn. And he had the connections and means to arrange everything.

Desperation shone in Aethan's blue eyes as he pleaded silently with Dorin.

A chair scraped against stone. Umbogo approached the prince, placing a hand on his shoulder and whispering something in his ear.

Dorin's lips thinned and he gave the subtlest of nods.

It's him. It's Umbogo. He's behind all of this! How could Dorin not see that?

Umbogo stepped back, folding his hands behind his back and making himself little more than a shadow behind the prince.

"I will speak with the twins myself," Dorin said at last.

Aethan released a breath of relief.

"You will remain in your quarters under guard until I summon you," Dorin continued.

Aethan flinched, but nodded in agreement, confident that the twins would vouch for him.

Dorin's gaze flicked to Roric. "Take the boy to the dungeons."

Roric emitted a muffled protest, yanking futilely at the guards' hold on him.

"No!" Aethan surged to his feet, dropping the knife on the table. The last thing he needed was a weapon in hand as he protested. "Leave him with me. We won't leave the room."

Roric calmed, but his eyes shone with fear that struck at Aethan's heart.

Dorin shook his head, almost looking sad and worn out. "The two of you must be kept apart until I've had a chance to investigate this further. Since he has proven himself slippery, I have no choice but to imprison him."

Roric cried out behind his gag.

Aethan deflated. He never should have let Roric leave the ship to join him here. "Can I at least say goodbye?"

Dorin glanced between Roric and Aethan, then nodded once.

Aethan rushed over to Roric and pulled the boy into a hug. "I'm sorry about all of this. We will get you out, Roric. I swear it. Cavis and Cormic will help us."

Roric leaned against Aethan, unable to hug him back in restraints, but eager for the affection all the same. He nodded against Aethan's shoulder, sniffling as he fought back his fear.

And as the guards pulled the two of them in opposite directions, Aethan admired his squire's tenacity. The fear that had shone in Roric's eyes moments ago winked out, replaced by a boyish show of bravery. Roric didn't whimper or cry, nor did he resign himself to his fate. The boy walked away with as much dignity as he could muster under the circumstances. He trusted Aethan completely, and that trust sent a shard of fear through Aethan's soul.

Both of their fates rested on Aethan's shoulders. If he couldn't exonerate himself from these treason charges, they were both as good as dead.

I can't fail Roric. No matter what.

CHAPTER 6

Palace Visitors

Empress, they call her. But there was never a wedding. The Empress rarely saw her husband, who—to her knowledge—was still only the imperial heir. Yet they all called her Empress, as if the name her parents gave her no longer existed.

Everything about this palace held an ominous weight, from the cold obistone walls adorned with tapestries of the first emperor's glorious victories in the War of Two Crowns over a thousand years ago, to the equally cold stone floors covered with thick, lush rugs and furs. Everything bore the imperial colors—black and silver. The only splashes of color in her rooms were those she had added herself since arriving over a month ago.

The Empress's suite was anything but small. With two bedrooms, three bathrooms—two of which had tubs with flowing water—a dining room, sitting room, and changing room the suite offered all the luxury the Empress could ever hope for.

Yet the space was lonely. Devoid of life. *Just as I feel devoid of life*. A fitting space.

The rooms draped with sheer decadence. The walls, adorned with intricate carvings and gilded moldings, seemed to drink in the soft glow of the chandeliers overhead. Velvet curtains of the deepest black draped the towering windows, their heavy folds muffling the outside world, sealing the room in an air of secrecy. The vast bed at the far wall, with its impossibly detailed headboard and silken midnight sheets, looked less like a place for rest and more like a throne in its own right.

A bed that size has no purpose in a place so empty and lonely.

Candlelight flickered from the elaborate candelabras, their silver arms casting twisting shadows against the walls that often gave her chills. A faint scent of myrrh and aged parchment clung to the air. Every surface gleamed with dark opulence—the carved mahogany furniture, the gilded accents, the lacquered floors that whispered beneath her hesitant steps.

What secrets will you share today? she wondered as the whisper of her steps followed her, a lone, lonely companion.

This was not a place of warmth or comfort. It was a place of dominion, where secrets had been spoken behind the glow of candlelight and veiled in layers of silk and shadow. A chill ran down her spine. She was no mere guest in this room—she was its heir, whether or not she willed it. *I have inherited all of the wealth and no one to share it with.*

No one ever came to visit her, save her maid and the servants who changed her sheets, washed her clothes, and cleaned her suite. And of those staff members, only the maid ever spoke—nameless and servile. She simply bowed her way out, murmuring "Empress" until she vanished from sight.

The silence had become suffocating. The young Empress was unsure how much more she could handle. Depression grew within her each passing day. In the past few days, she had begun speaking to herself, offering herself companionship.

This existence was abysmal. *Death would be a mercy. Has my purpose been fulfilled? Can I just... let go?*

Empress, they called her, yet she had no power over any of the five kingdoms. She didn't even have power over her own staff. While they bowed and scraped to ensure her comfort, some of her orders had gone ignored. Once, she had tried to fire a young woman who had silently refused to show her to the castle stable. The next day, that same young woman returned to continue her job as if the Empress hadn't excused her from service.

She harbored no delusions any longer. This title of hers was little more than an illusion, a form of courtesy. It meant nothing at all. I *mean nothing at all*.

The Empress smoothed out the skirt of her thick dress as it twisted when she turned toward the doors and marched out into the tall, wide, empty hallway. The material of her dress helped ward off the endless chill of this palace. A Black Guard closed in behind her, trailing her every step like a shadow. They never spoke. They never looked directly at her, as far as she could tell. They simply existed like shadows.

Do they realize their protection in this place is pointless? There is no one to guard me from.

No one had confined her to her quarters. The Empress was free to wander the castle, but the Black Guards constantly blocked off entire sections of the massive palace, restricting her movements to only a small portion of the grounds. Her suite. Her husband's suite, but only if he invited her to join him, which he never did. A library, formal dining hall, vacant ballroom, and garden without greenery. Even that space only housed manicured stone pathways and statues of the first emperor.

The Empress stopped before one such statue, peering up at the face of the first emperor, Narcisse. The freestanding mannerist style of the sculpture gave Narcisse a benign, gentle quality which history taught them he had been far from. This man had smooth features, kind eyes, and an overall strikingly handsome visage. He offered a sense of peace to the viewer, yet she knew him to have been a cruel, ruthless leader who killed any who opposed him.

If she cocked her head and squinted, the resemblance to her husband was uncanny. They could have been the same man. A ridiculous notion, since nearly a thousand years separated the two men from each other.

Slate stones shifted and crunched as booted feet shifted. Someone approached. From the corner of her eye, she spotted her Black Guard stepping back and bowing. She stiffened as her heart began racing, worried the emperor chose this moment to approach her at last. Without thinking, she curtseyed, holding her bow with her eyes lowered.

"No need of that from you, my love," Valen said.

She relaxed a little as she straightened, her racing heart slowing to a more steady rhythm. At least it was her husband and not his father. She dreaded meeting *him*. How could she live in the emperor's home for weeks and he had yet to cross her path? Not once had she laid eyes on Emperor Oxon. The only time she had ever laid eyes on him was as a girl at her mother's funeral. Was he avoiding her? If so, why?

"How are you feeling today?" he asked, stopping beside the statue without giving it a glance, as if something as beautiful and imposing as the statue were as inconsequential as a tree or shrub.

The Empress ran her hand along her cheek, feeling the cold skin. The few times she and her husband did speak, he inquired about her state. She couldn't recall exactly why, but that it had something to do with a previous empress... one of her predecessors.

"I am cold all the time," she said. Was it this place? Did it drain on her somehow? Perhaps that was why she was always cold. *Or perhaps I am just dying very slowly.*

"I will have a new lined cloak sent to you immediately," he replied. "How do you fare otherwise? Are you sleeping better?"

The first two weeks, she had hardly slept at all, hearing noises where there were none, sensing movement when completely alone. The palace was haunted. It must have been. Either that, or some dark magic took root in this place. Once he noticed, he had sleeping draughts sent to her each night to help her rest.

"Better, yes, thank you."

"Good," he said. "Your emperor needs your services."

Her stomach twisted, but she nodded. "Of course. What service will he require of me?"

"We will host a guest for a short while," he said. "Just keep her entertained. Be a good hostess and reassure her that the Imperial Seat remains strong."

"Is it?" she asked her husband.

His brows knitted together and for a moment anger flashed in his black eyes. "Is it what?"

She flinched, averting her gaze to the slate stone path beneath them. "Strong," she whispered, afraid the word would insult him. Once more, her heart raced, drumming in her ears as she waited for his response.

His silence terrified her. In seconds, that stillness between them made her tremble. She thought she might pass out from sheer terror. She couldn't gather the courage to look up.

Valen's finger hooked under her chin, forcing the Empress to peer into his dark, depthless eyes. A fierce determination, a certainty, filled those black voids, flooding through her skin and into her soul, shoring up her doubts and soothing away her fear. "It will be. You and I will make it stronger than ever, Sybil."

SybilSybilSybil. She repeated the name swiftly in her head. The name that her parents gave her. The name she had nearly forgotten because no one called her by name in this place.

Valen placed a gentle kiss on her forehead, and the tenderness of it chased away the rest of her doubts, as if they had never been. Then he whispered, "I cannot do it without you."

Gannon walked through the palace garden with Trystain and Iskra, a habit he had begun nearly as soon as Aethan left. They met every other day in various locations around the palace grounds, at the Pridell Manor, or at a tavern in Mordelic. With Aethan gone and Iskra leaving for Arithia as soon as her marriage contract with Cavis Dysart arrived, Gannon's pool of friends began running dry. He had a hard time trusting the motives of most, but not these two.

These were the only two in all Mordelic that Gannon could trust with any of his worries or secrets. For the most part. Some things Gannon was forced to keep quiet, even from his friends. If they knew that he and his father prepared for what they believed to be an inevitable war against the Imperial Seat, they would no doubt tell their families, and word would inadvertently spread.

Instead, Gannon spent as much free time with the two of them as he could, acting as if nothing bothered him and he wasn't terrified every moment of every day that war was coming to Vorovesti.

Iskra had changed since returning from Stormvalor. She had always been happy and doting with Aethan, but now she positively glowed with joy. Cavis Dysart clearly made her happy. Gannon was happy for her—especially since Aethan had found happiness elsewhere.

Iskra offered Gannon insights into the pulse of the noble class in a way no one else seemed capable of doing. He appreciated her intelligence and intuition more and more each time they spoke, and in the weeks since her return from Stormvalor, he had grown to think of her as a sister. He never had siblings of his own. Aethan and Sybil were the closest he ever had, and now they were both gone. One day soon, Iskra would be as well.

Gannon worried about Trystain. He had been utterly smitten with Sybil, even if he had acted flippant about it and flirted with other women. All of it had been harmless because Trystain would have done nothing to hurt Sybil.

Outwardly, Trystain acted like his normal self, flirting shamelessly with any girl who paid attention and waving off Gannon's and Iskra's concerns over his welfare now that the Imperial Heir had claimed Sybil for himself. "It is what it is," he would say. But Gannon knew Trystain almost as well as he knew Aethan. His friend was hurting deeply and acting it off. More than once, Gannon spied Trystain in the training grounds or stable lost in thought. One day, Trystain would finally break down. Gannon just needed to be certain he was there for his friend when it happened.

"No word from the emperor about King Orrin's demand for a High Council ruling?" Trystain asked.

Gannon shook his head. "It can take a while. But as long as the request has been made and the accusation remains unresolved, it protects Vorovesti from Novavito retaliation."

"You think war is coming," Trystain said, a hint of shock flickering across his face.

Gannon tensed. "That's exactly what we are trying to avoid, Tryst. If we can get the High Council to rule in our favor, Novavito will have no choice but to direct their demands for justice toward Umbr... toward the Bloodstones. If that happens, not even the emperor will protect any of them."

Not that Gannon wasn't worried the empire wouldn't just march on Vorovesti for daring to accuse the emperor's military advisor and his heir. But his friends didn't need to know that. So much hinged on the Bloodstone trial, on Aethan's successful mission. If one failed, they should be able to fall back on the other. If both failed... war would be inevitable.

Trystain turned his attention to Iskra. "So you haven't heard anything yet?" he asked as they wandered along the garden paths. Summer was in full swing, but the gardens hadn't recovered from winter. Several trees never budded leaves. Flowers bloomed and withered on the same day.

As if the world itself was giving up.

"No," Iskra said. "But they would only just be arriving in Arithia. Then Cavis and his father would have to talk through the contract my father negotiated with Cavis. And he would have to sign it and send it back. Father won't allow me to leave Mordelic until he has a signed contract." She shot Trystain a wry smirk. "Something about intentions being useless without the contract."

Gannon winced. Her father referred to Aethan's intention to marry Iskra before he left for Stormvalor. That had all changed when he fell in love with Aslyn. Not that Iskra hadn't benefited from their broken intentions as much as he had. Both were so much happier.

"Good," Gannon said. "It means I can selfishly hold on to you a little longer."

Iskra laughed as she took Gannon's arm and hugged it. "Oh my sweet, selfish prince. One of these days, a woman will come along and steal your heart. I'm just sorry I will miss it."

Gannon forced a smile. But he knew better. As crown prince, his options were restricted. He would be lucky if he felt affection for his wife. The king would make appropriate arrangements when the most beneficial offer came along. Gannon's feelings had nothing to do with it.

"Don't stress it," Trystain said with a shrug. "Love is overrated." The words sounded haunted to Gannon's ears, but Trystain smiled at him. And there it was again, that spark of sorrow in his eyes. It passed quickly, replaced by mischief. "It's what happens between the sheets that really matters."

"Tryst!" Iskra squealed, slapping his shoulder playfully.

He chuckled, but Gannon detected an emptiness even in that sound, like he was going through the motions but not truly feeling any of them. Like he was acting his part. "He knows I'm right."

Gannon laughed softly, shaking his head. "You're a terrible influence."

"Is there any other kind to be?"

H ouse Dysart was a family of lesser nobles who served the high houses of Novavito for several generations. Cavis and Cormic, as sons and potential heirs to the Dysart name, had trained with royal guards and would one day serve as lieutenants in the Novavito military. Their father, Lord Gerant Dysart, worked with his brother as one of the chief military leaders in Arithia. They were a far step down from generals, but Gerant Dysart had hoped that might change once his sons returned from the Stormvalor tournament.

Cavis had clenched his jaw against his father's private tirade upon their return home. Lord Dysart had been kind enough to the other competitors, offering them rooms and playing a personable host. But the moment he had his sons alone, he unleashed his genuine disappointment upon them both. Never mind that they had earned the trust and confidence of the future King Consort which would no doubt earn both prestigious positions in the royal guard soon. And ignore the fact that Cavis had snared the heart of a woman well above his station, a wife who would surely elevate him even further in social circles.

The fact that he had lost the tournament and several matches were the only points on which Lord Gerant Dysart could focus.

The moment the lecture had ended, Cavis cleaned himself up, saddled a horse, and rode to the palace to deliver the queen's ashes at dusk, per Aethan's request. Cormic accompanied Cavis on the trek, as did a few of the other Stormvalor men.

The palace courtyard had guards lined along every wall around the courtyard. An older man with peppered hair that Cavis recognized as Javon Nadier, the king's financier, waited on the lower steps of the palace with only guards around him. No Aethan. No Prince Dorin.

Cavis and Cormic dismounted first, followed by the other competitors. As Cavis marched forward and bowed to Javon, Cormic retrieved the urn and small chest from his saddlebags.

"Master Nadier," Cavis said formally. "We are here to speak with the prince."

"His Majesty is otherwise occupied," Javon said smoothly.

"We are happy to wait."

Javon's gaze slipped past Cavis's shoulder and his expression tightened. "What have you brought to us?"

Cavis glanced at his brother and the small cohort following behind. They all kept a respectful expression and distance. Cavis turned back to Javon. "I assumed Lord Starkling would have explained already. As I said, we would prefer to deliver this directly to Prince Dorin."

"And as I have said," Javon snapped, "His Majesty is otherwise occupied. He has entrusted me with the task of turning you away."

Cormic muttered something under his breath that Cavis knew would be very unlordlike. But Cavis had to maintain his composure. This was a horrible business, and Aethan had assured them he would prepare the prince to receive the news by the time they arrived.

"Very well," Cavis said evenly. He gave Cormic a sharp nod. His brother stepped forward and held up the urn in a large hand, offering it with a bow to Javor. "We wanted to return our queen in her beautiful glory, but the journey would have been too long for her to make the return in her radiance." Cavis's throat tightened as he gazed at the urn. That was his queen. The queen they had been forced to burn to avoid her rotting corpse from spreading illness on the ships. He drew in a breath as his eyes burned. "But we wanted to return her home all the same."

Javon stiffened, staring at the urn. He stepped forward, accepting it reverently from Cormic's hand. "How do I know this is Queen Giata?"

Cavis flinched, insulted that anyone would doubt his integrity, especially where his own queen was concerned. As if reading his mind, Cormic held up the small chest, then set it on the palace steps at Javon's feet.

"Those are the queen's jewels and crown," Cavis said. "My brother and I inspected, cleaned, and packaged them up ourselves, guarding them on this long journey." Cavis opened the chest so there could be no doubt that everything was there and accounted for, or that it contained what they promised.

Javon pulled the urn close to his heart as he peered down into the open chest.

"We had hoped to touch base with Lord Starkling before returning home," Cavis added.

"He is currently unavailable," Javon said swiftly. "I believe His Majesty had plans for Lord Starkling."

Cavis had no choice but to accept they would go no further than these steps. It was either that or he risked angering Javon, the gatekeeper who could bring the entire royal guard down on their heads. "That's unfortunate. Please let him know we would like to reconnect with him when he has time. And please send our deepest condolences to the prince. If he would like any of us to return for more information, for anything, just send word and we will be here within the hour."

Javon motioned for a guard to collect the chest as he hugged the urn against his chest. "I'm sure he will be reassured to know you are close at hand, should he need you. These are troubling times for the young Majesty, what with his father kidnapped, his sister gone, and his mother dead."

Cavis nodded solemnly. Not that Aslyn was missing. Cavis and Aethan both knew exactly where she was, and neither of them liked it.

As he turned to mount his horse, the others followed his cue.

Javon watched the small cohort ride out of the palace grounds, hugging the urn against his chest protectively.

The moment they passed out of the palace walls, Cormic edged his mount closer to his brother. "Something is wrong."

Cavis nodded. "Aethan mentioned the ambassador making a play for power. Do you think that, without the princess, he is somehow manipulating the prince?"

Cormic shrugged. "You're the brains. I'm just the much better-looking muscles. But I've never been turned away like that before."

Cavis grudgingly agreed. Something foul was afoot in Arithia.

CHAPTER 7

The Imperial Seat

From a distance, the imperial palace hadn't looked nearly as impressive as the palace in Arithia, but as Aslyn rode the narrow path between Marek and a squad of Black Guards, her head tipped back to take in the truly colossal size of the structure. With thick outer walls of obistone and several towers, the palace turned out to be much larger than she had first thought it to be.

Black Guards at the gate checked each of them and passed them through. The gate itself was made of thick reinforced blackened steel. Something about the weight of the place instantly settled over her bones, oppressive and grim and utterly dangerous.

Once through the ten-foot-thick obistone walls, the area opened into a courtyard of stone just as crushing as everything else. A fountain in the center of the courtyard displayed a statue portraying the first emperor, Narcisse, slaying a golden dragon. The blood that seeped from the dragon's wounds was red-tinted water that spilled out into the fountain below. Aslyn shuddered as her horse halted. That statue alone made a statement about the dominant nature of the imperial line. *We come from a line of dragon-slayers*, it said, *and we remain just as brutal and powerful.*

As Aslyn dismounted, she sought the guards who had accompanied them up to the palace. But as her gaze darted around the courtyard, she could no longer tell one guard from another. A dozen men in that demonic black armor held regular positions at each key point in the courtyard. If Blackblade was among them, he certainly was good at blending in. Not that it should shock her to learn as much. It was how they met, after all. Layers of deception she now refused to peel back.

Yet she missed the comfort of his presence, if only because it made her feel less alone. Blackblade hadn't returned since he urged her to read the letters and she rudely told him to leave. Maybe she had finally pushed him too far and he had, in fact, left her to take the Jewel of Arithia to his buyer.

So much for his oath, Aslyn thought with a pang of contrition.

If that were the case, Aslyn had no one to help her now. Kaiti remained at Bloodstone Manor at Lord Bloodstone's insistence, her only other companion in this place. If Aslyn wanted to escape her situation, and this place, she would have to save herself.

An ambassador waited at the palace doors in black robes trimmed in multi-hued ribbons that seemed to change color with each subtle movement.

"Your Majesty, Our Great and Revered Emperor is honored to host you," the ambassador said, his voice more like a woman than a man. Were there female ambassadors? Aslyn had never met one. "Please, allow me to escort you to the throne room where he will greet you."

Marek stepped up beside Aslyn, taking her arm as if escorting her onto the dance floor. Aslyn gritted her teeth and swallowed the revulsion climbing up her throat. She wanted to shake him off, shove him into the gravel beneath their boots. But she couldn't give away her absolute disgust toward him. Not when she stood on the front steps of the imperial palace. Instead, she raised her chin, took a deep breath as if it could ward off his touch, gathered her skirt in her free hand, and allowed Marek to escort her up the stairs and into the palace.

The palace entryway spread out in so far that the left and right wings of the space vanished into darkness. Across the wide space, a pair of iron doors at least thirty feet tall stood open, arching into the throne room. Aslyn stepped through confidently with Marek clinging to her arm as if hauling in a prize. Her amber eyes swept the doors as she passed. Murals inlaid in the doors shone with a glow from within, undoubtedly imbued with forbidden magic. The door she inspected depicted a battle scene from the War of Two Crowns.

Emperor Narcisse climbed to the peak of a mountain of bodies—human, elf, and dragon—hoisting his flag in victory. Some of the bodies still lived, bloodied and reaching up as if begging for mercy beneath the mound of the dead. Aslyn's stomach twisted taking in the violent scene. She swore that, as she examined the mural upon passing, some of the Black Guards at the base of the mountain of bodies killed the survivors.

Aslyn shook off the terror that scene pressed into her bones, doing her best to continue forward to the head of the throne room...

And the empty obistone throne. It was a cruel, twisted thing just as dangerous as the man who would soon sit upon it. Set at the apex of the throne, above where the emperor's crown would sit atop his head, a pair of sapphire blue and brilliant amber stones shone with a light all their own.

The throne room made every other part of the palace appear small. Pillars of obistone stretched high above, vanishing into darkness. Surely the throne room had a ceiling, but it was so high above, it disappeared into a void of nothing. The only light in the room shone through stained glass windows that reflected light on mirrors strategically placed around the vast chamber. The more the light from the stained-glass images reflected off glass, the more distorted and grotesque the art became. More reminders of Emperor Narcisse's great victories.

Per instructions, Aslyn halted at the base of the stairs leading up to the imperial throne. She gathered her skirt carefully, dipping down onto her knees, then rearranging her skirt around her. Marek joined her, both with heads bowed to stare at the tiles beneath them.

Tiles that once more depicted Emperor Narcisse killing each of the kings and queens who opposed him in the War of Two Crowns. King Malik of the Kruos elves, alongside his son Malikai. The elven Kruos princess Loralai and her husband, King Quade Martnarving of Novavito. King Khaelys of Oshon and his wife and heirs. King Tiberis Strong of Vorovesti and his two wives—Queen Solfia and Queen Vanna. Aslyn knew the stories of each one of their falls from her history lessons. And these brutal images made those lessons feel lacking. She struggled not to shudder as she kept her gaze on the tiles.

Placing these images in the tiles at the base of the imperial throne was a clear power play. Any who entered this throne room would kneel before the emperor and gaze upon these tiles as a reminder of what happened to those who opposed the emperor's rule.

Emperor Narcisse established the kingdom of Umbr after his victory, claiming lands belonging to both Novavito and Vorovesti as his own and carving out those pieces of power from the kings who had opposed him.

A staff banged against the tiled floor, followed by a booming female voice. "His Excellency, the Exalted, First of His Name, Ruler of the Five Kingdoms of Divica, His Imperial Majesty, Emperor of Divica."

Aslyn didn't dare sneak a peek at Emperor Oxon, a man she had only seen once in her young life, at the tender age of seven. She remembered him being cold and imposing, but little else. Her gaze remained fixed on the tiles, as did Marek's at her side. Both had their hands folded together in front of them, wrists bared to show they bore no weapons, as was custom. Only the Black Guards could carry weapons in the emperor's presence. Breaking that law was immediately punishable by death.

The thump of boots across the dais, accompanied by the soft click of heels, was the only sound in the still throne room. Aslyn could only see the black shine of his boots as he passed three steps up from her to take his seat.

Cloth rustled as he settled in place, followed by utter silence. Aslyn focused on keeping her breath even and steady. She would not cower like she was nothing, even if this was the emperor.

"Princess," the emperor said, his voice silky smooth. "I'm pleased to host you here in my home."

The voice sent a shock down Aslyn's spine and she nearly looked up but caught herself just in time. Still, that familiar voice subdued her.

"And Marek Bloodstone... I don't recall inviting you." Silence. Marek didn't move a muscle. Was he even breathing? "But this does save me the trouble of a visit with your father later."

Silence once more, broken by that smooth voice after an insufferably long time. "Speak."

"Imperial Majesty—" Marek began.

"Not you, Bloodstone," the emperor cut him off sharply.

Marek immediately fell silent.

Aslyn cleared her throat. "I bid you a good day, your Imperial Grace, and thank you for welcoming me into your home. Lord Bloodstone is relieved by your gracious offer after several of his Black Guards were killed."

The emperor hummed thoughtfully. "*His* Black Guards? Interesting choice of words, princess."

A beat of silence. Aslyn scrambled to find the right words, but before she could speak, the ambassador beat her to it.

"His Imperial Grace has bid you to gaze upon him now."

Aslyn's heart thundered against her ribs as she raised her chin proudly, despite remaining on her knees. Marek did likewise beside her, entirely silent. Yet their reactions mirrored one another as they gasped.

Prince Valen perched upon the throne, hands folded casually over the curled black arms of the seat. The imperial crown gleamed upon his pale white hair. No. He couldn't be Prince Valen any longer. Not if he sat upon the throne, wore the crown, and had others calling him the emperor. His father would tear him apart for impersonating the emperor.

A slow, devious grin split his youthful face. "I see she has already put the pieces together." He cocked his head at Marek. "This one's a little slower to get there."

At the left side of the throne, Lady Fia studied Aslyn, her burning gaze raking over every detail as her fingernails rapped rhythmically against the back of the throne. Aslyn didn't like the way she studied her, but she couldn't speak freely unless Prince Valen—*Emperor* Valen—gave her permission.

"Are you... emperor now?" Marek asked.

A blast of magic hit Marek in the chest and he struggled for air, doubling over and clutching at his chest.

"You will speak to the emperor when he permits you to speak," Lady Fia hissed viciously.

"Now, now, Fia," Valen chided. "Is that any way to treat our guests? They are welcome to speak freely."

Marek gasped hard as he gulped down breaths like a drowning man breaking the surface of water.

Valen ignored Marek, and his dark eyes sparkled as he smirked at Aslyn. "Though I expect a certain level of respect. This one has a sharp tongue."

With a flick of his fingers, he dismissed Lady Fia. She scowled at him over his shoulder before retreating to the exit. If Valen noticed her open contempt, he ignored it.

"What happened to your father?" Aslyn asked.

"It was time for Emperor Oxon to retire, just like those who came before him. Just as Valen one day will."

Aslyn couldn't help but wonder what happened to *retired* emperors or why he referred to himself in third person. No one ever heard from them again once they passed the crown down. Outside the Imperial Palace, no one put much thought into it. Aslyn knew her father assumed they lived out their days in the palace. As vicious as these men could be, retirement must have meant death or imprisonment. Anything else would open the reigning emperor to the violent heart of his predecessor.

Aslyn wanted to ask about Sybil, but didn't want to seem too eager.

"Lund Bloodstone sent his concerns regarding your safety," Emperor Valen said. "He issued a special request I would normally ignore, but I feel this might be mutually beneficial."

A chill raced down Aslyn's spine. Mutually beneficial for who? Her and the emperor, or Lund Bloodstone and the emperor? Either way, it didn't bode well for Aslyn.

"You will remain here until your wedding to Marek, under my protection," Emperor Valen announced. The way he made the proclamation made Aslyn certain she was more prisoner than guest. "I shall even provide you suitable quarters for your wedding night. In one month, I will host your wedding. That should give staff time to prepare."

No... Aslyn's insides writhed madly. *One month?* "Your Grace, I was promised the wedding would wait until my father was rescued. If you are pushing this wedding so soon, does that mean there is progress in locating him?"

"There are a few promising leads," Emperor Valen replied, but the way he said it made Aslyn sense something more devious at play. "Regardless, I have spoken. You will marry Marek in one month, with all the blessings of the imperial seat."

The finality of his statement pressed down on Aslyn, making it a struggle to keep her shoulders back proudly. If she couldn't get out of this palace, there would be no escaping Marek.

Beside her, Marek raised his chin, triumph gleaming in his dark eyes. He knew as well as her that there was no escaping this fate.

"Meanwhile, princess, you will be provided with quarters befitting a princess, and my wife will be available at any time to keep you company and show you around the grounds," Emperor Valen rapped his fingers on the arm of the throne.

His wife? Had he married Sybil without a celebration? Aslyn had been in Lemheller Gap for a month already. She hadn't heard anything about an imperial wedding. *Poor Sybil*. At least Aslyn would have the freedom to speak to her.

"Your Grace," Marek said hesitantly. He waited for Valen to nod before continuing. "I had hoped to stay here as well, if it's no imposition."

Emperor Valen stared at Marek so long and hard her "betrothed" shifted anxiously. "I'm not sure that would be in my best interest, Marek. You will be quite busy during the next month."

Marek's eyes widened in confusion.

"King Orrin of Vorovesti has requested a trial of the High Council for crimes of treason and sedition against you for your alleged involvement in the shadowspawn attack in Stormvalor," Emperor Valen said plainly.

Aslyn suppressed a smug smile. Was this Aethan's doing? A way to protect her from Marek when he couldn't be here himself? Gods, she loved him! It was a brilliant move and only made her more certain he would be a perfect match for her crown.

"Your Grace—"

"He also claims you were involved somehow in the murder of Queen Giata and her royal guards," the emperor cut Marek off sharply. "His statement claims it was an attempt to instigate war between Vorovesti and Novavito."

"But I had nothing to do with what happened in the royal suite," Marek protested.

Aslyn took a measured breath and turned a too-sweet smile on Marek. "My love," she crooned. "If you had nothing to do with it, I'm sure you have no reason to worry. Would you truly wish for war in a kingdom where you will soon become King Consort?"

Marek glared at Aslyn. As slow as he could be, Marek understood perfectly well what she insinuated. Some part of her prayed the High Council had information she didn't that would convict Marek and save her from this marriage.

For a moment, no one spoke, then Marek turned his attention back on the Emperor. "Your Grace, you told me at Stormvalor that—"

"Watch what you dare to say to me, Marek Bloodstone," Emperor Valen snapped. "I'm not above killing you myself. I know what I said. You needn't worry. I have a feeling King Orrin will have his hands full soon and he will abandon his quest for justice."

Hope evaporated from Aslyn's heart. They had planned this—expected this!—and already had a plan to deter King Orrin. What could that be?

Aslyn noticed a shadow growing from behind her. Terror clenched her heart.

"Princess Aslyn, you are dismissed," Emperor Valen announced. "The Empress is waiting to escort you to your suite."

Aslyn had a hundred questions she couldn't quite sort through, and she was nowhere near done with this conversation, but pushing the new, young emperor seemed like a good way to get on his bad side. If she had a month in this palace, that gave her time to find some answers, and maybe a way out.

As she stood and turned, Aslyn looked right past the guard who had loomed at her back toward the doors into the throne room where Sybil waited in thick layers. Her pale blond hair was twisted back from her face with perfect ringlets trailing down her neck. Aslyn approached, ignoring the guard completely, and noticed the vacant stare in Sybil's pale blue eyes, like she wasn't all there.

"Princess Aslyn," Sybil said softly, nodding respectfully. She reminded Aslyn of Aethan and it made Aslyn's heart ache for him. That distant look in Sybil's eyes vanished, replaced with something slightly sharper but still not quite right. "This way, please."

Aslyn followed with a humble thank you, eager to be alone with Aethan's sister.

CHAPTER 8

Something Rots Within These Walls

Bast watched Aslyn leave Bloodstone Manor from the mansion rooftop. The horses carried Aslyn and company up the treacherous, winding path to the imperial palace slowly. Aslyn didn't look back as she rode beside Marek with a casual calm Bast was certain she couldn't possibly feel. Two Black Guards rode ahead to ensure the path remained safe. Two more rode at the rear to protect their charges. Lord Bloodstone couldn't be bothered to escort the Novavito heir, as if it were beneath him. Nor did he allow Aslyn to bring along her maid, Kaiti. They dwindled into specs as he watched.

As much as Bast had wanted to venture to the palace with Aslyn, he had his own mission. Surely the emperor wouldn't imprison or harm the heir to one of his richest kingdoms... would he? *No, he's no fool*, Bast reminded himself. She was as safe as she could be... for now.

Once the horses and their riders were little more than specs of darkness moving along the mountain pass, Bast slipped down the walls of Bloodstone Manor and into the gardener's shed where he had hidden his Black Guard armor. He had gained access to the shed by duplicating the key while the gardener slumbered. It had been far too easy.

Once changed, Bast marched toward the Black Guard fort.

The Citadel loomed at the base of the Umbr Mountains, far below the Imperial Palace high above, like an ominous shadow against the jagged peaks. Its blackened walls had been forged from the same dark gray-black obistone of the Umbr Mountains and etched with runes of warding during the War of Two Crowns over a thousand years ago. The obistone drank in the light. Spiked towers jutted skyward, their silhouettes stark against the sky. It was a massive, impenetrable fortress where Black Guards were housed and trained.

Behind the Citadel, the narrow, treacherous path to the Imperial Palace wound up the mountain far above—a path guarded by the Citadel at the base of the mountain as well as the Citadel occupants.

Even from a distance, Bast could scent the soot and iron hanging in the air around the Citadel, faint but undeniable.

For a while, he simply observed the Citadel entrance from his hiding place behind a thick tree. Few came or went, and those who did all wore the black colors of the emperor. Eventually, a wagon pulled by two of the largest black horses Bast had ever seen wound around the Citadel. The occupants of the prison wagon were all men from age sixteen to forty. Their clothes were soiled and faces drawn in defeat. Even from his hiding place, Bast could see they had given up already. Were these magic users the Black Guard had captured? Why were they only able-bodied men? Where were the woman and children?

He continued waiting until the wagon disappeared before making his way cautiously around the side of the Citadel where it had vanished. After nearly an hour of inspecting the Citadel walls, Bast could find no point of entry. It truly seemed they had vanished.

Bast made his way back around to the front.

Massive gates reinforced with dark steel marked the only visible entrance, flanked by statues of faceless warriors clad in spiked armor, eternal sentinels carved to mirror the Citadel's infamous inhabitants: the Black Guard. Tales whispered of the horrors within—of recruits broken and reforged into merciless enforcers of the Emperor's will. The rhythmic clang of hammers on anvils or steel against steel were the only sounds to drift over the walls.

A sense of foreboding settled over Bast as he marched straight toward the front gate, wearing the armor he had pilfered off the now-dead Black Guard. The fortress seemed alive, a monstrous entity in its own right, radiating menace.

Bast's gray eyes flicked around the gates as he drew nearer, suddenly rethinking his entire plan. Those the Black Guard discovered with magic were captured all across the five kingdoms of Divica and brought to this very fort for judgement. Most were likely tortured and experimented on. The lucky ones were simply executed. No one with magic passed through this gate and came back out again.

Yet Bast crossed the threshold. His magic hissed in warning, urging him to turn back and abandon this lunacy. But he couldn't find answers any other way. What would the emperor think if he knew the infamous shadow assassin walked through his Citadel?

The moment he reached the other side, a barrier separated Bast from his magic like a dense fog between the two. He hesitated, but he had to get through this.

The plan was simple enough. Find a vacant room to claim as his own. Pose as a Black Guard. Spend as long as he dared investigating the secrets of the Citadel. Slip out with no one realizing who he was.

Bast kept his back straight and head high as he crossed the massive courtyard that also served as training grounds. He marched with the same practiced, stiff measures that all the Black Guard used when they walked anywhere.

The Citadel courtyard turned out to be much larger than Bast had anticipated from the outside. Once within the walls, he realized with horror that the emperor could house and train entire legions, and no one would be the wiser. As he marched across the courtyard, keeping close to the edge near the building, Bast observed hundreds of guards training in brutal combat.

He reached the entry to one of the many forges and paused, peering through the open door. The inner chamber was expansive, with more than a dozen forge fires and twice as many blacksmiths working them. Fire blazed and smoke belched up the smokestacks.

One blacksmith paused in his forging of a sword and met Bast's gaze. His brows drew slowly together, then his gaze swept over Bast from head to toe. As he eased his work-in-progress onto the anvil and stepped away, Bast realized somehow this blacksmith could tell he didn't belong. The blacksmith took a few steps in Bast's direction.

As casually as he could, Bast dipped around the doorframe and along the courtyard, losing himself in the mass of men in matching armor. He only dared to glance back once to spot the blacksmith inspecting the courtyard a few meters out of the doorway, looking for *him*. It was all the warning he needed to be careful who he made eye contact with.

Bast closed the visor, shielding his eyes from sight as he vanished into a crowd of men. When he experimentally reached for his shadows, they resisted. The magic had dampened the moment he entered the Citadel walls as if some barrier separated him from the power. Even as he realized this, dozens of men around him all ceased training at the exact same moment. Could they tell when he reached into his well of magic?

Great, Bast thought regretfully as he immediately released his hold. *Just what I need. Surrounded by men who will kill me in an instant and I can't use my magic to protect myself.*

He stopped moving a tick behind when they had, his assassin skills honed enough to warn him without him knowing why. Hopefully, they hadn't been aware of that second of delay. He examined the men around him, all without helmets or visors. Just as with the guard he had killed, these men were pale, with thinning, lank hair and empty black eyes. Every single one of them.

The truth hit him hard and he turned toward the Citadel gates as others began moving again. Bast had no chance of fitting in the second he removed his helmet. His thick, dark hair and stone-gray eyes would give him away, and likely already had if that blacksmith noticed the color of his eyes.

The gates were nearly beyond sight. Already, he had come so far. If he had to make a run for it, he would never make it in time. Especially not without his shadows to aid his escape.

This is why I prefer stealth over subterfuge, he thought bitterly. There was no turning back. His best chance of making it out alive would be at night, under the mask of darkness, which only allowed for a few hours to investigate the grounds.

As one, the men resumed their training and Bast resumed his march around the courtyard toward the entrance to the spires where the guards slept. Thankfully, he was not the only man wearing the helmet with the visor down. As long as he moved like they did and avoided his magic, no one would suspect him.

The guard quarters high in the Citadel's spires were as austere as the soldiers who occupied them. Each narrow chamber held a single cot, its thin mattress covered with a tightly stretched, unblemished sheet. The beds were all made, as though the act of resting was more a privilege than a necessity. The stone walls were devoid of any adornments or comfort. No belongings cluttered the spaces—no tokens or traces of individuality, nor of family or friends. Even the quarters seemed to enforce discipline and erase humanity, leaving nothing but soldiers honed for obedience.

None of this would have bothered Bast, except that he had hoped for some clue which spaces were unoccupied that he could use—if necessary—as a base for his operation. Instead, he had to abandon the notion of using a guard quarter for his own purposes.

A fellow guard marched past Bast as he lingered in a doorway. The man's helmet was tucked under his arm, and he gave Bast an odd look when he realized Bast still wore his helmet with the visor down. Perhaps none of them wore their helmets in the quarters. Bast took a stiff step backward, then pivoted and marched away as if headed for the courtyard. The ruse worked.

As Bast moved through the Citadel, he passed bathing rooms as unadorned as the quarters. Bare stone walls enclosed a series of trough-like basins fed by icy water from the mountain. The air was damp and cold, the space devoid of luxury or comfort.

Nearby, several kitchens hummed with quiet efficiency, their plain stone hearths and iron cauldrons churning out nothing more than the basics: dense bread and steaming vats of protein-rich broth with chunks of potatoes. Common rooms adjoining the kitchens held long wooden tables and benches, where guards ate silently in shifts. Bast found it eerie that, aside from the sounds of clinking dishes and slurping soups, all remained utterly silent. Not that this surprised him after his close encounter with the Black Guard he tortured and killed. Their vocal chords were severed to keep them from speaking.

Bast didn't dare linger and risk drawing attention to himself again.

Bast entered a second courtyard, where the stark obistone gave way to intricate floor tiles forming a map of the Five Kingdoms. The detail was precise, each kingdom delineated with sharp lines, as if mocking the notion of peace between them. Would commanders gather here to make plans? Were there Black Guard commanders?

Beyond the courtyard, Bast encountered a thick steel door. He checked the hall to ensure no one watched, then tested the door. It clicked and gave way with hardly a sound. Bast quickly slipped inside.

An armory. Chamber after chamber organized by weapon and weapon size. Each chamber was stocked with an arsenal of death. Racks of weapons lined the walls—blades honed to a lethal edge, shields polished to gleaming precision. The air carried the faint tang of oiled metal and aged leather, cared for as if preparing for use. The Black Guard were not merely the emperors enforcers. Every corner of the Citadel echoed with the purpose it was built for: unyielding war.

But war against who?

The sheer volume of the weapons and their apparent care, combined with the high activity of the forges, worried Bast. The five kingdoms of Divica hadn't known true war in hundreds of years. These weapons should be rusting from disuse, or at the very least covered in layers of dust.

But the emperor was gearing up, which only proved Aslyn right. Bast muttered a curse.

The imperial seat was up to something, and it could bring war to the five kingdoms.

"Is there a problem, commander?" The male voice startled Bast, and he moved faster than he should have in this armor.

In a heartbeat, Bast pinned the man to a wall, his sword at the man's throat.

Not just any man. He lacked the thinning hair and oversized muscles of the Black Guard. Judging by the black robes trimmed in crimson, this man was an ambassador—or an ambassador in training.

The hilt of Bast's sword heated right through his gloved hand. He dropped it reactively as burns melted the leather of his glove to his skin.

Magic!

Bast thrust himself into the well of his own power, only to tumble into it without reaching the source. Stunned by the retreat of his magic, Bast didn't notice the next blast of power until it slammed into his chest, knocking the air from his lungs and sending him skidding across the floor into a rack of halberds. They clattered around him.

"Who do we have here?" the ambassador asked as he straightened the sleeves of his robe.

Bast rolled, knocking a few more halberds to the ground, attempting to get his feet beneath him and get sufficient air into his lungs. The visor stifled every breath he dragged in, so Bast ripped it off.

The ambassador stood only a foot from Bast now, and when Bast looked up in a rage, knowing this man had to die, the smirk on the ambassador's face made his skin crawl.

"An infiltrator!" The ambassador readied another attack with magic. "Oh, you are a special one. The emperor will reward me well for you."

Bast reacted on instinct, yanking the man's feet out from under him. He fell with a sickening squelch, splitting his skull on the blade of a fallen halberd.

Moving quickly, Bast closed the door and stripped out of his armor, replacing it with the ambassador's robes. He would still lack the dark eyes that seemed prevalent to anyone in the emperor's service, but maybe he could pull on his magic like this one had.

Bast was also acutely aware that the ambassador's use of magic might have sent up a warning to everyone who could sense the use of magic. He had to get out of here.

The moment he slid the ambassador robes on, Bast's magic surged to the surface, like a caged, starved predator eager for release. The suddenness of it made him momentarily dizzy. Bast steadied himself with a hand against the wall, pushing the magic down. Then he ran his hands over the crimson trim. Someone must have designed these robes to give only ambassadors access to magic in certain spaces.

After tossing his armor in a pile in the back corner, over the body of the dead man, Bast pulled up the hood of the ambassador's robes, pocketed several daggers, and slipped out the door just moments before guards rounded the corner headed for the armory. He squared his shoulders as he saw ambassadors often do, then pointed down the hall, away from the armory door. He hid his injured hand behind his back to avoid detection. It burned, but he would suffer much worse if he was caught now.

"It's about time," he hissed. "I sensed something amiss down that hallway there. Deal with it already."

They nodded in unison, marching past Bast in the direction he indicated. The moment they turned the corner, Bast moved as rapidly as he dared in the opposite direction, listening for the heavy thump of approaching boots at every intersection.

The retreat brought Bast to the entrance of another of the Citadel's spires. He stepped through the entryway into a garden courtyard at complete odds with the stark, seemingly dead nature of the rest of the Citadel. Butterflies flitted from one bush to the next. A dozen or more men and women in black robes trimmed in various colors meandered along paths. Some read from books or scrolls. Others conversed quietly with each other. Bast moved with caution as he realized the crimson color on his robe would signify something to these people and he was clueless what it would mean.

Did these ambassadors know one another by face? Would someone realize he was not who he should be?

With his hands tucked into his long, wide sleeves, a knife in each palm, Bast strolled casually along the perimeter of the garden, using his peripheral vision to warn him of danger.

That was how he spotted the cluster of five ambassadors moving toward a closed door. One of the men traced his hand in a pattern along the door. Bast memorized the motions as he observed, slowly and casually closing the gap between them and him.

The door swung open and they all walked through. He took a few more steps closer, watching the courtyard. No one noticed him. The grinding of the door closing hastened his steps. Bast barely slipped through before it sealed shut.

Darkness settled around him. Bast pulled that darkness toward him by instinct and his vision sharpened enough to see wide stone stairs descended into nothing. He strained his ears to listen to the ambassadors who entered before him. Only distant whispers of their conversation reached him, making him confident Bast was alone in this space.

The only other option was the door at his back.

Taking a deep breath, he began his descent.

Chapter 9

Eyes and Ears Are Everywhere

Aethan had expected Cavis and Cormic to offer statements quickly and help him out of this situation. After the first day confined to his quarters, he assumed Prince Dorin had yet to send word to them. After the second day, Aethan wondered what held them up. But a week passed, and the only time his door ever opened was under guard when a servant came to bring his meals, change his sheets, or gather the dishes. Every time, they were escorted in by royal guards and right back out the moment they finished. No one said a word to him, despite his most charming and heroic efforts to engage the staff and guards.

As luxurious as the room was, Aethan knew what it truly was. His prison. And the longer he remained here, the more he doubted he would ever walk free again. He missed Aslyn, yearned for her not only because she could help him out of his current situation, but because he needed to see her. What he wouldn't give for one of her quippy remarks or sly smiles.

Even worse than lamenting his own ill fate was the knowledge that Roric remained in the dungeons, likely rotting away. Would they feed the boy and care for him even half as well as they did Aethan? His gut churned every time he thought about Roric in the dungeon. The boy deserved better. He was good in a way that many people weren't. Dorin wouldn't resort to having Roric tortured for information, would he? Every time that thought crossed Aethan's mind, he thought he might be sick. There had to be some way to get Roric out of there.

Aethan blamed himself for all of it. Aslyn had led him to believe her brother was kind and reasonable, if a bit lazy. The young man he had met might have been lazy and manipulated by the two men at his shoulders, but something about Dorin's eyes haunted Aethan's dreams. Something about him wasn't quite right.

As an outsider, Aethan's first instinct was to believe Aslyn's brother was after the throne. Perhaps he was a predator in hiding, waiting to pounce on his prey at the right moment. It would hardly be the first time someone in the line of succession usurped a throne in any kingdom. In fact, the emperor's line descended from a greedy prince who had done just that.

Aethan continued pacing the rug in his sitting room, ignoring his cooling dinner as his mind spun webs in every direction. Spending so much time alone with nothing but his own thoughts was a terrible place to reside. Aethan began believing the worst in people he should trust.

Why had Trystain truly refused to make this journey with him? Did he know somehow what would happen when Aethan arrived? Was he in on it? Aethan paused, peering down at his palm as he traced a fingertip over the scar from their blood oath. It didn't contain true power. That required magic, which neither of them had. It had been a symbolic gesture of brotherhood. But what if Trystain blamed him for what happened to Sybil? He said he was getting past it, but could Aethan believe him?

Stop it! He chided himself, gritting his teeth in frustration.

Trystain hadn't turned against him. He was suffering his own losses in his own way, and no doubt his father hadn't made any of it easier for him. Lord Cyrus demanded the sun and stars of his son and constantly berated Trystain when he failed to meet such unrealistic expectations.

But *someone* had set Aethan up. Maybe Cavis and Cormic weren't on his side as much as he believed. Just what did their loyalty to the crown mean? They were both Novavito men through and through, but did it matter to them which Kiernan sat on the throne? Perhaps they had struck some kind of deal to help Prince Dorin seize control.

If that's the case, I have no help coming, he realized. He would have to get himself out of this. The only reason he didn't escape was because running would make him look guilty. His friends would stand for him. The truth would win out. It had to, or his entire sense of justice would crumble.

Aethan had considered that perhaps Dorin wanted Aethan to fight back or try to escape. No doubt it would be a trap for Dorin to point the finger and prove to everyone that Aethan must be guilty. No, he would face this and find a way to come out the other side.

And what did Ambassador Umbogo or Master Javon Nadier stand to gain from putting the prince on Novavito's golden throne? *My palace*, Dorin had called it, as if he were already upon the throne.

Aethan raked through his mind for the thousandth time, recalling every detail, every word, every significant and insignificant gesture or movement of that conversation. Dorin acted casual, almost nonchalant. Then he would strike swiftly before returning to the carefree prince so quickly Aethan would have dismissed the change under different circumstances.

And that one moment Dorin had put the ambassador in his place with little more than a glare caught Aethan's attention over dinner. Who was controlling who in that relationship?

Aethan resumed his pacing across the full length of the room, pausing momentarily on his fourth pass of the bedroom door. Memories of his night with Aslyn came to him in flashes. *"You are a king without a crown,"* she had told him. Surely she wasn't in on this plot. But what if Aslyn had been sent to seduce him? What if this was a coordinated effort between the siblings to seize control of Vorovesti?

Aethan shook his head aggressively to knock that dangerous trail of thought away as guilt gnawed at him.

No. Not Aslyn. He would sooner believe Roric worked against him than Aslyn. How could he even consider such a thing? She had been nothing but kind, compassionate, and loyal to him. And the way she had looked at him when they promised themselves to each other had been honest and vulnerable. She loved him. He knew it and considering anything else was a betrayal of that love and faith she placed in him.

Aethan closed his eyes, remembering the feel of her, the sounds she made beneath his touch, and he inhaled deeply. The scent of jasmine and roses filled his senses.

When he opened his eyes, Aethan peered at the open window. This entire place smelled like her. It was torturous.

Aethan strode toward the open window, peering over the edge to the grounds below. The moment he leaned out, a nearby royal guard on the lower level rested his hand on his sword and watched Aethan. While Aethan could open his windows or venture onto his balcony, he could not leave.

Eyes were everywhere. He could not let them know of his worry. And so, just like every other time he encountered another living person, Aethan smiled and waved in his most friendly, charming manner. Then he attempted to strike up conversation once more.

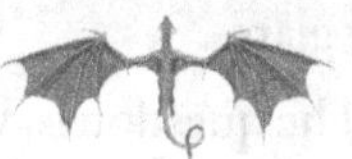

The Spotted Snapdragon didn't boast rowdy crowds or boisterous music, but as Cavis entered to meet with his friends and brother, the number of patrons and din of the tavern was enough to mask their conversation and hopefully make their group less conspicuous.

Cormic nodded to his brother from their table across the tavern. Von, Weylen, Kern, and Gorim were all seated at the long table, leaning close and speaking in urgent, hushed voices as Cavis approached.

Each had spent a few days exploring sectors of Arithia, hunting for information. More than anything, Cavis had hoped they would find nothing amiss, but his own conversation with one of his friends in the palace guard made him uncomfortable.

He sent a message to the captain of the guard, a stout man in his early forties who had taken Princess Aslyn under his wing years ago.

"—still haven't heard word of Aethan even being in the city from anyone," Gorim finished as Cavis settled on the bench beside Von.

A barmaid brought Cavis a watered-down ale and the others fell silent as she refilled each of their mugs. Kern handed over coins for their drinks and she happily strolled away, examining his generosity in the lamplight.

"It's like no one even knows he's here," Weylen agreed.

"I'm not surprised," Cavis said. He took a drink and winced at the bland ale. Why was everything so thin lately? All eyes turned to him. Cavis kept his voice low as he explained what little he had learned. "I just spoke with a buddy of mine in the royal guard. He said Aethan arrived at the palace, but hasn't left his room since. Only the guards chosen by Nadier and Ambassador Umbogo ever see him."

"What about Roric?" Weylen asked.

Cavis shook his head. "No idea."

Von wiped foam from his upper lip, brows drawn together. "Who's Nadier?"

"King Novin's financial advisor and ... well he's been at the ear of the crown for as long as I remember," Cavis supplied.

Cormic grimaced. "I don't like that guy. He always felt suspect to me with his forced smiles and condescending glares."

Cavis nodded in agreement. "The question is, why are he and the ambassador the ones pulling the strings?"

They all fell silent. They knew the truth, or at least a fair proximity of the truth. With King Novin and Princess Aslyn gone, those two men would pull all of Prince Dorin's strings. The prince wasn't exactly known for being proactive with anything but his own desires. Dorin was little more than a fop.

"There's more, and it might tie into all of this," Kern offered. "Not about Aethan, but the crown and the ruling class in general."

The others waited expectantly.

Kern glanced around the tavern, then lowered his voice. "There's a reason the ale is watered down. Rumor has it the Seoras Plains have yet to sprout much more than seedlings, and we are well into summer. Crops should be growing. The carts that do come in are rumored to be put in the royal stores." Kern glanced at each of them, concern darkening his eyes. "You must have noticed the number of hungry people in the streets, the state of what little is sold at market, and how much vendors are charging. People are pissed."

Cavis peered into his mug of ale. Arithia starving? The Seoras Plains were the largest crop fields in all five kingdoms. If they failed this summer...

"Oh..." Weylen's eyes widened. "Now it makes more sense!" He shifted on the bench and leaned closer to the others. "At first, I was looking for information about the rebels that might help us locate where they would have taken King Novin, but most people I managed to get information from had loved him. It wasn't until Prince Dorin stepped in after the king's disappearance that the people started forming these groups. At first, they gathered to commiserate about the inflation that hit the market right after the king was taken. But the groups started organizing."

Cavis's gut twisted. Groups organizing was never a good thing.

"They were all waiting for the princess to return," Weylen continued. "But when those ships showed up and she wasn't among those who returned... Let's just say people are starting to talk about a real rebellion, where there didn't seem to be one before."

"That doesn't make sense," Cormic grumbled. "If there wasn't one before, then what happened to the king?"

Silence. All six men exchanged uneasy glances.

"If it wasn't rebels, the prince lied to his mother and sister," Cavis mumbled under his breath. He hated speaking the words, but they all needed to hear it. "And if that's the case..."

"Aethan is in danger," Von finished, his expression hardening.

Cavis nodded once. "And the princess might not have a fiancé or a crown to return to."

Cormic hushed them all, peering over Cavis's shoulder toward the entrance. "Captain Shino incoming," he hissed without moving his lips.

Cavis turned to see the Captain of the Guard marching toward them with all the rigidity that came from years of discipline. It might have given him away even in his common clothes with the hood up to mask his face. Cavis waved him over.

"I invited him."

"Why?" Cormic hissed, anger pulsing off him.

Cavis pressed his hands to the table to rise and greet Shino. "Because his loyalty has always been to the king and the princess above all else." Cavis turned and offered a hand to shake with Shino. "I appreciate you coming to join me for a drink. We haven't had a chance to catch up since I returned from Stormvalor."

Shino shook Cavis's hand. "I hear you both did well in the tournament."

"Not as well as some others," Cavis admitted.

Shino nodded grimly and joined them as Cavis motioned to a space Weylen had offered, shifting to the side to make room at their table. He didn't lower his hood, which set Cavis's nerves even more on edge. Why would the Captain of the Guard be afraid of being spotted?

The barmaid returned with another mug for Shino and a pitcher to refill the rest of their drinks. They waited for her to leave before speaking.

"Before we say anything else, you should know there are ears everywhere," Shino said lowly. "The level of paranoia in the palace is at a peak right now, and... things aren't what you think."

By unspoken communication, Von and Kern kept an eye on the room around them as they continued.

"Cavis, you need to stop asking questions around the palace guard," Shino continued. "If your questions reached the wrong ears, they would have you thrown into prison for sedition." Shino ran his thumbnail along the handle of his mug anxiously as he continued, cutting off the question Cavis wanted to ask. "Before you ask any more questions, let me finish. I'm holding my position by the fingernails, especially after I spoke with Prince Dorin about concerns I had regarding the ambassador and the financier. They are watching me closely now. Just meeting you here could cost me dearly.

"I was not present when they met with Lord Starkling, but my men reported to me afterward, as required," Shino said. "Prince Dorin is preparing a trial."

Weylen cursed. Von appeared ready to burst into voracious protest.

Shino cut them both off with a glare. "There is apparently evidence that Starkling committed treason, and that he might be behind the capture of King Novin. It didn't help that his squire was caught spying and thrown in the dungeon."

Roric! The poor boy. He was smart as a whip. Cavis respected the hell out of that kid.

"And before any of you say a word, remember where you are," Shino said. "Tensions between Vorovesti and Novavito are high right now. High enough that, should anyone believe you a sympathizer for the young Vorovesti lord, it will likely result in your own death." Shino sighed, then cleared his throat. "We are on the brink of war."

"This is not what Aslyn wanted," Cavis said sharply, keeping his voice low. "I spoke with her. I saw her with him. There's no way that love isn't real." Cavis thought of Iskra. The way she looked at him set his heart afire, and he worshipped the ground she walked on. More than once, Cavis witnessed that same kind of love between the princess and Aethan. "Are you suggesting it was all an act? Because if so..."

"Bullshit," Cormic grumbled vehemently. "Bloodstone has his hand in this. I guarantee it!"

"Keep your voice down," Shino hissed, glancing around them from beneath the cowl of his cloak. He waited a beat for everyone to settle, studying each man and the level of anger and disbelief each displayed. Finally, he nodded. "I believe you. I know the princess well. She wouldn't make a choice like Starkling without being certain about his integrity. Aslyn knows it's about more than just a marriage. It's a crown and a kingdom. She wouldn't offer it without absolute trust. And seeing the way you are all quick to defend him only confirms my suspicions."

Cavis took a long drink of his ale and curled his nose. There had to be better ale elsewhere in Arithia.

"We must get Aethan out," Von said with devout determination.

"That's easier said than done," Shino replied. "He's being kept in his suite under guard—men selected by the ambassador and the financier. Men loyal to them and not the princess. I might be able to get him a message, but to get him out will take time and patience."

"Time he may not have," Von countered.

Shino nodded. "True. But if we do this wrong, we all die." The captain of the guard took a slow drink, unbothered by the watery flavor. Maybe there wasn't better ale elsewhere.

"What about the prince?" Cormic asked. "Is he in danger?"

Shino winced. "No. I have a couple of men who... well let's just say the prince and the ambassador seem to have an amicable relationship."

Cavis snorted as the implication hit him. There were rumors for a few years now that Prince Dorin didn't discriminate in his preference of male versus female partners. One rumor had claimed Dorin and Ned Corinth had been lovers even after Ned married Lady Darma. Another rumor claimed all three of them were involved with one another.

More disturbing were the rumors from the guards, who thought Dorin and Umbogo were lovers, and Cavis didn't doubt it could be possible. After all, if Umbogo was after the throne and he couldn't get Aslyn, he just might move on to Dorin. Worse than the disturbing thought of the two of them together was the realization that struck Cavis at that moment. Umbogo could have easily seduced the prince, then offered to help Dorin claim the crown. After that, they could rule together. And if Dorin fell for it, their collusion would be sealed with an Ambassador's Promise. Dorin wouldn't be able to back out even if he wanted.

"The charges against Starkling are steep," Shino said. "Kidnapping the king. Financing and stoking rebellion in the city. Manipulating the princess. Hiring Blackblade to kill Ned Corinth and the queen."

Gorim chortled. "I saw what happened in that suite. There's no way that was Blackblade's doing. He has a reputation for finesse. Clean work. What we saw was brutal and messy. One man couldn't have done *that* on his own."

"No," Cavis agreed. "But Bloodstone's men could have."

Kern blanched. "Wait, are you saying Marek had his own men kill the queen and her guards?"

"After what we saw him do in Stormvalor, would it surprise you?" Weylen growled. Fury made his neck pulse and redden any time Marek Bloodstone came up. He hadn't forgotten the way Marek killed his countryman without remorse. One day, Weylen would exact his revenge. Cavis was certain of it.

"What will happen to Roric if Aethan is convicted?" Cavis asked.

"Considering he was caught snooping around the palace, the boy will likely face the same penalty," Shino replied. "He may face it regardless."

A table nearby burst into laughter, silencing all of them as they waited to ensure they were not being listened to.

"If we can't get Aethan out, we need to rescue Roric," Cavis said.

The others nodded in agreement.

"Yes, if we manage to get Aethan out and Roric is still in there, he will storm right back into the palace to get the boy," Von said. "He feels a great deal of responsibility toward that kid."

"Is it even possible?" Cormic asked.

All eyes turned to Shino.

The captain of the guard considered the question a moment, then nodded. "Yes. But if we aren't careful, they will blame his escape on Starkling." He leaned forward, resting a forearm on the table. "Listen to me closely, gentlemen. Do not be fooled by the prince's tricks. He may allow others to believe he is just following the ambassador and financier, but I suspect he is at least partially in charge of all of this."

With the captain of the guard on their side, Cavis was confident they could succeed. Now all they needed was a solid plan.

CHAPTER 10

Cold, Dark Spaces

The halls of the imperial palace were stark and cold, even if the gothic architecture was beautiful. Aslyn walked alongside Sybil, who seemed content to say nothing at all. She remembered Aethan's sister being more reserved, but this version of Sybil was different, little more than a shell of the woman she had been. Sybil's skin and hair were paler, her sky-blue eyes bordering on vacant and present at all times like she teetered on the precipice of nothingness. Had Valen done something to her, or was it this place?

Aslyn examined the walls around them, and the grotesque paintings of the War of Two Crowns that dotted the walls on canvases larger than her bed back home. They passed few windows along the way and those Aslyn did spot offered little outside light. Instead, torches and mirrors cast the illusion of daylight.

Sybil shivered and rubbed at the thick sleeves of her dress. At least it wasn't just Aslyn who found this place unusually cold.

A Black Guard stood outside a pair of arching double doors carved of obistone. He bowed to Sybil, fist over his heart, then opened the door. Sybil slipped through like a ghost. Perhaps she was a ghost of the woman she had been.

Aslyn followed her through the doors, casting a wary glance at the guard who would no doubt spend sleepless nights guarding the door.

Aslyn stepped into the sitting room, her gaze drawn immediately to the towering glass windows that framed the gray sky beyond. Beyond the windows were jagged peaks of the Umbr Mountains, distant pines, and even more distant views of Lemheller Gap.

The gothic arches overhead cast long, twisting shadows across the polished black floor, where flickering candlelight danced in wavering pools of silver from the dismal light beyond the windows.

Two tufted velvet settees faced each other in the center of the room, their frames carved with intricate patterns of curling vines and beasts she could not name. The scent of the roaring hearth fire and smoldering wax filled the air, mingling with the faint perfume of the lush ferns that softened the otherwise cold space. A table, laden with unlit candles stood between a pair of matching chairs.

The furniture offered no color, in varying shades of black and gray. Even the wooden furniture seemed carved from ebony wood. The paintings on these walls were not as grotesque as those in the halls, but they still clearly depicted the first emperor Narcisse exerting his dominance over the five kingdoms.

Aslyn fought off a shudder and turned her back from his black eyes. Had Sybil noticed how much her new husband looked like Narcisse? How did they keep their bloodline so strong for centuries? Aslyn looked nothing like her ancestors, if their own paintings were to be believed.

They did not build this place for warmth. Aslyn ran her fingers along the arm of a settee, its surface cool beneath her touch. It felt like a place meant for watching, for waiting—as she would be forced to do for the next month if not longer.

Sybil stepped wide around the dancing shadows as if afraid they would snatch her away. What had this poor woman suffered in this place already?

"Sybil, are you alright?" Aslyn asked cautiously.

Sybil blinked at her as if she didn't understand the question. "What do you mean?"

"I mean, in this place... with him... how are you faring?" Aslyn eased toward the other woman like one would approach a skittish animal.

Sybil turned toward a curtain. "Just fine." She yanked it open.

Letting it go for now, Aslyn stepped into the bedchamber, her breath catching as the oppressive grandeur of the room settled around her. Darkness pooled in the corners, stretching long fingers across the obistone floor, broken only by the flickering glow of candlelight. Blackened iron candelabras stood like sentinels, their wax-dripped arms cradling pale flames that sputtered and wavered, casting eerie shapes along the gothic arches of the windows.

The bed, vast and somber, was carved from the darkest wood, its towering headboard an intricate spire of twisting designs, gilded with faint silver that caught the candlelight like ghostly veins. Black silk sheets lay undisturbed, smooth as glass beneath a heavy, velvet coverlet.

The cold air clung to her skin. Tall and foreboding windows framed the outside world in fractured panes.

Aslyn exhaled slowly, fingers brushing the edge of the bedpost. How could she ever sleep in such a dark and foreboding place?

Aslyn finished her tour of the sitting room, bedroom, walk-in closet already lined with everything she would need during her stay, and a massive washroom.

The faint scent of lavender clung to the air in the washroom. A great circular showerhead hung suspended from a wrought-iron pipe decorated with intricate metalwork. Sybil stepped forward to show Aslyn how to activate the wide showerhead. A curtain of water streamed through hundreds of small holes in the showerhead, gathering in the raised bathing tub beneath the massive showerhead.

Arched windows framed one wall with gothic style, and a table of towels and washcloths of pure white waited for her use. Aslyn exhaled, watching her breath mingle with the steam.

"The water comes in from the mountain peaks and feeds the palace reserves," Sybil explained, but her voice rang hollow as she spoke. "Servants stoke a fire to keep the water warm."

Those poor servants. Their only job was to keep the fire burning so a handful of people in the palace could enjoy warm showers?

Aslyn didn't find the quarters impressive. Her suite in Stormvalor had been more home-like than this place... and warmer, too.

The two women returned to the sitting room as a handful of servants set a meal at the table. They murmured greetings to their empress, bowing as Sybil passed.

Aslyn strode to the balcony doors and opened them. A cold gust of wind from the Umbr Mountains made her immediately regret the decision, but she wanted to take in the view and inspect the palace around her balcony. Just in case.

The view was breathtaking, if stark. To her left, the Umbr Mountains rose high into the clouds, their jagged peaks piercing the sky. To her left, Lemheller Gap and the Citadel appeared as little more than miniatures in the distance. It was farther away than she had expected. Had she truly come so high into the mountains?

Aslyn gripped the cold stone balustrade and peered over. The distance to the ground far below made her momentarily dizzy. The ground level beneath her balcony looked to be at least two dozen meters below. Nothing else offered her a route down. No balconies below or jutting rooflines to jump to. Aslyn turned, inspecting the smooth exterior walls of the palace. Not even a vine or crevice to hold on to. She tipped her head as far back as she could, staring up the smooth obistone wall of her tower.

Because this was a prison tower for her. Emperor Valen had selected this room to give her the illusion of comfort with no chance of slipping out.

"There is no way up or down," Sybil said, defeated.

She's already searched for this. Aslyn strolled back into the room, closing the door when she noticed the way Sybil hugged herself to ward off the cold.

"How are you doing here, Sybil?" Aslyn asked as she snatched a blanket off the back of her lounge chair and wrapped it around Sybil's shoulders.

"It's cold, but my sweet prince does what he can to make me comfortable," she replied.

Prince? Aslyn guided Sybil to the table and set her down in front of their meal. "You do know Valen is the emperor, now, don't you?" How could she not know?

Sybil sank to the seat, hugging the blanket around her to ward off the chill. Her features crinkled. "No. He said..." Her gaze turned inward, then her eyes widened. "That would explain why I haven't met his father."

Even the new empress hadn't had the courtesy of meeting Emperor Oxon before she married his son? Strange. Even stranger was her calling Valen "sweet". That certainly had never been Aslyn's experience.

"Do you feel safe here?" Aslyn asked.

Sybil stiffened, peering at one of the shadows dancing from the hearth. She stared at it for so long, Aslyn wondered if she forgot she was there.

Aslyn leaned across her field of vision. "Sybil? What's wrong?"

Sybil's lips parted and her fingers turned white as she gripped the blanket around her. "The darkness," Sybil whispered so softly Aslyn barely heard her. "He is watching."

"Who? Valen?" Aslyn asked, fighting the urge to peer into the shadows that captivated and terrorized Sybil.

She shook her head so slightly. "The emperor."

"But Valen is the emperor."

"Narcisse." The word is so softly whispered from Sybil's lips that Aslyn didn't realize what she said at first.

What could Sybil possibly mean by that? Sure, there were a lot of artistic pieces all over the palace declaring Narcisse's glory, but he died hundreds of years ago. Was Sybil going mad in this place? Did she believe the eyes of those paintings and statues watched her? *The poor woman.* Aslyn wished she had some way to comfort her.

Sybil closed her eyes and whimpered, murmuring something to herself with apparent fear. Aslyn nearly stormed into the hallway to demand a meeting with Valen when Sybil's eyes snapped open and she smiled so warmly at Aslyn it made Aslyn wonder if *she* had gone mad and imagined the Sybil who had been with her to this point. The empress tossed back the blanket and motioned to the meal.

"Please dine with me, Aslyn," Sybil said, and for the first time she sounded like the girl Aslyn met in Stormvalor.

What had just happened?

The screams reached Bast before the light. Men screamed in agony, begging for mercy, forgiveness, the lost gods... The utter desperation made Bast's insides twist. Was this where magical offenders were taken? What kind of torture did they endure down here to make them beg until their voices broke?

He followed the sounds around the bend, cautious of any other ambassadors or guards who might be monitoring these dark, narrow halls. Each step fell silently as he moved with the most caution he had ever harnessed in his life. If he was discovered down here and they learned what he could do, Bast knew he would be tortured like these other men until his own voice cracked. He liked to think himself strong enough to endure the pain, but every man had a breaking point. How long could he hold out before reaching his?

At long last, Bast entered a hallway with a handful of torches lining the long passage. The screams here were loud enough to make his ears ring. Bast edged toward one of many alcoves along the hall, peering in, wary of the torches nearby that might cast his shadow on the floor.

The alcoves were prison cells. Or perhaps a better description would be torture chambers. No doors were necessary to hold prisoners in. Not when the prisoner was chained to obistone table in the center of the room.

A single table in the cell had the chained form of a man younger than himself. Blood dripped from dozens, perhaps hundreds, of cuts on his skin. His face was tilted toward the door as if yearning for the freedom he would never find, eyes closed. Bast edged closer once satisfied they were alone. The young man's chest rose and fell in slow, unsteady breaths. His face twisted in agony even in sleep.

Bast examined his sleeping body. The cuts were not those of torture. They were precise, purposeful, and cleanly made. Bloody, straight lines in equal measure carved up various muscle groups from his neck all the way to his feet. As if the cutting wasn't bad enough, Bast's throat tightened as he looked down and saw the healed remnants of the young man's privates. Someone had surgically rendered him sterile.

Unable to look upon the gruesome state of the prisoner, Bast moved toward the cabinet along the back wall. Surgical blades soaked in a bath of bloodied water. A towel to wipe them down lay folded neatly beside the bowl, along with a few unused tools. Items to pry skin back and pin it open, to cleanly remove eyes, tweezers for gods only knew what.

Bast's stomach churned as he took it all in. He had done a lot of torture and killing in his time, but this... It was beyond even his expertise. What did they hope to get out of these men?

As he turned to leave, Bast noticed the neat stack of stones on the counter. He had nearly missed it. They blended in with the counter and the walls. Bast stepped closer, examining one of the stones, if he could call it that. They were all precisely cut in various sizes, but all in the same shape. He picked one up and the stone instantly sent a sensation of prickling along his fingertips. He grimaced, slipping it into his pocket to examine later.

The screams from along the hall never ended. At least two others were undergoing whatever torture this was. Bast needed to get out of here before anyone spotted him. Something told him he would find chamber after chamber of the same thing if he inspected each.

As he made his way toward the door, sticking close to the wall in case someone entered, the young man wheezed.

"Kill me..." He sounded like he had swallowed gravel. "Please..."

Bast turned his attention to the young man. His blue eyes were fixed on Bast. Tears slipped from the corners of his eyes, sliding along his nose and down his temple into the stone slab beneath him.

"Please..."

Bast glanced toward the entrance, waiting to see if anyone approached. When he heard nothing beyond the agonized screams of other men, Bast edged toward the slab. A knife dropped into his palm, but he wasn't sure he should kill the man. It would leave evidence of his intrusion behind. Thinking better of it, he tucked the knife away again and pulled a poisonous dragonleaf from his pouch. The poison worked quickly and left no trace, as long as they didn't inspect his insides for a cause of death.

He held the leaf for the man to see. "Answer my question and I'll give you this. It will kill you quickly."

The young man squeezed his eyes shut and whimpered, then nodded in agreement.

Lucid enough, then, Bast decided. "Why did they bring you here?"

"I didn't mean to do it..." The young man choked on a sob.

"Shh." Bast put a hand over his mouth. "If they find me, you won't get your end. Answer."

He waited for a somewhat lucid nod of understanding before removing his hand again.

"I... I... grew the... the crops."

Bast scowled. They didn't do this because the man grew crops. Which meant... "With magic?"

He nodded. "Please kill me. Please."

"Did they say what they are doing here with you?" Bast asked.

"Please."

Bast held the leaf over the young man's mouth. "Answer first."

He licked his cracked lips, eyes locked on the promise of death just out of his reach with desperate hunger. "Making me... b-better."

Better? What did that mean? There was no way they were healing him. Not in this condition. The young man's fingertips dug into the stone slab beneath him, rattling the chains holding him down. His fingernails were cracked, broken, or missing, and his fingertips bled on the stone.

Bast tried to pull more answers from him, but time would run out and the young man had nothing more to give him. Giving up on further questioning, Bast stuffed the leaf in the young man's mouth and held his hand over his mouth, instructing him to swallow. As he saw the bob in his throat, Bast released and walked toward the exit.

The young man was dead before Bast slipped out the door.

Exploring further would be risky, but Bast needed to know more. He moved like a shadow from one cell to the next, checking to be sure each had only a single occupant. Most of the men couldn't speak, or wouldn't. All of them had the same precise cuts along their muscles. A couple of the men he recognized from the wagon he saw just that morning, their bodies yet to be mutilated, though someone had rendered them unconscious.

One prisoner had cuts beneath his eyes. When he watched Bast move around the room, Bast noticed the black of his eyes. Just like the black, soulless eyes of the Black Guards.

"No one deserves to die," Aslyn had scolded him after he killed all those Black Guards in the alley. Bast had scoffed at her assertion. But as he considered what happened to these men, he had to admit to himself that she might be at least a little correct. How much agency did any of the Black Guard have over their actions anymore? Did they even know what they did in the emperor's name?

The realization hurried his steps toward the exit, eager to leave this place and never return.

CHAPTER 11

A Deadly Plan

The days in isolation passed slowly. Aethan tried to keep himself busy. He cleared a path around the outer edge of his sitting room and each morning before breakfast, he jogged laps around his room until his lungs burned. After breakfast, Aethan stretched, working his muscles with pushups and sit-ups. Then he finished the morning routine with extensive practices of his sword forms until he dripped with sweat by lunchtime.

After lunch and a bath, Aethan passed his afternoon watching the comings and goings around the palace from his windows and balcony to learn what he could about guard rotations, visitors, or anything else that might be useful. He wasn't sure he knew that any of it would help him out of his situation, but at least it kept his mind busy.

He spent his evenings reading the books on the shelf in the sitting room—most of which were cursory histories of Novavito's kings and queens. He absorbed the information in case any of it would come in handy. One book focused heavily on the reign of Novavito's first Kiernan king. Aethan had learned some of the kingdom's history in his own lessons as a youth, but bits of information in the book in his sitting room provided insights he hadn't known.

The first Kiernan king had been appointed by Emperor Narcisse after the War of Two Crowns ended—which Aethan already knew. The previous royal line of Martnarvings had been exterminated by the emperor in the weeks following the end of the war. Again, Aethan had learned as much already. What he hadn't realized was that the first Kiernan king had been married in a political alliance. His bride had been Emperor Narcisse's only daughter. Aethan hadn't been aware that Narcisse had a daughter at all. According to the historical record, she was a great beauty with eyes like sun-kissed amber.

Just like Aslyn's eyes.

Every time he thought of her, it made his heart ache. What would she say if she knew what her brother was doing to him? How would she respond if Aethan was killed on treason charges by her own kin?

A knock sounded on the door in the middle of Aethan's sword form practice. He glanced at the clock on the mantel. It was still an hour until lunch. This visit couldn't bring good news.

The door unlocked and began to swing open. Aethan sheathed Stormshard and leaned the sword against the stone wall beside the hearth. Having a sword in hand when someone entered would likely end in a beating, or perhaps they would seize the weapon assuming he would use it to escape—which he still refused to attempt. He wouldn't fall prey to Dorin's bait.

By the time his visitor entered, Aethan stood straight in the center of the practice space he had cleared on one side of the sitting room, hands folded in front of him so they knew he held no weapons. He was shirtless and sweaty, but little could be done about that.

The man who entered wore a royal guard uniform, and judging by the cords and stripes, he was highly ranked, an officer. He moved like a man with years of military discipline and had to be close to the same age as Aethan's father.

After closing the door, he studied Aethan with sharp eyes. Aethan didn't doubt he noticed everything. His gaze lingered on the dragon tattoo over Aethan's heart before meeting his gaze.

Aethan held his chin high through all of it, jaw clenched. Whoever this man was, Aethan worried that his visit meant something terrible was about to happen. He waited to be spoken to.

"Word on the street is *you* should have been named Stormvalor Champion," the officer said. He strode closer with slow, confident steps. Aethan swallowed. That hadn't been a question and he had nothing to contribute. But the officer's gaze shifted past Aethan to Stormshard. His brows lifted. "That's quite the sword."

The officer stepped around Aethan, and as he reached for the weapon, Aethan tensed. Not because he worried the man would use it on him. What if he felt that power whispering to him when he held it, too? He could take it. Aethan didn't want the weapon in enemy hands.

"I'm Captain Shino, head of the royal guard," Shino said as he wrapped his hand around the hilt and the other around the scabbard.

Aethan turned, still unwilling to speak. Anything he said could be used against him, and he would give Captain Shino nothing.

Shino didn't draw the sword, but he did loosen it a few inches from the scabbard to inspect the weapon. His calloused fingers brushed against the blue gemstones in the cross guard and pommel. Aethan held his breath, worried Shino *could* feel the same power Aethan felt when he held it. Suddenly, Shino thrust it back into the scabbard and returned it to where Aethan had rested it before. Aethan released the breath slowly.

"You could have used that on me when I came in," Shino said. "Why didn't you?"

"Why should I?" Aethan folded his hands behind his back.

Shino made a sound of consideration in the back of his throat. "Are you not worried about what will happen to you?"

"Obviously, but I'm more worried about my squire and Princess Aslyn than myself," Aethan said. It was as honest an answer as he could give.

Once more, Shino considered him carefully. "I've seen him."

Aethan took a step toward the captain before thinking better of it and stopping himself. "How is Roric? Are your guards taking care of him?"

"He's as well as can be expected," Shino said. Aethan's shoulders slumped, the air punched from his lungs. In a dungeon, that didn't mean much. "He has regular food and water, and keeps himself strong moving around his cell." Shino's gaze swept Aethan's suite. "Much like you. If I didn't know better, I would think the two of you planned all of this and have further plans for escape... or perhaps a coup."

Aethan lifted his chin, insulted by the insinuation that he would dishonor himself so much.

"He doesn't speak much to anyone," Shino continued, "and only asks about you."

It wasn't great news, but it lifted Aethan's spirits a little. At least Roric wasn't suffering too much in his cell.

"He's just a boy," Aethan said. "And he only does what I tell him to do, so if there is any blame to be had, it falls squarely on my shoulders."

Captain Shino raised his brows and smirked. "Funny, he said something similar about you. That he acted alone and none of it was your fault."

Aethan swallowed hard. Why was Roric lying? Did he think it would spare Aethan any punishment? Roric's crimes were far from the worst of what Aethan had been accused of.

"That kind of loyalty is hard to find," Shino said. "And it speaks volumes about the man who could inspire it."

Aethan snapped his jaw shut and grimaced, staring at the floor. That loyalty would get them both killed.

Shino relaxed into an armchair. Silence settled between them for a painfully long minute before Shino spoke again. "He isn't the only one I've spoken to who shows you such loyalty."

Aethan's gaze snapped up to meet the captain's, and the look in Shino's eyes was not mistrust, but curiosity.

"The Dysart brothers are particularly dedicated to your wellbeing," Shino said.

Cavis and Cormic! He spoke to them. At last, a break in this nightmare! Aethan's pulse increased with the first glimmer of hope in weeks.

"Almost as dedicated as they should be to the Novavito crown," Shino continued. "Cavis, in particular, insisted you would do nothing to put the princess or her crown in danger, that you are wholly dedicated to her."

Aethan swallowed the lump in his throat. "I am, which is what I tried explaining to her brother, but he didn't seem too interested in what I had to say."

Shino shook his head. "He wouldn't be."

Those three words startled Aethan. He sank into the plush armchair across the sitting space from Shino.

"I hope you remain wholly dedicated to my future queen, despite the circumstances."

Aethan connected the pieces quickly, pulling his shirt over his head. At the ball, Aslyn told Aethan stories about home. Stories about how the Captain of the Royal Guard had taken her under his wing and taught her how to fight and had been like a second father to her. She also told stories about her brother being afraid of the captain.

"I am. Until my last breath."

"Hopefully beyond that," Shino said plainly.

What did that mean?

Shino paused a moment before continuing. "There is nothing I can do for you in that regard, Aethan. Prince Dorin is unreasonable. He spends all his time behind closed doors with Ambassador Umbogo or Javon Nadier."

Aethan's stomach twisted. His suspicions had been correct. "You think they planned all of this?"

"The prince has always been an entitled, petulant boy," Shino said. "And I always suspected he resented his father for reasons I won't divulge here. Suffice it to say his parents got in the way of what he perceived to be his happiness and his right. The only thing standing between him and that right to his happiness..."

"The king, queen, and heir," Aethan finished. He cursed under his breath. What kind of hornet nest had he walked right into? "If you can't help me, I can't help her. What are you really here for?"

Shino smirked again. "Smart. I see why she likes you." He leaned forward, resting his elbows on his knees. A pained expression creased the corners of his mouth and eyes. "I failed my king. The day he was taken I... The ships burned first. King Novin and I were working together to organize the men to save as many ships as we could."

Aethan fell silent as he listened to the confession. This was the first anyone had spoken about what happened to the king, and it was clear Shino took this failure personally. *Just like I took my failure to help Aslyn and Sybil personally*, he realized.

"Then the rebels stormed the palace," Shino continued. "Their heads were wrapped in black that covered most of their faces. They moved with efficiency, like they knew the exact layout of the palace and where guards would be posted. King Novin was secured in the council chambers with myself and a dozen men guarding the door." He rubbed a hand across his chin and sighed. "When the fighting stopped and I opened the door, the king was... gone."

"Did they take him through a window?" Aethan asked, trying to sort out what he could.

Shino shook his head. "The windows are high and they don't open in that room. None were broken. No, they took him through the tunnels." The captain lifted his gaze to meet Aethan's once more, eyes hardening. "Only five people know about that emergency exit."

Aethan's stomach sank as he did the math. The royal family and the captain. Five people. He cursed softly under his breath. "If you know it was him, why haven't you done anything?"

"And then what? Leave Novavito in the hands of Ambassador Umbogo?" Shino shook his head. "Until Aslyn returns, I cannot do anything."

"What about the king's return?" Aethan asked.

"I fear King Novin is already lost to us," Shino said. "Prince Dorin would not allow even a chance of his father returning to unseat and punish him. Your quest to rescue him is a fool's errand. I don't know whether he lives, but whatever happened to him, he won't return here. Not as long as Dorin is in charge. King Novin tried to connect with his son, but Dorin constantly pushed him away. After Aslyn left for Stormvalor, Dorin's moods grew... darker. He spoke to his father less and less until he stopped altogether. The rift between them was clear and vast. I want to believe the king is alive, but I'm not very confident that is the case. This kingdom needs Aslyn, and to bring her home, we need you."

"But you just told me I'm already marked for death and there's nothing you can do to save me," Aethan responded. "And if he kills me, King Orrin will declare war against Novavito."

"Yes, and I suspect the prince will have the emperor at his back."

The room tilted as the implication of those words hit Aethan square in the chest. Vorovesti would fall to Novavito and the emperor's combined might. King Orrin would put up a fight, but it would end with the fall of Aethan's homeland.

Aethan leaned forward, pressing his face into his hands with a groan of irritation. Shino gave him a moment to collect himself. Finally, Aethan scrubbed his hands down his face and lifted his gaze to the captain at last.

"So how do I help Aslyn retake her kingdom from my grave?" Aethan asked.

"It won't be your grave."

"If you break me out of here before Dorin has his way, he will tear this city, this kingdom apart searching for me."

Shino nodded. "Which is why you have to die."

Aethan chortled and sank back into his seat. "You're contradicting yourself."

"Dorin won't take your head," Shino said confidently. "He wouldn't be able to stomach watching it happen and he will want to witness your execution. Odds are, he will want it to be a slow, painful death."

"That's reassuring," Aethan muttered.

"It should be." Shino tapped a finger on his leg, calculating something. "A gut wound will be easier to heal afterward. He won't have the nerve to watch the light leave your eyes. He will have you dragged out first."

The truth of what Shino suggested fell across Aethan's shoulders like a weight. "You're suggesting I *allow* him to kill me?"

"He will have someone else do it."

Silence settled thick over the room. This was a terrible, deadly plan. Aethan liked no part of it, but he saw no other way out. Dorin would never let him escape and risk exposing his true darkness. No one attached to him would be safe, and he would have nowhere to run or hide. Escape could put his entire kingdom at risk—his life for thousands. He couldn't be so selfish.

"It has to be you," Aethan said, resigned to his fate. It would be best for everyone, and if Dorin thought him dead… "You must put the sword through me. No one else can know, and if anyone else is given the *honor*, they might not miss something vital. Besides, if you insist on the honor, Dorin will be too scared to refuse. Aslyn told me her brother is afraid of you."

"I don't believe he fears me as he once did," Shino said grimly. "Not with the guards at his command."

Was Aethan really talking about his death so nonchalantly? Even if Shino knew what he was doing, Dorin might want to watch him bleed out too long for Aethan to be saved.

"It will work. He might even see it as a victory, bringing the Captain of the Royal Guard to heel." Aethan huffed out a breath to try steadying his nerves. "Okay, let's assume all goes according to plan, which it almost never does. What happens to me after?"

Shino rubbed his chin, and the gleam in his eyes made Aethan certain he had already thought through all of this. "I will have a few guards I personally select take your body from the room—only men I trust and know are loyal to the princess above all else. I will convince Dorin we should send your body out with the tides, so no physical evidence remains. Cavis and Cormic will be at the boat to help me with the healing before we send you out."

Aethan scoffed. "Your big plan is to patch me up and stick me in a boat at sea alone? How could that possible not go wrong?"

Shino scowled and Aethan regretted that he likely insulted the only man capable of helping him. "He will want to watch your boat float out with the tide."

"Wait," Aethan held his hand up, hoping to appease some of Shino's anger. "My ships. Have word sent to Captain Barrow to leave at least two days before my trial. I'll pretend they abandoned me when Dorin undoubtedly brings it up. Find out where the tides will take me and have Captain Barrow waiting out of sight from any Arithian scouts."

"Easily done," Shino nodded in agreement.

"Cavis and Cormic can't be the ones to help you, though," Aethan added as something else occurred to him. "Dorin will no doubt have them watched after what I said. I swore they would vouch for me, that they are loyal to the crown. I probably put a target on them both, which means they are doubtless already being watched. It can't be them. They need to remain in clear sight until I'm gone. If you don't trust your men to help, Gorim and Kern are both big enough men to help."

The two men fell silent as the treasonous plot settled between them. Aethan didn't like the plan if it involved dying before he could be saved, but he couldn't see another way out. If he escaped, Dorin and the emperor would hunt him down.

At least this way, if he survives, Aethan would have anonymity. They would think him dead, and he could use that blind eye to his advantage.

But how would he save Aslyn? By the time he healed enough to reach her and take on Marek—and likely a legion of the Black Guards—it could be too late to help her. They wouldn't kill her, but if the emperor wanted Prince Dorin on the throne instead of Aslyn, she would be held as a captive bride in the Bloodstone Keep for the rest of her days. The very thought of Marek touching her in ways and places he had claimed for himself made Aethan's blood boil with hate.

"Three more things before you go, Captain," Aethan said reluctantly. "First, Roric has to be somewhere safe when I face my trial. I will accept the blame for his disappearance. But he *must* be gone before they can hurt him. I won't leave unless he's free."

"Done." Shino nodded. "Not easily, but your friends already suspected you would insist on it and have worked out a plan."

That news lightened Aethan's heart a little. At least they were working with the captain as well. They wouldn't leave Roric behind.

"Second, Roric, Von, and Weylen need to leave for Lemheller Gap as soon as possible with all the food and coins you can spare them," Aethan said. Someone had to reach Aslyn before she heard of his death and she became trapped in Bloodstone Keep forever. "They are to find her and give word of my survival, as well as ensure she is out of that place if anything dangerous happens."

"I will try to meet with them tonight to discuss our plan, but they may not reach her before news of your death," Shino said. "What is the third?"

Aethan bit his lower lip and straightened, raising his chin once more. "I need you to send a message from me directly to King Orrin or Prince Gannon so that this doesn't start a war. I suspect that's what the emperor wants."

The imperial seat had a grudge against the rulers of Vorovesti ever since the War of Two Crowns. Likely because Emperor Narcisse wore one of those Vorovesti crowns before the war started and they stripped him of it. Aethan could be the catalyst that finally gave the imperial seat the right to wipe Vorovesti off the map.

"Have it ready when I return and I will do my best to see it delivered," Shino agreed.

The two stood, sizing one another up, then Shino offered his hand.

If this was a trap to pull Aethan into the treason charges, he had fallen squarely into it. All Aethan had to keep his hope alive was Aslyn's insistence that she trusted the Captain of the Royal Guard with her life. He was placing that same trust in this man now.

CHAPTER 12

Building Bonds

Aslyn had never known a place could feel so lifeless. Beneath the opulence, the imperial palace was a mausoleum, suffocating in its silence and secrets. That sensation was only intensified by the slew of art depicting Emperor Narcisse's glory in the War of Two Crowns.

She had spent her first days in the palace wandering the endless corridors, learning their twists and turns, cataloging which doors led where, and which ones were locked or guarded.

A thick glass door with intricate vines of obistone woven around and through it revealed a vast chamber full of ancient relics from the War of Two Crowns. Aslyn pushed the door inward and strolled slowly through the space, taking in everything. Weapons were labeled for their previous owner—all names of legend—as well as the battle in which the owner was conquered and the weapon seized. Swords and bows of fine elvish make. A battle ax engraved with ancient runes Aslyn couldn't read. Helmets and battle armor sliced open by weapons or claws, still darkened with blood. The armor and short sword of King Tibris Strong of Vorovesti. The staff of his wife, Queen Consort Solfia Strong. On and on. The history in the room should be impressive, but instead it gave Aslyn chills.

Aslyn's heart stopped, feet frozen in place as she gazed upon another ancient relic.

The battle armor before Aslyn had clearly been mended quite a few times. But the battle that claimed the owner must have been gruesome. Scars from claws and weapons marred what had once surely been a pristine golden surface, yet worse still were the gashes in the pauldrons, abdominal plate, vambraces, greaves, steel boot tips, backplate... The chainmail beneath the armor had been shredded. The green cloak fastened to the shoulders was in ribbons. Dark blood stained every part of the armor. Whatever had gotten this warrior had brutally ripped him to shreds.

It wasn't the condition of the armor that drew Aslyn's breath from her lungs. She reached up, tracing her finger lightly over the rose embossed disks that fastened the cloak in place. The rose of Novavito. Her gaze darted to the label on a stand beside the armor.

Lord Commander Quade Martnarving, King of Novavito

Last Stand – Goldwood

Beside his armor, fine elvish armor custom crafted for a female stood vigil on its own stand. This armor was not nearly as destroyed as King Quade's armor, but the owner certainly had put up a good fight as well. A shield was propped against the greaves in two pieces, broken right down the middle by something very powerful. A fine, slightly curved elfish sword rested on a wooden stand beside the armor. Scratches across the armor made it clear this bearer had been in battle as well. But unlike King Quade's armor, this had a single puncture in the chest plate. Right through the heart.

She read the placard.

Loralai a'Malik, Kruos Princess, Shieldmaiden, Queen of Novavito

Last Stand – Goldwood

Aslyn's brows furrowed. "Last stand?" she murmured to herself.

Either the history Aslyn had learned of the war had been wrong, or this placard was, which she highly doubted. This wasn't where she learned King Quade or Queen Loralai died.

"One of the last battles in the war," Valen said.

Aslyn jumped, glancing over her shoulder to see him approaching. He moved so quietly! She quickly ducked her eyes away before he took insult at her direct gaze. Instead, Aslyn once more studied the two suits of armor.

"I'm a bit confused by it though," Aslyn said, hoping he didn't mind her speaking freely. "It says Last Stand Goldwood, but I was taught that his final fight had been north of Barden, in a city now lost to time."

Valen stopped at Aslyn's side, dark eyes picking apart King Quade's armor. His spine straightened. "In a way, that is correct. You would know Goldwood as Deadwood."

Deadwood? Why had it changed?

"What happened to him?" she asked. "The armor is…" She shuddered, unable to find the right word to describe the condition of the armor.

Valen clasped his hands behind his back. Was that a smile on his face? "Quade put up quite a fight trying to save his beloved wife. But they had both committed treason against Narcisse of the worst sort—coercing Narcisse's allies, wielding the power of the gods in battle, attempting regicide on several occasions. When Narcisse demanded the blood of their son, they refused to comply. In their last stand, Quade fought off Narcisse's army in Goldwood as Loralai summoned magic she had no right to wield."

Valen turned to Aslyn, and the cool detachment on his face as he relayed this story chilled her to the bone. "The trees of Goldwood bore great power, a gift from the gods. The bark of the trees shone silver in the sunlight and in the moonlight. The leaves were as brilliant as molten gold. But the elf drained all the power from Goldwood to protect her son. In doing so, she killed the forest. It became a harbor for all dark manner of creatures and became one of the deadliest places in this realm. Loralai sacrificed the gods' gift for her own selfish ends."

Aslyn's mind turned like the gears on a clock spinning out of control. None of that story made sense. Aslyn had been taught that the couple were tried and executed by Narcisse upon his victory north of Barden. That their child had died with them.

"So, what happened to the child?" Aslyn asked, trying to make sense of what she learned compared to what Valen knew. He had access to the true history of the five kingdoms as emperor. Did he gain anything by telling her this?

Valen's cool detachment shifted as his jaw clenched and his expression darkened. "Dead, most likely. How could a babe survive without a mother or any of her allies?"

"Your records don't speak of what happened to him?" Aslyn found this hard to believe. He would have access to everything.

Valen turned and marched away. "Explore this room all you want, but touch nothing."

For a moment, Aslyn watched him retreat. If their son had died that day, Valen should know. His lack of answer bothered her. Narcisse didn't seem the sort to assume the baby had died without his mother. He would have dedicated his army to tracking the infant down. *Could it be possible... Did he survive?*

The question made Aslyn's stomach sink. If that baby survived, his own offspring could be out there somewhere... true heirs to her throne. Aslyn closed her eyes and drew in a deep breath to steady her nerves, but it did little good when a memory from Stormvalor surged forward in her mind.

Aslyn's eyes shot open. Von and Yun, two of the competitors from Elpisio, had spoken urgently of prophecies. She had listened to as much as she could without seeming suspicious. They mentioned the Slumbering Hero, and she assumed they thought he was Aethan. But what if they knew something more?

Loralai a'Malik, Kruos Princess, Shieldmaiden, Queen of Novavito

Lord Commander Quade Martnarving, King of Novavito

An elf and a human. With a son who vanished.

Just as the legend of the Slumbering Hero foretold. He was cast into eternal sleep to protect him from Narcisse's wrath and was foretold to return when it came to fight against the growing darkness. A Martnarving heir believed extinguished by the ancient emperor. Yet Von and Yun were raised in the one kingdom that held on to those old prophecies and still worshipped the lost gods. If they knew more than Aslyn did... Could they have been right?

What if Aethan descended from that line? Clearly, the first emperor kept the truth of this child to himself. He didn't want anyone else to know the legend might have any truth to it. That would also explain why the emperor worked so hard to keep Aslyn and Aethan apart, to keep him from returning to his place in Novavito...

To *his* throne.

This has nothing to do with me, she realized. Because if the legend was correct... would his arrival in Arithia signal the start of the fight against the growing darkness?

Aethan had every right to seize her kingdom, and she would be helpless to stop him.

The thoughts tumbled through her mind, picking apart all the pieces as she wandered back to her quarters.

No, Aethan wouldn't steal my throne from me, even if it's his birthright, Aslyn decided. Did Aethan's father know of this heritage? Was that why Lord Starkling had pushed Aethan so hard to win Aslyn's hand? It would be much easier to rule together than to fight for the throne. And she knew in her heart that he would never fight her for it. He would refuse his right for her, but they would still return the Martnarving bloodline to power through their children.

And if Aethan came from that bloodline...

Sybil does, too! Aslyn paused, surprised to find herself already standing outside Sybil's door.

Emperor Valen had figured it out. He tried to pry Aethan and Aslyn apart. He claimed Sybil as his own bride. If he and Sybil had a child, that young emperor would be a Martnarving—the true heir. He could claim the kingdom for the empire, fold it into Umbr. And if it came to it, Valen could use Sybil against Aethan.

Trembling, Aslyn knocked gently on Sybil's door, then smoothed out her dress and rubbed the gooseflesh from her arms as she waited.

She needed to know how much Sybil understood of the situation, but first she needed to ensure she could trust Sybil. While Sybil loved her brother dearly, this place had clearly done something to her, and Aslyn had to tread carefully.

The door opened and a servant waved Aslyn through.

Aslyn stepped into Sybil's sitting room, her gaze drawn first to the beautiful vaulted arches overhead, their dark wood curving like the ribs of some ancient, glorious beast. Candlelight flickered in lamps along the walls, casting long shadows that danced between the towering bookshelves lining the far end of the chamber, atop a slightly raised platform where an ornate desk rested untouched. Behind the desk, thick black and silver velvet curtains hung over the great windows that stretched toward the storm-heavy sky.

Nearby, a velvet chaise rested beneath the glow of a crystal chandelier, scattered with embroidered cushions that softened the room's brooding elegance.

A pair of high-backed chairs flanked a heavy, carved table near the hearth. Sybil sat at the table, situating each chess piece in place atop the board. Her blue eyes lifted to Aslyn, and they seemed brighter today than yesterday. She still wore a thick gown crafted by an expert seamstress, with a high neckline and not a shred of skin exposed from the neck down. Sharp bands of black and white twisted around the bodice, and through the pleating of the skirt. A white cloak draped from Sybil's shoulders. She was a vision.

"I assumed I would see you for a game again today," Sybil said.

Aslyn joined her at the table, arranging her blue and green skirt around her legs. "I do enjoy our games, even if you win most of them."

Chess had become one of their favorite ways to pass time. It gave Aslyn and Sybil a chance to talk, and Aslyn felt a little closer to Aethan's sister because of these games. But Sybil excelled at the game, often seeing several moves ahead. Sometimes Aslyn couldn't fathom what Sybil's strategy was until the game was over and Aslyn lost.

"Don't take it too personally," Sybil said with a small grin. "My brother often lost to me, too, though he improved significantly over time."

"Well, hopefully I will, too," Aslyn replied.

Hearing Sybil talk about Aethan made Aslyn's body ache for him in ways she hadn't known possible. Despite the few comments Sybil made about him, she never once said his name. Aslyn wondered why.

Sybil was the only warmth in this frigid place—a woman wrapped in silks and sorrow. She was not yet completely broken, though Aslyn saw the cracks widening. They spent their days together when they could, speaking in hushed tones, laughing softly like long lost friends. When Sybil smiled, her eyes never lost their detachment completely.

"Do you miss home?" Aslyn asked, making her first move on the board.

Sybil traced a fingertip along the arm of her chair, her gaze distant. "Sometimes. And sometimes I can't remember home at all."

How could she not remember? Aslyn hesitated before asking, "Doesn't that frighten you?"

Sybil let out a soft, humorless laugh. "It should, but in some ways it's a mercy. Home was safe once. Now, it's a place I can never return to. Perhaps it's better that I cannot always remember it. When I do..." Her face fell, gaze dipping to the chessboard as she examined it for her next move.

"It hurts," Aslyn offered gently, keeping her voice down. The two often spoke in whispers when referring to Aethan, Stormvalor, or her home and family. But this sentiment, Aslyn shared, because she felt it, too.

Sybil nodded, then shifted her piece. "Hurt isn't the right word, but yes. It's... more than that."

Aslyn studied her, noting the way Sybil's fingers tightened against the fabric of her gown. "If you could leave, would you?" Aslyn moved her piece.

Sybil looked at her then, truly looked at her, and for a moment, the mask slipped and terror took over. "Where would I go? There is nowhere beyond *his* reach." Her gaze slipped to the darkness in the corners of the room.

"Home," Aslyn said plainly, keeping her voice low. "To your father, your brother, your uncle. They would protect you."

"They couldn't." Sybil leaned in slightly, placing her finger on a chess piece. "And I cannot leave, Aslyn." She lifted her finger and ran it along the back edge of the board. "His success, his future, depends on me being here, in the imperial palace. If I were to run, I would doom him."

Aslyn's breath caught in her throat. She didn't need to ask who. She knew. Aethan. Did that confirm that Sybil knew of her family's origins? That Valen knew who Aethan and Sybil truly were, and she had to be here in this palace for Aethan to fulfill the prophecy?

Sybil smiled faintly, as if this truth of her situation had settled deep into her bones long ago. Perhaps it had.

For a few minutes, they continued their game in silence. Aslyn mulled over the prophecy and the possibility that Aethan could, in fact, be the Slumbering Hero... somehow. It became easier to put the pieces together the more she turned the puzzle in her mind.

Then, like a delayed afterthought, Sybil said, "Besides, Valen... he is not so bad. He treats me very well."

Aslyn smirked, tilting her head. "Not so bad, hmm? Does that mean you're enjoying your wifely duties, or is he as distant in the bedchamber as he seems in court?"

Sybil bit her lip and a hint of color flushed her cheeks. "We have not been... intimate."

Aslyn blinked, momentarily stunned into silence. How long had they been married? Didn't it nullify a marriage if it was unconsummated after a year? She figured Valen would be invested in preventing that.

"Not at all?"

Sybil shrugged, taking her turn and another of Aslyn's chess pieces. "He's held my hand, kissed my cheek, my forehead, hugged me."

The news startled Aslyn. She assumed Valen would want to work quickly to produce an heir with Sybil. Especially if her suspicions were true. If Sybil spoke the truth—and Aslyn had no reason to doubt it—then he hardly even showed interest in his wife. What Sybil described was little more than how Aslyn and Dorin had shown one another affection.

"Have you ever done it with anyone? Trystain?" Aslyn remembered how much Sybil seemed to adore Trystain in Stormvalor. Did she handle the forced break-up well?

"Trystain..." Sybil spoke his name as if tasting it, testing it, remembering it. Light sparked in her eyes, followed by sadness. "Yes. He was always so full of passion."

Yes, Aslyn could imagine that to be true, if his personality was any clue.

"How have you been doing with the loss?" Aslyn asked gently, taking her turn, and one of Sybil's pieces. She genuinely worried about Sybil's mental health. Losing her love, her lover, and being forced into this place with a man who showed little interest in her could be enough to drive any woman over the edge.

Sybil made a decisive move, removing one of Aslyn's knights and placing two others in position against the queen. "It was hard at first." Her eyes darted to the darkness in the corner and she cleared her voice. "But I haven't thought about it much recently." Tears welled in her eyes, and one slipped down her cheek, despite her conversational tone, as if two different parts of her were in play—the calm, logical brain and the dejected, lonely heart.

Or as if she were truly hurting but feared whoever she thought was listening.

Aslyn thought about Blackblade, of his ability to hide in the shadows untrace-able, the way he had done for more than a month while she traveled with Marek to Lemheller Gap, then during her stay in Bloodstone Manor. She never imagined she would miss his invisible presence, but some part of her wished he hid in these shadows, still watching over her like a dark and deadly guardian.

Blackblade would find a way into those forbidden chambers Aslyn had stumbled across in the palace. He would already know what was behind those doors. She needed to find out, as well. Because despite all her exploring in the palace, she had not yet found Valen's war room, his office, the officer's quarters. The few times Aslyn had come close to some of those forbidden doors, but guards would appear to encourage her away, or Valen himself would materialize as he had in that artifact chamber.

Perhaps Sybil was on to something. Perhaps Valen could hear or see something through those deep shadows. In fact, as she thought about it, Aslyn realized many of those forbidden doors were close to the darkest shadows of all, with no light on the doors. She needed to get into at least one of them. If she could distract Valen—or better, have Sybil distract him—she could explore behind a few.

Aslyn grinned broadly, taking on a playful tone. "If you're interested in Valen in that way, why not make the first move?"

Once again, Sybil's cheeks heated. She let out a small, breathy laugh, shaking her head. "It is not so simple."

"Why not? You are husband and wife." Aslyn shrugged and moved her queen, hoping to save it. "Aethan and I couldn't wait more than a few minutes once we were..." Aslyn swallowed. As much as she cherished that night of bliss with him, Aslyn feared speaking too much about it aloud in this place. Especially if Valen was listening.

"Really?"

Aslyn nodded sadly, staring at the board as Sybil considered her next move. When she found her voice, Aslyn spoke as quietly as she could. "It was the best night of my life. I miss him." She glanced at the dark corner. "Why would you leaving here doom him?"

Sybil made a decisive move. "Checkmate." She didn't even acknowledge Aslyn's question.

Perhaps another time I can get her to say more. "Again." Aslyn smiled at Sybil. "Maybe you have a point," Sybil said, picking up the pieces to put them away. "Perhaps it's time my husband and I had a... conversation. He must need heirs, after all. Why else would I be here?"

CHAPTER 13

Surrendering Power

The ambassador robes lay out on the small bed of the room Bast rented for a few nights. It was a cramped space, but he didn't need much. Lamplight flickered off the red trim on the robes, making it dance like flames. Beside it, the smooth obistone he stole from the torture chambers.

Bast stood at the foot of the bed, arms crossed, studying the objects.

Inside the Citadel walls, Bast had felt his magic, but had been unable to wield it until he put these robes on in place of the Black Guard armor. Something about it nullified the ancient runes of the Citadel that barred the use of magic within the walls. There could be no other explanation for why he could use his magic once he put it on in the Citadel.

First, Bast touched the tip of his finger to the smooth stone, embracing a little of his shadow magic to probe at the artifact. The shadows screamed in his head. Pain shot up his finger and forearm. He immediately jerked his hand away, rubbing at the stinging pain in his arm as his shadows fell away. Even after letting go, the pain didn't subside. It lingered for several minutes as if seeking somewhere else to go. He didn't dare touch his magic again until the pain subsided, and he wouldn't touch that stone with his bare hands again.

Bast ripped a strip of cloth from the edge of the bedding and used it to bundle the stone up tight so there would be no chance he could accidentally touch it later.

Then he turned his attention to the robes.

Experimentally, Bast reached for his shadows, sending only a trickle toward the robes. The shadows slithered around his ankles, then up the edge of the bed and along the threads woven into the garment. Bast focused, probing for runes. As the shadows slid over the edge of the red trim, they hissed and thrashed back.

Bast ran his fingers along the red. Open to his magic, he felt the snap of external magic hitting him. He staggered back a step, then gritted his teeth and reached out again. This time, with measured control of his own magic. Heat danced along his fingertips as if he held them over an open flame.

Fire magic.

Fucking hypocrites. The Imperial Seat spent centuries arresting and killing any who dared to wield magic while giving that power to his own chosen minions. Did that mean Black Guards had magic as well? Bast had never seen any of them use magic. Yet when he was in the Citadel, they had all sensed when he had tried to reach for his power.

What had that ambassador said to him in the armory?

"You are a special one. The emperor will reward me well for you."

A shudder rolled down Bast's spine. That bastard had intended to turn him over to the emperor the second he realized the magic Bast could wield.

Images of those prisoners deep beneath the Citadel flashed through his mind. The torture. The experiments. All of them with magic. That would have been him, if the ambassador had his way. What sort of dark heart did one need to become an ambassador? They were all little more than dogs doing their master's bidding.

If ambassadors all had magic, it made every kingdom vulnerable to the emperor's whims. At any moment, they could use that magic against those who might pose a threat to the emperor, and each of the kingdoms would be helpless without magic to protect them.

Bast growled and swiped the robes off his bed. They flew against the wall, then slid to the floor with little more than a whisper.

The magic had to be the reason mere mortals were bound to an Ambassador's Promise. In the Citadel, ambassadors had conversed quietly and studied together or alone. Bast had never witnessed so many of them in one place. Their education likely included speech manipulation so they could learn to trick innocent people into these promises without them being any the wiser until the trap closed around them, too late.

I will die before surrendering any piece of myself to them, Bast thought, clenching his fists tight at his sides.

A burning need to become a thorn in the emperor's side flared through his veins.

He stomped toward the door, snatching his sword from where he propped it against the wall. With a flick of his wrist, he fastened it to his back. A twitch of his fingers on the other hand and his own black cloak rode the shadows to his shoulders.

By the time he reached the exit, Bast's hood was up, his weapons stashed all around his leathers, ready for a fight.

It had taken all day to work up the courage to approach Valen. Sybil considered changing into something that might catch his attention but dismissed the notion for two reasons. The palace constantly chilled her to the bone. And she still hadn't convinced herself that she wanted this kind of intimacy with him. It made her ache for Trystain and felt like a betrayal to all those shared dreams they had whispered to one another. Most days, she couldn't remember Trystain at all. Sometimes, she remembered his smile or the light in his eyes, the sound of his laugh. A few times, she recalled their shared moments of passion with aching need.

Aslyn had pulled those memories from her, made Sybil yearn for Trystain's touch, his lips. But after that night at the ball, he hadn't even tried fighting for her. He just... gave up. It broke Sybil's heart when she realized it, and Valen had been quick to try piecing her back together.

He had never pushed her for more than she would give.

His words had soothed her broken heart and made her think that maybe, just maybe, this wouldn't be so bad.

Yet she still couldn't be certain if she was ready to give herself completely to him. She had to find out for herself, on her own terms.

Two Black Guards shielded the outside of Valen's chambers as Sybil approached. Both stood statue still as she drew near, but she knew with certainty that they were very aware of her presence. Just as she was about to boldly reach for the handle to Valen's outer chamber, they moved in sharp unison, snapping their halberds into a cross over the closed door.

Sybil's insides writhed at the sudden motion, but she raised her chin and glared at them. "I am your Empress and am here to see my husband. Step aside."

They didn't so much as twitch.

Just as Sybil drew in a breath to berate them, the doors swung inward.

Lady Fia waited on the other side, her sharp eyes cutting down Sybil. "He is busy, Empress. Perhaps another time."

What is she *doing in Valen's chambers at night?* It seemed that everywhere Valen went, Lady Fia hovered close behind. The woman appeared and disappeared from the palace often, no doubt on business for the emperor. That closeness grated on Sybil's nerves tonight in a way it never had before. Whether she chose this future or not was irrelevant. Valen was now *her* husband. Lady Fia had no place in his chambers at night.

"You are dismissed, Lady Fia," Sybil said, summoning as much of a commanding voice as her twisting nerves could muster.

Lady Fia released a low, soft laugh. "How cute. You honestly believe you have any power over me. Let me make things clear. You may hold the title of Empress, but it's strictly for ceremony. Any power you believe you wield in this realm, in this palace, is an illusion. I do not answer to you now, nor ever."

Sybil lashed out to slap the arrogant woman, but Lady Fia snatched her wrist and tsked.

At the contact, Sybil opened to her magic, reaching into the other women with her Sight. All she saw was fire. All she heard was an echo of Lady Fia's laughter rising from everywhere. All she felt was a raging inferno racing through her as if attempting to consume her whole.

"Enough!" Valen's voice clawed at Sybil's consciousness.

Lady Fia released Sybil's wrist and the pain and flame vanished in an instant.

What was that? Sybil's chest heaved as if she had run a mile. She trembled. Teetered. Collapsed.

Valen swept in to catch her before she hit the floor. He glared at Lady Fia as he marched toward the chaise with Sybil cradled in his arms.

"You know what you need to do next, Fia," Valen barked. "Go do it."

"I already have him lapping after me like a loyal dog," Lady Fia protested.

Who were they speaking of?

Valen settled Sybil on the lounge, then turned to Lady Fia, his expression turning dangerous. "Good. Make him beg. Make him so eager to please you he will surrender power." Valen smirked, and something about it made Sybil's blood cold. "We both know you excel at that particular skill."

Lady Fia's thick, red lips drew in a tight line as she shot a filthy look Sybil's way. "Fine."

She spun, her black skirt flaring and igniting in the light like flames. It sent a shudder through Sybil at the echo of her vision.

The door slammed closed.

Valen settled on the edge of the lounge, offering her water. Sybil took a slow drink, eyeing him over the rim of the glass.

"That was quite brave, attempting to hit her," Valen noted. "And foolish. She will never forget, and she can hold a grudge forever."

Sybil finished the water, attempting to digest everything she just heard and witnessed. Fire in the nearby hearth blazed, warming the room.

"What brings you here when you should be asleep, Sybil?" Valen slid the glass from her hands, setting it on the nearby end table.

The speech Sybil had prepared slipped from her mind as that vision of fire consumed her thoughts. Did he know of her gift? Valen had never said as much, and Sybil knew what the Imperial Seat did to those with magic. She couldn't risk exposing that part of herself to him. Not yet. Not until she was certain it wouldn't result in her death.

"You, obviously," Sybil said, her voice shaking.

For the first time since the doors opened, Sybil got a good look at Valen. She had never seen him so unguarded, so casual. His usual tailcoat and vest were gone, leaving only a light undershirt that hinted at the strength beneath. The fabric clung ever so slightly to his frame. His black trousers were tailored as if molded just for his skin, tucked neatly into polished boots that rose to his knees.

But it wasn't his clothing that held her attention. It was *him*. The contrast of his perfectly placed snow-white hair against the deep shadows of his eyes, dark as the midnight sky, made her breath catch. His chiseled jaw, the sharp angles of his face, the way he held himself with quiet, restrained power—it all left her unsettled in a way she hadn't expected.

She had married him for duty, for the future of the empire, for Aethan. And yet, as he peered down at her, something flickered in his gaze. Sybil's fingers curled at her sides, as if she could hold herself back from the pull of him. The truth settled in her chest like a whispered secret—she desired him.

But she still didn't know if she trusted him enough to give in to that desire.

"I suppose that is obvious," Valen agreed. "Since these are my chambers. But why now, tonight?"

Sybil licked her lips, heated by his gaze. "I've just been wondering why you have shown no interest in me."

A brow arched upward on his striking face, making him seem more man than imperial ruler. "No interest? Is that what you believe?" His jaw twitched. "She put that idea in your head didn't she? Aslyn?"

Sybil blanched. "I suppose, but she was only encouraging me."

His expression darkened. "To what end?"

Why was he angry? Did he think Aslyn toyed with Sybil's emotions? Did he think her so weak? So incapable of understanding her own mind?

Instead of answering, Sybil boldly brushed her lips over his. For just a moment, he tensed and she feared she had overstepped. Then he returned the kiss briefly before easing back. Valen leaned his forehead against hers.

"I told you I can't do any of this without you," he said with a certainty that made Sybil wonder why he believed it to be true. "But I'm also aware you had feelings for another before coming here. And my last wife... she never showed any interest in me. She barely allowed me to touch her, even up to the end."

He closed his eyes and took a slow, measured breath. As it released, the warmth of it spread across Sybil's face. Valen pulled back and the cold of this place once more wrapped around her.

"I suppose I assumed you were the same," he continued, and Sybil's heart ached for him. He thought she wanted nothing to do with him.

Sybil reached up, her fingers tracing along his jaw, then she cupped his face in the palm of her hand. His jaw twitched against her skin, like he prepared himself for the worst. Those dark, depthless eyes locked her in. Sybil swallowed. Then she reached out with a trickle of her magic. Nothing. Sybil increased the flow, digging for something to help her understand him, to help her decide if she truly wanted to give in to him.

His eyes narrowed. "What are you up to, Sybil?"

Her breath caught. Could he tell that she was trying to read him?

"I want to know you," she said softly. "Open yourself to me, Valen. Let me in."

Valen's hand slid up her arm. He took her hand and pulled it away from his skin. "Are you sure that's what you want? Because once that happens, there is no turning back."

"Is there now?" she asked.

His expression darkened, not with anger, but something much more dangerous. Something that made her heart race and her stomach drop. "No, there is not." He pressed his lips to her knuckles.

Sybil nearly gasped at what she saw in him. The flash of heat, desire, need. For her. All of that focus in the vision was on her. Intent. Intense. *Consuming*. Sybil licked her lips again, unable to break away from his gaze.

The words slipped past her lips before she could rein them in. "I want that."

Valen studied her, his dark eyes unreadable, but she could feel the weight of his gaze tracing over her curves. His presence filled the room, overwhelming and undeniable.

The space between them vanished as he braced against the back of the lounge. His scent—something dark and clean, like crisp night air—wrapped around her, making her pulse race.

Sybil tilted her chin, meeting his gaze, and any hesitation melted the moment he reached for her. His fingers traced the curve of her jaw, his touch lighter than she expected, almost reverent. He hesitated, as if giving her the chance to pull away, but she had no intention of doing so. Instead, she leaned in, her breath mingling with his, her lips parting just enough for him to understand her answer.

Then he kissed her.

It started slowly, almost tentatively, but the moment she melted against him, his restraint snapped. Valen's hand tangled in her hair, tilting her head to deepen the kiss. His other arm slid around her waist, pulling her flush against him. Sybil responded in kind, her hands pressing against his chest, feeling the steady beat of his heart beneath her palms.

The chaise lounge was too narrow, too confining, but neither of them seemed to care. Valen shifted, his weight pressing her back against the cushions as his lips traced a path along her jaw, down to the delicate hollow of her throat. Sybil's breath hitched, her fingers curling into the fabric of his shirt, anchoring herself to him. She had never known a kiss could feel like this—like a promise, like a storm waiting to break.

When he lifted his head, his breath was uneven. His dark eyes searched hers. For a moment, neither of them spoke. Then, with a slow, knowing smile, Valen brushed his thumb over her kiss-swollen lips.

"I should stop," he murmured, though he made no move to pull away.

Sybil arched a brow, her own lips curving. "Should you?"

His gaze darkened with something dangerously close to amusement. "You don't want me to."

She exhaled a breathless laugh, threading her fingers through the white strands of his hair. "No," she admitted, voice hushed. "I don't."

Valen made a sound low in his throat before he kissed her again.

The kiss deepened, charged with something ethereal. Valen shifted, pressing his glorious weight against her as his fingers traced the curve of her waist. His lips left a searing trail down her throat. Sybil shivered, her breath catching as he reached the delicate hollow of her collarbone. A soft sigh escaped her lips, and Valen stilled for the briefest moment, his breath warm against her skin.

"Tell me to stop," he murmured, his voice rough with restraint.

Sybil's thighs tightened against his hips. "I won't."

A slow, knowing smile curved his lips before he kissed her again, deeper this time, claiming and consuming. The heat between them built. Her hands roamed, exploring the firm planes of his back, feeling the tension coiled within him and delighting in the fact that she created that tension.

In a fit of need, Valen's fingers found the fastenings of her dress, peeling the fabric away from her shoulders. The thick material slipped down her arms, exposing her heaving chest. Valen's hungry gaze slid over her breasts. He stilled. His breath caught as his gaze fell upon the inked design over her heart—a dragon, its wings spread as if caught in flight. The firelight danced over the lines of the tattoo, accentuating the curves and detail of the mythical creature.

Valen drew back slightly, his fingertips grazing the blue ink. "What is this?" he asked, his voice edged with something she couldn't quite name.

Sybil's breath shuddered, her gaze lowering briefly before she met his eyes again. "A reminder," she murmured. "Of who I am. Of what I've lost."

His thumb traced the edge of the dragon's wing, his expression unreadable. "And what have you lost?"

Sybil swallowed, a shadow passing through her gaze. "Everything."

For a long moment, Valen said nothing, only studying her as if searching for the truth beneath her words. Then, with deliberate slowness, he bent his head, pressing his lips just over the inked mark, his kiss featherlight yet searing.

"Not everything," he murmured against her skin. "Not anymore."

For a glorious, agonizing minute his lips traced every line of the dragon tattoo. The attention made Sybil's heart beat faster than ever, and she became molten beneath him. Every touch sparked a fresh wave of need she was certain would swallow her if not sated soon.

Valen pulled back again, and she felt a chill only for a moment until noting the wild hunger in his dark eyes. Then he yanked his shirt up and over his head while Sybil pulled at the ties on his pants, but he grabbed her wrists, pinning them above her head as his weight settled over her.

"Not yet," he growled, the sound feral and hungry. "You are my little treat." His teeth raked the tender flesh on her neck and she moaned, pressing against him, needing more of him. Valen's nose nuzzled along her cheekbone, and his lips brushed her ear as he spoke. "And I'm so very hungry."

Seven Gods help me. If Sybil wasn't molten and eager for him before, those words certainly did the trick. How could his last wife ever resist this?

Then he moved his way slowly down her body, inch by delicious inch kissing and nipping at her skin. She panted and writhed beneath him, coming undone just by his touch alone. It made her tremble to even consider what else he might be capable of. Valen released her wrists the lower he moved, hands cupping her breasts, pinching her aching nipples while his mouth and tongue played games along her abdomen.

Sybil's fingers dug into the cushions behind her head as she arched into him. His palms slid down her sides, hooking into the fabric of the dress bunched at her waist. Sybil's skin pebbled as the heat of his touch left her skin. When she looked down, Valen was glaring at the cloth, then he yanked it down, working to free her legs from the fabric with savage need.

Valen's dark eyes met hers. His strong hands each grasped one of her legs, pulling them apart, resting them over his shoulders. Sybil shuddered in delight, her entire body burning with need that drew a moan from her lips. He slid his hand along her inner thigh, thumb flicking at that oh-so-tender spot. Sybil gasped as it sent a shock up her spine, through her core. Instinctively, she pressed down against him, needing his fingers, his lips, his tongue against her. But he resisted, pushing her back with his shoulders and a vicious smirk that did nothing to quell the heat burning through her body.

Only when Sybil melted against the lounge did he attack again. Valen's fingers slid along her, his gaze firmly fixed on hers.

"You're already soaked," he crooned.

Sybil inhaled as his finger slid into her. Then a second.

"He had no idea what to do with you, did he?" Valen asked, his hot breath rolling over her aching folds. His fingers worked slowly, creating wave after wave of euphoric bliss. She could hardly breath, hardly think straight as he hooked into her and increased the pace. Sybil's back arched as she cried out in pleasure. "I've been hungry for you from the moment I laid eyes on you."

"Please... Valen..." Sybil thought she might shatter into a million pieces if he didn't put his mouth on her soon. "I need..." A cry lifted out of her as he increased the speed and pressure.

"Tell me, my treat," he teased.

Desperate, Sybil lifted her voice, forcing the words out through panting breaths. "I need your mouth on me."

Valen lowered his head, still watching her every move with those predatory, hungry eyes. His hot breath hit her swollen folds and she whimpered, squirming. Valen pinned her with his palm against her abdomen while the other hand continued gifting her with pleasure she had never known before.

"You are mine now, my treat." His fingers slowed. "Not his. Mine alone." Sybil peered down as he licked his lips. Seven gods help her, she wanted that tongue on her. He grinned as if reading her thoughts. "Tell me you are only mine, and I will give you what you need."

It was so hard to draw in breath, as if his fingers somehow stole the air from her lungs. His gaze dipped down, studying her.

"I'm yours," Sybil breathed the words out. "Only yours."

Before she even finished speaking, his mouth fell over her, devouring her as if she were his last meal. Spots dotted Sybil's vision as she cried out in pleasure. As his lips moved over her, Sybil felt herself unravel. It was as if he traced fire across her skin, each stroke of his tongue and fingers sending ripples of pleasure through her veins, an intoxicating pull that left her breathless. The world outside this moment ceased to exist—there was only him, only the exquisite torment he wove with his mouth against her flesh. A sigh, raw and unbidden, escaped her lips as he probed her with an appetite that made her tremble.

Pleasure bloomed within her, a sensation so overwhelming it stole her breath, left her weightless, adrift in a sea of sensation. Each kiss, each stroke, sent her spiraling further, higher, until she thought she might dissolve into the very air around them. She clung to him, her hands fisting in his snowy hair, anchoring herself to the storm that raged between them.

"Surrender everything to me," he breathed against her flesh, his voice a low command wrapped in velvet.

Sybil shuddered beneath his endless hunger. She had already given him so much—her longing, her deepest desires, herself—but in that moment, she realized she wanted to give him everything. *Needed* to.

And so, she did. Sybil relinquished control to him, yielding to his skill, his hunger. He was hurried and unrelenting, worshipping her with a devotion that made her ache, made her whole, made her nearly break. And when she finally shattered, it was like falling into the stars, into a place where nothing else mattered but feeding every piece of herself to him.

Valen's eyes slid closed as he moaned in ecstasy, devouring every last drop she gifted him. Her vision shifted and blurred as her body relaxed back.

Then the exhaustion hit her square in the chest, as if she had drained herself utterly for him. It was all she could do to remain conscious long enough to feel him shift over her again, kissing at her neck and whispering in her ear.

"Perfection. You are everything I needed and more."

Those words relaxed Sybil, and she allowed the exhaustion to claim her.

CHAPTER 14

Boy with the Heart of a Lion

Nothing about Aethan's plan gave Cavis any comfort. Shino had relayed everything in detail and they had spent hours working out all the kinks the best they could. Two days ago, the Vorovesti ships hoisted anchor and sailed away. According to Shino, Dorin had been livid, demanding to know where they went. Shino posited that the rumors had reached the ships, and they abandoned Aethan before their vessels could be boarded and they would be executed with him.

Executed. That was Cavis's least favorite part of the plan. While Cavis understood Aethan's cold logic, he couldn't shake the urgency to plan a rescue instead of this.

Von insisted he could make a salve that would minimize Aethan's blood loss for a whole day. He claimed that, back in Elysia, his family became wealthy because of their well-known healing poultices, and his parents taught him everything they knew as he grew up. All he needed were the right herbs, and as long as the ships could reach Aethan in time to heal him completely, he would survive. But too much could go wrong. Aethan could still die. Most likely, he *would* die.

Cavis's spine itched, and he hoped that it wasn't a sign that someone was watching him. They moved through the guards' blind spots around the Arithian palace where Shino had directed them, under the cloak of darkness. He and his brother crouched beside the swaying trees along the edge of the Aryth Mountains. Ahead of them, the lush mountainside cradled the Novavito palace above the rest of the city. His gaze swept the landscape for the hidden door Shino had described. It would be unlocked for them, if Shino kept his word.

"Are you sure this is the right spot?" Cormic muttered as he also studied the mountainous wall for the door.

"He said it would be directly below the backmost palace spire," Cavis said for at least the hundredth time. He pointed up at the spire. "It should be directly below that." He traced down in as straight of a line as he could until he pointed at the base of the mountain. "It should be right there."

Cormic harrumphed, growing irritated that they hadn't found the entrance yet.

"I think I see it!" Von exclaimed quietly. Without waiting for the rest of them, Von began winding his way through the trees toward the mountain wall.

Gorim and Cormic followed.

Cavis glanced over his shoulder, but he couldn't see Kern or Weylen in their hiding places. They were to wait with the horses for the extraction. Once they emerged with Roric, the trio would take the horses through a mountain pass Shino had mapped out for them. The roads would be guarded, and the pass would make the journey take longer, but they couldn't risk being caught.

"Cavis!" Cormic hissed, waving him over to the wall where Von and Gorim worked together to push the door open.

Cavis flicked his gaze at the guard post on the palace walls, but no one was looking their way. They wouldn't, even if they heard something, by order of their captain.

If all went according to Shino's plan, they would be in and out with no one noticing until shift changes in the dungeon at dawn.

Cavis sprinted toward the open door, following the others into the black, dank tunnel. Von struck a flint and lit a torch, and Cavis pulled out the map Shino had given him as he followed along the narrow stone space.

The tunnels were close to the hidden mountain pass as a means of emergency escape for the royal family if the palace was lost. Cavis had heard stories about such tunnels, but he had never actually seen any of them. It was a well-guarded secret among the royal guards. The captain had been hesitant to even share it with them despite the circumstances, as it would be in breach of his vows to King Novin. But there would be no other way for them to get into the palace and out again without notice. Every other route risked exposure. As Shino saw it, he was aiding the future queen. Cavis didn't care, as long as it got them in and out without notice, Shino could tell himself whatever helped him sleep better at night.

Shino hadn't joined them. For their plan to work, he needed to go about his evening with business as usual. An hour ago, Cavis and Cormic had drinks with some of the guards Shino knew were loyal to the princess. After Roric was mounted and leaving with Kern and Weylen, they would return to the guard barracks to play cards with those men, firming their alibies for the evening.

If they followed the map Shino had given them, they would reach the dungeons through a passage with no resistance.

Cavis kept a watchful eye on the passage and map simultaneously to be sure they were following the directions to the letter. At the second junction on the left, Cavis instructed Von to follow the new path.

The four men moved in relative silence, focused on not kicking up too much dust or making too much noise, just in case someone was where they shouldn't be. A smell of stone and mildew permeated the tunnels. The walls were smooth, carved out thousands of years ago by ancient stone smiths.

"Nothing like a little light treason to help you sleep at night," Cormic muttered as he followed behind Cavis.

It was true, sadly. Cavis and his brother had dedicated their lives in service to the crown. They were both loyal and loved their kingdom and their king. But if Shino was to be believed, Prince Dorin had orchestrated heinous acts against his own family. Cavis knew he committed treason and prayed the princess would return to pardon them before they were caught and executed. *If I die, Iskra will kill me*, he thought as they turned at another junction. If he didn't save Aethan, she might kill him anyway. As much as she loved Cavis, he knew Aethan still held a special place in her heart.

After spending weeks pouring over the marriage contract, Lord Dysart had finally signed it. Cavis had watched the contract delivered into the hands of the messenger who would travel north to deliver it. It took a significant burden off his shoulders to have it signed before his father heard about Aethan's alleged treason. There was a good chance he would have refused had he heard the news. So far, Dorin kept it quiet.

What would father say if he knew what we were doing right now? Cavis mused to himself. Lord Dysart would likely kill them himself.

At last, they reached the dead end, as promised. A stone wall blocking their path.

"Now what?" Von asked.

"Hang on," Cavis whispered. He turned sideways to wedge past Von at the head of the group. The two barely fit past one another in this narrow space. He ran his hand along the edge. "Shino said the entrance would be concealed to be less obvious on both sides, but there would be a trigger under a stone crevice to activate the door and open it."

Cavis felt something shift beneath the tip of his finger and he turned to the others, holding a finger to his lips. Von slipped his torch into a mount on the wall. Cavis motioned for the others to ready themselves. Then he started a countdown with his fingers.

After reaching one, Cavis activated the trigger. The stone rumbled softly as it popped out. Cavis rested his hand on his dagger as he peered around the stone door into the dimly lit dungeon hall.

"Clear," he whispered back to them.

The four slipped out of the tunnel and into the dungeon halls.

Up one set of stairs. Fourth cell on the right. Two guards on duty at the far end of the hall. Those would have to be dispatched quickly before they could raise an alarm. Shino couldn't get his trusted men on this shift. Apparently, Prince Dorin wanted only men he selected watching his special prisoner.

The lower cells were for the worst offenders and were currently empty, according to the captain.

Cavis led them to the staircase, hugging to the inner wall like Shino instructed. They would be less likely to project shadows along the wall. They took each step slowly, making as little sound as possible.

At the top, Cavis peered around the corner cautiously. As Shino predicted, two guards were on duty, playing cards over a barrel at the far end of the hall. He counted the cell doors on the right to the fourth, where Roric would be. All he could see was a lump on the cot. Roric was likely asleep.

There would be no way to sneak up on these two. Quick attack would be best.

The guards engaged in bored conversation. Cavis leaned back toward his friends.

"Two at the far end. One will make a stand. The other will run for the alarm," Cavis said as quietly as he could. "Von and I will take the one who runs. Gorim and Cormic will take the other."

Cavis and Von were the faster runners of the four, so it made the most logical sense. The others nodded in agreement.

Just as Cavis was about to burst into the hall, Gorim lunged for him, pulling him back.

He placed a finger to his lips, then produced two throwing knives. "Quick and quiet," he whispered.

Cavis remembered watching Gorin with throwing axes in the tournament. He had been deadly accurate. But were knives the same?

"If you miss..." Cavis whispered.

"I throw, we rush," Gorim replied.

Cavis nodded and stepped back, making space for Gorim on the top step. The guards chuckled with one another, oblivious to the death coming for them. Killing his own countrymen was not something Cavis would relish, but these two were loyal to Prince Dorin and betrayers of the rightful heir. That choice would cost them.

Gorim glanced around the corner, crouching low to make himself smaller. He watched the guards for a moment. One knife flew from his hand, followed less than a breath later by the second. He held up a hand to hold them back as he waited for his knives to hit the target.

The second Cavis heard the guards become aware of the attack, Gorim dropped his hand and they launched up the steps and rushed.

The knives hadn't killed them, but one guard clutched the side of his leg at the knee where the knife stuck in the joint. The other stood, staring at the knife sticking out of his stomach. That would have been a headshot if he hadn't toppled his barrel to stand.

The four of them descended on the guards so fast the one with the stomach wound didn't make it to the stairs before Cavis pulled him back and Von sliced clean across his throat. When they turned, the kneecapped guard lay over the barrel they had used as a table. He hadn't even been able to stand and defend himself before they finished him.

"Dorin will be so pissed when he finds out about this," Cormic mused, frowning at the guard. "I knew this guy."

Cavis tried not to look too closely at their faces as he searched for the keys. "Don't let yourself think too much about it. They made their choice."

"Master Cavis?" Roric sat up on his cot, rubbing sleep from his eyes. He was a little thinner, pale, and dirty, but otherwise seemed to be in good enough health to walk himself out. Dorin probably kept him just healthy enough to use as a tool against Aethan. That was some luck.

Cavis pulled the keys from a latch on the guard's belt and rushed to the door, searching for the right one to unlock the cell. "How you doing, kid?"

"Been better," Roric replied truthfully. He examined each of them before his face fell. "Were's my Lord?"

"We will explain on the way out," Cavis said, testing another key. "Anything?" he called back to Von at the stairs.

"Not yet."

The lock clicked. Cavis yanked the door open and Roric stepped out slowly, eyeing the dead guards.

"This way," Cavis said, nudging Roric toward the staircases to the lower level.

Roric stumbled a few steps as the others moved toward the exit. He stopped and straightened. "Wait. We can't leave him!"

"Everything is under control kid," Cormic said sharply. "Our mission was you. Starkling's orders. Now move."

Roric turned to the dead guard slumped over the barrel, then rushed over and pulled the knife from the guard's belt, tucking it into his own before moving for the stairs.

The wrong stairs.

Gorim wrapped his strong arms around Roric's waist and hauled him up and over his shoulder like a sack of flour. "Nope. Wrong way."

"Put me down!" Roric snapped. "I have to get Lord Aethan." The pitch of his voice cracked and shifted in his desperation.

"Quite down or you'll attract more guards," Von hissed.

Roric beat on Gorim's back viciously, squirming to break free. Cavis admired his wholehearted loyalty to Aethan. Roric had the heart of a lion, but if this was the fight they were getting from him now, there was little chance they would get him on a horse and out of Arithia tonight.

The group rushed down the stairs, and Roric's protests abated by the time they reached the secret tunnel again. Gorim couldn't carry the boy over his shoulder. The tunnels were too short and narrow. He set Roric on his feet, holding tight to his arm.

"Listen, kid, your lord is the one who set all of this up," Gorim hissed. "Would you go against his orders?"

Roric sniffled and rubbed his dirty sleeve across his cheeks, trying to look strong and defiant, wiping away the evidence of his tears. He shook his head once as Cormic and Von led the way.

"Good. Go." Gorim pointed toward the tunnel as Von removed the torch from the bracket.

Roric looked up, as if he could sense or see Aethan, murmuring something that sounded like a vow. Then he dipped his head and shuffled into the tunnel. *Thank the seven gods*.

Cavis brought up the rear, swinging the tunnel door closed and engaging the trigger again, sealing it shut.

They moved swiftly. The only sounds came from their thumping boots and Roric's sniffles. They followed the map in reverse until emerging along the mountainside once more. Cavis closed the door behind him, then sprinted after the others to where Kern and Weylen waited with horses.

Had that plan actually worked? Dare they hope that the next plan would go as smoothly with Aethan?

When he joined the others, Cavis heard Roric once more protesting as Gorim hoisted him into a saddle.

"I won't leave without Lord Aethan," Roric said, stubborn determination setting in his young face. "He would never leave without me."

"Which is exactly why you have to go," Kern said. "Prince Dorin will have guards searching for you the moment he learns you've escaped. Aethan refuses to leave until he knows you are safe. The sooner you *are* safe, the better."

Cavis stepped up to the boy's side, placing a reassuring hand on his knee. "We have a plan to help him, but it won't work if you are still here. He has an urgent mission for you, Roric. Aethan needs you to go through the mountains with these two and head north to let Aslyn know he is safe, and to help her. She is all alone. He's placing a great deal of responsibility on your shoulders. Are you sure you can handle it?"

It wasn't entirely true.

Roric sniffled again, his eyes watery as he considered Cavis's words. "You swear you have a plan?"

"I swear it." A terrible plan, but Roric didn't need the details. "Can you handle your mission?"

"Deliver the news and help the princess," Roric said, as if confirming the orders. He gave a tight nod. "I swear it on my life."

"Let's hope it doesn't come to that," Cavis said as he stepped back. He turned his attention to Kern, then Weylen. "Ride. Don't look back. Stop only when necessary. We will meet again on the Cliffs of Hope."

With that, the horses turned and the trio galloped into the mountain pass.

"No alarms," Cormic noted.

Cavis murmured in agreement. "Let's go solidify our alibi." He eyed Von and Gorim. "You two know what to do?"

"Got it." Gorim patted Von on the shoulder and the two lumbered away.

Cavis turned to Cormic. "Let's go lose a small fortune to some special guards."

Chapter 15

Right of Ownership

All roads to the Citadel ran through Lemheller Gap. Bast set himself in a tree a couple kilometers from the city. He lounged back against the thick trunk, stretched out along the strongest branch he could find above the road. And he waited, trimming slices off an apple as his eyes remained locked on the only path into the city.

He couldn't be sure a wagon would come through, but considering how few he had noticed over the past few weeks passing through the city, Bast assumed they made the trek at night. It made sense if the emperor's minions wanted to keep their dirty torture chambers secret. And if nothing came by tonight, he would return the next night and the next until something did.

Really, Bast hoped that the Citadel sadists would ramp up their efforts with the recent death of several of their newest subjects—courtesy of his undetected visit—not because he wanted more people tortured, but because he desired, more than anything, to be a thorn in the emperor's side.

A cold wind swept through the trees, rustling the leaves. Then, at last, he heard it—the distant creak of wagon wheels, the rhythmic clop of horses' hooves. He tensed, his breath steady, and his heartbeat a measured drum in his chest. The wagon emerged from the bend, flanked by six Black Guards. More than he had anticipated. Black Guards were some of the toughest fighters in the realm. But he had beaten four before. He could handle six. Hopefully.

Bast's lips pressed into a thin line as he recalled the one he had interrogated. Efficiently, their vocal chords were cut to keep them silent, and their wills were broken in those torture chambers until they served without question. No warnings, no cries for help—perfect sentinels for the emperor's army.

The moment the wagon passed beneath him, he moved.

A flick of his fingers sent a tendril of shadow lancing down, snaking around the nearest guard's throat. With a swift jerk, the man was yanked backward into the darkness, his struggles brief before the shadows crushed the life from him. Bast was already airborne, dropping soundlessly onto the roof of the wagon as a knife flew expertly at the next guard. His blade plunged deep between the man's ribs, but it caught on the armor and the guard simply pulled it out while making a guttural sound of warning. How did that not kill him?

The remaining guards snapped their heads toward him, sensing the pulse of his magic in the air. Their hands went for their weapons, and this time, they were ready for him.

One guard fired a crossbow bolt at Bast, forcing him to flip off the roof of the wagon to avoid death. The tip of the arrow came so close he felt the air displacement near his neck. As he came down, Bast kicked his feet out at another guard while throwing a knife into the neck of the guard beside him. The knifed guard gurgled, then slumped, falling face-first in the dirt-packed road.

Two down, four to go.

The swordsman lunged as the guard Bast kicked moments ago recovered. Bast barely dodged the strike as a blade slashed through the shadows curling around his arm. Bast twisted, using his momentum to drive a dagger into the man's ribs. The swordsman staggered but did not fall, his strength unnatural.

The kicked guard recovered quickly, swinging a heavy axe at Bast from behind. Bast ducked, shadows surging around him to disarm his attacker. The soldier snarled as he felt the magic coil around his wrist, and he wrenched free with sheer brute force.

Bast cursed. These guards had been trained to resist magical attacks. No one had ever broken free of his shadows like that. Bast tucked and rolled under the axeman's swing.

As he came to a crouch behind the axeman, and the swordsman fell on Bast in a series of vicious swings of his sword. He blocked the strikes, feeling them jar his joints with each deflection with the dagger.

Click. Click. Click. The crossbowman prepared another bolt to fire at Bast. The string creaked.

In a flash, Bast kicked out at the swordsman's leg to buckle him away from the attack, rolled away from the axeman's deadly swing, and threw another knife. The blade buried in the eye of the crossbowman before he could fire. The bolt fired into a nearby tree as the crossbowman fell back, crossbow cracking as he fell on it.

Bast didn't have time to be relieved. While the crossbowman was down, the axeman and swordsman were working together to break through his defenses. Bast barely had a breath to throw a shield of shadows up as they both struck death blows. Their weapons rebounded off the shadow shield. Bast gritted his teeth as the force drove his knees deeper into the dirt.

If he couldn't get to his feet, he would be in serious trouble really soon.

Bast unsheathed his sword from his back, pushing out with his shadows shield to create more space as he rose to his feet. The swordsman hacked a swing aimed at Bast's side. He twisted his blade to block the attack, forcing the sword out of the swordsman's hand. The impact still made Bast's arm tremble.

Bast kicked up dirt as he kicked the handle of a discarded sword from an already dead guard. Both guards stumbled backward, and Bast seized the opportunity. As the discarded sword tipped up, he wrapped it with threads of shadows and threw it like a dart with the shadows.

The sword glanced off Black Guard armor, but the impact still sent the swordsman staggering backward. The axeman recovered, renewing his vicious attacks.

As he parried the axe swings, Bast reacted instinctively, lashing out with his shadows at the axeman's ankles. As the axe swung toward Bast's sword arm, he yanked the shadows, wrenching the axeman's feet from beneath him. By the time the axeman hit the ground, Bast leaped onto his chest, slicing his sword through armor, flash, and bone. The head rolled.

Sensing movement, Bast glanced to either side. The swordsman had recovered and, to Bast's horror, the crossbowman rose, blood spilling from the lost eye. How was he still alive?

The last two moved in unison, their swords flashing as they flanked him. Bast climbed to his feet slowly, eyeing each guard with his sword in one hand and a dagger in the other. With each breath in, Bast pulled his shadows around his body like a shield. They coiled up from the ground.

The guards attacked together. One struck high, the other low, forcing Bast to twist between their blades. He parried the first strike, his dagger scraping against steel, while he kicked the one-eyed swordsman back, buying himself a fraction of a second, then yanked him back from the fight with a tendril of shadow.

The other guard lunged again, sword arcing toward Bast's ribs. Bast sidestepped, catching the blade with his own sword, but the one-eyed guard had already recovered and closed the gap. His knife whistled through the air. Bast barely ducked in time, feeling the rush of wind as it passed inches above his head. He retaliated with a shadow-imbued strike, but they anticipated it, splitting apart to avoid the curling darkness.

He grimaced. They were adapting.

Gritting his teeth, he shifted tactics. Instead of reaching for more magic, he let them come. As the one-eyed guard surged forward, Bast caught his wrist, twisting sharply before driving his dagger into the man's neck. The guard staggered, blood spilling in eerie silence, but his partner did not hesitate. The swordsman came again. Bast flung the dying guard as his compatriot.

The final guard fell backward, giving Bast a chance to recenter himself. The swordsman shoved the dead one-eyed guard to the ground, then adjusted his grip on his sword. Bast tossed his dagger up to shift his grip, catching it deftly. He swung his sword back into the sheath, then replaced it with a thick band of shadows around his arm.

With a curl of his lips, the guard charged, swinging his sword down with terrifying strength and speed. Bast rolled away as steel bit into the dirt where he had stood moments before. That swing would have cleaved his body in half.

As the guard wrenched his sword from the dirt-packed road beneath them, Bast struck. He darted inside the man's guard, his shadows wrapping around the swordsman's neck and squeezing tight. His blade flashed once. Twice. The swordman jerked, then bones crunched under the pressure of the shadows. His lifeless body crumpled to the ground.

Bast exhaled sharply, surveying the fallen. He felt the blood trickling from a shallow cut on his neck. That had been far too close for his comfort.

Even in death, their faces held no fear—only the blank, unrelenting obedience that had made them such formidable foes. Whatever spark of life had once existed in these men was long gone before death.

The bodies lay scattered in eerie stillness. Not a single cry had rung out. The forest remained undisturbed, save for the whisper of wind through the trees and cries of the captives inside the wagon.

Bast gave himself a moment to collect his breath, then exhaled, turning toward the wagon. He cleaned his blades quickly, then sheathed them before stepping forward. He snapped the lock with his shadows.

The wagon doors groaned open, revealing a half dozen weary souls huddled together against the far wall of the wagon. Their eyes flickered with a mix of fear and disbelief as they beheld the dark figure standing before them. Throughout the fight, his hood had remained in place, and he bent shadows to mask himself from prying eyes. Bast gestured for them to step out.

"You're free," he said. "Head south along the river. Keep to the woods and avoid the roads. There's shelter if you know where to look. And if you value your lives at all, you will avoid using your magic at all costs. They can track it."

Some hesitated, casting wary glances at the fallen guards, but a few took cautious steps forward. Three males, barely men, followed a fourth. He was thin and reminded Bast of a young wolf cub.

The cub studied Bast carefully, assessing him, attempting to peer into the darkness of Bast's shadowed hood. "You—you're..." His eyes widened, then he gave a nod that felt far too deferential for Bast's tastes. "Thank you."

Bast gave a brief nod, then turned his gaze to the distant horizon, his instincts prickling. A faint sound reached his ears—the unmistakable thrum of approaching boots. Reinforcements.

His brow furrowed. How had they known? His ambush had been swift, precise. No alarms had been raised, no messengers had escaped. And yet, they were coming.

The last of the prisoners hopped out of the wagon, making their way into the trees.

But the four young men remained, their chins lifting and defiance in their eyes.

Bast unsheathed two knives and stepped back into the shadows. "Run. Now."

"We can help," the cub said. "I'm Pulto. These are—"

"Don't care," Bast snapped. "I didn't open that door so they can recapture you. And I'm not looking for friends." His ears twitched as he heard the approaching reinforcements drawing closer. "If you don't run, I'll leave you to your fates. And I've seen what they are. You don't want it. Now, fucking run."

Pulto and his followers hesitated only a moment before sprinting south toward the river as he had instructed.

Bast edged deeper into the forest shadows, cautious of drawing on his magic. Behind him, he could hear the panicked breathing, rustle of sticks and leaves, and pounding feet of the fleeing prisoners. They would get themselves caught from the noise alone. Bast had to buy them time.

Gritting his teeth, Bast reached as deep into his well of magic as he dared. Shadows and darkness flexed in the surrounding trees before answering his call. His muscles tensed as the magic poured into him as powerful as a thundering waterfall. He gritted his teeth.

The sound of booted feet approached. The reinforcements would arrive soon.

Magic inside of him hummed with a seductive call, a chorus of sirens all targeting him. Bast couldn't take these guards on again. More would arrive than had guarded the wagon. Perhaps dozens. Even with his skills, he couldn't hope to fight them all and survive. He needed a distraction.

They closed in. Soon, they would spot him in the tree line.

The retreat of the prisoners grew quieter.

There was no time.

Bast poured all the magic into one location. The wagon. He filled it with darkness so thick no light would penetrate it. When only a few drops of power remained, Bast curled his fingers, focused on the wagon door. It swung shut. Then he inverted threads of his shadows around the handles, setting the trap.

Time was up.

Bast released the magic, and backed silently into the forest, eyes on the road.

More than two dozen Black Guards rounded the bend. Without a word, they split like water around rock, streaming around the wagon to face the forest on all sides.

Bast ducked behind a tree, knowing he couldn't flee. But he also couldn't fight. Not these numbers. If he was lucky, he could take out a quarter of them before the rest either killed or captured him.

Three guards marched around the wagon, inspecting their fallen comrades with little more than a cursory glance. They stopped at the back of the wagon. One drew two vicious-looking curved dadao swords, then nodded at the other two positioned at either door of the wagon.

Bast steadied his breathing and readied his muscles. He would have but a heartbeat to run out of danger once the shadow bands on the doors broke. If he ran too soon, he would attract attention and some of those guards would escape with him. If he ran too late, he would die with them.

The second they pulled on the wagon doors, Bast turned and sprinted as fast as his legs could carry him. Before any of the Black Guards registered his retreat, the shadows inside the wagon exploded outward, plunging everything within a half dozen meters into deadly shadows.

He ran, barely outpacing the blast. The hood over his head fluttered but didn't fall. Bast didn't dare look back, feeling the cold of the shadows nipping at his heels.

But through that darkness, he heard the guttural grunts of death, the clatter of falling weapons, the clink and snap of breaking bones and falling armor.

He ran until his lungs burned and his muscles protested, circling wide around the catastrophic site before doubling back to the city.

There would be no hiding his presence from the emperor after that.

And he would send everything he had to find Bast.

When he reached the city, Bast slipped through the shadows toward the inn where he rented his room in the more rundown part of town. Fewer people looked twice at him in the slums, and there was little risk that anyone might recognize him from Stormvalor among the poor. Every few days, he switched inns to avoid detection. Unfortunately, Bast had been in Lemheller Gap for so long that his options ran thin. If he didn't get Aslyn out soon, he would be forced into the nicer inns.

As expected, the few who spotted him crossing streets hardly spared him more than a glance. Not when he wrapped the black and silver band of cloth around his upper right arm. It marked him as a loyalist to the imperial throne. A lie, obviously, but one Bast had to maintain in this city to avoid unwanted eyes.

Bast reached the inn and entered through the back where a guard employed by the innkeeper dozed against the wall, his head slumped against his chest and jaw slack in sleep.

Money well spent, Bast thought as he slipped past the guard without detection. Did the innkeeper know this guard slept through his night shift? Did he even care?

Bast climbed the back stairs to his fourth-floor room. Like most buildings in Lemheller Gap, this one was crushed close to its neighbor, forcing it to rise upward to accommodate guest space. Bast had asked for a room on the top floor. Fewer thieves looking for quick coins would climb so high. They would target the lower rooms first for an easier getaway. Or at least, that was Bast's logic.

Ten paces from his door, Bast stopped, then slid toward the shadows against the wall.

To the common patron, the door looked closed. Dark on the other side. But Bast noticed the lock turned the wrong way, and along the doorframe, a slight marring in the wood where the lock engaged in the frame.

Someone broke into his room.

Bast dropped a knife into one hand, then edged toward the closed door. With a twist of his wrist, Bast used his shadows to open the door instead of doing it himself. The second the door opened, he rolled into the room, tossing a knife to where he sensed a disturbance in the dark shadows.

Magic slammed against him. Bast skidded across the small floor until his back hit the wall. An invisible force pinned him in place. How could the emperor's men have possibly found him so quickly, before he even returned to his room?

"You are very intriguing." A male voice said from the darkness.

Bast focused his eyes toward the voice, reaching for his magic to help his vision in the dark. Instead, he hit a magical barrier just like the one he experienced in the Citadel.

"How did you come to possess Candidate Herund's robes?" the man asked.

"Lucky purchase," Bast growled.

"I don't think so." Boots shuffled across the wooden floor toward Bast. "We found his body in the armory. Were his robes not missing, it might have looked like he stumbled into the halberd rack and fell on one."

A shadowy form of a face came into view, closer than Bast had anticipated. "Not only did you sneak into the Citadel, break into the armory, kill the candidate, and likely several of our men in transition, but..." He breathed in deep, leaning close enough for Bast to make out the whites of his eyes and his sharp nose. "You reek of powerful magic. *Ancient* magic."

Bast spit in the man's face, still unable to move.

The man tutted as he wiped away the spit. A slap hit Bast before he even registered the movement. The Jewel of Arithia shifted in its hiding place between his tunic and the leather armor.

That's what he smells, Bast realized. *The ancient magic from the stone.*

The man reached behind Bast, drawing Bast's sword from the sheath on his back. He traced a finger along the black blade, then chuckled.

"Oh this just gets better and better. You aren't just any lucky thief—or perhaps unlucky, under the circumstances." His lips twitched into a vicious smirk. "You are the infamous assassin, aren't you?"

Bast didn't respond. It wasn't a question.

"I will admit I didn't dream what I would discover when I followed the trace of the candidate's robes to this place, this... dank hole in the wall inn." The man's fingers slid up the sword hilt to the gray stone in the pommel. "You don't even know the power you possess with this blade alone. Foolish child, stumbling around in the dark pretending to be superior. Really, you are as ignorant as all the other common shit festering in this realm."

Bast growled, pulling at the invisible force pinning him against the wall. *Ignorant? I'll show him ignorant!* Two could play this game, and the man had no idea that, while Bast's arms might be pinned, his legs could still move freely. As he squirmed, Bast pulled a knee up as if he wanted to push himself to his feet.

What power did the intruder think that blade held? Bast had never known it to be anything more than a sword. A rare one with a black blade that didn't reflect light, sure, but a sword nonetheless.

"To have *two* gifts from the ancients..." The man shook his head, studying the sword. "Emperor Valen will reward me with a huge promotion."

Valen? What happened to Oxon?

"I will bring him the blade, a powerful shadow wielder, and..." He reached toward Bast's leather armor and he knew what the man was after.

Flexing his arms to pull up the rest of his body, Bast twisted around, triggering the blade in his boot as he brought his heel down on the man's neck. But a magical shield blocked the strike and his blade didn't just deflect off the shield. It sizzled and snapped.

The man laughed again. "Clever, but not clever enough." He pulled on the chain around Bast's neck, tugging the Jewel of Arithia out of its hiding place. "I believe this belongs to someone else."

Bast grunted as he reached down and down and down into that well for his magic. He hammered against the wall blocking him, slammed into it with every ounce of will. Sweat beaded on his forehead.

The chain snapped as the man yanked it from his neck. The intruder touched Bast's sword against his neck where his pulse thrummed wildly. Bast closed his eyes, throwing all of his energy, his will, at the wall. It cracked.

"Once you are put through the transition, the emperor will have the best assassin in the realm at his beck and call," the man said. "I might even be promoted to Head of the Citadel for this." He turned the jewel in his palm, caressing it with his thumb.

The pendant called to Bast. He gritted his teeth, losing focus on his attempt to break through the shield blocking him from his magic as the pendant consumed his attention.

The man stood, stepping back with Bast's sword in his hand. He slid the pendant into his pocket.

No, Bast thought, though he wasn't sure where the thought came from. *He cannot have the stone.* To get that artifact, he had worked so hard, risked his life, burned bridges, betrayed the only person to ever show him kindness. He sacrificed *everything* for that pendant. It couldn't fall into imperial hands.

The pendant hummed in response.

The man turned from Bast, gathering the stolen robes.

"Give it back," Bast growled.

"I will see it returned to the rightful owner," the man said, tucking the robes into a pack.

As he tucked the robes away, the smooth obistone, still wrapped tightly in cloth, tumbled out. Bast watched it hit the floor and roll toward him. His pulse kicked up, but the intruder didn't seem to notice. If that man put that stone against Bast's skin, what would happen? What kind of horror would he face? He eyed the man, carefully moving his boot to cover the wrapped stone from unwanted eyes. He couldn't risk it.

Bast could see the intruder's movements clearly in the dark as a pulsing green aura seeped out of his pocket, wrapping around his body. Bone crunched. The sword clattered to the floor. The shield blocking Bast from his magic vanished at the same moment as the invisible bonds holding him down.

In a heartbeat, Bast was on his feet, filling himself with as much magic as he could drink down. But before he took a step and unleashed his fury on the intruder, the man's head rolled unnaturally to the side and he fell to the floor.

Bast edged toward him, knives in his hands and shadows ready.

The man's dark, empty eyes stared at the ceiling.

The jewel did this. It wound around him and snapped his neck.

Bast kneeled beside the body, his hand trembling as he reached into the pocket to retrieve the pendant. The green gemstone pulsed like a beating heart, then the light within it died. He turned it over in his hand, absently retrieving his sword to return to the sheath. As soon as the sword was on his back, it hummed like a happy cat.

What is happening right now?

Legends told that the Jewel of Arithia could not be taken from the rightful royal owner. It had to be given or the owner killed, or the Jewel of Arithia would retaliate. When Aslyn gave it to him, did that transfer ownership? He could think of no other explanation for how or why the stone would kill the intruder. But only Novavito royals—those of the right bloodline—could become rightful owners. At least, that was the legend he heard. Could it be wrong?

And why had the sword responded, too?

I have to get rid of the body, Bast thought, coming back to his senses.

But first, he traced the trim on the new robes with the tip of his finger, funneling a hint of his magic into them.

The trim on this one was so dark he almost couldn't see it in the darkness of the room. A chill slid along his magical touch. Not heat like the fire robes, but like a cool embrace.

He would get rid of the body, but it could never be found. Not if the robes were traceable. And he needed these robes for as long as he could keep them.

Bast set to work, swapping the fire robes for the mysterious dark ones on the intruder's body.

Then he hoisted the body over his shoulder and slipped out to burn the remains before dawn.

Chapter 16

Secret Partners and Deadly Threats

Aslyn had expected Sybil to consider her suggestion about making the first move with Valen for a few days before taking the next step, but just in case opportunity came, Aslyn kept an eye on Sybil's movements. Her father had trained her not to underestimate anyone.

The vigilance paid off much faster than Aslyn anticipated, and she thanked her father for his lessons. Late that same night, Sybil made her way through the halls much later than she would normally move about the palace. Aslyn followed at a distance, keeping her steps quiet and cautious of guards.

When Sybil attempted entering the chamber, two Black Guards abruptly cut her off. Aslyn waited for Sybil to change her mind and retreat. Instead, the woman straightened her spine and berated the guards in a way that reminded Aslyn of Aethan.

The door opened, and from her angle, Aslyn couldn't see who stood on the other side. The voice of Lady Fia shocked Aslyn. Why would that woman be in Valen's chambers in the dead of night? Apparently, Sybil wondered the same thing based on her reaction to the woman.

Then Sybil attempted to strike Lady Fia and the woman seized her wrist. Aslyn's stomach somersaulted as a strange sensation rippled out from Sybil. It came and went quickly, and when it vanished, Sybil collapsed.

What just happened? Aslyn wondered as she hugged her stomach.

Valen appeared, scooping Sybil into his arms before she hit the floor. But his commands to Lady Fia had Aslyn's mind churning. Who were they talking about?

Lady Fia stormed away in a huff, headed in Aslyn's direction. Aslyn's heart thumped as she rushed to hide behind a heavy curtain before the other woman spotted her. She held her breath, listening to the click of heeled boots approaching. The anger on Lady Fia's face was clear as glass, and Aslyn swore the hallway heated in the woman's wake. Sweat beaded on Aslyn's forehead as Lady Fia passed, and she counted to five before peering out to watch her retreating form.

With a glance back toward Valen's chambers, Aslyn slipped out of her hiding place and followed the trail of heat she was certain emanated from Lady Fia.

They climbed a spiraling staircase and torches flared to life the higher they climbed. Aslyn kept a cautious distance from the other woman. Her instincts warned her to turn back and continue as she had planned, but that intense curiosity to know what Lady Fia was up to overpowered the instincts writing in her stomach.

At last, they reached the top of the staircase. Aslyn kept close to the wall as she shifted around to see Lady Fia.

A door stood open at the top and Aslyn caught a flash of Lady Fia moving from one side of the room to the other. Aslyn edged closer to the door, doing her best to keep her breathing as even as possible despite her nerves. There would be no escaping notice if the other woman decided to descend the stairs again.

She reached the doorway and peeked inside. The largest bed Aslyn had ever seen dominated the space, covered in rich red coverlets and sheets. Above the bed, mirrors made the torchlight fill the room, dancing across every surface. This wasn't a tower prison. It was a richly decorated suite suitable for any royal.

Near the bed, Lady Fia stripped out of her surprisingly decent dress. It pooled around her ankles. Aslyn gaped at the woman. Not only was every curve of her body utterly perfect and smooth, but a massive tattoo of a red dragon spread across her entire back, the tail coiling around one thigh. It was the largest, most detailed tattoo Aslyn had ever seen. The red scales of the dragon shimmered in the torchlight as if it were a real, breathing thing. The detail was breathtaking.

Lady Fia slid her hands along her curves in a way that made Aslyn uncomfortable watching. But as her hands moved along her body, a translucent red nightgown bled into being over her body. The back dipped so low it revealed the tip of her crack and the dimples just above it. The nightgown stopped so close to the creases where her legs met her backside that Aslyn was certain it would reveal everything if she bent over.

With a snap of her fingers, Lady Fia's hair swept up into stunning curls that highlighted the fine, delicate slope of her neck. A slinky dress settled over her nightgown.

Aslyn felt utterly indecent watching this transformation, yet she couldn't look away. Envy for Lady Fia's effortless perfection flared through Aslyn.

Lady Fia stepped into a pair of stiletto heels that made the shape of her legs even more pronounced. If ever there was a woman who could turn the heads of any man, it was this one.

The magic required to create clothing from nothing made Aslyn's head spin. But the worst part was the blatant use of it. Magic was strictly forbidden in all five kingdoms. Yet the emperor's own right hand waved about magic like it was nothing.

Anger burned in Aslyn's heart. Men, women, and children, were put to death for being born with just an ounce of the magic Lady Fia had just wielded. Surely the emperor knew. He must know. What made this woman the exception to such brutal laws?

Aslyn's hand clenched into a fist around her skirt as she fought to control her anger at the flagrant hypocrisy.

Magic could destroy their fragile world. Only by holding back the use of magic and the destructive toll it took on the world could they hope to survive. That was what everyone was told, and people were put to death for it. But if Lady Fia walked freely, waving about her magic like an extension of herself, surely the Imperial Edict had it wrong.

Aslyn couldn't decide what to do with this information.

Just as she was about to retreat down the tower stairs, flashes ignited in Lady Fia's room, freezing Aslyn in place. The sparks intensified, forming an oval of flickering firelight that flitted around it like fireflies. The inside of the oval shimmered with a translucent opalescent light, then an image solidified in its place.

That's no image, Aslyn realized. It was a doorway to elsewhere. A magical doorway. Aslyn didn't even know such a thing was possible.

She studied the space beyond, squinting into the darkness—a courtyard of what appeared to be a noble estate. The onyx walls of the manor and sloping roof nearly blended into the late-night darkness. But the silver trees, Aslyn could easily identify. They only grew in one place.

Mordelic, seat of the kingdom of Vorovesti.

The man she and Valen spoke of is from Vorovesti! Aslyn's insides became a mess of apprehension. Was it the king Lady Fia had targeted for the emperor? Or perhaps... the crown prince. Surely he knew the dangers of tangling with this woman. Aethan made his cousin sound so sensible and intelligent.

"On time as always," a man voice said from the darkness.

Something about that voice tickled at Aslyn's memory. She knew it. She heard it before. But where?

"I wouldn't dream of keeping you waiting," Lady Fia said with a seductive allure in her voice that hinted at much more than a casual conversation. She stepped toward a shadowed figure leaning against one of the trees. "A promise is a promise, after all."

He chuckled, low and hungry. "Updates?"

Aslyn squinted to get a better look at him, but the darkness was so deep where he stood she couldn't make out more than his form.

Lady Fia practically purred. "Later." Then she slipped into the darkness, and Aslyn could make out just enough of the two of them to see her sliding her fingers into his hair as he pulled her against him.

As the doorway slid closed, Aslyn caught a glimpse of sandy hair as he tilted his head in a kiss that was far from chaste.

Then the sparks vanished, leaving Lady Fia's chamber in the dark.

Aslyn pressed her back to the wall, her head spinning as she attempted to put the pieces together. She heard that voice before, and his response to Lady Fia echoed in Aslyn's head as she struggled to place it. A Vorovesti noble with sandy hair and a familiar voice. Surely that limited the potential candidates.

The mystery plagued Aslyn all night. Once she finally found sleep, the mysterious man appeared in her dreams. He transformed as the dream went on from one man to another. All with sandy hair. All with the same voice. But their faces changed. Men she didn't know, and some she knew very well. Not all of them truly had sandy hair but in her dream, Aslyn couldn't tell the difference between her brother, Cavis, Cormic, Marek, Prince Gannon, Trystain, Ryker... Aethan.

The next day, she sat outside with Sybil after lunch, she considered asking her friend if she knew anyone matching that description. But 'sandy hair' was hardly much to go on among Vorovesti nobles. Aslyn didn't even know how old he had been.

Aethan said his father took a new wife so he could produce another Stormvalor heir. Could it have been him? Perhaps he didn't recognize Lady Fia, or he had been tricked somehow with magic to not know it was her. While his hair had been darker than either of his children, Aslyn thought it hadn't been sandy.

I hate my memory sometimes, she thought as she sat beside Sybil in a lounge chair the guards had brought outside—one for each of them.

Sybil had slept in until nearly lunch, and when she had agreed to meet with Aslyn, she insisted they do so outside in this courtyard. "Sunlight is good for the soul," Sybil had said. Not that there was much sunlight.

An army of servants moved around the two of them, keeping their tea hot, bringing delectable finger foods, stoking a brazier between the two that warded off the chill of the mountain air.

Across the stone courtyard, another statue of Emperor Narcisse stood proudly, a monolith of polished obistone and gold that gleamed even in the overcast light. The emperor stood atop a mountain of fallen enemies, his armored form both regal and imposing. His sword, a masterpiece of dark steel, was raised high like a beacon of unchallenged dominance. Around him, sculpted figures of his silent enforcers stood in eerie stillness, their blank expressions carved with perfect precision, as if even in death, they awaited his command. At his feet, an inscription was etched deep into the stone:

"By his will, the world is shaped. By his hand, order is kept. By his blade, all kneel."

Aslyn studied the statue as Sybil regaled the events of last night in more detail than Aslyn expected the young woman to share.

Once more, Aslyn was struck by the likeness of Valen to Narcisse. How did the imperial line remain so utterly pure that all the heirs resembled those who came before all the way back to Narcisse? Was that likeness the reason Sybil insisted on this location, so that she could gaze upon the statuesque figure so like her husband?

"And then, just... blissful nothing." Sybil sighed in contentment.

She was different today. She positively beamed with contentment, yet her pallor seemed changed. Not the healthy glow of a woman in love, but a paleness that contrasted with her bright mood.

"Wait," Aslyn suddenly realized what Sybil said. "It was so good you blacked out?"

"Uh-huh," Sybil hummed, sipping her tea with a little smirk.

"With just his mouth?" Aslyn asked in disbelief.

"And his magical tongue and fingers, but yes." There was no flush in Sybil's cheeks as she spoke, no timidness as there had been the day before.

Magical... Aslyn shuddered, connecting that word to what she witnessed last night. It couldn't have been true magic, could it?

A servant rushed forward to stoke the brazier of coals when she shuddered, assuming the cold around them caused it.

While Aslyn's own experiences had certainly been glorious, especially with Aethan, she couldn't recall a single time she had ever been so overwhelmed by pleasure that she blacked out from it.

"And then you woke in your own bed?" Aslyn asked, her face scrunching up as she attempted to understand the experience.

Sybil nodded. "I assume he brought me back when it was clear I was out for the evening." She peered up at the statue, shifting her legs together.

"So you still haven't actually had sex," Aslyn countered.

"Seven gods, Aslyn," Sybil laughed. "I just told you about a blackout-inducing orgasm and you are still worried about consummation?" She shook her head, then drew in a deep breath and let it out slowly. "I can't even imagine what that would be like. World-shattering, most likely. I intend to find out."

Last night, Aslyn had felt bad that she had manipulated Sybil into even attempting anything with Valen. Now, she was almost sick of hearing about how glorious it had been already. *At least I don't need to carry that guilt around*, she thought, taking a drink of her tea.

And as long as Sybil wanted to return to his bed, Aslyn would have the distraction she needed to continue investigating restricted places in the palace.

Sybil melted against her lounge chair, still gazing up at the statue. "And Fiara help me, the things he said, the way he said it..."

Aslyn was certain now that Sybil looked at that statue and saw Valen, not Narcisse. At least this had sparked some life back into Sybil. When Aslyn arrived, Sybil had been a husk of the woman she had been in Stormvalor. Now, the situation clearly agreed with her.

But Aslyn was done listening to Sybil go on and on about how amazing Valen had been. It turned her stomach to think of him in such a way.

"Hmm, I understand that," Aslyn purred, flipping the conversation. "Aethan's mouth had been glorious, but he shattered me over and over again with his—"

"Ugh, enough of that," Sybil groaned, her face twisting in disgust. "That's my brother. I don't want to think about him in that way."

Aslyn laughed. "So you can dish it but can't take it."

"If I said such things about *your* brother—"

"If he laid a finger on you, I would end him," Valen said, stepping around the chairs from the palace behind them.

Sybil's eyes immediately snapped to him, watching every move he made as he approached and perched himself beside her on the edge of her lounge chair. Aslyn startled, wondering how long he had been listening to their conversation.

"You are mine, remember?" he asked, his voice lowering.

Sybil bit her lip and nodded, heat flushing her skin.

Aslyn looked away as he leaned toward Sybil and whispered something in her ear. But Aslyn's gaze fell on the statue and once more that likeness struck her. With him in their presence, it was even more obvious. She glanced at the newlyweds from the corner of her eyes as Valen slid a hand between Sybil's legs. Discomfort immediately settled in Aslyn's stomach.

"I know when my presence is unnecessary," Aslyn said, setting down her cup and rising. She couldn't escape fast enough.

When she reached the double doors, Valen called to her and she froze. "Aslyn, stay out of the south tower."

He knew. How did he know?

Aslyn dared a glance over her shoulder, fingers wrapped around the doorframe so tight it hurt her nails. Valen leaned close to Sybil, but his predatory gaze burrowed into Aslyn with more than just caution in the dark depths. It was clearly a threat. Sybil moaned, melting against the lounge, already lost in bliss as his fingers moved beneath her skirt.

Heat flared across Aslyn's face and down her chest, and she murmured in agreement before rushing inside.

The utter indecency of that display in front of her... Aslyn wouldn't get that image out of her mind for a long time.

Nor the dangerous look in his eyes.

He had Sybil under some spell. How else could he get such a reserved woman to completely abandon all sense of propriety?

Seven gods, I hope I never see that again. It made Aslyn embarrassed for Sybil. What would Aethan think if he knew how easily his sister gave in to the emperor out in the open?

I might as well take advantage of this distraction, she decided as she rushed up a flight of stairs and around a corner, eager to put space between her and the newlyweds. She would stay out of the south tower. But she wouldn't stop probing the other restricted spaces for information.

CHAPTER 17

Without A Trace

Aethan woke before dawn, unable to sleep any longer knowing that Roric's attempted escape had happened overnight. He hadn't heard alarms in the night. That had to be good sign, but not knowing what happened drove him out of bed early.

By the time daylight lightened the sky, he was dressed in the finest clothes he had. Today could very well be the day Dorin executed him. He would walk into his trial proudly and not give an ounce of ground to the prince. He was a Starkling and nephew to the king of Vorovesti and he would act like it.

Commotion in the hallway stopped Aethan's pacing as someone commanded the door be opened. Aethan straightened his spine, squared his shoulders, and lifted his chin, folding his hands in front of him so they didn't suspect him of hidden blades.

The door opened and Shino stormed in first, hand on his sword and his face a cloud of anger. An act. Relief flooded through Aethan. Roric made it out. He must have or the act would be unnecessary. Unless the others were caught...

Shino's gaze swept the room as if searching for something. "Clear," he called into the hallway. A handful of guards entered, spreading out to search the suite.

Dorin strode in, arrogance all over his face. He marched right up to Aethan, not bothering to worry about whether Aethan had a weapon. Foolish man. Not that Aethan did. He wouldn't kill Aslyn's brother. She likely would never forgive him if he did.

"Your spy escaped without a trace last night, killing both guards on duty," Dorin seethed. He stopped closer than Aethan was comfortable, nearly toe to toe with him.

"A pity, I'm sure."

"How did you do it?"

"Do what?" Aethan asked cooly. He remained statue still, staring down at Dorin.

"How did you orchestrate his escape? Your friends did it, didn't they? The Dysart twins have committed treason against the crown."

Shino snorted, peeking behind curtains as two guards entered the bedchamber to search. "I told you those two were saturated with alcohol, and a dozen of your men vouched that they were with them all night drinking and losing a small fortune at cards. It wasn't them."

Dorin stepped back, rounding on Shino. "Well someone is responsible!"

The captain glowered at the prince, and Dorin withdrew, averting his gaze to the floor for a moment before his attention fell once more on Aethan. "What about the others who came from Stormvalor with you? Maybe it was them."

"I warned you about keeping him in the dungeon," Aethan said calmly. "Roric is just a boy."

Dorin bared his teeth. "So be it." He spun on his heel, fuming as he marched toward the door. "Captain, prepare the guards and notify the court. I will pass my judgment on Lord Starkling tomorrow morning and they are all to attend by order of the crown."

"Your Majesty," Shino said, dipping his head in acceptance of his orders.

Aethan released a low, rumbling chuckle. "You've actually convinced yourself that the throne is yours. It isn't. Nor is the crown. They belong to your sister before you. The people will never accept you as long as she lives."

Dorin froze, his spine stiffening. For a moment, Aethan thought he wouldn't take the bait, that he would carry on out of the room. But Dorin turned slowly. Something sinister blazed in his brown eyes. *Does Aslyn know her brother at all?*

"They will bow to me," Dorin said. But the way he said it gave Aethan a chill. The people's love would be forced if not given freely. "Especially since the emperor has already passed the crown to me." His gaze flicked to Shino and his jaw twitched. "I gave you an order. Why are you still here?"

"Because you are, Your Majesty," Shino said as if it should be obvious Shino stayed to protect his prince.

Dorin considered the words, then nodded. Aethan nearly released a breath of relief. Dorin didn't suspect Shino.

"I appreciate your concern, but there are other guards here," Dorin replied. "Please go see to the orders."

Shino scowled, then turned a deadly glare at Aethan.

He's good at this. Too good. Which part was an act? Who did he truly support? Perhaps Aethan had in fact walked right into a trap.

Shino grumbled his agreement before leaving the room.

Dorin watched him leave, waited a few moments, then smirked at Aethan. "Do you truly believe I would go to all this trouble without ensuring my place in the line of succession?" He chuckled and shook his head. "I struck a deal with Umbogo months ago. One that benefits us both. Tomorrow, the people will see me crowned and see the man who killed their king and queen dead. And my sister? I love her, but she's soft. She lacks the courage to take what she wants. All those years sleeping with her guard in secret made that clear enough."

Aethan flinched, remembering the hate in Elisio's eyes the day they fought in Stormvalor, right before Elisio killed himself.

"She will remain in Lemheller Gap, marry the Bloodstone heir, and never return here," Dorin said plainly.

"You can't possibly claim to love your sister while forcing her into a marriage to that brute," Aethan scoffed.

Dorin picked imaginary lint from his pristine jacket and shrugged. "From what I hear, she liked him until *you* got in the way. They can find that spark again."

Aethan considered strangling the life out of Dorin right then and there, but the guards searching his room for Roric would stop him before he had the pleasure of seeing the light leave those brown eyes. Once more, he imagined Aslyn's anger and disappointment if he hurt her brother.

Shino's assessment of Dorin proved accurate. He was arrogant and entitled with a chip on his shoulder and something to prove. But one day, when the dust settled, Dorin would find himself surrounded by only predators.

"Kill me if it makes you feel like a bigger man, but know this." Aethan stalked slowly toward Dorin, his hand clasped so tight behind his back now that his fingers ached. If he let go, he would wrap those hands around Dorin's neck and choke the life out of him for everything he had done. *I'm doing this for Aslyn,* he reminded himself. Then, Aethan pushed the impulse deep down. "You are wrong about Aslyn. And one day, she will march back here with an army at her back to yank you off *her* throne."

Dorin's pallor turned a little green, but he recovered quickly, bursting into a full belly laugh. "What army?"

Mine, Aethan thought. But he didn't dare say it aloud and give Dorin a hint at their plan to keep him alive—hopefully. Instead, he said nothing.

Dorin shook his head and pivoted, striding out the door. "You are delightful. Pity you must die."

The guards followed him out and the door slammed shut, locking from the outside. Then something slid over the door with a thump.

He was barred into the room.

At least Roric was safe.

Gannon sagged over the desk in his study, chin resting on his palm as he reviewed the records from the Vorovesti iron mines. The amount of paperwork a king delt with on a daily basis was beyond what any normal mortal could rightly handle in a day. It was no wonder his father had so many advisors assisting with each aspect of ruling. Because Gannon was Crown Prince, his father insisted he learn everything himself first.

"Advisors can assist you," his father had lectured him, "but you must know how to run this kingdom."

Unfortunately, that meant hours of endless study on finances, food stores, housing developments, diplomatic relations... the list seemed endless.

And today, it was annual iron and steel production.

Gannon reviewed the balance sheets. Hours laborers worked. Iron carts produced. Coal and limestone reserves. Steel yielded. Gannon would never admit it to his father, but he actually loved the math, tedious as the job may be. He frowned and blinked at the balance sheets. Something about numbers didn't add up.

Straightening, Gannon snagged a spare sheet of paper and began rechecking the math. Month after month, production had reduced. The amount was so small it could be easy to overlook if one wasn't watching closely enough, but Gannon saw it clearly. Production of steel had reduced, but the items required to produce it had not. He frowned. Where had their steel gone?

Vorovesti boasted the richest mines in all five kingdoms. It was a large piece of profit for the kingdom both financially and politically—that and Murandy Hills wine. If someone was bartering under the table, it undercut the crown. Who would risk treason?

Gannon gathered his ledger and the records and hurried from his study.

The corridors of the Vorovesti palace were the only home Gannon had ever known. Most of his life had been spent in these halls. Only a few times in his life had he ever traveled beyond Mordelic's outer wall, and even fewer beyond the borders of Vorovesti. He knew these halls by instinct. All the shortcuts, servant corridors behind the onyx walls veined in silver, how to avoid certain offices or suites. Gannon was fairly confident no one knew this palace as well as he did. More than once since his teenage years, Gannon snuck out through corridors and passages others seemed to forget existed just so he could enjoy a day in the city of Mordelic. Sometimes, being the heir to a kingdom was exhausting and he just needed a break.

He took the quickest route to his father's office on the second floor, eager to share what he had uncovered from the ledgers. But the shortcut brought him up short at the sight of two people down the rarely used hallway.

Gannon froze in his tracks.

Trystain and Lady Fia, one the emperor's closest advisors, stood far too close to one another as they spoke in hushed tones. Gannon couldn't hear the conversation, but the way she tilted her head as she gazed at Trystain and the way he responded with a coy smirk made it clear this was more than just friendly. Trystain's hands rested on her waist as hers slid up his arm. *What in the name of the seven gods?*

Not wanting them to see him watching, Gannon dipped into an alcove, hugging the ledger and his notes to his chest.

Lady Fia tucked hair back from his ear, then leaned close, her chest pressing into his. Trystain's hold on her tightened. She whispered something in his ear, then kissed his cheek and sauntered away, hips swaying. Trystain turned to watch her go as he adjusted his jacket.

Once she disappeared, Gannon strode toward his friend.

"Trystain, what was that?" Gannon asked.

Trystain startled, spinning to find Gannon standing behind him. He smoothed the alarm from his face and adopted his usual casual expression. "Does it matter?"

"Yes. Is she the reason you keep insisting you're fine without Sybil? Do you have any idea what you're doing? Her loyalties are to the emperor first." Gannon couldn't believe he had to explain this to his friend.

Trystain's face hardened. "Aren't we all?"

The words sent a chill down Gannon's spine. In a way, Trystain was correct. The empire demanded loyalty to the emperor first and foremost. But Trystain knew that wasn't strictly the case. And after Sybil was stolen away, Gannon would have expected Trystain to resent the emperor. There had to be an explanation.

"What are you hoping to accomplish?" Gannon asked, exasperated.

Trystain stuffed his hands into his pocket and cocked his head. "I think that's pretty obvious."

"Getting tangled up with a woman like her is dangerous," Gannon said.

"And I'm incapable of handling myself?" The words had struck Trystain as an insult. Gannon hadn't intended it that way.

"That's not what I meant."

Trystain rolled his eyes and snorted. "She's right. You and Aethan don't really respect me. I'm your token friend."

Gannon flinched. "What in the realm of Morumbris does that mean?"

"It means you two always push me around, talk down to me, imply that I don't know what I'm doing or the trouble I'm getting into." Trystain took a step closer, lifting his chin arrogantly. "I know exactly what I'm doing with her, and I can handle myself."

Gannon edged back half a step. Trystain's words stung him deeply. They were friends. "I care about you."

"You know what I think?" Trystain sneered at him. "I think you're jealous."

"Don't be ridiculous."

"Oh, it makes perfect sense. You want love and passion, but you're harnessed to your crown. You're bitter and jealous of what I could have because you can't." Trystain shook his head in disgust, then stepped around Gannon. "I'm done being your token friend," he shot over his shoulder.

Gannon pivoted, watching Trystain stroll away, dumbfounded by this shift in him. Maybe the breakup with Sybil truly had broken something in him. But how could Gannon help Trystain see sense when he harbored so much resentment?

The words stung him all the way to the king's office. Trystain and Lady Fia. What game was she playing with his friend? Gannon knew he would have to get to the bottom of it if he wanted to help Trystain out of whatever trap she was setting for him. He would have to recruit Iskra's help to see it done.

The office door was closed and two guards posted outside of it. That meant his father was in the office for certain. They bowed to him as he approached, neither stopping him as he reached for the handle and let himself in. Few would be allowed to simply walk in on the king when the door was closed. Gannon happened to be among the precious few.

King Orrin sat behind his desk, reviewing a message with furrowed brows. Across the desk, Ambassador Zambul turned toward Gannon. He said nothing as Gannon closed the door, but those black, hawk-like eyes were locked on the prince as he approached the desk.

His father sighed, pinching the bridge of his nose. Gannon waited patiently for his father to acknowledge him.

King Orrin finally lifted his gaze to Zambul. "So be it. I will have my response for you to send to the emperor before the end of the day."

"Of course, Your Grace." Zambul stood, bowing to the king. His gaze slid over Gannon again as he made his way to the exit.

The blackwood door clicked shut and Gannon raised his brows. "What did the emperor say?"

His father passed the message to Gannon without a word. Gannon skimmed it quickly.

"He agreed to the High Council against Marek Bloodstone," Gannon said as he read it again. "That's a good thing, isn't it?"

"Yes, but did you notice that they will not convene until Aethan can stand as a witness against the accused?" King Orrin shook his head. "He's stalling."

Gannon had noticed that and hadn't thought twice about it. That seemed logical to him. After all, it was Aethan who raised the charges initially. He *should* stand as a witness. But Gannon realized his father was also right. Aethan would be gone for months and the emperor must know that.

"What do you think he gets out of stalling for so long?" Gannon asked, sinking into the seat Zambul had vacated.

"Look at the signature, Gannon."

Gannon frowned and looked down at the paper again.

Emperor Valen.

The world rocked for a moment before steadying again. He murmured a curse that made his father scowl.

Valen had been in Stormvalor when everything happened. He had stoked the flames of animosity between Marek and Aethan, using the princess as leverage according to Aethan. Then he took Sybil and left. None of this could be a coincidence.

"You think he's up to something?" Gannon asked quietly, worried that Zambul might eavesdrop.

"Our spies report an influx of activity around the Citadel," his father said. "And Princess Aslyn has been moved from Bloodstone Manor to the imperial palace. For safety, they say, because someone attacked and killed her guards in the street. No one has found the killer yet."

"Do you think the attack was staged by the emperor to force the princess into the imperial palace?" Gannon asked, setting the message on the desk.

King Orrin leaned back in his leather seat. "I hadn't considered that, but I see no other way the killer could kill his Black Guard and vanish without a trace."

Gannon rubbed his neck as he considered the options. What would the emperor stand to gain from the princess in his palace? She was heir to her kingdom. He wouldn't keep her there. But perhaps he thinks he can poison her against Aethan if she is with him. It seemed like a lot of trouble just to keep her and Aethan apart. Unless...

Gannon raised a finger thoughtfully. "What if, at the High Council trial, the emperor plans to turn events on Aethan?"

"What makes Aethan so special that the emperor would choose to target him?" his father asked, but Gannon could tell his father was considering it.

"Maybe he just got in the way." Gannon shrugged. "Aethan seemed convinced the emperor wanted Marek to marry Aslyn. Now he has to get rid of Aethan to pave a path for his man to marry the future queen."

The terrible reality of those words settled over them like a smothering blanket.

"How does Sybil play into all of this?" his father wondered aloud, speaking to himself.

Still, Gannon answered. "Collateral. The Starklings won't turn against the emperor and risk harm to Sybil."

King Orrin drew in a deep breath and let it out slowly. "All the same," he said softly, and he sounded utterly exhausted. "War is coming."

Gannon's mouth went dry as he remembered the reason he had come to the office in the first place. "About that... Someone is smuggling our steel."

King Orrin's gaze snapped to him. Gannon presented his evidence, showing his father the numbers in the charts and his math.

"We need to find the trail," the king said. "I'll speak to General Lassiter and ask him to visit the mines himself to investigate for himself."

CHAPTER 18

The Trial of Aethan Starkling

Aethan took a deep breath as he stood before the towering doors to the throne room. The pair were an awe-inspiring masterpiece of craftsmanship. Constructed from ancient bonewood, their white surface shimmered in the brilliant lights from the archways across the hall. Intricately bound around the wood were thick vines that twisted and curled around the expansive frame of each door. Their tendrils formed an elegant lattice.

The vines shimmered with inlaid gold, each leaf a delicate filigree, each thorn sharp and gleaming. Interspersed among the twisting vines were golden roses, each petal shaped with breathtaking precision. Their surfaces caught the light and cast soft reflections onto the marble floor. The roses appeared almost lifelike, as though they might bloom further at any moment, while the thorns, though beautiful, gave the doors a sense of foreboding. That sense of foreboding matched Aethan's current inner turmoil.

At the very center, where the doors met, two large roses sat in perfect symmetry, their golden petals creating an ornate handle. No wonder Aslyn adored her home. Thinking of her opened that ache in his heart once more. *Please let me make it through this to her.*

The two guards escorting Aethan each held one of his arms, waiting for the doors to open.

Aethan tried his best to put on a confident façade, but inside he was a complete mess. If this went wrong, he was walking straight to his death. If it went right, he was still walking to his death. None of this comforted his aching gut or calmed his pounding heartbeat. One way or another, Dorin would see Aethan bleed today.

Manacles had been locked into place before he was allowed to step out of his room, binding his wrists together in front of him. A chain dangled from them, connected to the chained that connected to the manacles around his ankles. At least he had been permitted to wear his boots and clothes. If he walked to his death, he would do it with dignity and pride.

The doors groaned softly as they slowly swung inward, pulled open by guards inside the throne room. Hundreds of sets of eyes turned his way. The entire Arithian court had been summoned for this event. Dorin called it a trial, but Aethan knew better. He would have no chance to mount a reasonable or logical defense.

People whispered to one another as he was nudged forward, chains rattling as he shuffled along with his guards, head held high. He wore the chains like links of gold, ornamental and not restricting.

A long, wide aisle led Aethan toward the head of the throne room and the golden throne upon the dais. To the figure there.

Dorin. Seated in his father's throne, wearing his father's crown, taking the place that belonged to Aslyn. This guy had balls.

Aethan tried to ignore the whispers and insults, did his best not to make eye contact with anyone except Dorin. At the base of the dais, Shino stood in full formal armor, an emerald green cloak draped from his shoulders. His hand rested on the hilt of his sword as he watched Aethan. For a moment, Shino's gaze flicked to the crowd.

Aethan couldn't help but glance in that direction.

Cavis and Cormic stood beside an older man and woman who bore some resemblance to them. Their parents, Lord and Lady Dysart. Aethan averted his gaze swiftly. He wouldn't allow Dorin to catch him watching his friends. Von and Gorim wouldn't be present. They would be waiting at the boat to patch him up, out of sight and out of mind. Aethan hoped.

On the other side of the dais, at the front of the crowd, Ambassador Umbogo's black eyes gleamed with delight. If Aethan survived this plan of theirs and returned with Aslyn, he would take great delight in killing Umbogo.

At the base of the dais, the guards yanked Aethan to a halt and pushed him to his knees. He didn't fight back, even though it made his knees ache and his teeth crack together. Beneath him, a giant golden rose was inlaid into the tiles of the marble floor.

Javon Nadier climbed the first step of the dais at a motion from Dorin, turning to face Aethan. "Lord Aethan Starkling, nephew of King Orrin of Vorovesti, you have been accused of high treason against the kingdom of Novavito."

How nice, Aethan thought bitterly, *to drag my king and kingdom into this*. He was more certain than ever that Dorin had plans to attack Vorovesti.

"The crimes you have committed against the crown are as follows." Javon unfurled a scroll, cleared his throat, and read the list in a loud, clear voice. "Funding, aiding, and abetting a rebellion in Novavito with the aim of kidnapping the king in an attempt to manipulate the Crown Princess's hand in marriage. Hiring the shadow assassin, Blackblade, to murder Ned Corinth, Queen Giata, and her royal guards, the latter of which were promised safety within the walls of Stormvalor where the Starkling family rules. Manipulating the Crown Princess into marriage with the intention of stealing her crown and her throne. Orchestrating the escape of a prisoner and known Starkling spy. Ordering the death of King Novin upon imprisonment here in Arithia."

Death? The king is dead? Fuck. There was no way he was surviving this. Aethan swallowed down the lump in his throat. Aslyn would be heartbroken. He had failed to keep his promise.

"Do you have a statement you would like to make?" Javon asked.

Aethan's gaze remained locked on Dorin, who stared right back, his face utterly neutral. "I assume you have evidence of these alleged crimes?" Let them be forced to show their hand.

"Do you deny the charges?" Javon asked.

"I am guilty of nothing more than falling hopelessly in love with Princess Aslyn during the Stormvalor Tournament," Aethan replied, not flinching his gaze from Dorin. As he spoke of his love for Aslyn, Aethan allowed true, raw emotion to burn in his words, praying the people of the court would hear the truth of his words. He would do anything for her. Everything for her. "If we could get word to her about this, she could straighten it all out."

Dorin straightened on the throne, glancing at the nobles before sniffing derisively. "I think it's best if my sister be kept out of this, for her own protection from your manipulations."

Of course. Because Aslyn would toss her brother off that throne, rip that crown off his head, and order Aethan's release. Dorin couldn't have that. Aethan lifted his chin and glared at Dorin, even if his heart broke as the truth of his situation pressed down like a great weight. If this didn't work, he would never see her face or feel her touch or hear her voice again.

Jasmine and roses drifted through the open windows, like tendrils of Aslyn reaching out to him. Aethan swallowed down the misery threatening to spill forward.

"Just yesterday your squire and spy escaped from my dungeons, no doubt with your aid," Dorin added.

Aethan knew how this would end no matter what he said. Better to get it over with as quickly as possible. "I'm sure it's a significant cost for you to lose an *innocent* fourteen-year-old child. A child you had your men throw into the dungeons and then left there. He plays no part in any of this."

Dorin smirked and leaned forward. "So there is a part to play, despite you claiming to be guilty of nothing more than love. Considering the charges, I think we would all find that hard to believe."

"Your guards locked me in a room the evening I arrived and kept me strictly confined for weeks," Aethan said. "No one so much as spoke a word to me the entire time. Not when they laundered the sheets or brought my meals. Not even the guards said more than a word of warning. I fail to see how I could have helped Roric escape the dungeon when no one spoke to me and we were kept apart from day one."

"Then you deny all charges?" Dorin asked.

Nothing he said would help him now. But perhaps he could create a crack in the court for doubt to slip in.

"Congratulations are in order, *Your Majesty*," Aethan said, the title dripping with derision. The chains rattled as he shifted. Cold from the tiles seeped through his pants into his knees and shins. "It looks like your deal with Ambassador Umbogo and the emperor has paid off. You wear your father's crown, just like you wanted. I'm sure your sister would be so proud of you."

Dorin's jaw twitched. He stared at Aethan for several silent seconds. No one else in the court made a sound. Then Dorin broke into laughter.

"You continue, even now, bound and on your knees," Dorin said through his false amusement. "Are you accusing me of something?"

"What happens when Aslyn returns to find you on her throne?" Aethan asked, baiting Dorin into a trap. How would he explain crowning himself while she still lived without inciting the anger of the court? *I hope she tears you apart.* That rogue thought made his love for Aslyn swell.

Dorin raised a brow at him. "You can't sway my court away from me, Starkling."

Aethan answered him with silence. He would say nothing more until Dorin answered his question.

"They already know the emperor has given me this right, by imperial decree, to maintain the stability of Novavito while he protects my sister from you," Dorin replied. "She will return to her place when the emperor determines it safe for her."

Shit. Dorin answered the question far more smoothly than Aethan had expected and even twisted it to make it sound like Aethan was the reason their princess was kept away. Who knew what tragedy could befall her if this turned into war? *I can't let it happen. I can't let her kingdom fall to war and ruin because of me.*

"You wanted evidence, Starkling, and so you shall have it," Dorin announced. "Bring in the first witness."

A side door to the throne room opened and a rather harried-looking man in a suit entered, adjusting his spectacles. He carried a tome under his arm with a ribbon dangling from a marked page.

"State your name and title," Javon commanded as the man stopped ten feet from Aethan.

"Me-Megret Acos, Managing Director of the Bank of Arithia," Megret said, a tremor in his voice.

"Present your evidence," Javon said, motioning toward the tome tucked under Megret's arm.

Aethan's stomach writhed madly as Megret opened the tome and began. "Upon close examination of bank records, a rather large sum of funds was transferred to the Bank of Arithia under the name Flint Trith. Funds from this account have been divided into several accounts in the Bank of Arithia. One of which includes traces back to the assassin, Blackblade. Another has been discovered to be a slush fund for a Novavito rebellion."

"And where did these funds transfer from, Master Acos?" Javon asked.

Seven gods, they had covered their tracks so expertly Aethan wondered if the bank director even knew he read fabricated evidence.

Acos adjusted his glasses again. "The Bank of Mordelic, in Vorovesti. The account there is owned by a third-party organization owned by the Starkling family."

Murmurs rippled through the crowd.

"It-it's all here in the ledger," Acos said as if he needed to calm the crowd, hoisting the tome a few inches to indicate the ledger.

"Would you say that this account links the accused to the rebellion and to the assassin?" Javon asked.

Dorin sank back on the throne, a hand over his mouth as if in shock, but Aethan suspected he simply hid his smile.

"Yes."

"Thank you Master Acos," Javon said. "You are dismissed."

The words were nearly swallowed by the commotion from the gathered nobles. Even if Aethan survived and returned with Aslyn, he would need to prove those documents were false to gain back the respect of the nobles gathered here. If there even was a way.

Aethan knew his fate was sealed before he stepped foot in the throne room, but some small part of him had held onto the hope that he could sway the court. A foolish hope.

"When your ships arrived in Arithia, seven others disembarked alongside you," Javon continued. "Two who are loyal to the crown and claim only to have hitched a ride home on your ships. Upon your imprisonment, you stated that these two men would speak as character witnesses for you."

A lump rose in Aethan's throat. He regretted saying those words now. Dragging Cavis and Cormic into this didn't rank high on Aethan's list of things to accomplish under the circumstances.

"Cavis and Cormic Dysart, please step forward," Javon called.

Aethan bowed his head as the court murmured and shifted. His heart sank to the floor. *Please have the sense to protect yourselves*, he thought desperately. When he lifted his gaze from the golden tiles, the brothers stood together at the front of the crowd of nobles, their heads held high.

"Do you have anything you would like to say on behalf of the accused?" Javon asked.

Dorin studied the brothers from his perch on the throne. Aethan wanted to punch Dorin in his smug face. Instead, he turned his attention fully on the brothers, begging them with his eyes to say nothing to incriminate themselves. Aslyn would need them when the time came to depose her brother.

Cavis's dark eyes burrowed into Aethan's, sorrow in the lines of his face. Aethan gave a subtle shake of his head and Cavis's lips thinned momentarily. He understood and didn't like it. But nothing he said could redeem Aethan. Dorin would kill Aethan no matter what they said. He just hoped his friends didn't go down with him.

Cavis cleared his throat before speaking. "No, nothing."

Cormic's eyes bulged, turning on his brother. Aethan held his breath, waiting for a typical Cormic outburst. But Cormic clenched his jaw so tight Aethan could see the muscles in his neck straining.

"Nothing," Cormic grunted.

A hush fell over the gathered court. Dorin leaned forward slightly, watching the brothers and Aethan closely. Aethan gave him no reaction to cling to.

"Interesting," Dorin noted. "The two of you spent months with the accused, and you have nothing to say on his behalf?"

Cavis turned his dark eyes on the prince. "He fought well in Stormvalor. He showed seemingly genuine interest in Princess Aslyn and had regular contention with Marek Bloodstone and others from Umbr. His sister, Lady Sybil, is now betrothed to our future emperor. If he has truly duped the princess as you claim, it's fair to assume any comradery we shared was also part of his act."

"And your own bride, a lady of the Vorovesti court, has no connection with any of this?" Dorin asked.

Cavis paled, fists clenching at his sides. Aethan gritted his teeth. How dare Dorin drag Iskra into this? No doubt Cavis had hoped to keep her out of it as well. Just how much did Dorin know about Iskra already? Aethan hoped Cavis knew how to balance on this blade's edge.

It took Cavis a moment to rein in his anger, and Aethan was fairly certain the prince noticed, but he said nothing.

"She and Aethan were an item before the tournament," Cavis admitted. "However, when he heard that Princess Aslyn was attending the tournament searching for a husband, he spurned Iskra. It hurt her deeply to have him toss her aside for the princess."

Tossed her aside? Iskra was the one who tossed *him* aside! Cavis spoke the truth, or as near to it as Iskra likely told him. Even if Cavis exaggerated the details to protect Iskra now, as he should, Aethan couldn't help but wonder just how close to the truth that testimony hit.

"And how do we know she did not choose you to be another disruption in the Arithian court?" Dorin asked.

Cormic glared at Dorin, speaking in a low, dangerous tone before his brother had a chance to form a response. "Iskra Pridell is a victim, not a spy. Her parents hold little love for the Starklings."

Aethan winced, but Cormic barreled on. "I saw her with my brother. She's a bright woman who very clearly adores my brother completely. Implying anything else is an insult to my brother and my family."

As much as Aethan appreciated Cormic's rescue of his brother, that certainly wouldn't help him. Not that Aethan had any hope of redemption.

Dorin drummed his fingers on the arm of the throne, studying the brothers and Aethan as if attempting to sift the truth from the lies. Sadly, everything they said was the truth. Finally, he flicked his fingers and Javon dismissed the two of them, thanking them for their candid statements.

"Bring forth the prisoner," Dorin commanded.

Prisoner? Aethan held his breath as the doors opened again, and guards dragged a bulky, limp body along the aisle to the head of the throne room. They deposited their prisoner in front of Aethan.

The breath caught in Aethan's chest as he recognized Gorim. He sported a swollen left eye and fat lip that still trickled blood. The usual dark braid of his hair had been hacked off, leaving his hair sticking out at odd angles from one side where he hadn't shaved it bald. As he attempted to push himself off the floor, clearly weak from whatever beating the guards had given him, his one good eye swept over Aethan. The moon and stars tattoo on his face was a mess. Blood seemed to halo the moon and connect the stars together in a web of crimson.

"What is the meaning of this?" Aethan demanded, lifting his gaze to Dorin.

If they caught Gorim, what happened to Von? *Seven gods help me if Von was caught*, Aethan thought. Any hope of surviving vanished with Von's capture. Not that he wanted either of his friends in the hands of this mad prince and his court.

"Your friend here was caught sneaking around the palace walls in what I can only assume was a botched rescue attempt," Dorin said calmly. "Another man was with him, but your friend here stopped and put up a hell of a fight so that the other could escape. He killed four of my guards before his capture."

Gorim, why did you do that? But Aethan knew. Gorim put himself between the guards and Aethan's only hope of survival. Von.

"After spending some time with my guards, it seems he has a confession to make," Dorin said. "He would like to share a few words about you, Aethan Starkling."

Aethan's gaze locked on Gorim, and for a moment he saw sorrow in Gorim's dark eye.

The guards pulled Gorim to his knees. That sorrow in his eye transformed into something else Aethan could not identify. Desperation to save his friend clawed at Aethan's heart, his mind. Heat spread through his veins as his anger intensified.

"Speak," Dorin commanded.

Gorim's neck flexed. His eye shifted to the open archways and waterfall and mountains beyond the throne room. To the storm clouds brewing overhead, darkening the daytime sky.

"Beware to those who walk in the realm of envy," Gorim said. His voice cracked but gained power as he lifted it high and deep across the throne room. "You who have been deceived shall kneel or die when He rises."

Aethan frowned. What was Gorim going on about? He glanced at Dorin, whose face turned into a cloud of fury. Clearly he had expected Gorim to say something very different. Aethan's own panic climbed as he grew more certain his friend's death loomed near.

"All usurpers will be swallowed in the tide," Gorim said with fanatical reverence, gaze locked on the storm outside.

"What are you doing?" Aethan hissed at his friend, hoping no one else heard him.

Thunder rumbled. Aethan's panic increased. Nobles near the archways to the mountains pressed further into the throne room, forcing the entire crowd to shift away from the openings.

Gorim met Aethan's gaze reverently. "I have known no other man with as much strength on the battlefield as intelligence off. Aethan Starkling is a man of supreme honor and mercy. I would rather die in his defense than live in silence."

"Stop," Aethan hissed.

Another peal of thunder rumbled through the mountains, making the throne room tremble. Members of the court momentarily cried out in alarm.

Dorin growled low and dangerous. "Kill the prisoner!"

"No!" Aethan tried to throw himself at Gorim in a feeble attempt at defending his friend, but his own guards yanked him back so hard the manacles around his wrists cut into his flesh.

"He comes with the fury of the gods and calls forth the storm to strike down the blackened hearts of men," Gorim said above the commotion of the throne room. A guard bared his blade, preparing to carry out Dorin's command. Gorim raised his chin proudly, blood slipping from his wounds down his face.

Another boom of thunder.

"A storm is coming," Gorim proclaimed.

The guard plunged his sword through Gorim's chest, buckling the large man over the blade. Aethan cried out, trying to reach for his friend as tears sprang to his eyes. The sword was yanked free without mercy, spraying blood on the pristine floor. The guards holding Gorim released his body and he slumped over on the ground, his one good eye meeting Aethan's blurry vision.

Gorim's lips moved and Aethan strained to hear over the thunder and lightning cracking beyond the palace walls.

"Justis take me now into the heart of the storm," Gorim murmured, each word breaking as he fought for breath. "So I may aid His coming."

"Gorim..." Aethan's voice cracked.

The light left Gorim's good eye, peace on his face despite his horrific death.

The fury in Aethan's veins crackled and burned, consuming him with grief. He growled low and angry, his mood matching the storm brewing outside. As he lifted his gaze to Dorin, it gave him no pleasure to see the worry on Dorin's face.

And near his side on the dais, Ambassador Umbogo studied the storm with awe. Aethan bared his teeth as the ambassador turned those black eyes on him—and they widened in shock. He whispered something to Dorin and the prince paled, nodding.

"Aethan Starkling, you are sentenced to death for treason against the Novavito crown," Dorin announced, his proclamation nearly swallowed by another rumble of thunder. "Your actions have reached into my soul, creating a gut-wrenching grief. And so, your punishment will fit your crime. A sword through the gut, so you can feel the pain you have caused me and my kingdom as you die."

"Your time on that throne is limited, Dorin," Aethan announced, loud and clear enough to be heard over the commotion of the nobles as they pushed away from the thunder and the brewing storm outside the open arches. "Your actions will be met with vengeance." He glared pointedly at Dorin as the prince leaned back in his seat as if trying to put distance between them. "My friend is right. A storm is coming."

Dorin cleared his throat and raised his voice. "Kill him, Captain Shino."

Shino bowed to Dorin, then drew his sword. Lightning cracked outside, reflecting off the polished blade. No one else seemed to notice the blade he wielded was not his own. They were too busy fleeing the storm's reach. Aethan prayed his suspicions about the sword were correct. Stormshard wanted him for something.

Aethan raised his chin high. "I die as I lived. With strength, honor, and valor."

"Arrogant to the end," Dorin said.

Aethan straightened, abs tensing by instinct to prepare for the blow. Sweat beaded on along his hairline. Regardless of the plan, he still feared his death. The guards placed a hand on either shoulder to hold him in place. His breaths came sharp and quick as he waited, shoulders back. He would not beg. He would not cry. He would not show weakness.

I love you, Aslyn.

First came the biting cold of the blade, like ice sliding through his gut, followed by fire. Every nerve lit with that fire, as if he burned from the inside out. Aethan grunted, bucking against the hands holding him instinctively. He lifted shaking manacled hands to his gut, watching the blood pour between his fingers. It pooled beneath him. His vision narrowed.

Voices around him quieted as his heartbeat thumped loudly in his ears.

Dorin's voice broke through the muffled din. "Get them out of my throne room!"

Hands grabbed Aethan and he floated, head hanging back as he fought to remain conscious. His eyes drifted shut. Cold overtook his body.

I love you...

A shock of heat pulsed through Aethan's body. He couldn't open his eyes. He could barely draw breath.

"Come on, Aethan," a familiar voice grumbled. "Hang on."

He wanted to. For Roric. For his king. For Aslyn.

But all he felt was burning heat and death.

"He has to go now," another familiar male voice said. Shino. "We're out of time. If this doesn't work, there's nothing more we can do anyway."

"If I had more time..." Was that Von?

Movement. A splash. Something heavy weighed against his chest.

Then the world drifted away.

CHAPTER 19

Shadows and Claws

For a week, Bast moved from inn to inn every night or two as Lord Bloodstone's men searched for the mysterious wagon attacker. During that time, he probed at the dark gray trim of the ambassador robes he took off his attacker, testing the threads fastening it to the rest of the robes, cautious of any magical triggers. He also wanted to be sure that removing the trim wouldn't remove whatever magic allowed the wearer of the robes to harness magic inside the Citadel—or the imperial palace, should he need to enter that forsaken place to help Aslyn.

The only thing that reassured him she would be fine was the knowledge that the Bloodstones and the emperor had plans for her, and for that, they needed her alive. What that plan was didn't concern Bast. As long as she was alive, he wouldn't suffer the consequences. Aslyn was so damned stubborn with him that he preferred the distance over watching the way her eyes dilated and her face heated with rage whenever they spoke. And he certainly didn't miss the way she clenched her jaw and fists, chest rising in short, angry breaths.

No, he didn't miss her resentment and contempt at all.

Bast gripped the robe in both fists and ripped. The sound of it tearing satisfied his irritation, and he continued following the tear along the trim of the robes. After a week of testing, he determined that the magic was imbued directly into the dark gray trim and not the entire garment. That made his task so much easier.

Aslyn could suffer her own fate if she was too stubborn to want his help.

Rip.

He didn't care.

Rip.

He didn't need her.

Rip.

He didn't need anyone.

With the final tear along the trim, Bast's chest heaved with enraged breaths and he clenched his jaw so tight it ached. The gray trim pulsed against his palm as he examined the back of it, pushing all thoughts of that irritating woman from his mind.

It wasn't just cloth. He could see the threads like any other piece of clothing, but something lived between those threads, like a second weaving, but of the magical sort.

Experimentally, Bast wrapped the trim around his forearm, holding each end in his fist, then drew in a trickle of his shadow magic. He wrapped the shadows around his forearm and nearly gaped at the increased strength. Yet it wasn't the power of those shadows that alarmed him. Ambassadors had magical conduits inlaid into their clothing that allowed them to use forbidden magic without detection and despite runes warding against the use of magic. They automatically inverted into something untraceable. That was why he had never sensed the ambassadors using their magic around him. Their robes masked their magic. But why?

The most obvious conclusion was that it prevented ambassador magic from interfering with the Black Guard ability to sense the use of magic. An efficient system.

He eyed the wrapped obistone he pilfered from the torture dungeons, flexing his shadows around his arms.

Transition. That's what his attacker had called it. That's what had been done in those Citadel dungeons. Those magical prisoners were transitioned into Black Guards meant to serve their superiors without question, without emotion, without complaint. It explained why Black Guards could sense when Bast used his magic. They had it.

One thing he learned at a young age was that those with magic could sense it in others when it was active. But why didn't the Black Guards ever access their magic to use against people? Instead, it had somehow been reduced to a magical sensor instead of a weapon. Was the emperor afraid of what might happen if his magical guards turned on him?

Bast tightened his fist on the trim, flexing the wrap around his arm. His magic hummed and pulsed, eager for release. Experimentally, Bast spread his fingers toward the wooden chair in his cramped inn room. Shadows shot out like arrows, puncturing wood, splintering it. Then he snapped his fist closed and the chair shattered into wooden shrapnel.

A smile curled the corner of his mouth as he unwound the trim from his forearm with great care.

Then he set to work. Hours passed as he threaded the trim into his own armor with great care, careful to avoid harming whatever magic had been woven into it. He would take the emperor's own tool and use it against him.

And no one would sense him coming. Not even the emperor himself.

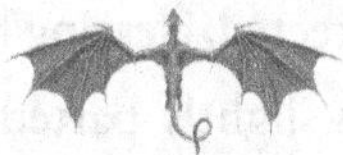

Gannon waited patiently for Iskra to process his concerns for Trystain, and what it might mean for their friend. He had invited her to meet with him in one of the palace parlors for a game of stones. The game now sat between them, untouched. The windows of the parlor were open wide, allowing the warm summer breeze to blow inside, making the silken curtains ruffle. There were a hundred other things Gannon should be doing, but he couldn't ignore the potential danger Trystain was in to continue due to his own inaction. His friend needed him, even if he denied it.

As the seconds ticked by, he rested his elbows on his knees and cupped his hands around his mouth anxiously, propping his head up on them. His sea-green eyes fixed on her, watching the gears grind behind her own eyes as she processed the information. The news bothered Iskra, as Gannon had hoped. He needed her help but didn't dare ask for it until he knew they were of the same mind.

Lady Fia's name was known in every estate and palace in the five kingdoms. Though few had crossed her path, and those who did never had good news to share. Her presence was like death or decay—the victim either succumbing to their own pride and arrogance until their downfall, or they simply vanished. That Trystain hadn't vanished could only mean he would suffer the former over the latter. Wherever she went, whomever she visited, she carried with her the will of the Imperial Throne. Lady Fia's infamy traced through countless stories over centuries, which made no sense to Gannon. No one was immortal. But since he spied her with Trystain, Gannon had returned to the royal library to dig up as many of those stories as he could find.

And all of them were consistent with description and devastation.

Finally, Iskra bit her lip, then broke her silence. "I think this goes back further than you realize."

Gannon blinked. "What do you mean?"

Iskra swallowed, hugging her arms over her chest. As she spoke, Gannon could tell she still sifted through the information to make more sense of it. "When Prince Valen—"

"*Emperor* Valen," Gannon corrected, clearing his throat.

Iskra froze for a moment, lips slightly parted, digesting this news. "Emperor Valen. When he made his appearance at the ball and stole Sybil's attention away from Trystain, Lady Fia was the one who escorted Trystain out of the ballroom. Cavis said he and Aethan searched for Trystain together only for him to show up in Aethan's room waiting for *him*. I don't know much beyond that, but... it's possible she used Trystain's weakness that night to sink her claws into him."

Gannon rubbed his chin, then sagged against the back of his cushioned chair. He muttered a curse that would have made his father furious. He recalled what Aethan had told him of the strangeness of Trystain's behavior. "Yes, Aethan mentioned that. He found it odd that Trystain just accepted that he had lost Sybil without even putting up a fight."

He rubbed as his temple, peering out the open window at the silverbark trees beyond. What had Aethan told him Trystain had said to him? "A vow of silence," he muttered. "That's what Aethan said she pulled out of Trystain that night. She told Trystain his future was safe, and Trystain told Aethan that Sybil's future was secure and everything else was in hand."

"In hand?" Iskra's face paled and she picked at her fingernails. "What could that possibly mean?"

"It means I'm right to worry about him," Gannon said. His jaw twitched as he considered how he would punish that woman for twisting his friend's mind. "You're right. She has her claws deep in him. Heart, body, and mind."

Agitated, Gannon surged to his feet and began pacing the thick rug. He ran his fingers through his hair, lacing them behind his neck and stretching his chin toward the ceiling.

"We have to do something for him," Iskra said as if reading his mind.

"Agreed," Gannon grunted. "The problem is, he wants nothing to do with me. Ever since he told me off in the hallway he has avoided me or ignored me."

Iskra sighed. "Then I suppose it's up to me. I will see if I can learn anything from him, and if we are lucky, I can find a way to get through to him that won't drive him further away."

Her hand fell on his arm, turning Gannon to face her. He hadn't even noticed her rising from her own chair. Iskra's green-rimmed hazel eyes softened, forcing him to meet her gaze. She eased his arm down. Iskra was a beautiful woman. He understood what drew Aethan to her, even if she didn't stir those feelings in him. Iskra was like a cousin or sister, and he couldn't imagine anything else ever happening between them. He cherished her as he had cherished Sybil.

"You have enough on your plate, Gannon," she said softly. "I will do everything I can to help Trystain with whatever time I have left in Mordelic."

He placed a hand over hers, grasping it affectionately. "Thank you, Iskra. If there's anything I can do to help, just ask. And please be careful. I don't want you to become a target of Lady Fia's ire."

Hopefully, he wasn't putting Iskra in any real danger. He would never forgive himself if anything happened to her. Nor would Aethan.

CHAPTER 20

Lost to the Tides

The storm clouds continued to hover over Arithia. Cavis stared out his window, leaning against the frame with his arms crossed, staring into the great beyond. Citizens bustled along the streets of Arithia as if nothing happened. Trees swayed in the ocean breeze in the distance. Cavis could just make out the waves of the water. The view from his family mansion was nowhere near as spectacular as the palace, but since the trial, Cavis hadn't the heart to step onto the palace grounds again. He would have to... eventually.

One day. That was how long Von had said his patch job would hold for before Aethan needed medical help. Long enough for the Vorovesti ships around the western edge of the continent, out of sight of the new *king's* spies, to find him. Aethan had lost a significant amount of blood by the time Von patched him up. A worrisome amount.

That night, Cavis hadn't been able to sleep, worried for his friend, guilty for speaking words that surely helped condemn Aethan to his fate. It didn't matter that it had been the plan. He still played a part in Aethan's execution. He should have stood up for his friend, as Gorim did. He should have planned Aethan's rescue instead of his execution. He should have stood up for what was right, even if it meant his own death.

The agony and rage in Aethan's eyes when Gorim was killed had made Cavis dare to hope that Aethan would somehow break free and strike Dorin down. But he hadn't. Because even in the end, that wasn't who Aethan was.

"I die as I lived, with strength, honor, and valor." Those final words haunted Cavis, and he swore that day he would dedicate his life to them as well.

Cavis reached into his pocket and ran his thumb along the edge of the letter Aethan had asked Captain Shino to give to him. It remained sealed. Cavis didn't want to read it. Not yet.

Two days passed with nothing. No signal. No Aethan. Then three days. Four. A week. Every day that passed significantly reduced Aethan's odds of survival. Cavis couldn't give up hope. He couldn't accept that his friend was gone.

Von had left as soon as he finished with Aethan. He was to meet up with the ships to help finish the healing once they found him. But Von couldn't heal a missing man.

"Staring out that window won't change anything," Cormic grumbled as he entered Cavis's room. "We need to accept that the plan failed and plot our next course of action."

Cavis glanced at his brother. Cormic didn't look much better than Cavis felt. Several days of growth darkened his chin and dark rings circled his eyes. "Not yet."

His breath caught as he turned his attention back to the window and saw the group riding into the small manor courtyard. His heart sank when he spotted a grim-looking Von. Cavis bolted for the exit as his brother peered out, then cursed and followed on his heels.

Startled servants darted out of the way as Cavis bounded down the stairs two at a time and across the foyer as the doors opened. He skidded to a halt as Von entered, accompanied by a few of Shino's selected guards. Sorrow creased the hard lines of Von's face as he spotted Cavis and Cormic. Then he gave a small, sad shake of his head.

The floor dropped out from beneath Cavis. Cormic's hand fell on his shoulder to steady him.

"What happened?" Cormic asked when Cavis couldn't find his voice.

"The ships spotted the boat," Von said, his voice thick with grief.

"He was dead by the time they got there, wasn't he?" Cormic asked.

Von swallowed and turned his gaze to the floor. "Hard to say. They hoisted the sails and did their best to reach the small boat but... the waves pulled him into the Isles of Storm."

"And they continued after him," Cavis said, his voice hard as if it were an order and not a desperate hope.

"There's no piercing the stormveil and surviving, Cavis," Von said. "He's lost to the tides."

Grief tightened Cavis' throat. His hands clenched into fists at his sides. No. He would not accept this. Every muscle in his body trembled with rage.

Cormic cursed, dropping his hand off his brother's shoulder.

Stiff and angry, Cavis turned and climbed the stairs as numbness spread through him. At first, Cavis wasn't sure what he was doing as he entered his room, moving automatically. He pulled a few changes of clothes from the closet, stuffing them in a bag, and strapped his sword belt around his waist.

"Cavis, what are you doing?" Cormic asked as he watched his brother's manic behavior.

Cavis opened a drawer, pushing items aside in search of his hidden coin pouch. "I'll find him myself."

"I swear to Morumbris, if you try, I'll knock you out," Cormic growled.

"Someone has to have the balls to do it," Cavis said, stuffing the coin pouch into his pack and buckling it.

"You're not a sailor or a strong swimmer," Cormic snapped.

Von joined them, shaking his head as well. "Listen to me, Cavis. No one has ever entered the Isles of Storm and returned to tell the tale. *No one*. I understand your driving need. Believe me, I do. But this is suicide, and it isn't what he would have wanted."

"How can you know?" Cavis snapped, once more running his thumb over the unopened letter from Aethan.

"Because I knew him, just like you."

"He's. not. dead," Cavis growled.

Von stepped forward, peering at the storm clouds beyond the window. "He is. The plan failed. The best we can do is monitor the stormveil to see if a miracle returns him to us. But Captain Barrow won't send his men to their deaths to search for a dead man."

Cavis trembled, not with rage, but grief. His legs gave out and he sank onto the edge of his bed. How could he ever look Iskra or Aslyn in the face?

Von took a knee in front of Cavis, resting an arm on his own knee. "We have something much bigger to prepare for. All the signs have indicated it is time for Him to rise."

"What are you on about?" Cormic asked, crossing his arms over his thick chest.

"The prophecy. The chosen shall pierce the stormveil. He who is born of the storm shall rise from the ruins of darkness. He comes with the fury of the gods and calls forth the storm to strike down the blackened hearts of men." Von signaled his heart, then pointed at the sky. "A storm is coming."

Cavis stilled.

Von often spewed some nonsense about prophecy, but now Cavis recalled something else Von had said to Gorim during their voyage to Arithia. Or the general gist of it, anyway. They believed Aethan was meant to fulfill their prophecy. Gorim hadn't been as devout in the assertion as Von had been. But the way Gorim had watched the storm in the throne room, the way he had died looking directly at Aethan as he made his declaration with those very same words Von now spoke couldn't be coincidence. Not when he directly references the chosen piercing the stormveil. Cavis's mouth went dry.

"Nonsense," Cormic grumbled.

"You think he'll come back from the dead," Cavis breathed. "That's why you won't go after him. Because you think he *must* pierce the stormveil to rise as your Stormborn savior."

Cormic scoffed. "That's not what he means."

Von didn't flinch as he lifted his chin, staring Cavis down. "It is," Von said.

"Fuck your prophetic poppycock," Cormic snapped. "The gods are gone. No fancy words or empty prophecy will change anything."

"My father is a master healer in Elysia, but my mother is a High Priestess of the Sun Temple," Von said quickly. "She and a handful of others guard dangerous secrets from even the emperor, because if he knew the truth he would burn all of Elysia to the ground just to destroy it. You know the myth of the Cavern of Lost Souls."

Cavis groaned.

"A fairy tale," Cormic said.

Von shook his head. "It is not a fairy tale or a myth. It's real. There is a reason that no one pierces the stormveil and survives. The Cavern of Lost Souls exists within, but only He who is worthy of the blessings of the Seven Gods can enter and survive. He will pierce the stormveil, enter the cavern and undergo the trials. It is a test of that which the gods wielded. One for each, penned to take place through a series of tunnels and caverns deep within the Cavern of Lost Souls—Determination. Patience. Strength. Balance. Wisdom. Pride. Mercy."

The brothers stared dumbly at Von as if he grew another head. Then a horrible truth settled over Cavis. Von *wanted* Aethan's boat to go beyond the stormveil. He likely watched it happen.

Anger burned in Cavis's chest and he stood, pushing Von back and hoisting his pack. "I agree, Cormic. Fuck the prophecies or myths. I'm going after him."

He marched toward the door, but Cormic jumped in the way, barring it with a thick arm. "Hang on, brother. That's not what I meant either. Whether or not their prophecy is bullshit doesn't mean you can survive the Isles of Storm. He's right about that place. No ships have ever returned. Not a single survivor. They go into that storm and vanish for good. I won't let you throw away your life. You said Aethan left you a note. What did he write?"

Cavis swallowed, staring down his brother before looking at the pocket where he kept the letter. "I haven't read it," he whispered.

"Now seems like a good time."

Now? His stomach sank.

Cavis pulled out the letter, running it between his fingers. Von and Cormic watched him, waiting. *I have to do this sometime.*

Gritting his teeth, Cavis broke the seal and opened the letter.

Cavis,

I will guess you didn't bother reading this until receiving bad news. I didn't make it. We both knew it was a long shot. Do what is necessary to protect Iskra, Aslyn, and her crown. Don't seek vengeance on your own. Aslyn will need loyal men and women in her court if she has any hope of reclaiming the crown. You, Cormic, and Captain Shino are her best chance.

Dorin is working with Ambassador Umbogo. He and Umbogo have worked out a deal that removed the king, queen, and Aslyn from any position of power so that the emperor can place Dorin on the throne. I'm not sure why, but the emperor is after Novavito. They tried to manipulate Aslyn. She told me of the plot herself. When it didn't work, they likely turned to her brother.

Help Weylen, Kern, and Roric rescue Aslyn. Dorin sold Aslyn into marriage to Marek. He told me as much, likely believing I would have no one else to tell. I don't think the wedding has happened yet, but it won't be long after my death. I'm certain of that. Knowing Aslyn, she is using me to cling to hope and as soon as Marek can rip that hope out from under her, it will be too late. I had hoped to do this myself, but it seems fortune isn't in my favor. And please, do what you can to keep Vorovesti from declaring war against Novavito. If you need help, reach out to my cousin Prince Gannon, or my uncle King Orrin. I've already sent a letter.

Whatever you said at the trial, please know I don't hold it against you. I consider you one of my dearest friends no matter what end I meet.

Your friend,

Aethan Starkling

Cavis read the letter again, allowing everything to sink in. Anger burned in his stomach.

Dorin was no king. He was a usurper who orchestrated the death of the king and queen, and sold his sister into marriage just so he could claim the crown. Cavis clenched his jaw, carefully folding the letter, then he placed it in an oiled pouch and tucked it into his bag.

Once the letter was secure, Cavis turned to Cormic and Von, one waiting patiently and the other a little less so.

"You're right," Cavis said. "We have one more mission, and it's a big one."

Chapter 21

Ancient Runes and Lost Prophecies

Aslyn trailed Valen through the halls of the palace, keeping a distance to avoid being spotted. For weeks she had searched high and low for answers to whatever the emperor was up to and had come up short. Locked doors barred her lackluster lock pick skills. Black Guards barred passage to certain areas of the palace. Even when Valen was distracted with Sybil, Aslyn came up empty.

Sometimes, Aslyn's palm itched. Other times it seemed to pulse with warning. She couldn't explain why. Did it have something to do with Blackblade? A few times, she stared at the small scar across her palm where Blackblade had cut her and given his oath. Where had he gone? Did he abandon her in this place? It shouldn't have bothered her as much as it did. But, while the scar made her wonder where he was, she had a task to complete and little time to carry it through.

Answers. She needed them, or at least clues as to what the emperor was up to and how her kingdom played a part in those plans.

Nothing in the imperial library offered further insight. Some tomes were so old she feared opening them would ruin the binding or pages. Most of the books and scrolls contained stories or history she had already learned back home. A few offered some fresh insight into the War of Two Crowns, but nothing too shocking. Certainly not as shocking as what she had discovered in that artifact room. If Valen had books or scrolls containing anything that would help her, they would be secured in his office.

Except she didn't know where his office was, so she followed him, hoping he would reveal his sacred space. Surely after nearly two weeks she should have found it. *Any day now, if the lost gods smile upon my quest*, she told herself.

As she peered around a corner, Valen opened a door blockaded by deep shadows and two Black Guards. Aslyn squinted to glimpse the interior of the room and her heart lifted as she noticed the answer to her desperate pleas.

His office! It had to be, judging by the wall of books.

Aslyn couldn't just stroll up and knock. The door was guarded and she suspected Valen would refuse her entry.

I will return later when he is occupied with Sybil again. That wouldn't be long. The two were always tethered by some invisible, insatiable need for each other that Aslyn didn't understand.

She bit her lip and ducked back around the corner, memorizing the path as she returned to her chambers.

All she had to do was wait.

Dinner was, as usual, a detached affair.

The grand dining hall loomed in cold, unyielding darkness. Towering walls of shadowed stone absorbed the light of the flickering chandeliers above. Massive columns lined the edges, their surfaces smooth and colorless, adding to the lifeless austerity of the enormous space. The only banners were the black and silver of the imperial seat. No paintings adorned the walls. The stark weight of stone and silence filled the space.

At the heart of the room stretched a long, obsidian table, polished to a mirror's sheen but void of warmth. It could seat forty-two in total—twenty on each side and one on each end—yet most of the chairs remained vacant. How long had it been since this table was full of occupants? Had it *ever* been?

At one end, the emperor sat with only two of his minions flanking him—Lady Fia on one side and a man in Ambassador robes at the other side. Aslyn could see their lips moving but heard no sound at all from their end of the table—not even the clink of silverware against plates. The urgency of their expressions and movements made Aslyn terribly curious.

At the opposite end, Sybil sat in regal solitude with Aslyn as her sole companion.

The table bore a grand feast at either end, a lavish display of roasted meats, golden-crusted bread, and jeweled goblets of deep crimson wine. Platters of fruit gleamed under the dim candlelight. Yet the abundance did little to soften the starkness of the setting, nor did it ease the weight of unspoken tension that lingered between the distant figures seated at opposite ends of the hall.

Aslyn would have given almost anything to hear their conversation instead of Sybil's. She knew Aethan's sister was just as intelligent as him, yet since she finally opened up in this place, Sybil's conversation had become as vapid and pointless as any other courtly lady Aslyn had dealt with. Had this place somehow twisted Sybil's mind?

Throughout the meal, Aslyn spied Valen eyeing Sybil like she was his next meal. Sybil preened under his hungry gaze, shifting in her seat, straightening as she fumbled over her words, losing track of her own sentences, or adjusting in a way that women often did to highlight their chest. Aslyn stuffed another morsel of meat into her mouth to distract herself and avoid rolling her eyes. It was jealousy to some degree, and she knew that. Aslyn missed Aethan.

It only took about five minutes for conversations to stall at either end of the table.

Valen stood and Aslyn tensed as he stalked to their end of the table. Did he know she had found the office? Not that she had gone in yet, but she knew how to find it again.

"Everyone out," Valen commanded as he neared their end of the long table.

Aslyn dared a glance at him and realized his dark gaze was ravenous, fixed on Sybil. She glanced at Sybil, noting the way Sybil sat back in her seat, heat spreading across her chest.

With a stab of disgust, Aslyn tossed her napkin on her plate, grabbed her goblet of wine, and rose, marching to the exit. She hadn't even left the room before dishes clattered to the ground and Sybil moaned like she was in heat. Aslyn would be lying to herself if she didn't admit she was a little jealous. Not of Sybil and Valen, but of the desire and need that drove two people into such a frenzy of passion.

Aslyn missed Aethan so much it made her heart break every time she thought about him. She wanted that passion with him. She wanted the freedom to do anything—*everything*—wherever and whenever they wanted. Mostly, she just wanted *him*. His companionship, dedication, jokes, smiles, scent... Aslyn didn't know when she would see him again. How long would she have to wait to feel his touch, his kiss, his breath on her skin, or the utter bliss of him moving inside of her again?

Lady Fia and the ambassador didn't even acknowledge Aslyn as they passed.

Turning from the dining hall, she quickly downed her glass of wine. Allowing her mind to wander down that path did no good. All she could do was hold on to the hope that it *would* happen again.

If Sybil detained Valen in the dining hall for a while, Aslyn planned to find a way into his office.

Aslyn set the goblet on a display table as she passed down the hall.

When she reached the office corridor, Aslyn paused, confused by the lack of guards at the door. Why were they no longer there? The shadows cast over the doorway were long and dark, making it nearly invisible if she didn't know where to look. Perhaps Valen thought those shadows were adequate protection. Fool.

Aslyn hurried toward the door, testing the shadows with the long sleeve of her gown to be sure they weren't dangerous. Nothing. Holding her breath, she reached for the handle.

The instant her hand touched the handle, Aslyn's heart began racing more wildly than ever before in her life. Stark terror seized her limbs, freezing her in place. The darkness pressed down on her like a crushing weight.

It whispered to her in her very bones a lethal warning. *"Turn back or die."*

Aslyn trembled violently, frozen in place by this gripping darkness. Could such darkness kill? Aslyn drew in a breath, as if preparing to plunge into icy waters. Then she turned the knob.

The bolt in the doorframe clicked and the door eased against open. Aslyn cast another glance up and down the hallway, still holding that breath as if it contained her life, and opened the door wider.

The shadows around her undulated violently as she stepped fully into the darkness around the doorway. They coiled around her, squeezing. Her steps halted in the doorway as if encased in ice. Aslyn squeezed her eyes shut, waiting for the darkness to crush her or snap her neck. But they settled again like a caress. Were they responding to Valen's current emotions?

With a shudder of disgust, feeling dirty standing in them, Aslyn peeked into the office.

Empty.

She slipped inside, closing the door. Then she shook off the sensation of something crawling over her skin as she considered the way that darkness had touched her.

Valen's office was as austere as the man himself—cold, imposing, and devoid of anything unnecessary. Hewn from the same dark stone as the rest of the palace, the walls lent the chamber an oppressive weight that not even the open window could fully dispel. Aslyn glimpsed the distant Lemheller Gap lit up by lamplight in the darkness when a faint breeze stirred the heavy curtains. From this window, the emperor could see the entire palace grounds, the Citadel, and the city, as well as every key point of entry toward the palace.

One entire wall was lined with towering bookshelves, floor to ceiling, filled with tomes bound in deep blacks, muted grays, and faded browns. No gilded lettering adorned their spines, no embellishments hinted at their contents—only an unbroken expanse of knowledge, locked away behind timeworn covers. The scent of aged parchment and ink clung to the air, mixing with the ever-present chill that seemed to permeate the stone.

In the corner behind the door, an ancient set of polished armor stood on a stand. Aslyn had seen its likeness before etched into statues of Emperor Narcisse scattered throughout the palace grounds. Here stood the actual armor of the first emperor. The plates were heavy and battle-worn but well-preserved. Dim lighting nearly obscured the faint patterns on the dark metal. It was more than a relic; it was a symbol of conquest, of the weight of an empire built on blood and steel.

Beside the armor, displayed on a beautifully carved wooden plate with golden hooks attached to the wall, rested a sword unlike any Aslyn had ever seen. Its craftsmanship was unmistakably elvish—sleek and elegant. The blade still gleamed with a silver sheen despite its age. This was the sword of the first emperor. The weapon that had carved out the foundation of the empire itself. It had not been made for men, yet it had been wielded by one. A blade meant for grace repurposed for war. How many legends had died upon that blade?

On either side of the sword, two more wooden display plates hung empty. Had the swords been stolen, or had the emperor given them to another? Then something else occurred to Aslyn. What if one of those was meant to hold Nova, the sword of the First King of Novavito, and the other the sword of kings in Vorovesti? The emperor probably kept those display plates up as a reminder that power given could also be taken. Her stomach twisted at the thought.

There were no personal touches anywhere in the office, save the armor and sword. Only history, power, and the weight of rule, as suffocating as the walls that surrounded it.

A massive desk of polished ebony dominated the center of the room. Aslyn made her way behind the desk, placing herself in clear view of the door with her back to the open window. She glanced out the window and noted the carvings in the stone that would allow her to shimmy down to a nearby balcony. Good. She didn't want to walk through that doorway again.

The chair behind the desk was tall, its high back an unspoken symbol of authority. It was a throne of paper and decree, where fates were sealed no longer with a swing of his blade, but with a stroke of ink.

Aslyn focused her search on the contents atop the desk first. A box of messages from ambassadors in all corners and courts of the empire intrigued Aslyn, but not nearly as much as the stack of books with pages clearly bookmarked by sheets of research notes.

Bingo!

One book lay open atop the desk. Aslyn's gaze slid over the pages, alarmed to discover it to be a study of ancient runes. Aslyn slid her finger over the parchment atop the book. Valen had scrawled a series of repeating runes at various angles. At the bottom of the parchment, his sharp handwriting scratched antiquated Vorovesti. Aslyn had studied the language, but since Vorovesti had evolved over the centuries, that outdated language was no longer spoken or written anywhere. Aslyn struggled with the old language. She needed time she didn't have.

Something about the runes tickled at Aslyn's memory. The placement of them, the shape they made together. As she traced a finger over the runes, the memory hit her. She had traced them before. She had learned their patterns—or some of them, at least—the same way she memorized the planes of Aethan's chest, his abs, his arms and back. These were the same runes in his dragon tattoo. Aslyn had touched them, kissed them.

A lump welled in her throat as tears pricked her eyes. She missed him so desperately sometimes, like a piece of her soul had been left behind with him in Stormvalor. Did he still hold her close to his heart as she did him?

Aslyn swallowed and blinked back her tears. She could allow herself to wallow in his absence later, but not now.

Aslyn searched the unlocked drawers of the massive desk until she found a fresh sheet of parchment. Then she copied the old language and runes quickly. Once she figured it out, she would need to burn it in her hearth so she wouldn't be caught with his notes.

What were those runes and why the emperor was so interested in them. How did he even know about them?

Her mind drifted back to when she had been in the artifact room. When she convinced herself that Aethan descended from the lost Martnarving heir. What if the emperor suspected something? How would the runes play a part? Did they somehow shield the truth of his bloodline from everyone? It would explain Valen's obvious obsession with discerning the runic meaning.

Aslyn kept a cautious eye on the door as she reached for the first book on a neat stack. The cover bore nothing more than a series of symbols in ancient Elpisian. When she opened the tome, Aslyn gaped.

Someone had translated an ancient text about the Circle of the Seven Gods, and the lost prophecies, leaving a trail of personal notes in the text. She flipped to the last page and noted the name of a member of the Temple of the Sun in Elysia. Nowan, a specialist in ancient prophecies.

Aslyn licked her lips and flipped back to the beginning.

The book opened with stories about the Circle of the Seven Gods. How each protected immense power to maintain balance in the world.

So much has been scrubbed from ancient records since The Scouring, not the least of which are the prophecies of the Saints of the Seven. But memory through whispers linger.

It is believed by the highest in our order that the Fables of the Seven Gods are only a partial truth. That something more is hidden beneath those fables. Something dangerous.

During the War of Two Crowns, another war raged in secret. The Whisper War, in which our first and glorious emperor and liberator challenged the Seven Gods themselves to obtain the tools necessary for victory—and for imperial supremacy.

At the time of The Whisper War, our first and most holy imperial lord was but a king without a throne, but his vision and will proved greater than any other mortal man. He saw the truth of the world—the destruction that magic and the will of the Seven Gods brought upon everything. To save the world from this destructive force, he hunted the Seven Gods in secret.

The first came to pass in the city of Lemhaldruun, a fortress of the black stone and sentinel of the river border. That name's gone now... but the stone remembers. It remembers the magic that erupted from this ancient, lost city. It holds that power still.

As the War of Two Crowns raged outside the walls of Lemhaldruun, Narcisse ventured into the belly of the Citadel, so far from the realm of mortals that no light could pierce the endless void. And in that endless dark, he challenged a god.

What followed was not a battle of swords alone, but of dominion, of death against unbreakable will. Morumbris moved like a shadow unmoored, a towering figure of cloaks and cold, while Narcisse's blade tore through the veil with every strike. As their battle raged, a maelstrom of darkness swirled over the Citadel, making all mortals tremble in terror.

As the final blow was struck, Morumbris screamed—not aloud, but in magic, in soul. The god's form ruptured, and with him, all of Lemhaldruun shattered. Buildings crumbled in silence. The stones of the city warped and melted. People disintegrated where they stood as their souls were reaped. The death-god's magic, unanchored and wild, surged through the ruins in a terrible flood, seeping into earth and bone.

Only the Citadel remained—untouched, unmoving, and sealed by powers known only to Narcisse as he emerged from the darkness imbued by remnants of that god-power.

From the ashen waste, the very stone of the mountains became infused with catastrophic magic.

Aslyn released a breath, her fingers trembling as she turned the page. Could he truly have killed Morumbris and taken his power? Did that power pass to the descendants? It would explain why the imperial seat always worked so hard to keep a tight leash on the bloodline.

But to kill a *god*! How could such a thing even be possible?

The next page told another tale of The Whisper War.

Fearing their deaths, the remaining gods bound their powers together to push back Narcisse's glorious advance and store what remained of their powers for only the most worthy to wield. If myths from the creation of the world and the gods within are to be believed, the Seven Gods protected something far more powerful than themselves. A dark force that seeks to devour creation itself—and only the united power of the Seven Gods keep its prison sealed deep within the roots of existence.

And thusly the legends of the Champion of Justis and the Saints of the Seven were born.

Aslyn couldn't help but wonder what force could worry gods. Yet as she continued turning pages, she found no answers. Just cryptic prophecies offering a glimmer of hope.

In the heart of this darkness, it was foretold that a single light would rise to restore hope to the world. His name shall echo where valor is shown, his heart burning with fury. And at that moment, the skies answer.

His name shall echo... Aslyn's eyes widened and she turned the page to find another prophecy proclaiming that ancient blood would rise. Another stating that he of pure strength, honor, and valor would claim what no man before could—a power unmatched; a gift from the gods.

He shall enter the impenetrable Cavern of Lost Souls, face his own soul in deadly trials set forth by the gods. Should he fail, all will die. Should he succeed, he shall be born again of the storm.

Aslyn knew bits and pieces of each of these prophecies, and she had heard some of the Elpisian competitors likening the signs ... to Aethan.

Aslyn closed the book and took a deep breath. It couldn't be.

But if the emperor was researching these prophecies, there must be some warrant in them. Some threat to the empire. Valen's fixation on Aethan couldn't be ignored, either. Aslyn hugged the book to her chest as she tried to steady her heartbeat. Instead, images raced through her mind.

Aethan in Stormvalor, competing as the crowds echoed his name off the walls.

His fight against Marek in the gauntlet... and the storm that broke over them as they fought. It ended when the fight ended.

Strength. Honor. Valor. The Starkling family motto. She knew there was something different about him from the moment she first met him in that hallway, disguised as a commoner. Her heartbeat increased just remembering that moment, and her thoughts shifted to their night in his bed, the night he proposed. Heat flushed er cheeks, and longing for him created a fresh wound in her soul.

Aslyn released a shaky breath, and her eyes fell on the title embossed into the leather cover of the second book in the stack.

Legacy of the Darkhold

Aslyn glanced at the door, listening for anyone approaching, then she set the first book down and picked up the second with trembling hands. When she opened the book, a paper slipped out. She picked it up and unfolded it to find a hand-drawn map of the five kingdoms of Divica. An angry "x" had been slashed over various locations on the map. The Vorovesti mines. Arithia. Murandy Hills. The temples of Elysia. Deadwood. The Arithian dam. Several others were circled. The caves of the Varyova Ice Cap. Stormvalor. The Isles of Storm. And around Mordelic, where the city had been crossed off, a circle had been drawn around the city again and again, breaking into the paper.

A hasty note in broken Vorovestian was scrawled beside Mordelic. *They would hide it right under my nose. Tear the city down to find it!*

How old was this note? Did Oxon write this, or did Valen? Was the emperor planning an attack on Mordelic?

Aslyn flipped through the pages of the book, tucking the map back inside. Most of it was written in a mixture of ancient language and modern, allowing her to understand only scattered pieces of the text.

The general sense she got from the text hinted that only He of pure darkness, light, and ancient blood could locate the final seal locking the Darkhold. And only He could unlock the darkness within to access infinite power. Was the imperial seat searching for this power? Did they believe *they* were the ancient blood?

A violent chill raced down Aslyn's spine as she realized that could, in fact, be true. The emperors were all that remained of the ancient lines dating far back before the War of Two Crowns. Narcisse had killed any who might bear that lineage when he won the war. Have the emperors been searching for the entrance to the Darkhold ever since?

And what would happen if someone like Valen unlocked such infinite power? She had heard of most of the prophecies in the first book, but never the Darkhold or the warning she sensed in her bones but could not understand as she read it on the page. Votha'kel Nyrrhadax. Was it a name? An ancient phrase?

One thing was certain. If the imperial seat gained infinite power, there would be only the kingdom of Divica. And any who dared oppose them would likely be exterminated, just as Narcisse had done at the end of the War of Two Crowns.

Aslyn added the words Votha'kel Nyrrhadax to her sheet, then folded it and tucked it safely into her dress before carefully setting the books back.

Then her attention turned to the box of messages. She needed to get out of the office before anyone caught her, and surely time must be running short, but she couldn't help from flipping the lid of the box open to peer inside at the messages.

The top message was from the Elysian ambassador, and mostly spoke of continuing to monitor the research of the clerics and scribes in the temples. But at the bottom of the note, a warning:

The whispers have become a din and continue to grow. The Elysians believe the prophecies are being fulfilled even as I write this warning. They say He comes with the fury of the gods and calls forth the storm to strike down the blackened hearts of men, and a storm is coming.

Aslyn recalled Von speaking of something similar back in Stormvalor. Could it really be true?

Could it really be Aethan?

She flipped to the next message, unable to recognize the name, then flipped to the next, searching for something from Umbogo. If she could find his messages to the emperor, perhaps she could decipher what he was up to in Arithia.

Just as she spotted his familiar name, she heard footsteps approaching. Valen might have plans for her future, but she was certain that, if he caught her in here, he would kill her without hesitation. Still, she had come for exactly this purpose. Aslyn quickly skimmed as much as she dared, but the steps stopped outside the door. No time. She quickly closed the lid.

Her heartbeat hammered as she rushed to the window and climbed out, clinging to the stonework just as the door opened.

"Foolish idiot." Aslyn recognized Lady Fia's muttering.

She held her breath as the woman continued moving around the office, searching for something.

"He insists on running when he should walk," Lady Fia grumbled to herself.

Thumps from within the office made Aslyn wince. Lady Fia continued her muttering. The noise ceased, and Lady Fia sighed in delight. "Ah, there we are lovely."

For a moment, Aslyn feared she had been spotted. But nothing happened. Her racing heart was so loud she worried it would give her away. After a few careful breaths, she dared to peek around the windowsill with one eye, making herself little more than a sliver as her fingers ached.

Lady Fia faced the bookshelves, flipping through one of the old books. She spoke in some flawless, ancient language, rolled her neck, and walked out the door with the book tucked under her arm. What book would interest Lady Fia?

Aslyn didn't dare to reenter the office after that. She cautiously worked her way to the nearby balcony, peeked inside the empty suite, then slipped back inside. Dirt marred the front of her dress and her fingers had cramped.

It didn't take long to return to her room, and the second she did, Aslyn stripped out of the dress and started a bath. She would wash the evidence off herself and her dress. Because even if she tried to tuck the soiled dress into the bottom of her laundry, someone would think it strange since she had no reason to be so dirty. Better to wash it herself and pray no one noticed.

Chapter 22

Valen's Perfect Little Possession

Sybil's laughter rang through her sitting room—sweet, sharp, unrelenting—as she once more fell into another endless string of detailed praises for Valen. Aslyn sat across from her, irritation crawling beneath her skin and a half-empty cup of wine cradled between tense fingers. Seven Gods, Sybil's eyes lit up at the mere *mention* of his name. She couldn't possibly be this happy with him.

Aslyn joined Sybil in the empress's suite for evening libations on Sybil's invitation. She had only just finished her bath and had dressed in a nightgown, prepared to remain in her room for the rest of the night when Sybil sent the request. Aslyn had dressed and begrudgingly ventured to Sybil's suite, knowing full well what she would have to listen to for the next hour.

She wore a different dress from dinner, though Sybil had already established that Valen had destroyed the last one. But something about this dress was different. The material was the thickest thing Aslyn had ever seen, with several layers all worked together in an intricate tapestry. Despite the warmth from the dress and the crackling fire, Sybil still wore a heavy, fur-lined cloak... like she was about cross through the Varyova Ice Cap and not sit in her perfectly comfortable—if not a little hot—sitting room.

"—and then, he tucked a strand of hair behind my ear, so gentle, so *intentional*, and said he couldn't imagine a world where I wasn't beside him," Sybil sighed, all bliss and breathlessness.

"I'm sure," Aslyn said absently.

"You should've seen his face, Aslyn," Sybil didn't even notice Aslyn's irritation as she carried on. "I think—no, I *know*—he means it when he says I've changed everything for him."

"No doubt." Aslyn stared into her cup, utterly bored. If she had to listen too much more of this, Aslyn was likely to snap.

"He even had the cook prepare that lemon tart I liked from the ball in Stormvalor." Sybil beamed. "He remembered. I didn't even have to say a word."

Aslyn's jaw clenched. "How generous of him." Seven Gods, how much more could she possibly have to say about him?

Sybil didn't seem to hear the edge in her tone. "And at dinner," she giggled like some dumb, moonstruck girl, "he took me right there on the table. Seven Gods, I didn't even *care* who heard."

"I was there." Aslyn downed the rest of her wine in a gulp as irritation crawled along her skin. "Everyone heard."

"It's like he can't *breathe* unless I'm—"

Aslyn cut her off. "Do you ever grow tired of it?" If she had to listen to one more detail, Aslyn thought it might break her.

Sybil blinked. "Of what?"

Aslyn met her eyes, voice low but shaking with suppressed anger. "Of praising him. Of recounting every moan and murmur as though the rest of us exist only to marvel at your perfect romance."

Sybil's smile faltered. "I didn't mean—"

"I'm tired of it, Sybil. All of it." She set her cup down with a hard clink. "I'm tired of hearing about every breath Valen takes, every look he gives you, every damned time he touches you. I'm tired of hearing how he *worships* you. Tired of being dismissed like some inconvenience just so he can 'devour' you over dinner like some prize he *owns*. And I'm especially tired of pretending that I'm not hurting while you sit there, blind to it. Do you even see what that does to me?"

The fire cracked. Sybil's mouth parted, but no words came.

"I sit beside you like a ghost," Aslyn continued. "You speak of love as if it's the air you breathe, and I—gods, I can't breathe at all in this place."

Sybil's smile fell. "Aslyn—"

"You didn't even notice, did you?" Aslyn snapped, unable to stop herself now that she had started. She needed to get so much off her chest. "You never ask how I'm doing anymore, or why I can barely *look* at him without wanting to claw the smugness from his face." Her voice cracked. "You never ask how I feel about being forced into this marriage to Marek instead of *your brother*."

Sybil straightened in her chair, brows drawn. "That isn't fair."

"No. It's not." Aslyn's hands shook. "But neither is watching my only friend in this horrible place vanish behind the shadow of a man."

Sybil opened her mouth, but no words came. Aslyn glowered, then gave up and strode toward the door.

After a few moments of hesitation, Sybil followed, her slippers near-silent behind Aslyn's storming stride. "Aslyn, wait! You can't just—"

Aslyn spun, her braid whipping behind her. "Can't just what? Speak for once instead of nodding and smiling like a well-trained handmaiden while you prattle on about every way he possesses you?"

Sybil froze, mouth parting. "That's not what I—"

"Oh, isn't it?" Aslyn stepped forward, voice rising. "Because that's all you are lately—Valen's perfect little possession. Do you even *remember* who you were before him? Or did he devour that out of you with his magical mouth, too?"

Sybil blanched. "That's not fair."

Aslyn scoffed. "No, what's not fair is watching you throw yourself into his arms like he's the sun and stars."

Tears welled in Sybil's eyes and she hugged her arms over her chest, trembling. "I thought you were happy for me."

"I *was*," Aslyn said, voice cracking again. "And I tried. I tried so hard to continue to be happy for you. But seven gods, Sybil, you don't see *anything* anymore. Just him. And you don't even care that he treats me like an afterthought, like he would rather be rid of me."

"He doesn't! He wouldn't!" Sybil said, defensive now. She took a bold step toward Aslyn, face scrunching up in irritation. "You're just—"

"What?" Aslyn hissed. "Bitter? Jealous?" Aslyn threw her hands up. "Maybe I am, Sybil. Maybe I'm sick to death of watching you disappear. Maybe I'm tired of being strong and quiet and *alone*."

Silence stretched between them. Aslyn's throat caught as she once more thought of Aethan and how much she missed him. Did Sybil even care how much she hurt, how much she loved Aethan, needed him, *craved* him?

Aslyn's voice dropped, lower, harder. "You think you're in love. Maybe you are. Or maybe Valen just tells you what you want to hear. Maybe you're too caught up in the way he looks at you to notice that he's swallowing you whole, because I don't believe for a second that he loves you. I don't even think he's capable of love."

Sybil's face heated. Tears welled in her eyes. "That's cruel, Aslyn."

Aslyn laughed bitterly. "No, *cruel* would be telling you that you've become shallow. Selfish. *Obsessed*. That you use his love like a mirror to feel *worth* something."

The silence that followed that landed like a slap.

Sybil took a slow step back. "You don't mean that."

Aslyn opened her mouth—but the words refused to come. Of course she hadn't meant it. Not really. Not *all* of it. But the fury kept her standing tall, because if she let it go and allowed her own aching heart to take over, she might break apart entirely.

"And what if I do?" Aslyn paused, but Sybil gave no response outside of anger in those blue eyes—Aethan's blue eyes. It made her heart twist in agony. *I miss him so much.* "Never mind. You don't care about me."

Aslyn pivoted on her heel and stormed out the open door as Black Guards eyed her like they debated whether or not to kill her.

Aslyn couldn't tell Sybil the truth, that—while she was irritated beyond belief with the endless nonsense—her pain wasn't really about Sybil at all.

It was about Aethan.

About the ache in her chest that had only grown more painful since the day they said goodbye.

Chapter 23

The Empress is Dying

S weat beaded on Sybil's forehead, but her very bones were chilled to the core. A fire blazed in the hearth across the room, but the warmth didn't reach her. All her muscles ached, tense from the cold grasping her in its icy fist. She moaned and stirred, blinking through blurry vision to make out the shapes moving about the room with her.

"Shh, don't move, Sybil." Valen's familiar voice caressed her as he ran a cool cloth over her forehead.

But it was so cold. Sybil needed that cloth off her skin, away from her body. She fumbled her hands from beneath layers of comforters to push his arm away.

"I'm trying to help you," he said a touch sharply.

"Too cold..." Sybil murmured. Her teeth chattered and her body trembled.

"Fia!" There was no panic or desperation in his call. Valen's tone was sharp, commanding. His dark eyes turned away from Sybil and she wanted them back on her.

The bone chilling cold had been creeping up on Sybil for some time. She knew it, felt it, but hadn't realized the extent to which it affected her. She hadn't expected it to make her feel like she was dying. *I can't be dying... can I?*

Yet there was no denying this strange sensation of death looming. When Sybil blinked her blurred vision, she was certain she saw the figure of death looming over her, waiting to collect her soul. It felt absolute. Inescapable.

Blinking once more, that figure of death vanished, replaced by Valen bundling more blankets over her prone form. Not that the blankets helped. Nor did the blazing fire in the nearby hearth.

Sybil knew death could hurt. She had read about it in enough books and heard enough stories to understand that much. But this... the word hurt didn't do justice to the torture deep in her bones. She attempted to relax her muscles by laying flat and not moving, but that agony ripped through her all the same. That cold still consumed her. So she curled into a ball—or as close to it as she could with her body refusing to obey her commands. For a moment, a split second, she felt relief.

Then it consumed her again.

What was happening? Or she supposed the better question was... why? She had seen her mother die of the wasting illness and it hadn't looked like this. Her mother had been weak, but smiling, happy, right up until the end.

Sybil didn't think she would ever smile again, that the only thing she would know until her death was pure, icy torment.

The last thing Sybil remembered was entering Valen's bedroom distraught over her fight with Aslyn. He had taken her in, comforted her, worshipped her. They spent hours moving through wave after wave of carnal bliss and she had let him do whatever he wanted because, seven gods, it had been utterly divine. They had eventually fallen asleep in his bed, tangled in one another, entirely spent.

Since that first time on the chase lounge, they had hardly been able to keep to themselves. At first Sybil had attempted to use her magic to See something when she touched him. His past. His future. His intentions. It failed every time, and while that should have bothered her, she couldn't hold it against him. This was where she was meant to be.

While Valen was away from her running the empire, Sybil counted the seconds until he would appear again. And every time he was near her something drew them together. An ache. A need. A hunger that drove them both mad. When they were around others, they did their best to restrain themselves, but more than once he had sharply dismissed everyone else in the room just so he could sate his hunger. And seven gods help her if she didn't quiver in anticipation of each time. In the courtyard, the hallways, the throne room, on the dining table where dinner went cold and guests had been kicked out.

Was there such a thing as too much coupling? Because the more they coupled, the more she felt so utterly cold until she couldn't stand it any longer, until only his heated desire could warm her again. Sybil tried reaching for him, hoping to curb this icy torment with his heat once more, but her arms were bundled securely beneath a mountain of blankets. She could do little more than move her finger, and even that made a fresh wave of pain lance up her arm and through her body. *What is happening to me?*

Fia materialized beside the bed, her face inscrutable as she studied Sybil, then she shot a hard, knowing look at Valen. "I warned you. I told you to slow down."

Valen tucked the blankets so tight around Sybil she couldn't move if her life depended on it. His features creased with worry.

He does *care about me.* For a while, Sybil hadn't been sure. He desired her, yes, but she hadn't gotten the sense that he truly cared.

"I'm in no mood for I told you so. Help her."

Fia snorted. "What do you expect me to do? You got greedy. This is *your* fault."

Sybil moaned as her muscles twitched. Could they coil tight enough to snap? It certainly felt that way.

He glowered at Fia. "I already told you—"

"I know what you told me!" Fia snapped, cutting him off. "And I told you not to take so much. Do you know how long this one could last if you could just pace yourself? *Decades.* But flames help us you have no self-control. After everything you've learned, you are still just a babe pretending to be a man."

Valen growled.

Sybil blinked slowly, trying to make sense of their argument but the gears of her mind jammed. *Help me,* she thought pitifully, yet couldn't muster the strength to speak the words.

Valen climbed off the bed and Sybil wanted to reach for him but couldn't move. He prowled toward Fia until he stood so close his nose nearly touched hers. His voice filled with cold fury. "Need I remind you that I still have power over you? Perhaps I've allowed you free rein for too long."

Deep silence filled the chamber. Sybil couldn't even hear her own breathing or heartbeat. She studied Valen's body. Every muscle had tightened, and not in the way she had become so familiar with. This was dangerous. Powerful. Dominating.

Fia shifted, but she didn't back down. "She's dying, and it's your fault," she hissed. "Why should I help when you threaten me?"

All the air in the room seemed to thin. Sybil struggled for every breath.

Fia choked, trembling.

A pulse of darkness spread through the room like a deadly warning. The floor shook. "You need oxygen," Valen said darkly. "Never forget I have the power to take it away."

Sybil didn't understand what was happening anymore, except that she couldn't breathe. Was Valen doing this?

"I will outlive her," Fia rasped, peering past Valen at Sybil. "And you will... have nothing... to sustain... yourself."

Valen turned and his face twisted in rage, then the air returned. Sybil drank it down. Before Fia could react, Valen grabbed the hair at the back of her head and shoved her toward the bed, never relenting in his grip as he leaned behind Fia.

"Fix her or join your brothers and sisters before the sun fully rises," Valen growled in Fia's ear.

"They are *not* my brothers and sisters."

Fia attempted to remain dignified, but it must have been hard when he manhandled her in such a way. Sybil felt a pang of sympathy for Fia. Valen was desperate and his mood had shifted so quickly. Sybil hadn't wanted to cause anyone trouble.

"Let me go first," Fia hissed through her teeth.

Valen shoved her as he released his death grip, and something about him grew imposing, like death waiting to claim Fia's life. This was a side of him Sybil never wanted to see again. Unforgiving, dangerous, and utterly deadly.

Fia yanked the blankets back and Sybil tried to protest, but her grip was weak as she pulled at them to keep herself covered. Not only was she freezing, but she was naked. Fia placed a hand over Sybil's abdomen, never touching her skin, and warmth spread through Sybil's body. She relaxed. Her muscles finally unbound. She sank back with a sigh. It was like a warm hearth fire beneath her skin.

Had I truly been dying, or was I just that cold? Either way, Sybil was thankful for whatever Fia did to chase away that bone cold, muscle tightening chill.

Fia continued feeding heat through Sybil, and she could sense death fleeing. But the effort strained Fia, as if something blocked her from further chasing death away, and she bared her teeth as if straining. Fia's gaze fell on the blue dragon tattoo over Sybil's heart. Her eyes widened and she gasped sharply, snapping her hand away.

"Why didn't you tell me about that?" she hissed at Valen.

He sank onto the bed beside Sybil, examining her as if making sure she would survive a little longer. His depthless, dark eyes stopped on the dragon. "I was working on it myself."

"Stumbling like a babe," Fia grumbled. She reached toward the tattoo, tracing a finger over one of the runes on the dragon's wing.

Sybil smacked her hand away, uncomfortable with Fia's hand so close to her chest.

Fia ignored the slight, turning her burning gaze to Valen. "It has a distinct pattern for a reason. Unlock it."

"Why? What is it?" he asked, staring at the tattoo now.

Sybil pulled the blankets up, suddenly self-conscious with them both staring at her. But Fia refused to let her cover the tattoo, peeling the blankets back far enough to keep it exposed.

"It's nothing," Sybil said.

"It is not nothing, child," Fia snapped, making her sound much older than she looked. "Unlock it, Your Grace, and this will *not* happen again. And what you could do with it..."

Valen frowned, leaning closer to Sybil and tracing his fingers along the runes. "But you said decades. This won't kill her?"

"Why would the tattoo kill me?" Sybil didn't understand what was happening. What did they mean by unlocking it?

"No." Fia crossed her arms and stepped back, ignoring Sybil's question completely. "Quite the opposite. Forget *decades*."

Valen's eyes burned with hunger in a way that made Sybil blush in front of Fia, a way reserved for only them.

"This is why you chose her, isn't it?" Fia asked.

Valen's touch made Sybil shudder in such a delightful way. "After her mother, I suspected something, but I wasn't sure. The runes. They're a charm, aren't they?"

Fia nodded.

A charm? What were they going on about?

"It's just a tattoo," Sybil protested, still weak but slowly recovering. "It's a Starkling tradition that goes back generations. My brother has it. My father. His father."

Valen cursed so colorfully Sybil recoiled, terrified of him for the first time since she met him. His nails scratched at the runes as his lips curled.

"Valen?" Her voice trembled.

"All this time they were right under our nose!" Valen growled.

"Unlock it," Fia said, her voice smooth and coaxing this time. "Find out."

"Get to Arithia," Valen ordered Fia. "I need her brother here, in whatever condition he's in."

Arithia? Aethan? What had just happened and what did it have to do with her brother? Valen's last five words sank in and Sybil's stomach twisted in knots. What condition would Aethan be in? Shouldn't the Arithians welcome him now?

"And find Lux Starkling."

No. Panic settled in Sybil's body.

Then Valen yanked a knife from his boot. "Let's try to unlock it then, shall we?"

By the time Sybil realized his intention, she couldn't move, couldn't speak. The knife slowly carved into the runes as Valen murmured in some ancient language.

And Sybil screamed.

Chapter 24

A Humiliated King

Cavis's grief transformed into a fiery anger over the next few days. At himself. At Captain Barrow. At Von. At *King* Dorin. A searing need for vengeance ignited a flame deep within him. Dorin was not now, nor would he ever be Cavis's king. Not as long as Aslyn breathed.

But to accomplish his mission, to pave the way for Aslyn's return, Cavis had to kneel to the so-called king.

So he did. In front of the entire Arithian court. In front of his parents. Beside his brother. He kneeled and spoke the fealty oath he vowed in his heart he would never keep. It was the only way to keep Dorin from watching him too closely. The so-called king would suspect Cavis of treason for his alliance with Aslyn and Aethan if he didn't speak the words in front of everyone.

Usually, Arithian kings and queens only bound those in their inner circle to the ancient blood oath magic, allowing all others to simply speak the words. But Dorin was not like his predecessors. He made each and every noble swear it on the oath stones. How many others silently pledged themselves to Aslyn?

"I kneel before you, my king, and pledge my life to your service," Cavis spoke loud and clear.

I pledge my life to the true heir to the crown.

"Your will is my command, your enemies my own. I shall guard your throne, uphold your justice, and defend your realm." *Princess Aslyn*, he added mentally after each statement. "By blood and oath, I am bound until death or release." Cavis sliced his palm and dripped blood on the ancient oath stones as he pushed all his will into his mental vow to fight and preserve this kingdom for the princess and rightful heir of Novavito. The blood sizzled and for a moment his insides truly burned—long lost magic that bound him to his oath of fealty. It only lasted for a moment. He gritted his teeth and finished the vow. *Princess Aslyn...* "This I swear to you, now and forever."

Seven gods help him if that didn't work.

Before Cormic could repeat the process, the side door of the throne room, used only by the royal family and their guards, opened and Lady Fia stormed in with a stream of Black Guards.

Cavis quickly wrapped his palm as he rose and stumbled back, ushered to the side of the chamber by the Black Guards.

"Lady Fia!" Ambassador Umbogo's eyes widened. Clearly they hadn't been expecting this visitor. "To what do we owe this—"

"Silence," Lady Fia snapped.

Umbogo choked on his own tongue, face paling. He bowed his head and edged back beside Dorin as Lady Fia's eyes turned to the new king.

"I come on behalf of Emperor Valen," she announced.

Whispers rippled through the court, matching Cavis's own shock. Valen was emperor now? What happened to Oxon?

"Everyone out!" Dorin commanded. Though his voice didn't carry the regal command like his father's had, everyone eagerly filed out the doors.

Cavis grabbed his brother's arm and pulled him along in the crowd.

"Cavis and Cormic Dysart!" Dorin bellowed over the commotion. "You stay. I'm not done with you yet."

The brothers froze, turning slowly as the rest of the court streamed around them and out the doors until they were the only two left. Why them? Did Dorin have some other plan for them once they completed their vows?

The doors thumped closed.

"I prepared an update," Dorin said to Lady Fia. His hands gripped the arms of the throne, but Cavis noticed the slight tremble in his muscles. "Umbogo was prepared to deliver it as soon as we finished here today."

"I'm not here to play your messenger," Lady Fia said. Something about her utter calm set Cavis on edge. "I'm here to collect Starkling on Emperor Valen's orders."

Dorin's mouth floundered like a fish out of water before collecting himself well enough to respond. "He—he's dead. That's what I was going to—"

"His body will suffice," she interrupted.

Why did Emperor Valen want Aethan's body?

As all the color flushed from Dorin's usually golden complexion, Cavis fought off a smirk as a hint of vindication passed through him. Oh, this would be delightful.

"After I had him executed, I ordered my men to send him out to sea," Dorin said. "To get rid of the body. I watched the boat float out myself. He's... his body is lost to the sea by now."

Lady Fia's long fingers flexed. Heat rippled through the room. Within seconds it became suffocating. Cavis felt the sweat bead on his brow almost instantly. Cormic tugged at his collar.

"Things are not progressing so smoothly for you, *King* Dorin," Lady Fia said. "The emperor gave you what you asked for, yet you have delivered him nothing you agreed to."

Lady Fia prowled toward Dorin. "You promised him Blackblade."

"He slipped my spies," Dorin said.

"But you know what he looks like."

"So do you." Dorin lifted his chin but was smart enough not to smirk at the woman. Cavis remained utterly silent and still, praying his brother would do the same. He needed to learn as much as possible. "You've seen him yourself. In Stormvalor."

Cavis frowned. Blackblade had been in Stormvalor?

Lady Fia connected the pieces much faster than Cavis and released a small gasp. "Khrahar."

Cavis blinked, uncertain he heard her correctly. There was no way Khrahar was Blackblade. He was too young and... normal. He had danced with Aslyn, courted her! What game had he been playing? *No, this is nonsense. Khrahar isn't Blackblade.* But for some reason, Cavis couldn't even convince himself. And if Blackblade targeted the princess in Stormvalor, she could be in worse danger than Cavis thought. Marek. Valen... Blackblade.

"When Bloodstone and his thug went after my sister, Blackblade vanished into thin air. There are only rumors of his whereabouts." This time, Dorin did dare a smirk. "And you know where that is, too."

Cavis's heart sank. He glanced at a grim-looking Cormic. Blackblade still hunted Aslyn. They had to do something.

Cavis glanced at the guard nearest him, eyeing the axe on the man's hip. Impulse made him yearn to snatch that axe and kill the guard, but it would be suicide. Even if he killed one and his brother followed quickly enough to dispatch a second, there would be no way to win against so many.

The guard sensed him staring and turned black, empty eyes on Cavis. He tightened his jaw and refused to look away. After a moment, the guard's hand fell on the axe head as if he could read Cavis's thoughts.

A sharp crack broke Cavis from his staring contest with the guard, snapping it to Dorin.

Lady Fia now stood directly in front of the throne. Dorin sagged to one side, rubbing his cheek where an angry red welt in the shape of Lady Fia's hand already bloomed to life. Hate burned in Dorin's eyes as he glared at her. But he smartly said nothing.

At his side, Umbogo winced, averting his own gaze.

"Emperor Valen *requires* Starkling's body," she hissed so softly Cavis hardly heard the words from where he stood. "Produce it or he will have to rethink your agreement."

Cavis's previous anger toward Dorin instantly turned into a fury so righteous he had to clench his fists. His fingers dug into the cloth wrapped around his cut hand and he felt it reopen. Blood dripped on the floor at his side. How much of Novavito's recent royal tragedy had been Dorin's doing?

Dorin straightened slightly and said through his teeth, "It's gone over a week now. The waves would have dragged him under. I cannot *produce* it."

Cavis flinched as Lady Fia struck again, this time wrapping her hand around Dorin's throat. She pinned Dorin to the back of his throne hard enough that the crown slipped from his head and fell into his lap. Instead of clawing at her arm as Cavis would have expected, Dorin held onto the arms of the throne like they were the only thing keeping him grounded. His face reddened as he struggled for breath. Cavis didn't dare hope that Lady Fia would kill the usurper for him. And if she did, he worried something far worse would take Dorin's place.

"I don't care if it takes the rest of your pitiful life," she said. Cavis shuddered at the silky-smooth calm in her voice. "You will find him. You will present his body to the emperor. And if you fail, the deal you made with the ambassador on the emperor's behalf will be voided."

Tears pricked at the corners of Dorin's eyes as his face shifted from red to purple. Cavis bit his lip, praying to whatever god might remain that Lady Fia would kill the so-called king for him, even if he was smart enough to know she was there to deliver a message for the emperor, not an execution... not yet, anyway.

"Do I make myself perfectly clear?" she asked.

Dorin tried to answer but couldn't draw the breath. Instead, he nodded.

Lady Fia released her strangle hold. Dorin coughed as he desperately drew air into his lungs. Where her hand had been, a red mark remarkably like burns remained on Dorin's throat. He swallowed hard as she backed up and marched toward the exit.

"Find him before your sister's wedding to Marek Bloodstone," Lady Fia said casually, as if she hadn't just slapped, choked, and threatened a king.

Aslyn was marrying Marek? No. That couldn't be right. She would never... But Aethan had said as much in his letter. He warned Cavis that this was coming. The horrible truth settled over Cavis as Lady Fia rounded the doorway, the Black Guards following her in systematic lines.

Dorin had, in fact, made a deal with the emperor. Kill the king and queen, then force Aslyn into marriage to Marek so he could have the throne. In exchange, Dorin no doubt gave the emperor of his ambassador a promise he could never break.

How far back did this arrangement go? Was that the reason Marek had turned into a crazed lunatic in Stormvalor after he was named champion? Dorin had promised his sister to Marek as part of the deal, and when she chose Aethan, Marek set out to force her hand.

Once Lady Fia and the Black Guards were gone, Cavis and Cormic turned to Dorin. Neither dared speak as Dorin's humiliation at Lady Fia's hands lingered thick in the air.

Cavis recalled the massacre in the Novavito royal suite in Stormvalor. The blood and dismemberment and evisceration. The absolute butchery of every royal guard and servant in the suite. Bile crawled up his throat as the images flashed through his memory. He had no choice but to help clean up the mess to ensure anything valuable to the royal family was returned. Armor. Gold. Jewels. Weapons... the queen. Dorin hadn't even bothered greeting Cavis to accept his mother's ashes.

Oaths be damned. He would kill Dorin himself. Slowly. Painfully. He would butcher the young king the same way those guards had been butchered. And he would make sure Dorin remained alive to feel every ounce of pain.

Driven by blind rage, Cavis stepped forward. Cormic followed a half second behind.

"Look what we have here," Dorin snapped, glaring at the brothers. "Volunteers." His voice sounded like someone had ground it over gravel. "Since the two of you were so eager to step forward, you will lead the search party."

Like hell he would! Cavis bared his teeth, preparing to condemn Dorin for all he had done and proclaim him a usurper and traitor to the Kiernan family.

But Dorin didn't give him a chance to speak. "I suggest you not delay. You will have one ship. You will find the body, whether it's above or below the tides. And if you fail, I vow that whatever is waiting for me at Emperor Valen's command will be a paradise compared to what I will have done to you." He leaned forward, but the menace in his brown eyes was dulled by the angry red marks Lady Fia left behind. "And you will return to me with the body before my sister's wedding at the end of the week."

Cavis wanted to tell Dorin he could jump into the fires of Mount Fjaroe for all he cared, but Cormic's hand fell on his shoulder. Cavis snapped his jaw shut as his brother spoke for them.

"It will be done, Your Majesty," Cormic said with so much deference Cavis wanted to smack him.

What was he doing? There was no way Cavis would spend the next week combing the ocean for a body he knew was lost to the Isles of Storm.

"Then get out of my sight," Dorin hissed. "You're wasting time. Gather your crew and leave. Now!"

Cormic pulled Cavis toward the exit.

When they were away from the throne room and away from the royal guards, Cavis rounded on his brother.

"What were you thinking?"

"I was thinking he just gave us a ship and a crew," Cormic replied. He glanced around to be sure no one was around. "Much faster to find the others by sea than land."

Cavis gaped for a moment as the truth of his brother's words settled over him. He was right. It was brilliant.

The wedding was only days away. Even with a ship, they couldn't hope to reach Lemheller Gap before the wedding. The trip would take at least two weeks. But Weylen, Kern, and Roric were headed that way already. With any luck, they would arrive to help Aslyn.

Meanwhile, Cavis and Cormic would take their crew and their ship northwest to the Cliffs of Hope. Hopefully, they could rendezvous with their Kern, Weylen, and Roric as planned. Making the trip on a ship would be much faster than over land. The timing just might work out perfectly.

And then he would have to face Roric and tell him the truth, that they failed to save Aethan.

Roric will never forgive me.

If there were any gods left, the trio would arrive at the Cliffs of Hope with Aslyn. Then they could follow her lead to gather a force to return and retake her throne.

CHAPTER 25

Shame Creates a Tighter Fit

Aslyn made her way toward Sybil's chambers, turning her practiced words over in her mind. Between the quickly approaching emperor-enforced wedding and Sybil's endless chatter about her husband's utter perfection and sweetness toward her, Aslyn had snapped. Overwhelmed, she couldn't bear to hear Sybil praise the man forcing her to marry Marek Bloodstone. The display in the dining hall hadn't helped matters.

Aslyn's words had been sharp and cruel as she snapped at Sybil, and she regretted taking her frustration out on her only friend. Because the truth was, after spending the rest of that evening in tears, missing Aethan, she had to admit that she had lashed out in large part because she needed him.

Three days passed since Aslyn's outburst. Sybil hadn't made an appearance or invited her for lunch, tea, conversation, or games. Aslyn hadn't *seen* Sybil since she stormed out on her. Now, guilt gnawed at Aslyn's heart. Sybil was Aethan's sister, and by extension would be her own. She needed to apologize and have an adult conversation about boundaries. Sybil had been Aslyn's only comfort in this cold, suffocating place, and now she felt utterly alone.

When Aslyn approached Sybil's door, two Black Guards barred the entrance. Neither glanced at Aslyn, but their presence clearly indicated that no one would pass.

The door was open slightly and Aslyn was about to call inside when the voices halted her.

"...days and it doesn't seem to have done anything," Valen said from deeper in Sybil's suite.

A woman sighed, and when she spoke, Aslyn instantly recognized Lady Fia's voice. "Perhaps you did something wrong. Besides, she is healing and you said yourself that she seems stronger now than she had been before. So even if it didn't break like we hoped, something obviously changed."

Why had Sybil needed healing? It had to be her, otherwise why have this conversation in her chambers? And what did they try to break?

I've been a terrible friend, abandoning her when she needs me as much as I need her... perhaps more.

Valen responded, his voice too low for Aslyn to hear the words, as was Lady Fia's response. Then Valen said, "It's time. I'll give the order today. You promise it will be done swiftly?"

"Have I ever failed you?" Lady Fia asked, her voice sultry and supplicating.

"Would you like a list?" he hissed back. "Get it done. We can't afford for this to go wrong."

Something buzzed in the air. Then Aslyn spotted Valen moving toward the door.

Afraid of being caught eavesdropping, Aslyn called through the narrow space in the doorway. "I would like to see Sybil!"

Valen pulled the door open wide enough for Aslyn to see inside. Sybil wasn't in the sitting room, and her bedroom door was closed.

"The Empress is quite tired and isn't up to visitors," Valen said sharply. His black eyes slid over her and his lips thinned in irritation. "Spying wins you no favor."

"I wasn't—"

Valen struck like lightning, quick and unexpected. One moment they stood on either side of the doorway. The next, Aslyn's back slammed into the far wall of the hallway with Valen's firm grip on her jaw pinning her in place. His fingers pinched so tight it made Aslyn's eyes water. Instinctively, she grabbed hold of his arm, trying to pull it away. She was certain his fingers would leave bruises. He possessed so much strength in one hand that Aslyn feared he could crush her bones. She didn't want to appear weak or scared, but it was impossible to control her rapid breathing as he leaned close. Something vicious consumed in his black eyes and it terrified her to her core.

"Don't lie to your emperor," he growled. "First you insult my empress to her face, now you dare to lie to mine? I have *killed* for less. Don't presume that you are safe from my blade because you are heir to a kingdom. If history has taught us anything, it's that no one cares who sits on the throne as long as they have food in their bellies and a roof over their heads."

Tears rolled down Aslyn's cheeks and she hated herself for allowing it in front of him, yet she couldn't stop herself if she tried. Aslyn attempted speaking, but the way Valen's fingers dug into her skin made it impossible to move her jaw. All she managed was a feeble sound in the back of her throat.

With a sneer of disgust, Valen tossed Aslyn aside. She stumbled and fell, barely catching herself before her face hit the tiled floor. Burning with humiliation, Aslyn glared up at Valen, only to find him standing over her, straightening the sleeves of his jacket as if preparing for court.

"I wanted to apologize to her," Aslyn said, and her voice trembled in a way that deepened her humiliation.

"Stay away from the empress," Valen hissed.

After a quick command to the guards to allow no one else into Sybil's chambers, Valen marched up the hallway, stepping over Aslyn as if she were nothing more than a dung heap at his boots. "Don't you have a dress fitting? Your wedding is only days away. I suggest you focus on your future with Marek Bloodstone, *princess*."

The condescension in Valen's tone slashed into Aslyn's skin.

He vanished down the hall.

Aslyn attempted to regain some of her dignity, rising on shaking legs. She took a moment to straighten her dress, then lifted her chin high and marched back toward her room. No one had ever handled her like that before. Not even Valen himself when they were in Stormvalor. She vowed to herself that she would never be so helpless again.

Her anger converted into alarm as she entered her sitting room to find a small team of men and women waiting. A crimson dress was spread across her sofa. The moment they spotted her, the team descended like vultures.

As if the humiliation of Valen handling her as he did hadn't been enough, these people stripped Aslyn of her current dress, tightened the bindings around her breasts to boost them higher, and swept her hair up with a swift twist and clip against the back of her head. Aslyn stumbled as many hands made quick work of changing her into the crimson dress despite her blundering protests.

After seconds that had felt much longer, the team stepped back. Aslyn peered down at herself. The dress was a masterpiece of crimson silk, flowing like liquid fire with every movement. Its bodice, cut daringly low, clung to curves with delicate boning, while sheer panels along the sides hinted at bare skin beneath. Around the plunging neckline and cinched waist, red gemstones shimmered like fresh drops of blood, catching the light with every movement. The skirt, a cascade of rich fabric slit high along one thigh, promised both grace and temptation. Every fastening was cleverly hidden, designed for effortless removal, as if the gown itself anticipated the inevitable unraveling of the wedding night.

Despite the grace of the gown, it sagged on her frame around her breasts and at the waist, and the length clearly needed to be brought up.

Was this to be her wedding dress? Regardless how beautiful it was, Aslyn felt utterly indecent in such a revealing dress. And crimson? Shouldn't she wear the colors of the Novavito royal family?

None of this truly matters, Aslyn reminded herself as the seamstress set to work pinching and tightening fabric for a perfect fit. Aslyn had no intention of being present for her own wedding to Marek. She would escape and find her way to Aethan... somehow.

Not that she had found a way out of the palace yet. Every path to an exit was heavily guarded. She could barely step outside before a dozen Black Guards descended around her to keep her where she belonged. Imprisoned in this mountain palace.

As the team worked on her dress and plotted her jewels and hair for the big event, Aslyn's mind drifted away. To her guilt over the way she had treated Sybil. How she needed to make things right. When she needed to escape the palace. The way Valen had handled her and tossed her aside like trash. His warning about heirs and thrones.

She thought about Aethan. Seven gods how she missed him. What would he suggest she do to get out of here? Would he find her father? Could she dare to hope that he already had and that he was on his way to Lemheller Gap to help her escape this place? Guilt swirled around Aslyn's stomach as she considered the possibility that she wouldn't escape before being forced to marry Marek, or before he forced her into his bed. She had toyed with him for months and he had promised he would have his way. Soon.

Aslyn's throat clenched and suddenly she felt sick. Her head spun.

"I need air," Aslyn murmured through the thickness in her throat. "I need air!" She shoved the seamstress and her team out of the way and rushed to the balcony.

The moment she was outside, Aslyn sucked down mouthfuls of air, but it didn't help. Her hands gripped the cold stone rail of the balcony. Leaning forward, she peered down.

The world shifted and the drop to the grounds below seemed to pull even further away.

What have I done? Regret pulled at Aslyn, threatening to yank her over the rail to her doom. She had come here willingly, thinking she might find answers. But answers to what? The emperor's plans? Would they even be the same now that Valen was in charge?

As her mind spun, Aslyn spied the new arrivals dismounting in the courtyard far below. Three of them.

The Bloodstones.

As if sensing her gaze, Marek looked straight up at her. From this distance, it was hard to tell, but she fairly certain he grinned.

I can't marry him. Aslyn would rather throw herself from this balcony than marry Marek Bloodstone.

Yes. That would be the plan. If she couldn't find some way to escape before the wedding, Aslyn would jump from this balcony before tying herself to Marek.

The dress no longer mattered. Nothing did except finding a way out of the palace.

Aslyn turned and marched back toward the seamstress and her team.

It would be better not to put up a fight so they suspect nothing.

After the fitting ended and Aslyn was once more back in her own dress, she settled in an armchair facing the glass balcony doors, her mind probing for answers as she mentally walked the palace halls.

The door opened and she peered over her shoulder, hoping Sybil had come by to visit her. She owed her friend so many apologies.

Marek strolled in as if it were his room and not hers. His lip curled up arrogantly and she tensed at his approach. "My bride. Glad to see you haven't run off in my absence."

"I thought the High Council needed you," she said. Had they dismissed the charges? Had Aethan been there?

Marek waved a hand dismissively, then kneeled in front of Aslyn. She wanted to recoil as he took her hand and brought it to his lips. His other hand slid along her thigh and Aslyn slapped it away. Marek's lips tightened and anger simmered in his eyes.

"Deny me all you want now, but in a few days, I will still have you," Marek said. "Even if it means I have to tie you down. Though I would much prefer you spread yourself open for me willingly."

"And you think that forcing me to fuck you will change anything?" Aslyn snorted and rolled her eyes. "All it will prove is that you are a brut who has to take what he wants instead of winning it fairly."

"There was a time you were very interested in what I had to offer," Marek said.

Aslyn shuddered because, as much as she hated it, he had a point. "That was before I saw the *real* you. I thought you were tender, that you cared about something beyond yourself, that you cared about *me*." She glowered at Marek with as much condescension as she could muster. "You only want me because of the crown."

"The crown was a bonus. What I really want is between your legs, and soon I will have a taste of that, too." Marek grabbed the back of her head and pulled Aslyn into a hard, biting kiss. It was all brutal possession and hunger.

Aslyn pressed her hands against his chest, trying to push him back, but he was so much stronger. For the second time that day, Aslyn was helpless and she hated it more than she hated him.

Marek broke the kiss, biting her lip, a grin on his face and consuming hunger in his eyes.

I won't be able to stop him.

That realization made her even more certain that she would rather die than marry him.

"Be a good girl for the next few days," Marek purred. "I have work to do for Emperor Valen, but I promise I will be back for this." His hand slid down her body and Aslyn shuddered. "And then I'll break you to make you a good little wife, if I have to. Just like my father did to my mother."

Marek stood and strode toward the exit, pausing to eye her up and down once more in a way that felt like he was stripping her with his gaze and imagining everything he would do once he had her tied and at his mercy.

The door whispered shut, but the sound echoed in Aslyn's ears.

She curled up, hugging her knees against her chest, and allowed herself a few moments to weep.

Then she would gather herself and find a way out.

A way back to Aethan.

Chapter 26

Tethers and Tyranny

Bast had been in Lemheller Gap for too long. He arrived when Aslyn did months ago. It was the longest he had ever remained in one place, and he was running short on inns he hadn't yet rented a room from. Staying on the move had always served him better and made it harder for the Black Guard to track his movements. And they *were* tracking him. Or at least, they were trying.

Each week, Lord Bloodstone increased the bounty on his head, hoping that someone in the city would turn him in. But no one knew who he was. Bast masked his face in shadows for a reason when he moved around as Blackblade, and he gave no clues away when he moved around the city as a citizen.

Despite all of this, he couldn't leave.

At least twice a week he left Lemheller Gap, headed in any direction as long as it was away from the city. Every time, something stopped him, some force that pulled at him, that burned within him. Sometimes he only made it a couple of kilometers before that force drove him to his knees. Most of the time, he could manage a little over a league. Once, he had gotten as far as two leagues. That had been the worst pressure of all. His palm burned like someone held a branding iron to his flesh. If he spent more than two days in the wild, a sickness spread through his gut. It vanished once he was again in Lemheller Gap, within sight of the palace. He knew the reason for these limits.

Aslyn. The blood oath. Bast cursed himself each time it seized him, berating himself for acting so foolishly and giving her that oath in Stormvalor.

Each day, Bast trailed city guards, listening to them talk about incoming shipments to the Citadel. These men weren't Black Guards, but lowly foot patrols whose sole job was to make sure citizens obeyed the emperor's laws. To their own discretion, of course.

Bast watched several take bribes or favors in exchange for letting minor infractions slip. He had killed one guard who tried to force himself on a girl whose only crime had been swiping crusty old bread for her family. She had cried and begged his mercy, and he had promised to give it to her. When she resisted him, he had thrown a few well-placed punches that reduced her resistance to little more than whimpers.

Flashes of his childhood, his stepfather abusing his mother, had made Bast see red. Shadows snapped out from his hiding place, wrapping around the guard's throat and ripping him violently away from the girl. He feebly scratched at his own neck, trying to free himself pointlessly as the shadows dragged him across the ground on his back. He came to a stop at Bast's feet. Bast held a knife in hand, ready for the kill. He had cursed the guard and noted the recognition in the man's eyes as Bast plunged his knife into his heart. The girl, he had left weeping in the alley. Her survival instincts would have her running for safety soon enough.

Almost as bad as the disgraceful guards were the loyalists. They existed everywhere in the realm, but those in Lemheller Gap were the worst, most stubborn idiots. These people were so diluted by the empire's lies that they believed the emperor was the only one who could protect them from the horrors of their world. Never mind that their crops continued failing, market prices continued to climb, produce grew progressively withered and tainted, and crime ran rampant everywhere. To a loyalist, these were all issues the emperor would fix, and they remained stubbornly committed to the lies regardless of the truth in front of their eyes. Bast could not understand them. Were loyalists truly so blind?

Anyone not wearing a loyalist band could become the target of unwarranted violence. To a loyalist, if one didn't support the emperor, they deserved to have some sense beaten into them. City guards in Lemheller Gap did nothing to stop them because, aside from these acts of violence against non-loyalists, they followed the emperor's laws to the letter.

Not everyone in a loyalist band truly was a loyalist, though. Bast saw it in their eyes. The way they avoided certain loyalists or remained at the back of a group when acts of violence against non-loyalists happened. The band around their arm was like a suit of armor protecting them. Their cowardly behavior would disgust Bast, but he had no room to judge. He strolled through the streets of Lemheller Gap with the band on just to avoid unwanted attention.

More Black Guards marched the streets of Lemheller Gap each week, on high alert. They searched for him. He knew it. He had kicked the hornet's nest and they were angry. Thankfully the pieces of the ambassador robe he had stitched into the back of his armor performed admirably, masking his magic and his trail. It gave him a freedom he had never been allowed in the past. He could use his shadow magic without the Black Guard being any wiser—until he struck. But still, they continued their search for him, forcing him to move around more and more frequently when they sniffed a little too close for his liking.

Most nights, Bast would go as far as that blasted blood oath would allow to watch the roads, making cautious, circuitous routes around the roads leading to Lemheller Gap. He kept his patterns irregular to avoid the Black Guard catching on and setting a trap for him. Every time a wagon of magical prisoners approached, Bast attacked. Since that first attack, his movements and use of his shadow magic had become more efficient, despite the increase in Black Guards around the wagons.

Yet each time he struck, reinforcements arrived quicker than the last time. They were learning. Watching. Waiting. Hoping to catch him off guard.

Bast had adapted as well. As reinforcements arrived quicker, he learned to create a path of shadows and darkness to mask the prisoners during their escape. As long as they remained within the path he created for them, they could escape to safety without the Black Guards tracking them. A few had strayed from the path in a panic, only to be caught again. Bast couldn't help a second time.

The Black Guard modified their tactics, and the last wagon Bast had waited for, he had been forced to allow to pass through to the Citadel. A company of one hundred Black Guards lined the road for several miles leading into the city. Even if Bast had tried attacking one of the weaker sections, the rest of those guards would close in on him before he could escape, and he certainly couldn't release the prisoners in time.

Bast watched helplessly as the wagon rolled between the lines of Black Guards, who then formed ranks behind and around the wagon as it passed. The emperor grew desperate for magical recruits to send so many Black Guards. In a way, Bast felt a sense of pride. He had rattled the cage so much that they had to send a full company of Black Guards to stop him.

Once the wagon and guards were out of sight, Bast followed, tracking their movements around Lemheller Gap toward the Citadel.

The open space around the Citadel gave him nowhere to hide. Bast studied the imposing walls. If he used his shadows to mask his movements, they could still track those strange shifts in the darkness. Angry, he gritted his teeth and circled wide, keeping to the rocky outcroppings and barren trees for shelter.

Around the southwest side of the Citadel, a man in ambassador robes greeted the wagon. The Black Guards formed a semicircle around the wagon from wall to wall. Even now, Bast couldn't hope to liberate those prisoners.

The ambassador led the way and the wagon simply vanished into the wall. Once it was gone, the Black Guards made their way around to the front gate.

Bast rubbed his eyes and squinted at the wall. *It vanished!*

Smooth obistone rose high into the sky all along the wall. No door. No signs of cracks or crevices. No knobs or mysterious markings. What kind of magic did the emperor employ to create a doorway that wasn't a doorway?

Bast glanced in all direction, cautiously moving toward the wall, darting from one rock to another, crouching to scan the area, then moving again. When he reached the wall, Bast ran a hand along the stone. It was cold, and that sense of suppression of magic slid over his fingertips.

But there was something else, too. Magic he couldn't use or identify. Experimentally, Bast tried to press his magic into the wall to see if he could make it work for him at all. A light ripple pressed back against him like a warning. He couldn't get through with the magic he controlled. What kind did it require?

Bast moved like a shadow along the jagged cliffs that ringed the emperor's Citadel, careful to keep to the darkness where the torchlight from the battlements could not reach. He had to find answers. Without the Black Guard armor or ambassador robes, he couldn't stroll through the front gate as he had done before. Could he hope to find a way in so he could venture into those torture dungeons and kill the poor souls within? He had seen the process before, watched men stripped of their voices and remade into the emperor's enforcers. The sight haunted him ever since. It was the very reason he spent so much time trying to save whoever he could. The most he could do for them. What happened to them after he freed them was on their own heads. He warned them as best he could but he wouldn't babysit them.

The land around the Citadel was stark, the mountains rising like jagged teeth. The plains around the outer walls were large enough to hold an army. Large enough to keep Bast from getting too close unnoticed. He pressed on, circling northward where the rocky terrain offered natural cover. As he crested a ridge, the moonlight revealed something he had never seen before—a hidden pass threading through the mountains like a wound in the landscape that had gone unnoticed even to his trained eye.

His pulse quickened. It wasn't this previously unknown pass that worried him, but what he saw moving through it.

Stretching before him, thousands of Black Guards stood in perfect, unbroken ranks, their armor glinting dully in the moonlight. Their faceless helms turned in eerie unison, movements precise and mechanical. There was no chatter, no shifting of weight, no sign of individuality—only perfect, unyielding discipline.

Bast crouched low, muscles coiled, eyes sharp as he tracked their movement. Row by row, the army advanced, slipping into the narrow pass with the silent efficiency of a blade sliding from its sheath. Where were they going? Whatever their destination, the emperor did not intend for prying eyes to see his army coming. They moved with a stealth that terrified him.

A whisper of unease slid down his spine. If the emperor had been forging an army in secret, it was for war. And if these soldiers were on the move, then their target was already lost. No one would see them coming until it was too late.

Steeling himself, Bast followed them into the mountains, careful to keep his distance. The jagged cliffs and shifting shadows provided ample cover, but he knew better than to rely on luck alone. These were the emperor's finest, trained to sense even the faintest disturbance. He moved in silence, pressing his body against rock when needed, taking advantage of every blind spot. Hours passed, the sky lightening with the slow approach of dawn, but he did not slow.

Then, just as the first slivers of light crested the peaks like the sun wanted to break through the overcast sky, Bast's body seized. Pain flared in his chest, white-hot and searing, as if invisible chains had wrapped around his ribs and yanked him back. His breath hitched. His knees buckled. The blood oath.

Aslyn.

That gods forsaken oath refused to let him take another step.

Bast gritted his teeth, cursing under his breath. He could go no farther. Whatever lay ahead remained out of reach, and the magic binding him to his oath would not let him defy it. He slammed a fist against the rock beside him, frustration burning in his veins. He had come so far—only to be stopped by his own damned oath.

Panting, he turned his gaze back toward the pass, watching the Black Guards disappear.

CHAPTER 27

Justice Shall Rise

Betrayal. Deep, agonizing betrayal stung deep in Sybil's heart. While the first month in the imperial palace had been a hard and lonely one, Sybil felt she and Valen had broken through that uncertainty and discomfort. The passion between them had ignited instantly once they lowered their defenses. It blazed hot and fast for weeks.

Sybil curled in the comfy plush chair in her sitting room, wrapped in a blanket, utterly miserable and alone once more.

She had trusted Valen, despite the warning of his dark intentions for the world. Sybil had allowed him to disarm her, to sway her, to consume her. She forgot the ominous visions she had witnessed in Mordelic, long ago. A spreading darkness. Kingdoms falling. The world dying. And at the heart of it, she had seen the Imperial Throne and Crown. While the face had been foggy in that vision, the intention had been clear.

Only darkness and death would follow. When she saw that vision in Mordelic, Sybil had known her place would need to be here beside Valen. The end for her had been set before she even laid eyes on her husband.

Still, Sybil had dared to hope that the vision had been wrong, that Valen could change, that he would change for her. A foolish wish from a child.

Sybil tenderly placed a trembling hand over the scars on her chest where he had mutilated her dragon tattoo, where he had tortured her, destroyed her heart and soul. Tears spilled down her cheeks, but she made no sound as she cried. Her breathing remained steady, like the calm in the eye of a storm.

Whatever ailment had nearly killed her had long since healed, but the scars over her heart would remain forever.

Aslyn had been right all along. She mistrusted Valen from the start, as Sybil should have done. And still, Sybil had pushed her away when Aslyn tired of hearing her endless chatter about how utterly perfect Valen was.

How blind she had been. How he had blinded her.

Aslyn hadn't returned since that day. Sybil had sent messages to her, unable to muster the courage to face her friend and admit her mistakes. The messages were always returned to her unopened with verbal apologies about how the princess would not receive her message. Sybil supposed she deserved it, but she still had wished her friend would forgive her.

Tears dripped from her chin onto her arm as she covered the scars beneath her dress. Sybil would never wear anything low cut again in her life. However long that life might be.

Valen came to Sybil far less often than he had before mutilating her flesh. Not that she minded. He ignored her completely, only to enter her room, her bed unexpected and uninvited. The moment he entered her bedchamber, Sybil told herself she wouldn't give him what he wanted. But he knew exactly how to draw her in so that she couldn't deny him even if she tried—a touch in the right place, the correct words whispered in her ear and she melted to his whims as if by some magic. Once satisfied, Valen left with no words of comfort or affection. He simply dressed and marched out.

Sybil understood what he endeavored. He needed an heir. But so far nothing had taken root within her and she knew he wouldn't be satisfied until she gave him a son. What would happen if she gave birth to a girl instead? There had never been a woman on the imperial seat. Would her daughter be sent away or killed? No, she couldn't allow herself to venture down that road. If she had a girl, she would find some way to hide her away.

How many past empresses strived to do the same? She thought miserably.

Sybil turned her face toward the open window, wishing the light outside would warm her skin. It never did. She didn't feel as cold as she once had, but there was still a chill she could never escape. A chill that grew worse around her husband. She closed her eyes, and the moment she did she saw Valen's face. Not the glorious look of bliss she craved. It was anger. Wrath. Hate. The look in his black eyes had been that of pure disgust as he gazed at her tattoo that day. She had nightmares about him slicing her flesh again, flaying her tattoo from her skin. Chanting and drawing dark creatures from the runes he carved into her flesh.

The day he carved into her flesh, Sybil had unlocked a secret. One she would never share with him. One she would take with her to the grave because it was the only way she could lash out in defiance—by denying him the information he needs to protect his own interests, his crown. A vision of light and darkness. Amber and sapphire. Great powers congregating and tearing Valen's army to shreds. Ancient power found and ancient power destroyed.

The end of the empire was her defiant little secret. Her hope. Her doom. And she welcomed it, because in the end justice would rise.

Then, she would finally smile again.

Aslyn paced her bedroom floor, finger absently tracing the handle of the knife tucked in her belt. After Marek left yesterday and she recovered herself, she fished out the knife Blackblade had given her in Stormvalor. A sedative, he had told her. She used it once, months ago, on a Black Guard. It had worked perfectly. If Marek returned, she wouldn't be helpless again.

In her other hand, Aslyn clutched the parchment she had copied in Valen's office nearly a week ago. Each day, she took time to study the runes. Each day, she grew more certain they were, in fact, the runes of Aethan's dragon tattoo—the same one she had memorized in that heated night of love and passion. Remembering that night renewed her yearning to see Aethan, to stand united with him against this tyranny.

But for now, Aslyn swallowed her broken-hearted need. How had Valen known about the tattoo and the runes in it? And what did he think they meant?

She chewed her lip as she paced, eyes glued to the parchment. If she could solve this first, maybe she could use it as leverage. What would be more valuable to Valen? Her marriage to Marek, or the truth of these runes?

Earlier in the day, she had tried once again to visit Sybil and been denied access. She worried for Aethan's sister. Lady Fia had told Valen that she was healing. Had something happened to Sybil, and how bad had it been?

Aslyn ceased pacing abruptly as her stomach dropped.

Aethan wasn't the only one with the tattoo. Sybil had one as well. Aslyn couldn't be sure if it was exactly the same, having only glimpsed the edge of it once or twice. But it was clearly very similar, if not the same. That was how Valen knew about the tattoo. He saw it on Sybil. This collection of runes had likely been burned into Valen's mind by this point, and he sought answers.

With hurried steps, Aslyn rushed to her desk and pulled out her quill and ink. If it took her the rest of the day, she would find out what his notes said, what the runes meant. She had learned some of this language from her language tutor. Now she would use that to the best of her ability to translate this ancient Vorovesti for answers. She had to find out before him.

Her quill made fierce strokes each time she thought she found the meaning for the archaic Vorovesti note. Sometimes she had to scratch it out in place of another word, but slowly, the notes came together. Aslyn sat back, frowning at the ancient Vorovesti translation. It made little sense to her. It spoke of the elves, how they had undermined his quest, how they taught the outlanders ancient runes even his texts could not translate.

It made no sense. Valen's notes made it sound as if *he* had been ruling during the War of Two Crowns. Did emperors somehow pass memories and knowledge down from one generation to the next?

Even more cryptic was the prophecy Aslyn had never heard or read in any text before.

Bloodlines thought buried shall stir once more,
When the half-breed heir reclaims their throne,
Eyes of light shall pierce through darkness,
Eyes of storms shall breech walls of stone.
The mighty shall falter, false thrones shall fall,
And justice shall rise with the blood of kings,
Bearing the weight of ages, to shatter your reign,
A legacy restored, for the rightful shall justice bring.
And then the storm will come for you.

The first line aligned with what Aslyn had been suspicious of for weeks now, ever since the artifact room. Bloodlines thought buried shall stir once more... like the lost Martnarving heir. Most of the rest made little sense to her except for the final line. She had heard something similar somewhere before. Using "you" in a prophecy like this felt very specific and targeted, like the curse belonged to one person in particular.

Could this prophecy be the secret to the fall of the imperial seat? *If so, I need to figure out who the half-breed heir is,* she thought. Aethan wasn't a half breed... unless he *was* descended from the Martnarving line. Then the blood of the elves flowed through his veins, even if diluted by time. It hardly made him a half-breed, but it was a mixed breed, for certain. And it explained his good looks and charisma, something stories claimed all elves had.

A legacy restored, the blood of kings... All the pieces came into focus, but they weren't quite in the right place.

I need more time. Unfortunately, time wasn't on Aslyn's side. But if she could find her way to Mordelic, perhaps she could find Lux Starkling and demand answers. He must know *something*. Then he could help her reunite with Aethan at last.

Aslyn knew of only one way out of this palace. Assuming she could, in fact, take that path.

I must try.

CHAPTER 28

Blissful Ignorance

Bast stepped through the narrow, cobblestone streets of Lemheller Gap. The city came alive with relentless revelry. Streamers of bright cloth hung between the narrow gaps between buildings, flickering in the lamplight. Laughter and music spilled from every tavern and alleyway. The people partied day and night, dancing through the streets, singing songs exalting their glorious emperor with slurred voices, and drinking until they collapsed in the arms of strangers. Alleyways became dens for sexual encounters, sometimes with more than one pair coupling at the same time. It was chaos—but joyous, unburdened by despair.

He didn't know what they were celebrating at first, nor did he much care. Snatches of conversation drifted through the air. Bits and pieces of drunken ramblings all led to the same conclusion.

A new emperor.

Valen had taken the throne from his father, Oxon. Whether by succession or force, Bast could only guess. It hardly mattered. The name of the man who ruled from the Imperial Seat meant little to him compared to what he had seen two nights past. Thousands of Black Guards marching through the pass. The memory lingered in his bones, an unshakable weight pressing against his chest. Something was coming.

No one else mentioned the massive army's movement, as if they hadn't even noticed. If he didn't know better, Bast would have believed Valen sent out the announcement to distract the people from what he was truly up to. He must have known the city would erupt into celebration and they would all be too drunk to pay attention to him. Ignorance could be bliss.

Bast did his best to cast off his worries and allow himself to melt into the festivities. A drink, at the very least, would dull the edges of his unease. After securing his sword and most of his weapons in his room—loath to leave his leather armor behind with the concealment it gave him, yet unwilling to risk wearing it around—Bast placed traps around the entrances to snare or kill intruders. Then he left, slipping into a nearby tavern.

The scent of spiced ale and hearty stew wrapped around him the moment he walked through the door. A barmaid shimmied through the crowd and pressed a foaming tankard into his hand before he even had to ask, winking as she moved on to another patron. He took a long drink. Lemheller Gap spiced ale had more of a bite than anywhere else in the five kingdoms. He wasn't sure how they distilled it to accomplish the feat, but he relished the burn all the way down his throat.

The room whirled with movement. Dancers swayed and spun to the frenzied tune of a fiddler in the corner. Men and women locked in heated games of dice, wagers made and lost with reckless abandon. Laughter exploded from a corner as a large man told a joke that the drunkards around him found hilarious.

Bast let himself fade into the background, observing, as always. He had spent years keeping to the shadows, gathering what he needed before moving on. Old habits were hard to break.

A group of men at a nearby table spoke in hushed but eager tones, their voices slurred with drink. All three wore the loyalist bands.

"Valen's taken the throne," one of them said. "Finally."

"Oxon should've been gone years ago. Bastard held on too long." The second man lifted his drink to his lips as he spoke.

"Means change is coming, aye?" another man asked, his voice a touch too loud compared to the rest of his group.

"Aye," the first man said, raising his tankard and sloshing spiced ale over the rim. "And gods know we need it."

Bast studied them for a moment before turning his attention elsewhere.

Change. The word left a bitter taste in his mouth. Change could mean salvation—or ruin. And while the rest of Lemheller Gap drowned themselves in celebration, he couldn't shake the feeling that whatever had left the Citadel that night ensured the latter. *Doesn't matter whose ass sits on the imperial throne*, he thought bitterly, *they're all the same. No change is coming. Only war.*

Still, he drank. After his third drink, Bast relaxed, allowing the music to wash over him. For a little while, he could be just another man in the crowd.

As the evening wore on, Bast made his way from one tavern to the next, enjoying a drink or two and listening to the chatter before moving on. He wasn't the only one partaking in the citywide tavern crawl. It seemed everyone who was old enough to hold a tankard in their hand had the same idea.

He danced with a few women in the street, allowed himself a laugh at jokes he heard here and there, and gave himself permission to let go of his burdens for the night. Everyone had to find some time to relax occasionally, and he justified his drinking, dancing, and occasional gambling as just what he needed.

As he clapped along to a rather talented fiddler at one of the countless taverns, Bast's gaze slid to the woman swaying to the beat as she approached him. He knew what she wanted before she even reached him and he downed the rest of his drink, barely finishing before she took his hand and pulled him into the throng of dancers. She spun into his arms, her body pressed deliciously close to his own.

Yes, delicious was the perfect word for this woman. Her dark hair clung to her neck with sweat as she moved in easy rhythm with him. They twisted, swayed, and spun together. And as the swell of the music shifted to something a little slower, her fingers teased at his neck, sliding into his hair. Bast's hands slid along her supple curves and she arched into him. Something about the way she gazed up at him through her lashes cut at something familiar. A moment he had before. Not in Lemheller Gap, but dancing in the street with different raven-haired beauty. The reminder of Aslyn unsettled Bast, but he didn't immediately pull away.

For a fleeting moment, he let himself indulge in the warmth of her touch, the rhythm of the dance, the illusion that he could lose himself in something simple. She smelled delicious—a blend of holiday spice and sweat. But as her fingers threaded into his hair along his neck, tracing seductively, Aslyn once more invaded his thoughts.

Irritated, he stepped back, offering the woman a fleeting smile before murmuring an excuse and retreating toward the bar. The music carried on.

The world spun in blissful ignorance, and he had allowed himself to get caught up in it while that blasted woman remained in the palace, invading his thoughts even from a distance. *Curse that woman.*

His dance partner followed him, undeterred by his retreat. As he leaned against the bar, nursing a fresh drink, she squeezed in beside him. Her fingers traced a slow, deliberate path along his arm.

"Running already?" she asked, her voice smooth as silk, laced with amusement.

Bast glanced at her, noting the mischievous glint in her dark eyes, the way her lips curled into a knowing smile.

He exhaled, shaking his head. "Not running. Just drinking."

She laughed, low and sultry, and leaned in close enough for him to catch the intoxicating scent of holiday spice, sweat, and something else—something dangerous. "Then let me join you," she said. She signaled for a drink, not bothering to look at him as she said, "Unless you're afraid of a little companionship?"

Bast hesitated, the ghost of Aslyn lingering in the back of his mind. But the woman's touch was real, her presence immediate, pulling him into the moment. For just one night, perhaps, he could let himself forget.

"I thought *you* might be," he retorted.

"With you?" Her dark eyes slid over him in a way that made it very clear how she hoped this would end. "Hardly."

He hummed deep in his throat. "Not subtle, are you?"

"Would you prefer me demure?"

The question gave him pause and he stared into his tankard as he mulled it over. "I'm not paying for it." He took a long, deep drink.

She snorted. "Charming. I should slap you for that."

His gaze darted to hers as she arched a brow at him. "What should I call you, then?" he asked.

"Azoria," she said, pressing closer.

Azoria. *Az.* Bast's jaw twitched. *This is a terrible idea. Walk away now.* But he didn't. He couldn't. Bast knocked back the rest of his drink, his head fuzzy from all he had consumed throughout the evening. Just enough to allow him to ignore that voice in his head telling him to go back to his room, alone, before he did something he might regret.

A knowing smirk played across her lips. "What would you like me to call you?"

He slammed the empty tankard on the bar and slid his arm around her waist. "Let's dance, Az."

Idiot.

He ignored the voice, allowing the bliss of ignorance to wash over him as the two of them moved together to fast songs, slow songs, and everything between. As their bodies pressed together, she hummed against him. He buried his face into her neck, inhaling the smell of her. His nose nuzzled against her ear, and he slid his fingers into her hair.

Not that he needed to encourage her. She seemed to understand, tilting her head to the side as his lips slid along her neck, blazing a trail along her throat, her jaw. Then he captured her lips. Or maybe she captured his. He didn't care. He allowed himself to let go, sliding his tongue along her lips. She parted slowly, teasing, drawing him in.

Azoria's hands moved down his chest, sending shudders of need through his body. Gods help him.

"Tell me to stop," he said between heated kisses, wanting her to stop him. *Needing* her to.

"No."

Bast groaned.

Azoria pulled away just enough to look into his eyes, and judging by her reaction, she must have seen the same desire mirrored in his as he saw in hers. "Shall we find somewhere a little more private?"

Bast couldn't even form a response as she stepped out of his arms, took his hand, and guided him through the packed common room and up the stairs. All the way up, his gaze fixed on the sway of her hips, on her luscious dark hair. "You have a room?" he asked.

This wasn't where he slept, and she seemed to know where she was going.

"I do."

They stopped outside a door, and she pulled him into a long, hard kiss. He pressed her back against the door, pinning her beneath him. The little gasp of delight she breathed into him only fueled his aching need.

Azoria nudged him back, reaching between her breasts with two fingers. He wanted to reach in there instead. She produced a key on a chain linked around her neck and turned to unlock the door. Bast grabbed her hips, pressing against her. She ground against him as she opened the door, and he groaned in pleasure.

The moment they were both through the door, he kicked it shut, stripping out of his long coat and black shirt as her hands worked frantically to untie his pants. Their lips devoured with insatiable hunger.

Bast knew the moment he pinned her to the closed door and buried himself in her that he would regret this in the morning. Not because he felt beholden to Aslyn, but because he was doing this for all the wrong reasons. Azoria reminded him just enough of Aslyn that, in his somewhat intoxicated state, he could convince himself that she *was* Aslyn.

They stumbled across the room and fell onto the bed in a frenzy of heat. Months of pent-up need poured out of him. She made a good enough companion, touching him and grinding against him and pulling on him like a wild thing. He wrapped her silken hair around his hand, reveling in the feel of her hair between his fingers. Heat built to glorious levels as he felt himself reaching closer and close to the edge. All he saw was the supple curves and dark hair.

Fuck. Bast sank onto his heels on the bed, his head tipped back as he came down from the high. The alcohol had worn off in the final throes of passion. With a groan of irritation with himself, Bast slid his hands up over his face and wrapped them around his head. The instant shame and self-loathing created a bottomless pit in his stomach. No. This wasn't fair. Aslyn hated him. Why should he feel like this? He had every right to do whatever he wanted with whomever he chose. But telling himself that only turned that pit into a yawning chasm.

Azoria kissed her way up his chest slowly. "So many scars," she murmured between kisses.

Bast wanted to push her off. He wanted to throw her on her back and bury his face between her legs. The two conflicting needs rendered him immobile as her lips reached his neck, her fingers tracing each scar on his chest slowly.

"That was much more fun than I anticipated," she breathed against his skin.

Bast tensed.

Her lips grazed his ear and his arms fell around her, sliding along her bare back.

"Would it be too awkward of me to ask you to be my companion for the event, or have you come here to break up the wedding?" she murmured in his ear.

A shock raced down his spine, electrifying that sick feeling in his gut. "Wedding?"

She released a sultry laugh that made his body ache for more even though his mind told him to stop. Azoria pulled back, smiling as her hands slid down his bare chest.

"I assumed that was why you were here, Zayne," she said. "But I figured I would take a chance that you might need a companion for Princess Aslyn's wedding to Marek Bloodstone."

Bast's heart stuttered to a halt. The pieces of the conversation from the last few minutes finally penetrated his thick skull. Zayne. She called him Zayne. He had been too distracted by her mouth and hands to notice immediately.

Bast pushed her away and climbed off the bed. "I don't know what you're talking about." He scavenged for his clothes, hastily pulling his pants up, then tugging his black shirt over his head.

"Denial. Alright. Then you *are* here to break up the wedding." Azoria crawled to the edge of the bed and sank back on her heels, legs spread just enough to be enticing. Bast averted his gaze.

"I don't think so," he grumbled.

"Then why are you in such a rush to get out of here?"

Bast paused as he laced up his boots, meeting her gaze.

"Let's not play games. Why else would you be in Lemheller Gap?" Azoria asked. "Business?"

He grimaced and resumed tying his boots. "Why are *you* here?"

"I own half the inns in this city," Azoria said. "Several of which you have rented rooms at recently. Why the constant movement?"

Bast paused, glancing around the room. He took notice of it for the first time now that he wasn't driven by blind lust. Fine furniture. Oversized bed. Rich decorations. He mentally cursed himself. This was an innkeeper's room. And a nice one, at that. And Azoria had been watching him for a while now, or at least found a way to connect his trail despite the different names he used. *Fuck, I'm in serious trouble.* Should he kill her? Would she tell the emperor?

"We danced in Stormvalor," she said. "I assumed you remembered me, but you really don't, do you? You were too blinded by the princess like all the other ambitious men there."

Fuck. Fuck! Bast slipped on his coat. His cover was completely blown.

"You have me mistaken for someone else. I came here because I heard there might be a transition of the imperial seat and knew this was the best place to add some coins to my purse."

She smirked and shook her head, sliding off the bed and swaying those fantastic hips as she approached him. "No. I would never forget this face." Her hand slid along his cheek. "No woman would."

Bast smacked her hand away. "Don't touch me. Don't follow me."

Azoria scoffed, hands on her hips. "After what you just did to me—"

"With you," he corrected. He wasn't sure why, but he felt like it was a line that needed to be clearly drawn.

"You're just going to leave like that was nothing?"

"Yes." Bast wrenched the door open. She tried to stop him, but he shook her off, jerking the door closed behind him. She couldn't exactly run after him nude, but he didn't bother slowing down to find out as he rushed down the steps, through the crowd, and out the front door.

Aslyn's wedding was in two days...

To Marek Bloodstone.

Bast growled as he stomped back to his inn—praying it wasn't one Azoria owned. Curse that fucking princess! He warned her. Now he would have to find a way into the palace to save her ass before that jerk had his way with her. Just thinking about Marek forcing her to do anything with him made Bast's blood boil.

When he at last reached his room and slammed the door closed, Bast threw his cloak on the ground with a howl of rage. Why couldn't he escape Aslyn?

Because you bound yourself to her, you fucking idiot.

Bast had been perfectly happy for a little while tonight, living in blissful ignorance. But now his cover was blown. Azoria knew he had been around the city for a while. She recognized him from Stormvalor. Who else would? Who else had already? Did the Bloodstone's already know he was in town? No. They couldn't know. They were looking for Blackblade and there was a chance Marek would make the connection if he knew Zayne Khrahar was in town.

Bast hurried around his room to collect his personal effects. He needed to get Aslyn and get out of Lemheller Gap before anyone tracked him down.

Searing, gut-wrenching agony ripped through him, sudden and unrelenting. The familiar pain of the blood oath. The warning that he had strayed too far from Aslyn—but this time, it was tenfold worse. His veins blazed molten fire, burning from the inside out. His breath caught in his throat. His vision blurred.

Bast's knees buckled and he hit the floor with a dull thud. The world narrowed to pure, blinding pain. His pulse pounded in his skull. Every heartbeat was like a hammer driving deeper into his bones. He tried to move, to push himself up, but his limbs were leaden, trembling uselessly beneath him.

Darkness swam at the edges of his sight. He clenched his teeth, a strangled groan escaping him as the pain refused to relent. The oath tethered him to Aslyn, and now it was as though it sought to punish him for daring to forget, daring to give in, even for a moment. But it couldn't result from what he had done tonight.

It was Aslyn. It had to be her.

The world spun violently before tipping into nothingness.

CHAPTER 29

Nothing Good Happens in the Dark

Aslyn had no intention of waiting two days to try and escape this horrible marriage. She would leave now. But she needed a little help from an unsuspecting accomplice.

The idea had struck her as she mulled over the translated notes she copied from Valen's office. Only one person had his favor and, to some degree at least, his trust. And that person had the ability to open portals, somehow. Aslyn suspected Lady Fia preferred making her visits abroad at night, when fewer would be awake to watch her appear from nowhere.

Aslyn admitted the idea hadn't been her brightest, but currently, it was her only one. Everything else she had tried over the past month had failed. Time wasn't her ally, and if this plan failed, Aslyn wouldn't have another opportunity to escape.

After dinner, Aslyn kept a careful eye on Lady Fia's movements around the palace. She didn't know if the other woman would even travel anywhere, but Valen seemed to have numerous plans in motion. Aslyn hoped that meant Lady Fia would as well. Aslyn didn't even care where she ended up. Anywhere was better than here.

Lady Fia entered a room Aslyn remembered as always having a locked door. Curious, she tiptoed closer and listened first.

"Everything is ready, Mistress," a man said. The strange title he gave Lady Fia confused Aslyn, but she tried to keep her focus on the conversation.

"Yes, the legions are all in position and awaiting your signal," another man said. "The emperor has given permission to strike as soon as you wish."

"Wonderful." Lady Fia sighed and Aslyn could practically picture the satisfaction on her face. "It will be tonight. I need an hour... two. Then I will have word sent to the guards inside the walls."

Walls. So whatever they plotted, it had to be a city. Arithia didn't have walls. The mountains and ocean provided all the walls her beautiful city ever needed. But from what Aslyn could recall, plenty of towns and cities across the five kingdoms were surrounded by walls. If there were guards... that narrowed the list a little. Stormvalor, Port Verix, Barden, Bleakburn, Elysia.

Mordelic.

Aslyn's heart stopped. Lady Fia had visited Mordelic once before. Was Aethan there now, or still searching for her father? She bit her lip as she hoped, prayed, Lady Fia would visit Mordelic again, even if the city was about to be plunged into battle. Perhaps Aslyn could slip in without notice and find someone to warn.

I have to try. Aethan would do it for me. I must do it for him.

"Gentlemen, this is only the beginning," Lady Fia declared. "Our glory will rise at last and the world will bow at my feet." *Her* feet? Was she working to undermine Valen's plans, his rule? The very notion intrigued Aslyn. The right hand feeds, but can choke just as easily.

"Flame be with you, Mistress," both men responded.

Someone snapped their fingers. "Flame is always with me," Lady Fia purred.

Feet shuffled, and Aslyn quickly darted away from the door, slipping through an open one across the hall. When the footsteps faded into the distance, she crept back toward the other door again. She peered in just in time to watch Lady Fia open another one of her portals. But unlike the last, this one led to a chamber indoors.

As Lady Fia stepped through and made her way across the chamber on the other side, Aslyn hustled across the room and peered through the portal just as Lady Fia leaned against a doorway to another chamber beyond.

Worried that the portal would close, Aslyn held her breath as she stepped through, then ducked behind a nearby sofa. The portal closed so close on her heels it trimmed the hem of her gown. That had been too close. Pain pulsed in her palm, clenching her insides into a fist. She hesitated, getting control as best she could.

"Well, look at you," Lady Fia cooed, and Aslyn tensed, expecting the woman to round the furniture and catch her any second, distracted by the pain.

Instead, that familiar male voice spoke from the other room. "If I had known you were coming, I would have been better prepared." Aslyn's heartbeat thumped loudly in her ears as she strained to listen for signs of trouble, rubbing her hand against her aching chest. She heard bare feet against the floor in the other room. "Or at least decently indecent," he added, closer this time.

"That certainly would have been delectable," Lady Fia purred.

This room, from what she could see, came from wealth. Not as rich as a palace, but not without grandeur. A noble estate, for certain. But whose?

A door about ten feet to Aslyn's left likely led out of this room, but between Aslyn and that door were also ten feet of open floor.

Please let them move into the other room, Aslyn thought.

She held her breath, then dared a glance around the back of the sofa. Her own pain dulled as a hard *thump-thump* pounded in her ears. Lady Fia's hands moved down over the expanse of his chest. Aslyn instantly recognized his face.

Trystain.

His sandy hair was tousled, and he wore only sleeping pants, leaving his muscled chest exposed for Lady Fia's obviously familiar touch.

"You said when next I saw you, it would be time," Trystain said. "I can't say I'm not relieved. Gannon and Iskra have been sniffing around a lot lately."

Aslyn dipped back around the sofa, covering her mouth and squeezing her eyes shut to block out the betrayal, but it just burned into her heart. Aethan would be devastated.

In Stormvalor, Aethan thought Trystain took the loss of Sybil too casually. He expressed his worry to her and even wondered if that nonchalance was an act. Now the truth became clear to Aslyn. He had let go of Sybil without a fight because he found what he likely thought was an upgrade. Sybil was a beauty, but even Aslyn admitted Lady Fia was gorgeous enough to draw anyone's attention. In fact, of all the men she had seen around Lady Fia, Valen was the only who seemed able to ignore her obvious appeal.

"You won't need to worry about that now," Lady Fia said. "But there has been a slight change of plans."

Trystain made a sound that seemed guarded. "This has taken forever to get into motion. I can't just change things now. And you gave me a vow."

Lady Fia tsked. "I would think you wouldn't doubt me any longer. You will get what you were promised... and then some." The allure in those last three words made it clear to Aslyn that the extra would come from Lady Fia herself.

"So what has changed? Are the men in position?"

"As of about an hour past full dark."

"And you're certain they can't be spotted by the guards in the watchtowers?" Trystain sounded doubtful, worried.

Lady Fia laughed lightly. "Not a chance. Not until it's too late. Not even the moon shines in the darkness tonight. It's pitch black. The change is that the emperor now requires Lux Starkling. Preferably alive."

Trystain's laugh sounded disbelieving in Aslyn's ears. "There is no way he will allow himself to be taken alive."

Aslyn's heart sank even as the endless pain twisting her insides didn't relent. The emperor wanted Aethan's father alive. That couldn't possibly lead to anything good. Worse, Aethan's best friend betrayed his family. His people. An attack was coming to Mordelic tonight, led by Trystain. What did he stand to gain from this? There was no way the Vorovesti king would allow Trystain to live once he learned the truth!

Another truth hit her square in the chest. One she didn't want to believe but somehow knew deep in her bones. *"No one cares who sits on the throne as long as they have food in their bellies and a roof over their heads."*

King Orrin wouldn't survive the attack. Aslyn had to get out of there to warn someone, but until the traitors entered the other room, she didn't dare move from her hiding place.

"It's not negotiable, my love."

Aslyn nearly gagged. *My love? Seriously?* Trystain couldn't honestly believe Lady Fia loved him. She was using him to do the emperor's bidding and when they had what they wanted, she would discard him. How did he not see that? Or did he just not care? Aslyn had thought him smart and loyal in Stormvalor. Had her assessment of him been all wrong?

"Fine," Trystain sighed. "I will make sure he is taken alive. How long do we have?"

"I told them to give me two hours," Lady Fia replied.

"That's it? It only gives us an hour to ourselves before we need to get everyone in place."

"You can't afford to expend all your energy before the fun begins." A beat of silence, then, "And by dawn a new day will rise in Vorovesti."

"Well then, my wicked queen," Trystain said with a grunt. "Better not waste another second."

I'm going to be sick, Aslyn thought miserably. And why did he call her his wicked queen? Lady Fia wasn't a queen. She was nothing more than the emperor's right hand.

After a minute, trembling and in pain all over, Aslyn dared to peek, only to spot them heading into the bedroom, much to her relief. Aslyn nearly released a breath of relief before stopping herself. It might give her away and she needed to sneak out.

Counting off the seconds for a full minute to pass, Aslyn waited. It didn't take that long to deduce what happened in the next room. She seized the opportunity and crouched, half crawling ten feet to the door. When she reached the door, Aslyn checked over her shoulder to make sure they hadn't noticed her, then she opened the door quietly, just enough to slip through, before closing it just as quietly behind her.

Once in the hallway, Aslyn stood and surveyed her surroundings. Her bones ached, pulling her toward... something.

She was completely exposed to the entryway below. Aslyn edged forward cautiously, resting her hands on the carved stone railing as she peered down at the grand entryway. The only light came from a few lamps below. The light cast pale beams across the polished marble floor, half illuminating the sweeping staircase on either side. Each spiraled downward in elegant curves, their bannisters adorned with intricate carvings of twisting vines and mythical beasts.

She had little time before someone might stir and find her wandering their halls. To her left, a long hallway stretched along the overlook, its evenly spaced columns breaking the view of the doors beyond. Another similar hall lay to her right, shadowed and still. The silence was thick, broken only by the occasional shift of a guard's boots against stone. Aslyn couldn't tell where those guards were stationed, but she was certain that they wouldn't take kindly to a stranger prowling their halls.

The cut from the blood oath burned painfully in her hand, but she gritted her teeth and did her best to ignore it. But she couldn't completely ignore the fire in her veins. That was a problem for later, once she found a way out of this estate. She had to find her way to the palace to warn King Orrin before it was too late, and she was aware of how long she had. One hour to allow them to prepare. Two hours until the attack began. And if she saved him, maybe he could help save her, one monarch to another.

Aslyn exhaled slowly, scanning for movement. The stairs were wide open and would leave her exposed, but she couldn't see any other way out. The servants' corridors would be safer, but she had no idea where they might be found in this place. At least the door was straight ahead. If she could get down and across the entryway, maybe she could slip out into the night unnoticed.

Her pulse quickened. If she wanted to slip past unnoticed, she would need to be swift—and silent. Aslyn drew a slow, steady breath and slipped toward the right staircase. It offered her a fraction more shadow to work with.

She kept one hand lightly on the banister, her fingers tracing the smooth stone as she moved. Halfway down, she froze. A faint shuffle of boots echoed from the hallway above. A guard? A restless resident? She didn't dare turn to check. Instead, she pressed herself close to the banister, body angled to the deepest part of the staircase's shadow. The noise faded after a moment.

Aslyn resumed her descent, breath slow and measured. The entryway loomed before her, vast and empty. A grand chandelier hung overhead, its many crystals dimmed for the night. The double doors leading outside stood just ahead, locked or guarded, most likely. If she stepped out that door she would likely find at least a couple guards on duty. Even if they were slacking in their midnight duties, she couldn't afford the risk.

Aslyn reached the final step and paused, hunched lower to make herself smaller as she listened. A clock from another room on the first floor ticked loudly. No voices. No footsteps. Where had the guards moved off to? She swore she heard them before.

As Aslyn's gaze swept the entryway to guess at the best course of action, her eyes fell on a small, nondescript door tucked along the far wall. A less conspicuous exit that led to the courtyard. The servant door. It would be barred from the inside, but a simple latch—far easier to undo than the heavy locks on the main doors.

Keeping low, she moved swiftly across the marble. The servant's door was just within reach. Her fingers found the bolt—cool iron, smooth from years of use. Carefully, she slid it back, unlocking the door. It gave the softest of grinding against the frame as it pulled back. Aslyn winced, once more surveying her surroundings. She was out in the open here. If someone walked in, they would catch her without a doubt. She had to get out.

A breath, then another. Her lungs hurt like never before. Aslyn eased the door open just wide enough to peek out. As she suspected, two guards were posted outside the main door. Both men seemed lax in their duties, practically falling asleep at their posts. Aslyn slipped out as silently as possible.

Warm summer air brushed against her skin, and she stepped outside, pressing the door closed behind her with aching slowness until it latched once more.

She was out. Now all she had to do was find her way off the grounds without being spotted.

The burning in her palm spread through her fingers and into her wrist. That crushing, invisible force pulled at her again. Aslyn winced, rolling her wrist as if that might ease her pain. It did no good.

Choosing a circuitous route around the shadows of the courtyard, Aslyn moved in the opposite direction of the front doors. She wasn't foolish enough to think that those were the only two men on duty. In fact, it was safest to assume that, if the entire Cyrus family was in on the plot, their estate would be heavily guarded. Especially tonight. She needed to find a less conspicuous exit. Marching out the front gate wouldn't be an option.

As she made her way through the shadows, Aslyn sought an exit. Servants wouldn't use the main gate. They would have their own exit. If she could find it, she could slip out without notice. Guards might even think her a servant out on a late-night run for the lord or lady of the house.

More than once as she examined the wall around the estate grounds, Aslyn had to duck behind trees or shrubs to avoid detection from a passing pair of guards. Yes, they had increased their security, which had to mean Trystain wasn't acting alone. Aslyn would be sure King Orrin knew that, as well.

Perhaps she should find the Starkling estate instead of heading straight to the palace. Lord Starkling would need warning, too. For some reason the emperor wanted him taken alive. He was close to the king, so it would be easier to get King Orrin to listen to her if she had an ally. And to be honest, a deep part of her heart hoped to find Aethan there, too.

Around the back of the estate, Aslyn spotted the stable and knew she had to be close to a secondary exit. With a quick glance in either direction around the stable grazing grounds, Aslyn rushed across the open space.

A wall of flame burst up across her path, forcing Aslyn to skid to a stop to avoid catching fire. The hem of her dress swirled around her legs, catching on the flames. Aslyn quickly stumbled backward and patted the fire out before it burned her skirt off.

"What a clever girl you are."

CHAPTER 30

Shattered Hopes

Aslyn turned slowly at the sound of Lady Fia's mocking voice, pulling her sedative dagger from her belt. She wouldn't go down without a fight.

Lady Fia strolled across the grazing grounds as if crossing her own throne room. "You followed me here, which I assume means you also heard my conversation. I thought I sensed something in that room."

Aslyn hated how she trembled. Part of it was the pain in her body, but mostly it was fear. Fear of returning to Valen... to Marek.

To strike at Lady Fia, the other woman had to get within arm's reach. Her eyes darted around, searching for any means of escape. She couldn't go backward. Not with that wall of flame at her back.

On a balcony above, Trystain stared out at Aslyn, hands wrapped around the stone rail in nothing but his pants. Even from a distance, Aslyn could see the irritation on his face. Was he angry that Aslyn had caught him committing treason against his king, or that she had interrupted his time alone with Lady Fia? Aslyn no longer cared what he thought of her. He had no leg to stand on in an argument about right and wrong. His opinion held no weight.

Lady Fia strolled closer. Aslyn reversed her grip on the knife at her side like Blackblade showed her. Just a little closer, and she could strike. Then she would run and pray she found a way out before the guards caught her.

Another step. Another.

"I can't wait to throw you at his feet and see what he does to you," Lady Fia purred.

There! Aslyn lunged, aiming for Lady Fia's obnoxiously beautiful face, but any part of her skin would do.

Lady Fia dodged back. The blade grazed her cheek. She spun, grabbing Aslyn's arm and twisting it in the process. Heat burned at her wrist and she dropped the knife with a cry. It was all Aslyn could do to keep the pain at bay.

Lady Fia used Aslyn's arm to shove her to her knees, then spun around behind her, grabbing a fistful of hair. Every movement was faster than Aslyn could keep track of. Why hadn't the sedative taken root yet?

With a flick of her wrist, Lady Fia opened one of her portals. Aslyn instantly recognized those oppressive walls on the other side.

She reached back, pulling at Lady Fia's hand desperately as pain brought tears to her eyes. "No. Please."

"Pitiful creature," Lady Fia spat. "You need a lot more than a minor sedative to stop me." She dragged Aslyn toward the portal by her hair.

Aslyn struggled, but she couldn't stop the inevitable half stumble, half crawl forward. Tears spilled down her cheeks. Feebly, she tried reaching for her knife, but Lady Fia yanked at her hair and she yelped. No one had ever handled her in such a manner. Not even Marek in his darkest moments. Not even Valen when he pinned her to the wall. Lady Fia dragged her kicking and screaming without horrible coldness.

The open portal called to Aslyn's palm as the two women wrestled through. Aslyn gave in to her tears. Not only had she failed to escape, but now her only weapon against Marek had been lost.

It wasn't until Lady Fia threw her on the cold, hard floor at Valen's feet that Aslyn realized she was in the emperor's office.

"Keep this one locked away," Lady Fia snapped. "She had the guts to follow me to Mordelic as if she thought I wouldn't sense something. I caught her trying to escape the Cyrus grounds."

Aslyn pushed herself into a sitting position, arms trembling violently as they held her up. Her scalp hurt terribly, but the other pains vanished instantly.

Blackblade had to be close. Could he sense her danger? Would he even bother coming to help after all she had said and done to him?

Valen peered at Aslyn over steepled fingers from the other side of his desk. "I warned you to close those portals faster. She followed you once before."

Aslyn scrubbed the tears from her face. *Stop crying like a child! Pull yourself together and outsmart them.* If she couldn't, Aslyn knew she would either die, or worse end up locked in her rooms until the wedding, perhaps even after, a brood mare to Marek's urges. Her lip trembled and she hated herself for it, but at least the tears had stopped.

"I told you to lock her up before," Lady Fia snapped back. "Deal with her. I have work to do."

Before Valen replied, Lady Fia reopened her portal to Trystain's family estate. Aslyn scrambled toward it, desperate to escape.

Valen simply chuckled lowly at her efforts. The portal snapped shut in her face. Aslyn's heart sank. She turned furious eyes to the emperor.

"What do you have to gain by killing one royal family while tearing another apart?" Aslyn snapped, pulling her courage together as best she could despite the tremble in her body. "You rip my family apart and sell me off in marriage and for what? So you can put *Marek* on the Golden Throne?"

Valen tapped his fingers together as he studied her. His silent assessment unnerved her. Finally, he said, "You truly are stubborn and blind. If you think I want that idiot on any throne, you aren't nearly as smart as I gave you credit for."

Aslyn slowly pushed herself to her feet, gripping the back on a chair to help stabilize her until her legs stopped shaking. "They why force me to do this?"

Valen rolled his eyes as if bored with her. "If you are looking for a villainous monologue, you won't get one from me. I've been doing this far longer than you."

Aslyn gritted her teeth. All her pain and humiliation transformed into molten rage. "I know what scares you most."

"I doubt it."

"The prophecy."

Valen paused, then narrowed his eyes. "You think I buy into fanatic beliefs? You get dumber by the second."

Aslyn wanted to lash out at him. She wasn't dumb. And she had one more card to play. Better to die now than be forced to marry Marek. And if this pushed his hand, all the better. She lifted her chin and straightened her spine.

"No. Not fanatic beliefs like those Elysia waves around like banners." Aslyn shook her head. "The oncoming storm. Buried bloodlines and half-breed heirs. The true heir who will rise to shatter your reign." A hint of satisfaction played on Aslyn's lips as Valen's eyes widened ever so slightly. Yes, she rattled him. "You fear the Starklings." She leaned forward. "You fear *Aethan*."

Valen's hands clenched into fists as he lowered them to his desktop. His arms trembled as every muscle in his body seemed to tighten. Then he smiled in a way that made chills dance along her skin. The smile spread into something wicked. Aslyn straightened again, uncertain what caused this reaction. She had been so certain she had struck a chord.

"Aethan Starkling is dead."

The world dropped out from beneath Aslyn. No. It couldn't be true. Wouldn't she have heard the news? Aslyn didn't even realize she moved until she seated herself in the chair, unable to trust her legs to hold her up a moment longer.

"No."

"Yes. Would you like to know how it happened?"

Aslyn couldn't respond. All she could do was sit in stunned shock. Aethan couldn't be dead. She would *know* somehow, wouldn't she?

"He was tried and executed for treason," Valen continued. Each word that spilled from his lips felt more and more insane.

"Lies," she breathed. *Treason? Aethan? Never.*

"The evidence against him was irrefutable."

Aslyn shook her head, denying it all because her heart couldn't take it if that were true. The evidence was fabricated. It had to have been. "You set him up because you wanted him dead."

Valen leaned back in his highback chair, looking immensely proud of himself, utterly satisfied. "Only because he was a nuisance getting in the way of my plans. But it wasn't me who tried and killed him." He smirked. "It was your brother."

"I don't want you dead, but your brother does. He wants your crown." Blackblade had tried to warn her. Repeatedly. *"Compare the letters, Aslyn."*

It couldn't be true. Dorin. Her sweet little brother, so passionate. So loving. He had always been her closest companion. She trusted him like she hadn't trusted anyone until Aethan. And he was responsible for killing the man she loved? She wanted to scream. She wanted to cry. But for the moment, she needed to keep herself together, even if she felt like she was falling off a cliff with no one to catch her plummeting toward the bitter end.

Aslyn closed her eyes to fight off the tears, swallowing the sorrow climbing up her throat, suffocating her. She tried to recall the last thing Dorin said to her before she left Arithia. *"I'll miss you. I love you."* And she could see it. That sorrow hiding behind his eyes. Did he know she wouldn't return even then? Could what Valen and Blackblade said be true?

Aslyn took a deep breath just to make sure she could still breathe, then opened her eyes slowly, meeting Valen's gaze. "What treason was Aethan accused of?"

"It was quite an extensive list." Valen shuffled through a stack of papers on his desk—in that box she had inspected barely over a week ago—then he pulled one out and passed it to Aslyn across the desk.

With trembling fingers, she accepted the paper and her heart sank at the sight of the royal rose seal beside Dorin's signature. Aslyn scanned the list, and her stomach dropped further with each item. It couldn't be true. Aethan certainly hadn't manipulated her. If anything, *she* manipulated *him* to get what she wanted. But the financial trail...

The final, crushing blow hit her as her eyes stopped on one of the charges on the list. One that threatened to rip her open. It took every ounce of her determination not to break down in front of Valen. She refused to break down in front of him, knowing it was exactly what he wanted.

"My father is dead?" she whispered.

Valen said nothing. He didn't confirm it. He also didn't deny it.

Aslyn's entire world had been turned upside down—by her brother. Dorin betrayed her, just as Blackblade warned her would happen and she had been too stubborn, too sure of her brother's heart to listen. Aethan was dead, the only man she had ever dared give her heart to. Her father as well.

Keep your head up, Aslyn, she chided. But it was hard. So hard to hold herself together in front of Valen when inside every part of her fractured. Grief clawed its way up her throat, but she swallowed it down. She just had to make it through this meeting. Then she could fall apart.

Another piece of the evidence against Aethan made no sense. If he allegedly hired Blackblade to kill Ned Corinth and steal the Jewel of Arithia from her, why did Blackblade insist it was her brother?

The truth, Aslyn realized, was that Valen didn't know that she knew Blackblade, that the assassin had sworn a blood oath to her. Her mind raced through the evidence, through conversations she had with Aethan and Blackblade, and neither seemed to be connected to the other. *"He wants your crown,"* Blackblade had told her of Dorin, not Aethan. She hadn't believed him, because why would she ever believe an assassin over her own brother?

Aslyn's gaze dropped once more to Dorin's signature and what little air remained in her lungs escaped, leaving her breathless.

King Dorin Kiernan

Aslyn dropped the paper onto the desk from numb fingers, too stunned to move. Dorin wouldn't call himself king while he knew she still lived. Unless Blackblade had been telling her the truth all along. He had wanted her to compare those other letters to come to the conclusion for herself. But now it stared back at her.

King Dorin Kiernan

"I hope you see now that marrying Marek Bloodstone is your best way forward," Valen said, sounding far too pleased with himself. "Your lover is dead. Your crown belongs to your brother. As I see it, Bloodstone is the best you can hope for. And you will be protected and well cared for. As long as you do your duty in the marriage bed."

No. No, this couldn't really be happening. The people wouldn't accept Dorin as king while she still lived, would they? Didn't the nobles fight for her at all? Had everyone abandoned her?

Aslyn couldn't move.

The weight of the heartbreak became an aching thing that pressed against her ribs as if her own body were caving in under the grief. Aslyn had known pain before—cuts and bruises bled and healed with time—but this was different. This was the kind of hurt that didn't mend, the kind that settled into the marrow and never left. The kind that irrevocably changed her, breaking her world into millions of pieces, never to be whole again. And then despair swept in.

What am I even fighting for?

They had all turned against her. Everyone she had trusted. Everyone she had once clung to. It was an axe to her heart of glass, shattering it irrevocably. The people she would have bled for, people she risked her life—her *future*—to protect had cast her aside like she was nothing in favor of her brother.

Her mind raced trying to make sense of it, but her thoughts were so fragmented she couldn't piece them together. Had she been blind all along? Had their smiles always been hollow, their words laced with falsehoods? Or had she simply not been *enough*—not worthy of their loyalty, their love?

She wanted to scream, to rage, to demand why. But the words choked in her throat, drowned beneath the crushing weight of betrayal... and loss.

Instead, she sat in the wreckage of what had once been her world, impossibly broken. Aslyn would never, could never, be the same again.

Lost in her shock and grief, Aslyn didn't notice when Black Guards escorted her back to her room. She hardly even registered the click of the bolt sliding into place.

Aslyn was numb, as if her heart had been so shattered by this news only a hollow shell of her remained. Tears rolled unchecked down her cheeks, but she didn't make a sound. Instead, she moved without thinking, digging through the drawer of the desk for the letters she had buried beneath everything else. At last, she retrieved them and gazed at the seal of the Novavito royal seat—the rose. Both seals were broken. Both letters had been read before, she knew.

With trembling fingers, Aslyn opened each and set them side by side. The first was the letter her mother received in Stormvalor, explaining the situation and what had happened to their father, signed "Your Loving Son, Prince Dorin Kiernan".

Loving son... What a joke. A lump swelled in her throat as her gaze darted to the second letter as tears blurred her vision.

The second letter was much shorter than the first.

I grow impatient. Finish the job.

Blackblade had been after the Jewel of Arithia for Dorin, because it belonged to the heir and Dorin wanted to use it to further validate his claim. Maybe Dorin thought Blackblade would kill her and save him from further trouble. Maybe Blackblade had actually considered killing her.

Everything—*everything*—she thought she knew had broken. Blackblade had used her, lied to her, considered killing her. For some reason, the fact that he considered killing her hurt far worse than the other crimes he committed against her. And she gave it to him. She *gave* him the Jewel of Arithia, and he didn't run back to Dorin to collect his dues.

He gave her a blood oath and followed her here... to the most dangerous place in the realm. Why?

If Javon worked with her brother... He was the chief financial advisor to the crown. He could have planted the records used against Aethan in his trial. No one would ever suspect them of framing Aethan. They would follow the paper trail right to him.

And she had sent him right into their arms—right to his death.

In a fit of grief, Aslyn snatched the letters in her fists and threw them into the hearth fire.

Her parents were dead.

Aethan was dead.

Her people had turned their backs on her.

Her brother had betrayed her in the worst possible way.

Blackblade abandoned her in this cold, dark place.

A sob clawed its way up her throat as she stumbled toward her bedroom. The sob turned into a wail. Aslyn fell to her knees as the numbness melted away and the grief hit her square in the heart. A scream ripped from her lungs, taking everything. Every bit of air, every hope and dream, everyone she loved. She clutched her skirt in her fists as if trying to hold on to the world.

"Make the best choice for the future of Novavito." Those were her father's last words to her and Aslyn sobbed, because how could she possibly do that now? *I've failed him completely. I'm sorry, father.*

Aslyn clawed her way into her bed, curling up tight beneath the blankets as she cried. Her body trembled and her skin turned cold.

"I am offering you my heart, my loyalty, and my love, should you find me worthy of it." Aethan's promises, his proposal, his fierce love haunted her. It filled her with pain the likes of which she was sure she would not survive.

"If you truly find me so worthy, let me prove myself once more." Everything inside of her hurt. Her lungs couldn't draw breath fast enough.

I did this to him. I sent him to Arithia to rescue my father. He would still be alive were it not for that promise, were it not for me.

Aslyn squeezed her eyes shut, but all she saw was Aethan. The way he looked at her like nothing else in the world existed. How his pale blond hair had curled around his forehead to make those beautiful blue eyes shine. The way he had touched her, held her, kissed her, worshipped her.

You will always be my king without a crown.

Aslyn clung to those memories of him like the most precious thing in the world. She stored each and every one of them tenderly in her memory, the pieces of him she needed and could never have again. The pieces of him she would never let go.

And she wept until the tide of exhaustion pulled her under.

CHAPTER 31

Flotsam and Bone on Black Sand

A rumble slowly grew to a crescendo, followed by the rhythmic *whoosh-slap*. The earth shifted with a tide of warmth before receding back into itself. Then the pattern repeated. Each surge pushed him through the lukewarm, salt-laden water until he lay sprawled on the wet sand like flotsam.

Consciousness hovered just beyond reach. Sounds of crashing waves lulled him with a dull, disorienting hum. His fingers twitched, digging into the coarse, damp grains beneath him, anchoring him to a world he could barely grasp. His mind drifted between wakefulness and darkness, the world around him a blur of crashing surf. Shadows pulled at the edges of his mind, and the shore, though solid beneath him, felt like a fleeting, fragile refuge.

His clothes clung to him like a second skin, heavy with sand and the ocean's weight. Saltwater burned in his lungs as he coughed weakly, vomiting the briny water into the sand. The taste of blood lingered on his tongue as his chest heaved with shallow, labored breaths.

Lukewarm water once more lapped against his body before retreating with the tide, but he remained still, too weary to move, barely aware that he was alive.

He dug his fingers into the sand, attempting to open his eyes as he clawed his way further ashore. Agony ripped through his gut, and he gasped in pain as another wave crashed over his body. The gasp turned into a choke as he swallowed more saltwater and his body rejected it. But even the act of coughing up water made the pain worse.

He groaned, once more reaching further up the shore his burry vision could barely make out in the gloom. Something cool brushed beneath his hand and, as if by some instinctual reflex, he grasped it, fingers wrapping around it. Heat like lightning shot up his arm and through his body, attacking the source of his pain.

Another wave washed over him from the waist down. The tide receded.

Slowly, his mind began making sense of everything. Who he was. Where he came from. Why he ached.

"I die as I lived, with strength, honor, and valor." The words rose to the surface of his memory.

Aethan Starkling, nephew of the king of Vorovesti, heir of Stormvalor, sentenced to death by the prince who played king. Captain Shino carried out the deed.

Aethan's grip on the object in his hand tightened as he recognized it for what it was. Stormshard. His sword. Shino must have placed it in the boat with him as instructed.

Drawing strength from the power of the weapon, Aethan blinked away the haze in his vision, grimacing in pain.

The blurriness hadn't been entirely his vision. A dense mist hung in the air, obscuring much of the landscape from sight. Beneath him, the sand was as black as night, as if scorched by some great beast. Aethan lifted his head, scanning the haze around him. Pure turquoise waters lapped the shore. If he squinted, Aethan thought he could see some kind of shelter further up the shore.

Moving his body required immense focus and strength. Several times, he attempted to push himself to his hands and knees only to collapse in a roar of pain from the impact. Instead, he rolled onto his back, using Stormshard as an anchor in the sand. He reached down with his other hand, trembling violently as he touched the wound in his gut. It was still painful, but something had crudely stitched and burned him back together.

Aethan dug Stormshard into the sand and used it to pull himself into a seated position. Striking pain shot through his body, momentarily flashing blinding light in his vision. He metered his breathing the best he could and waited for the world to right itself, then he looked down.

His shirt was unbuttoned all the way down to the wound. He peeled the soaked, sand caked and dirty material away from his skin, hissing as the abrasive sand ground into his wound.

An angry jagged line surrounded by red, swollen skin marred his gut. Bits of black sand clung to the wound as if probing for entry. Aethan carefully scooped water from beneath him to wash the sand away. Salt burned into his flesh. Aethan screamed, his knuckles turning white around Stormshard's hilt. He once again metered his breathing until the agony passed, then he repeated the process over and over until the wound was as clean as he could get it.

Slowly, Aethan's strength returned enough to push himself to his feet, listing a few steps to his left before catching his balance. He needed medical attention, which meant he had to get off the beach and find help.

A splitting headache made it hard for him to keep his eyes open for long, but he gritted his teeth and staggered forward, dragging Stormshard with him.

The ships must have lost him in the mist, and somehow Aethan had washed up on shore. How far was he from Arithia?

The distant shape Aethan assumed would be shelter grew thicker and taller the closer he came. When the mist shifted and cleared away enough for him to see, Aethan groaned.

It was a monolithic stone spike. He ran a hand along the cool, damp stone as he followed alongside it. It dipped away, only to be replaced by another spike. Then another. And another. Skeletal remains scattered near the rocks.

Aethan didn't know how long he stumbled along the rock formation, tripping over brittle bones, before his strength gave out. He collapsed to his knees and let out a roar of frustration. It echoed off the stones until it blended with the rumble of thunder.

Unable to rise again, Aethan curled up beside the stone, hugging Stormshard to his body as exhaustion pulled him under.

Hunger gnawed at Aethan's stomach, forcing him awake again. He blinked away sleep. How long had he been asleep? Everything looked the same. Neither day or night. Just gloom, mist, turquoise water, black sand, and stone. He moaned as his stomach heaved, reminding him it needed sustenance.

Aethan sat up, cautious of his wound, and leaned against the stone.

Mist rolled like waves in the air, ebbing and flowing. It cleared just enough for Aethan to make out the shadow of a tree through the mist perhaps twenty paces away. He rose on trembling limbs and approached it.

Aethan's eyes fell on something far more precious than the large fronds. A splash of color—bright, yellow-green, and curved. He paused beside it, examining the strange object, then looked up at the fronds of the tree. Dozens of the yellow objects weighed down one of the massive leafy fronds.

Fruit! He raised Stormshard to chop the fruit from the frond, but hesitated. What if it was poisonous? He had never seen this fruit before and didn't know if it would be safe. His empty stomach gurgled in protest, and Aethan sliced the bunches of dangling fruit from the tree. Starvation would kill him anyway. He needed something in his stomach to survive.

Aethan sank down, back braced against the tree and Stormshard resting in his lap. He used the edge of the blade to cut into a piece of fruit to get to the meaty center. The first bite flooded his mouth with a sweetness so vivid it felt like sunlight on his tongue. Or perhaps that was the hunger. The soft, yielding flesh melted as he chewed. Hints of caramel warmth lingered beneath the sweetness, a richness he hadn't known he craved until now. Each swallow sent a tremor through his body.

The outer skin was thick and bitter, and he tossed it aside, slicing into another. Aethan gorged on the bunch he had cut from the tree. Some were softer and sweeter than others. The greener, the more bitter and firm the meaty inside was.

When Aethan had his fill, at least a dozen more remained. He pulled off his ripped nobleman's jacket and turned it into a sling to carry the food with him. Who knew how long it would be before he found anything more to eat?

Aethan's strength returned gradually as he continued exploring the beach for some way deeper inland. He couldn't tell if it was day or night, or how long he walked before taking a break to eat more fruit. Just one, this time, to ration his provisions. He hadn't spotted another tree bearing fruit. Just more stones and skeletons.

More sleep was necessary. More fruit to hold him over. But Aethan knew if he couldn't find fresh water, he would die of dehydration.

Something white glowed against the black sand. Aethan moved toward it with caution, gripping Stormshard tight in his hand. When he could make out the source, Aethan froze in his tracks.

Bones. Piles upon piles of them. Human skulls, ribs, arms legs, and weapons. A graveyard of others trapped on this beach like him—far more than he had seen already. Despair clawed at his aching gut. How many others had washed up on this shore only to die? Would he die despite surviving against all odds? Where *was* he?

He moaned pitifully, forcing himself onward after a quick prayer for the dead.

Time held no relevance in this place. After what he assumed had been the second day, Aethan stood on the shore, gazing out at the endless mist and waves. Driftwood lapped at the beach.

No, that's not driftwood, Aethan realized. It was the boat they had put his body in before casting him off from Arithia. Or what remained of the boat. Only scattered remnants remained. *Have I circled back to where I started?*

He turned back the way he had come, then peered ahead. If that was the case, he would come across the tree again. With hurried steps, Aethan rushed across the beach as quickly as he dared in his condition, stopping short in front of the frond tree with its freshly cut branch. Skins from discarded fruit were half buried in the black sand.

Aethan sank to his knees, staring up at the large fronds. He had gone in a circle, but never turned back the way he had come from over the past two days. Which could only mean one thing.

I'm on an island. He turned his gaze toward the stone spikes that lined inland along the beach. It had been the same all the way around the island. Nothing but black sand, lapping turquoise waves, and stone spikes.

In a panic, he dropped his fruit sling and Stormshard in the sand beside the tree and rushed into the water, attempting to swim away against the tide. It tossed him to and fro, refusing to allow him to swim far from shore. It pushed him back toward the shore no matter how hard he stroked against the waves. But still he tried, kicking and paddling until something sharp sliced his leg open. Deadly rocks beneath the surface. In pain as the salt water burned into the fresh cut on his leg and through the angry wound in his gut, he screamed in frustration, then lost steam and flopped on the beach ten paces from the tree.

Stranded on an island who knew where with no way to make a watercraft, no way to swim elsewhere, and no fresh water.

"I survived Dorin to die here," he said to himself. His voice was rough, weak. "Or maybe I died and this is the afterlife."

Aethan slung an arm over his eyes as he closed them, succumbing as the tide lapped at his wet boots. Thankfully, this place wasn't frigid. He would die of the cold before thirst if the temperature dropped too far.

His thoughts drifted to Aslyn. The smell of her. The softness of her wavy black hair. The light in her amber eyes. The way she laughed. Was she safe? He missed her so much it created a pit in his stomach that only she could fill. All he wanted was to help her, hold her, love her. It seemed a distant dream, and he allowed it to pull him under, content to be with her in his mind if not in reality.

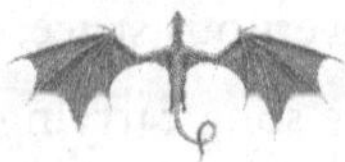

Something cool brushed along Aethan's arm, like a shadow blocking out the sun. Aethan pulled his arm away, unaware if he had slept at all. Had he dreamed of Aslyn, or simply thought about her?

Above, the mist swirled in a frenzy of whorls. Stormshard called to him. He couldn't explain what it felt like. The sword didn't use words, but a sense of urgency that settled over Aethan, demanding it be in hand. The message was clear.

Danger.

Aethan scrambled over to where he left the sword and his only food, then surged to his feet, holding the sword in a defensive stance.

Stormshard buzzed up his arm and he wasn't sure if it was the dehydration causing hallucinations or not, but the blue stones in the cross guard and pommel pulsed with dim light.

A shadow rippled overhead toward inland, sending the mist into another mad frenzy of whorls. Aethan swallowed, slung his fruit over his shoulder, and edged inland with Stormshard ready for a fight.

But the stone spike he had expected to encounter was not what he found. Magic rippled across the surface of the stone creating a doorway not unlike the one he encountered beneath Stormvalor. The entrance loomed before him, an arch of smooth blue stones fitted together with impossible precision. Their surfaces faintly glowed with an inner light that pulsed like a slow heartbeat. The surrounding air crackled with quiet energy, a whisper of something ancient and unseen.

Beyond the archway, a cavern yawned open, its depths shrouded in impenetrable darkness, the edges of jagged rock disappearing into the void. A chill curled outward, brushing against his skin like the breath of something waiting. Instinct warned Aethan not to enter.

That wasn't there before, Aethan thought, fairly certain he had examined every inch of the stone wall holding him on the shore.

Thunder rumbled, followed by lightning that illuminated the mist.

A massive shadowy form of a creature perched high above the cavern entrance. Aethan edged backward. The tattoo on his chest itched.

Yet somewhere within that cavernous space, the soft trickle of water echoed through the emptiness, its gentle song carrying a prospect of fresh water. The sound drew Aethan forward, his steps hesitant but inevitable, as if the very sand beneath him urged him onward. The scent of damp earth and something faintly metallic lingered in the cool air, filling his lungs as he crossed the threshold. Shadows swallowed him whole, and the light of the gateway dimmed behind him, leaving only the unknown ahead.

Then, lichen glowed along the cavern floor, revealing a path forward and the terrible truth.

He was sealed inside.

CHAPTER 32

The Hero of Vorovesti

Something in the air kept Gannon from sleeping. He tossed and turned in bed, shifting, throwing blankets off, hugging them up tight. He even tried calling for a draught of tea that usually helped him fall asleep. Nothing seemed to work. Eventually, he gave up and accepted the restlessness of the evening.

Gannon wasn't sure what time it was when he left his chambers. Late, for certain. He wandered the silent halls of the palace as night shift servants worked to clean floors or chandeliers while the rest of the palace slept. They bowed to him and ducked out of the way with murmured "my prince" or "Your Majesty". Gannon responded with a small nod of his head each time. The palace wouldn't function without the servants, and he felt they deserved respect as well.

In seemingly aimless wandering, Gannon found himself outside of his father's office. A soft light glowed from the slightly open door. Gannon frowned and edged toward it, rapping his knuckles gently before pushing it open. The sound still seemed loud in the silence of the palace.

King Orrin sat behind his large desk, clearly exhausted. Dark shadows ringed his eyes and his lids sagged. He had been leaning on his hand, but sat up straighter as Gannon entered.

"You can't sleep either?" Gannon asked.

His father grimaced and returned his attention to the papers in front of him. "I can't stop thinking about the mines. General Lassiter has been gone for too long. He should have returned by now, and the last message I received is more than a week old. I don't know what's holding him back, or if..." He trailed off, but Gannon understood the end of that sentence.

"He can't be," Gannon said with certainty. "General Lassiter is one of the toughest men I know."

"And most dependable, which is what worries me," his father finished. "Something must be—"

A distant horn cut off the conversation. Both men froze, staring out the window. Gannon couldn't see much in the moonless dark, but he knew that horn. His heart dropped.

"Who is attacking?" King Orrin asked.

"I'll find out." Gannon jumped to his feet and was out the door before his father could protest.

After swiftly strapping on his armor and sword back in his chambers, Gannon rushed to the stable where soldiers and guards were already rushing around, readying for battle. The stable master nodded to Gannon and offered the reins to Gannon's dapple horse.

"It's coming from the western gate," one of the guards reported.

Gannon mounted and charged out, calling for as many men as he could gather to follow him to the western gate. Guards and soldiers quickly answered their prince's call.

Citizens of Mordelic peered through doors and windows at the late-night commotion, but none dared step into the path of the charging horses and Vorovesti soldiers. Gannon could feel the fear pulsing through the city, yet he trusted the men who had been trained to protect it. Mordelic's walls were thick and unbreakable. No army had breached the gates in over a thousand years.

As they neared the western gate, Gannon breathed a sigh of relief to see it closed. He dismounted as quickly as his mount skidded to a halt, dropping gracefully and sprinting to the stairs up the tower wall. An army naturally spilled at his back, climbing on either side of the gate to spread out their forces along the western wall. Archers lined the embrasures atop the seventeen-meter-high wall, ready to defend the city from invasion.

Gannon raced along the onyx battlement to the commanding officer who sounded the horn.

"What do we have?" Gannon asked as he reached the officer.

"An army, Your Majesty," the officer answered. "Hard to see in this darkness, but it's there." He handed over the telescope.

Gannon took it and stepped toward a lookout gap, lifting it to his eye.

"To the southwest," the officer directed as Gannon swept the landscape.

He was right. It was impossible to see much more than fifteen or so meters beyond the wall in the impossible darkness, but Gannon spotted it. Now that the horn had sounded and the dark army had been spotted, they marched forward in perfect unison. Gannon couldn't spy any battering rams or other siege machines. Just endless lines of dark, shadowy figures advancing toward the gate.

"Send word to all of your captains to have the archers ready to send a volley into the darkness the moment they are withing range," Gannon commanded. He closed the scope and handed it back to the officer. "And get those tar trebuchets moving. I want fire out there. With any luck we will take out a number of those troops before they even reach archer range."

"Yes, Your Majesty," the officer said, taking the scope with a bow. Then he pivoted on his heel and marched along the line, shouting orders as soldiers took up position behind the archers and formed ranks inside the gate.

Gannon gritted his teeth. No one would breach the walls today.

He raced to a tower, ready to climb the steps as the trebuchets began launching flaming balls of tinder out into the fields beyond Mordelic. They exploded with a blast of light, spreading flames in their wake.

The sight froze Gannon in place and his breath caught in his lungs. Thousands of Black Guards formed perfect ranks, marching in lockstep toward the onyx walls. He had never seen so many at once, had never imagined the emperor had such numbers.

As dozens were killed or maimed by the fireballs, the remaining men didn't break rank or stride. They carried on as if nothing happened.

Gannon cursed under his breath. Why was the emperor attacking Mordelic?

By the time the second volley of fireballs launched, three more horns sounded. Gannon turned, gaze sweeping the city. He listened as the horns sounded again. All four gates were under attack. Were there as many Black Guards at the others as here?

"Hold the wall!" Gannon bellowed, racing along the lines on the battlement. "We have never been breached before. Today will not be that day!"

The men straightened at his call, bolstered by the prince's confidence.

By the time the third volley of fireballs streaked across the night sky, Gannon heard the *whump* of hundreds of archers releasing arrows.

Were they so close already?

Gannon rushed to an embrasure, peering through over an archer's shoulder as the man reached for another arrow. The Black Army advanced at inhuman speed. He squinted, searching for ladders. But there were none. If they had no ladders and no siege weapons, how did they hope to breach the walls? Surely the emperor knew he couldn't take Mordelic by sheer force of numbers. No one ever had. A siege then? But why approach?

Archers continued raining arrows on the army. The Black Army didn't break ranks, didn't stop the march, didn't even flinch.

"Explosives!" Gannon shouted at the trebuchet master. He nodded once curtly, then barked out orders to his men, sending runners in every direction to spread the word.

Gannon nudged the archer in front of him back. The man nearly protested until his eyes fell on the prince. He stumbled back without a word.

At the embrasure, Gannon watched the Black Army gather outside. They would be on the wall in less than a minute at this pace. Half a dozen explosives snapped through the air. As they impacted, each exploded in a deadly blast. Gaps in the Black Army formed, but still they marched ahead, stepping over the fallen as if they were nothing more than rock in the way.

Within ten feet of the wall, the Black Army stopped, shifting their ranks around the gate. They fell to arrows, but this close the trebuchets could no longer safely attack.

Gannon held his breath, heart thundering as he waited to see what would happen. Nothing. No battering rams advanced through the army. No Black Guards even bothered drawing weapons. They simply... stopped.

What are they up to?

A horn blasted from another gate. One long warning, followed by a short blast.

The army was inside the walls.

How in the name of the seven did they get in? Gannon thought furiously as he rushed toward the steps, descending as quickly as his legs could carry him.

"Defend the wall!" He called out as he descended. "Concentrate forces on the gate!"

Vorovesti soldiers followed him down the stairs as men descended on the other side as well. They formed ranks with the soldiers already guarding the gate.

Gannon turned to the commander at the left flank of the guard gates. "Hold this position unless you hear me send up the retreat call. Send out the call if they breach the gate. No matter what tries to come through that gate, do not break ranks."

"Yes, Your Majesty," the commander said with a nod of acceptance.

Gannon ran to his horse and mounted swiftly, then pivoted and raced toward the south gate where the call had gone out that the army was inside. The horse darted along the city streets, dodging and weaving as necessary. Calls went out for any able-bodied citizens ready to defend the city to gather arms and aid the nearest gate. It created a din of chaos that slowed his progress, forcing him to call out and command people out of his way.

The south gate was defended by House Cyrus during an attack. Had they fallen?

A fifth horn blasted as Gannon spotted the southern towers looming over houses. The palace horn.

Gannon's hammering heart skipped in fear. He yanked the reins so hard his horse reared back, but he held his seat. His eyes darted to the palace, where fire blazed in the night sky.

Father! Forgetting the south gate, Gannon turned his mount toward the palace. Fury burned in his veins. If anything happened to his father, he would make the emperor pay for this invasion in much more than blood.

As he raced toward the palace, Gannon's horse darted past men in commoner clothes and uniforms racing toward the palace to defend the king. He passed a few skirmishes between soldiers and Black Guards and loyalists wearing the bands. His stomach sank. The imperial seat insisted on a presence of Black Guards in every city across the five kingdoms, and fanatical loyalists existed in all five kingdoms.

The attacking force had allies inside the walls, and the south gate was closest to the palace.

He unsheathed his sword, taking out enemies from horseback as he continued toward the palace. Most of the time his sword glanced off the black armor. Only a few stumbled or fell to his blade. The men fighting for their kingdom rallied as they saw their prince fighting with them. His presence bolstered their confidence.

When he reached the palace gate, soldiers and guards littered the ground—most were his own men, but a few Black Guards and loyalists joined the dead. Gannon slowed his horse, then dismounted in the courtyard.

A flood of men had followed Gannon through the open gate. "Find your king! Defend him at any cost!"

The people loved his father. He was just and fair. He took care of his people as well as any king could in this dying world. He had protect them for years, just as Gannon had done. The way the reinforcements surged forward gave him some confidence that hope would not be lost.

Gannon led the way through a side door, knowing better than to take the most direct route. Whatever had burned before had been put out. Gannon couldn't even spot the smoke within palace walls.

The inside of the palace contrasted starkly from the silence he had been met with earlier. Now, screams ripped through the air in all directions. Weapons clashed. He headed up a set of servant stairs to the floor with his father's office, taking the fastest route he knew of. Once more, he was glad he had spent much of his youth memorizing every hidden passage in the palace. Odds were King Orrin had moved elsewhere, but the office would be the best place to start.

When he reached the office door, it rested wide open, the light still glowing within. Gannon motioned for men to continue toward the royal quarters, war room, and throne room. The stream of soldiers split, taking citizen soldiers with them.

Gannon stepped into the office, searching for clues. His father's sword was gone. He checked the desktop and spotted a letter from Emperor Valen at the top of the stack. With a glance at the open door, he picked it up and skimmed the contents. With each word, his heart sank further.

He demanded Lord Lux Starkling be handed over to the imperial seat. But worse than that, Gannon's hand trembled as he read the words he couldn't dare to believe.

Aethan was dead.

Gannon dropped the letter as the room tilted. He gritted his teeth, leaning against the desk for a moment. Had his father known this when he was here just a few short hours ago? *There will be time for mourning and anger later. First, I need to find my father.*

As he was about to leave the office, Gannon spied another letter bearing Aethan's familiar script on the front. It was still sealed. He pocketed the letter as he dashed from the room. There was no time to read it. He could review it once the chaos ended. And if the worst happened, he wouldn't leave Aethan's last words in enemy hands.

Collecting himself, Gannon straightened, then rushed out the door. Lux Starkling was in the city. He had seen his uncle after dinner.

Gannon raced down the hall as he heard the horns of a rally call from outside the palace walls. Dare he hope this nightmare would end soon? Someone had rallied troops to push the Black Army back.

But his mission was his father. Then Lux Starkling.

Gannon rounded a corner and skidded to a halt as a squad of five Black Guards surged toward him, their dark armor reflecting the flickering torchlight. He scanned for the servant door, only to find it on the other side of the guards. He had no choice but to meet them head-on.

With a cry, he drove forward, his sword a blur as it met the first attacker's blade. The impact sent a jolt up his arm, but he gritted his teeth and pressed on, sidestepping a second guard's swing before ramming his blade into the man's gut. The guard crumpled, but two more took his place. Gannon barely ducked in time as a sword whistled past his ear. Then he countered with a vicious slash that sent another enemy to the floor.

The final guard sliced his arm before Gannon cut him down. His blade was slick with dark crimson blood. His breath came in short, sharp gasps, his pulse hammering against his ribs like a war drum. But he was alive despite the pain in his arm. He could hear the distant clash of steel and the screams of dying men echoing through the palace corridors, but he had no time to linger. His father was somewhere within, and if the Black Guards reached him first, they would surely kill him.

He shoved the thought away and took the steps two at a time, his boots slipping on the blood-slick marble.

At the bottom, a hallway stretched before him, gilded walls marred with soot and splashes of crimson. The bodies of the emperor's loyalists lay dead all around the hall. Gannon couldn't imagine how loyalists breached the palace walls unless they came in on the heels of the Black Guards. The scent of death choked the air.

A sudden movement to Gannon's left sent him spinning just in time to block a descending sword. The force of the blow sent shudders down his injured arm. His opponent pressed forward with brutal efficiency, seeking to drive him back toward the staircase. Gannon gritted his teeth and shoved against the man's blade, twisting free before striking low. His steel bit into the guard's thigh, forcing him to stagger.

But the Black Guard did not fall. Baring his teeth at the prince, he swung again, a diagonal slash aimed at Gannon's ribs. The prince barely raised his sword in time. Sparks flew as their blades clashed, and pain flared in Gannon's side. His breath hitched—hot blood seeped beneath his armor and tunic.

Ignoring the agony, he drove forward with a growl of rage. A feint to the left, a quick pivot, and his sword sliced across the Black Guard's throat. The man collapsed, gurgling as his life spilled onto the marble floor.

Gannon pressed a hand against his wound, cursing under his breath. He couldn't afford to slow down. The pain would have to wait. He forced himself onward, past the bodies, past smoldering banners and broken chandeliers, through hidden passages, taking the quickest route to the throne room. He had to reach his father before everything was lost.

A distant crash made him quicken his pace. He turned the final corner and sprinted toward the throne room doors, his heart hammering with dread. He could only pray he wasn't too late.

Through the partially open doors, he caught sight of Lux Starkling, his sword a streak of silver as he battled a dozen Black Guards alone. Royal guards lay in scattered heaps in the hallway and throne room entryway.

Lux moved like a tempest, weaving between strikes, cutting down foes with ruthless precision. Beyond him, Iskra ushered a group of nobles and frightened servants toward a hidden passage behind the throne, covered by a few bleeding and battered guards and noblemen. Her face was pale but determined as she guided them to safety, throwing quick glances toward Lux, as if she, too, feared he would be overwhelmed.

Gannon surged forward, blade flashing as he cut into the nearest Black Guard, taking him by surprise.

Lux barked a curse at him between strikes. "Get to the tunnel, Gannon!"

"I won't run!" Gannon snarled, parrying an overhead blow and driving his sword through an enemy's chest. "I can fight. I won't abandon you!"

Lux gritted his teeth as he blocked another strike and there was a flicker of something else in his expression—grim resolve. "Your father is dead," he said, voice sharp as steel. "You are the last hope for this throne. If you die here, everything is lost."

Gannon faltered for half a heartbeat, shock slicing through him even deeper than his wounds. But there was no time to process the grief, not with death pressing in on all sides. Not with his kingdom on the line.

His grip tightened around his sword. "All the more reason to stay!" he shouted, slashing through another foe. "I won't leave my people to die! I won't abandon my kingdom!"

Lux attacked a guard quickly, throwing his foe off balance, then he shoved Gannon backward, his expression hard. "Trystain and I have this under control! You need to go!"

Before Gannon could argue further, a hand seized his arm. He turned to see Iskra, her face drawn with urgency. "Gannon, please!" she pleaded, tugging him toward the tunnel. "If Lux says to go, you must go. We can't lose you too!"

He resisted for a moment longer, but the determination in Iskra's eyes, the desperation in Lux's, and the unrelenting tide of enemies forced him to reconsider. With a frustrated growl, he allowed Iskra to pull him toward the passage, his heart raging against the retreat.

Once behind the safety of the secret passage, Gannon paused again, blood dripping from his sword as his gaze fell on the body behind the throne.

King Orrin lay facedown on the ground, his sword still in his hand. The crown had tumbled from his head and come to rest at the base of the dais. Gannon couldn't see his father's face, but there was no mistaking the truth. He was dead. A pool of blood covered the marble floor beneath the king.

Tears sprang to Gannon's eyes and he gritted his teeth. After taking a few deep breaths, Gannon darted out at a crouch.

"Stop!" Iskra hissed behind him.

Gannon grabbed his father's sword, the sword of Vorovesti kings, and was about to rush forward to snatch the crown when Iskra seized his arm and yanked him back into the passage once more, his finger still outstretched as if he could reach it if only he tried harder.

Lux screamed in agony.

Iskra pulled the tapestry covering the exit back into place, jerking on Gannon's arm.

Steel clattered to the ground.

Gannon's heart couldn't possibly sink any lower. In one night, he lost everything. He and Iskra both froze at the mouth of the tunnel as a familiar voice rang in the throne room.

"It's over, Lord Starkling."

Gannon's jaw clenched so tightly it sent a throb through his skull. He dared to peer around the edge of the tapestry with Iskra.

Lux kneeled on the throne room floor, held in place by two Black Guards. In front of him, a man Gannon didn't recognize held a blade to Lux's throat. He growled something so low Gannon couldn't hear the words.

"Marek Bloodstone," Iskra breathed.

That was Marek Bloodstone? Gannon should have been angry at the audacity of a Bloodstone attacking his throne room, but he couldn't be angry at Marek when he saw the man and woman standing side-by-side behind Marek.

Lady Fia and Trystain.

"You were never helping us secure the palace," Lux spat at Trystain.

"I absolutely was. But not for you."

"I'll fucking kill him," Gannon growled under his breath.

He took half a step before Iskra restrained him with a shake of her head.

Trystain committed treason. The south gate didn't fall. Trystain opened the gate and let the Black Army in!

"Where is Gannon?" Trystain asked.

Lux spit at Trystain. "You were their friend and you sold them. For what?"

Trystain snorted. "They were never my friends. They used me. And Sybil... she was more than happy to move on to something better. From what I hear, she's been very eager in her new position. None of them gave a fuck about me."

I did, Gannon thought miserably. *We did*.

Lux said something low and deep. Gannon strained to hear it but failed.

"I'll ask again," Trystain said. "Where is Gannon?"

"Dead," Lux snapped. "By your treason. He burned in that fire your witch started in the garden." The lie slid past Lux's lips so easily. A lie to save his prince and the last heir to the throne.

Lady Fia glided forward, almost ripping Lux Starkling's shirt clean off with one hard yank that nearly impaled him on Marek's blade. He grunted, jerking back to avoid death.

What are they doing? Gannon wondered.

"As suspected," Lady Fia purred. "He will come with me. The emperor will be happy to experiment on him."

Trystain didn't argue.

Gannon's grip on the swords in his hands tightened so much his palms ached and the leather bit in deep.

Her gaze lifted, and for a moment, Gannon thought she saw them hiding behind the tapestry before realizing the true object of her attention.

The Vorovesti crown.

Gannon struggled against Iskra as she hugged her arms around him to hold him back.

"Please," she whispered so quietly he almost couldn't hear over the thump of his pulse in his ears. "We need you. Please."

"Gather men and start the search immediately, Trystain," Lady Fia commanded.

She glided across the throne room with Trystain. His eyes locked on the crown with covetous desire. Then she lifted it and placed it on his head.

Gannon opened his mouth and Iskra slapped her hand over his lips to silence his outrage.

"As promised," Lady Fia said. "King Trystain, the hero of Vorovesti."

Trystain preened, lifting his head high.

He can't have my crown. I'll cut off his head for this!

Tears blurred Iskra's eyes as she pulled Gannon back.

The last thing Gannon saw before Iskra dragged him down the secret passage was Trystain pulling Lady Fia against him in a hard kiss.

CHAPTER 33

Forever a Monster

Bast woke on the floor of his rented room just before dawn, aching but otherwise no worse for wear. With a groan, he pushed himself to his feet, rubbing away sore spots in his shoulders and back, flexing his jaw. The stiffness would wear off soon, he knew. It wasn't the first time he woke up on a floor, but it was the first time he had nearly been ripped apart in pain.

Gathering his weapons and armor, Bast strapped everything to his body, ready to move out of Lemheller Gap. But first, he had to get to Aslyn. Experience taught him that he couldn't go far without her.

As he rolled his neck and stepped into the street with the coming light, Bast wondered what had happened to her in the middle of the night to make that blood oath react the way it had. He was alive, which meant she had to be. But how much danger was she in? He had no way of knowing until he could see her for himself. To do that, he had to find a way into the palace, so he headed toward the mountain pass leading up to the palace, climbed as high as he dared among the spikey rocks, and waited for an opening.

The imperial palace loomed above him, its obistone walls glowing with ominous darkness as the first light of morning reflected off the surface. A fortress of power and arrogance, its sheer cliffs and towering gates dared any intruder to try their luck. No one had ever dared try.

Proving I'm a fool, he thought bitterly.

The pass leading up to the palace was a narrow, winding path cut into the mountainside. It was the only approach, and it left him woefully exposed. Even now, the silhouette of guards patrolling the thick obistone walls shifted in the dawn's light, their weapons glinting. At the blackened steel reinforced gate, every wagon, every crate, every beast and visitor would be stopped and searched. The emperor left nothing to chance with the wedding tomorrow.

Bast needed a way in.

Shadow magic was of little use in the morning light. There were too few places for darkness to pool, too many open stretches where he would be laid bare. He watched as servants, merchants, and performers made their way toward the gate, their wares and official orders scrutinized by vigilant guards. He could not risk going in with them.

He turned his gaze along the rock face, studying the natural formations. Climbing was impossible—the palace had been built to make certain of that. The walls rose too high, too smooth, and even the lower levels had overhangs were designed to stop any would-be infiltrator. Bast's fingers flexed with frustration. If he couldn't find a way in, he was useless to Aslyn.

For a moment, he considered turning back to the city and killing a Black Guard to steal their armor, but dismissed the idea. Their armor was heavy and he would have to shed his own armor to wear it. If he and Aslyn had to make a quick escape, he would be too slow in that gear. He couldn't risk hunting down and killing another ambassador if their robes so easily identified them. Someone on the inside of the palace would realize he was an infiltrator, and his mission would end swiftly.

A wagon carrying barrels creaked along the pass, drawn by two weary-looking mules. No doubt, the brewer was delivering casks of ale or wine to the wedding feast. A plan took shape. A terrible one, but he had no other ideas.

Bast slid from his hiding place and moved low to the ground with purpose, keeping to what little cover the terrain allowed. Timing was everything. He reached the path just as the wagon passed a sharp bend in the road. Without hesitation, he lunged forward, rolling his body under the wagon, grabbing the underside, and pulling himself up into the shadows beneath it. His limbs locked tight against the wooden beams as the wagon rattled onward.

He kept his breathing even, forcing himself to stay still as the wheels bumped and jolted over the uneven path. Dust filled Bast's nostrils. The scent of damp wood and spiced ale pressed close. It felt like an eternity before the wagon rolled to a stop at the palace gates. He didn't dare a peek for fear of being spotted under the wagon.

The clank of metal. Voices. Bast held his breath.

"Wine for the feast," the brewer grunted. "Came up from the valley this morn on Lord Bloodstone's orders."

Boots moved toward the wagon and a guard paused a breath from where Bast's hand clung to the undercarriage. He held his breath as a wisp of dark magic slithered under the wagon. Bast quickly pulled tighter to the shadows beneath the wagon, praying that magic couldn't sense him. He didn't dare reach out with his own magic to protect himself. Not if the guards could sense him.

Several heartbeats passed before a guard thumped at one of the barrels. The wood rang solidly. Another did the same.

Then the wagon lurched forward again, and Bast allowed himself the ghost of a smirk as he released a slow breath of relief. Challenge one overcome.

The wagon passed through the walls. Bast turned his head to watch as best he could beneath the wagon. The walls were thicker than he anticipated. At least ten feet of solid obistone guarded the imperial palace from invasion.

Once inside the walls, the real challenge began. The courtyard was bustling. Servants scurried with armfuls of flowers and linens, soldiers marched in formation, and a few of Lemheller Gap's elite strolled in groups, basking in the grandeur of the occasion. No one had been invited to the palace for an event like this in memory.

As the wagon rolled through the courtyard and past the palace entrance, Bast spied the ghastly fountain dominating the space. A massive statue of the first emperor, Narcisse, slayed a dragon. The blood that seeped from the dragon's wounds was red-tinted water that spilled out into the fountain below. He grimaced at the hideous display.

Even beneath the wagon, Bast could see clearly up the shallow palace steps into the towering entrance of the palace, a structure of blackened iron and deep-shadowed arches. A grand staircase curved upward, its crimson carpet like a river of blood spilling from the second story. Chandeliers swayed gently above and matching candelabras lined the sweeping staircase, their candlelight flickering against the vaulted ceiling, casting long, dark shadows across the statues that stood in silent vigilance. A fortress of power and darkness, and he was slipping past its gates unseen.

The moment the wagon reached the delivery station, Bast slipped free, ducking into the narrow space between a stack of crates and the wall.

He needed to disappear—fast.

The only doorway he could access without calling attention to himself stood at his back. The thick, heavy hardwood surface was closed. Bast tested his luck to see if it would open, keeping a watchful eye over his shoulder. It didn't budge. Crouching low, he sent a wisp of shadow into the lock, feeling his way around until it clicked far too loud for his liking. He wouldn't make that mistake again.

Holding his breath, Bast watched the activity on the other side of the crates. No one had noticed or heard. He sent out a sound barrier with his shadows before opening the door, preventing it from creaking. Bast didn't dare open beyond what was necessary to slip inside.

When he had it closed, Bast listened along the sloping corridor for guards, but was met with silence. He straightened and followed the corridor downward. The scent of damp stone and mold curled out like a warning. Dungeons.

Bast hesitated only a moment. The upper levels were too exposed. But the underbelly of the palace... that was another matter. And he would bet his life the emperor had an entrance inside the palace leading down here. The door Bast took must have been for loading prisoners into the palace.

He descended into the darkness, footsteps silent against the cold stone. The deeper he went, the more the air thickened with the scent of decay, feces, and stale water. Most of the cells were full of deep darkness even his magically enhanced eyes couldn't pierce. Above those cell doors, ancient runes were scratched into the stone. A few cells held little more than skeletal remains, as if those prisoners were simply forgotten, left to death and rot. The emperor had little use for prisoners—at least, not here.

As Bast moved through the corridors, his steps slowed. A faint hum vibrated against his chest. He froze, one hand instinctively pressing against the Jewel of Arithia tucked beneath his shirt and leathers. It pulsed against his skin, a subtle pull drawing him forward. He narrowed his eyes, scanning the cells.

Then he saw him.

A man curled in the shadows of a cell, barely more than a husk. His beard had grown long and unkempt, tangled with filth. Once finely made, his clothes were reduced to little more than tattered rags on his gaunt frame. His skin was sallow, stretched thin over his sharp cheekbones, and streaked with grime. His wrists bore the raw, chafed marks of iron bindings, darkened with old blood and bruises. The cell around him was a pit of neglect. The stench of rot, feces, and damp stone hung thick in the air.

A cracked wooden bowl sat untouched in the corner, its contents long congealed. He lifted his head at Bast's approach, flinching deeper into the shadows. Hollow eyes glinted dully in the dim torchlight, and something in his wasted face struck a chord of recognition.

Bast stiffened. He had seen this man before, in Arithia—though not like this. Not broken, not starved.

Realization struck like a blade to the gut. This was King Novin. Aslyn's father.

The Jewel hummed louder, its magic thrumming between them. Novin's weary eyes locked onto Bast's, and in them, confusion flared.

Bast stepped to the iron bars, gripping them tight. Whatever plans he had made for this infiltration had just changed, because if he didn't help Aslyn's father, the king would die down here. Soon.

His jaw clenched and his nostrils flared as anger tore through him. Aslyn risked everything because she thought Aethan would save her father. But she had sent him on a fool's errand without even knowing. Emperor Valen had her father down here the whole time. The rebels who allegedly kidnapped the king were the emperor's men, likely aided by a power-hungry prince.

Bast muttered a curse. This escape just became much more difficult.

"Can you walk?" Bast asked quietly.

The king's eyes sharpened but he shook his head. "I cannot stand. My legs..." His voice trailed off.

Bast growled, tracing the lock on the cell door with a finger as his shadows slipped into the mechanism and unlocked it. As the gate swung inward, King Novin pushed himself back harder against the wall.

"I won't hurt you, but we have to get you out of here," Bast said as he stepped into the cell, showing his hands to try and alleviate the king's distress. "She won't leave once she knows you're down here. Not without you."

Wrinkles creased the corners of the king's eyes. "Aslyn," he whispered.

Bast approached slowly as he would to a skittish animal, then crouched beside the king to inspect his legs. In seconds, Bast noted the protrusion. A broken bone they had never bothered to heal. They just left him down here to suffer or die of the injury. Bast checked the second leg to find it in barely better condition.

The king couldn't walk without a lot of healing. And even then, it would take months. He could carry him out, but not until he had Aslyn with him.

"I'll go get her and we will leave," Bast said.

The king shook his head fervently, his eyes wide. He grabbed at Bast's coat, pulling him closer. "Get her out of here. She's in danger."

"I know that."

"No. You don't." His voice cracks as he neared hysterics. "You don't know. He knows. He knows!"

Bast eased King Novin's hard grip from his coat. "Who knows?"

"The emperor. He knows who... who she is. Save her. Please. Save her and you can have anything. Everything."

The scar on his palm itched, reminding him of the blood oath. But King Novin's words didn't make sense. "What do you mean, who she is? She's your daughter."

"Yes." Madness burned in the king's eyes. "Yes, but she's so much more." Tears carved rivers through the grime on his face. "She is light and hope. She is *his*."

Bast pulled his waterskin and offered a drink. King Novin eagerly gulped down the contents. "You aren't making any sense. I need you to calm down and explain it to me clearly, logically, or I can't help."

King Novin swiped water from his chin with the sleeve of his tattered coat. "I know who you are, and I trust her safety to no one else."

Bast blinked dumbly at that.

"Besides," the king continued, "you are the first... the first person I have seen aside from the emperor and *her* in... I don't... I don't..."

Bast's fingers flexed around the empty waterskin. He capped it, unable to meet the king's eyes as he exposed himself further. "As long as I breathe, she is safe with me. She has my oath." He showed his palm.

King Novin's brown eyes snapped to the scar on his palm, his lips moving but no sound came out. "Good. Good. She is the queen now. It's her. It must be." The king tried to steady his racing thoughts so clearly to Bast, but it was still hard to understand what the king meant. "The prophecy. Light and dark. Amber and sapphire. It's her. Light. Eyes of sun-kissed amber. I didn't... didn't push her toward him for nothing. Light and dark. Amber and sapphire."

Him. Starkling. But there was nothing dark about that prude.

King Novin scrubbed a dirty hand over his cheek to wipe away his tears.

Bast leaned closer as the king slumped lower. "I don't understand."

King Novin's eyes locked on Bast's chest, widening, then he looked up at Bast. "You..." He closed his eyes, murmuring something to himself that Bast couldn't discern.

"Novin, I will get her and come back. We will get you out and to a healer."

"Kill me."

Bast reeled backward, stunned by the determination and lucidity of those two words.

"No," he breathed, knowing what killing the king would do to them.

"As you said, she won't leave without me, and I can't slow her down." Something in King Novin had shifted in the past few seconds. He straightened, sliding a simple, golden band off his left pinky finger. "I won't survive an escape. I'm broken, weak, dying slowly. And I won't be the reason she is forced into this. The emperor... he wants to breed her with the Bloodstone boy. And once she gives birth, he will kill her and take the child. He needs it. She cannot remain here another day."

Bast's gut churned at the idea of Aslyn being turned into a womb and discarded once she produced an heir. His shadows reached up the corridor as if in response to his anger and worry.

King Novin pressed the golden ring against the scar on Bast's palm, then folded his fingers around it. "Tell her to run. Tell her it's more than our people depending on her. It's all five kingdoms and beyond." He squeezed Bast's hand around the ring. His gaze dipped to Bast's chest, as if he could see the Jewel of Arithia through the armor. "Keep it away from the emperor. Guard it and her with your life." He released a small sigh. "Tell her I love her."

Everything inside of Bast raged like a wild storm. His shadows swayed, lashing out at the walls and the iron bars of the cell. If he killed Novin, Aslyn would never forgive him. Any hope that he could make up for his deception in Stormvalor would be pointless.

But if he didn't kill King Novin, it could cost all three of them their lives before this day was done.

Bast hadn't realized he pulled his black dagger from his belt, but he gripped it in his fist, angled over King Novin's heart. Grief clawed at him. Not grief for the king. He begged for this end. No, the grief that ripped into him was so much worse. With this act, he would lose her forever. And for the first time, he admitted to himself that he had actually hoped for it. For something.

King Novin's face settled into peace as he leaned back, exposing his chest. When Bast hesitated, the king wrapped a hand around his, guiding the dagger into place over his heart.

"I'm sorry it must be like this," the king said softly, sincerely. Then he tightened his hold and pressed the tip into his flesh over Bast's hand. Pain flashed in his brown eyes.

It had to end quickly. That was the least Bast could do for her father.

Bast thrust the blade into the king's heart, and the king drew his last breath. Tears blurred Bast's vision.

He would forever be her monster.

CHAPTER 34

Floods and Unsteady Ground

Thirst drove Aethan forward, following the path of glowing lichen and slowly increasing sound of flowing water. If he didn't find fresh water soon, he would be in serious trouble.

The ground beneath his boots was uneven and slick with moisture. The air was damp, heavy with the scent of earth and the faintest hint of something ancient. His breath echoed faintly as he pressed on. The only light came from the soft, ethereal glow of lichen that clung to the tunnel's jagged stone walls. The lichen bathed the path in an eerie, blue-green light, casting long, dancing shadows shifted with every movement he made.

The tunnel wound its way through the earth, twisting and turning in unpredictable directions. Aethan's eyes adjusted to the dim glow, though the light was never enough to reveal the true shape of the cavern beyond the immediate path. His fingers brushed against the cold stone walls. The texture grounded him and helped keep his heartbeat steady as he moved toward the sound of water. The ceiling of the tunnel dropped so low that Aethan had to duck or crouch to avoid scraping his head against the rock.

As he moved, the silence was oppressive, broken only by the soft shuffle of his footsteps and the growing sound of trickling water echoing from somewhere deeper in the earth. The lichen flickered faintly, as if responding to his presence. Their luminescence glowed brighter in the darker stretches of the tunnel before dimming again as he moved on. Aethan's hand rested on Stormshard's hilt, the sword at his side providing the only sense of security in the unknown.

The deeper he ventured, the more Aethan could feel something watching him, hidden in the shadows.

Aethan had been walking for what felt like hours, and his strength waned. The cut in his leg had stopped bleeding, but it still crippled his ability to walk at a normal pace. It forced him to limp increasingly more as he went, until he was dragging that leg behind him.

Just as he was about to give up and rest, Aethan rounded a bend and came upon a small pool nestled in the heart of a tall cavern. Water flowed down from high above, creating endless ripples in the pool.

Aethan's throat ached with thirst, and the thought of fresh water was a life-saving relief. He kneeled awkwardly at the edge of the pool, dipping his fingers into the water. It was cool, not cold enough to be dangerous, and there was no rancid smell. He tasted a drop on his finger—clean and crisp, with no briny edge. The tension that had been building in his body loosened. Aethan lumbered deep into the pool of water to where it flowed down from above. Tipping his head back and opening his mouth, Aethan let the refreshing, cool water bathe him and slide down his throat.

He drank deeply, savoring the relief as it slid down his dry throat and splashed against his face. Once he drank his fill, Aethan sprayed fresh water over his face, through his pale blond hair. He scrubbed away all traces of black sand from the beach.

Finally, Aethan wiped drops of water from his face as he stepped away from the waterfall. The pain in his leg no longer hindered him, nor did the wound in his gut. Aethan frowned, peering down at his stomach.

Nothing more than a puckered scar remained. Experimentally, he pressed a finger against it and the skin bounced back with no traces of pain. Then he peered around at his calf through the slice in his pants. It was gone. Completely. He rocked his weight onto the leg, testing it.

A delirious, glorious laugh bubbled up. Healing waters. *Maybe the lost gods haven't forsaken me yet*, he thought.

Water sloshed around his boots as he moved in a slow circle back toward the entrance he came from. But the entrance was gone, replaced by solid stone as if by magic.

The lichen that had guided him here no longer glowed. Only those in the small cavern pulsed with gentle light.

With his thirst now sated, wounds healed, and food at his back, Aethan took a moment to absorb the moment. He wondered where he was and how to get out of this underground space. Somehow, he had to make it back to Aslyn.

Last he knew, Aethan had been in Arithia and Dorin had ordered his death. The plan had been to put him in a boat, patched up, and intercept the boat away from the shores.

Once more, Aethan glanced down at his scar. Von must have done something for him to survive this far. It was after he was sent out to the ocean waves that things must have gone wrong.

Aethan couldn't help but muse at the irony of being stuck in a cavern on an island, alone after all that Von had spoken of on the way to Arithia. The stormveil. The Cavern of Lost Souls. It was ludicrous, of course, but what would Von say if he could see Aethan now?

A tunnel stretched into darkness out of this small cavern to his left. He couldn't go back because the entrance to the cavern had closed behind him. Aethan turned to his left.

It was only then that he noticed the sound—the faintest shifting of water beneath his feet. Aethan's eyes widened. His heart quickened. He hadn't noticed when the water had started to rise, but it was undeniable now. The water surged faster than he'd expected, creeping higher quickly. He instinctively moved back toward the dry ground, but the rising tide followed, flooding the tunnel with alarming speed. Did this cave fill at high tide?

Aethan's pulse thudded in his ears as he moved faster, pushing forward into the tunnel on his left, now certain that the water would drown him if he didn't act. There was no time to think. He pressed onward, stepping over rocks, pushing against the current that had risen to his waist, slowing his steps. The water climbed faster than he could move, pulling him back.

Aethan's breath came in ragged bursts, and his hand instinctively grasped forward, as he attempted pulling himself up the tunnel as the current tried pulling him back. It didn't matter how strong he was—he couldn't control the water, couldn't change the flow. He could only hope to survive it. The only thing that mattered now was finding a way out.

Aethan's breaths were shallow as he moved forward, scanning the walls for any sign of an exit, anything that might offer a way out of the ever-encroaching flood. Any pocket of air he might cling to. But the tunnel stretched on before him, dark and endless. The water rose enough that he could swim and use grips along the tunnel walls to propel himself forward.

A soft, unsettling groan emanated from the stone above. The walls closed in, and the ceiling lowered. Aethan was certain the earth itself would push him down into the water and drown him. Panic stirred at the edges of his mind, amplified as he pulled at the path ahead, kicking his feet. He reached out desperately and came back not with stone, but bone.

The water level rose, or the tunnel shrank, he wasn't sure which, and the panic in his chest made him pause. Only inches of air remained in the tunnel. Soon, the water would swallow him.

Aethan pulled in a deep breath as the final inches of air were replaced by water. Then he was underwater, swimming desperately against the current pushing him backward. Aethan forced himself to stay focused. He couldn't let fear control him. He needed to think. He needed... He needed air.

Lichen glowed softly along the tunnel walls, giving him just enough light to spot debris charging down the tunnel toward him.

No. Not just debris. Skeletal remains, broken shields, rusted armor and weapons. Aethan twisted and turned to avoid a collision and injury. The water surged faster, pushing against him with an almost deliberate force. Aethan's mind raced. The flood had to have a source—there had to be something in the tunnel that was causing the water to rise and flow back toward the pool. But where?

Aethan's lungs burned, desperate for air. If he couldn't find a way out soon, he would be another of those skeletons attacking the next poor soul to venture into this place.

Stormshard buzzed at his hip, as if attuned to his distress. Aethan glanced down at the sword, unsure of what it was trying to tell him.

His eyes darted around once more as he fought against the current, finally catching a faint shimmer near the far wall of the tunnel. It was small, almost imperceptible, but it was enough to give him hope. Without hesitation, he swam for it.

As he drew closer, he spied a small crack in the wall, just large enough for him to squeeze through. It was barely visible beneath the lichen's faint glow. Aethan reached for the crack, using all his strength to wedge his shoulder into the stone.

The water tugged at him, threatening to pull him under, but he wedged his way deeper into the narrow gap and gulped down glorious air.

The opening was tight, forcing him to twist and squeeze through, the stones scraping against his back. With one last, desperate push, he heaved himself through and into a small hidden alcove.

For a moment, Aethan lay still, his chest heaving as he refilled his lungs. The floodwaters raged past. The crack he'd squeezed through had somehow closed, preventing him from returning to the tunnel once the water cleared. What kind of godly magic haunted this place?

When the water's roar had quieted, Aethan pushed himself to his knees, scanning the new space. The alcove was small, barely tall enough for him to crouch.

Upon inspection, Aethan noticed only two pieces of fruit had made it through the flood with him. He grimaced, folding them more tightly into his makeshift sling so they wouldn't fall out. Could he eat the lichen? Some were poisonous, and he had no way of knowing which surrounded him. No, he had to save his fruit for when he truly needed to eat.

Stormshard buzzed lightly against his side. Aethan peered down at the sword, stroking the handle with relief. At least he still had the sword.

As his gaze slid past the sword, Aethan noticed a small hole in the floor just large enough for a fully grown man to slip through. He leaned over it, peering into the darkness, wondering what might be on the other side. Not that he had a choice. It was this or he stay in the cramped space until he died. It was time to keep moving.

Aethan slid through the narrow hole carefully, holding the edge as he peered down, hanging midair. Clenching his jaw, he let go and braced for impact against stone.

He hit the ground with a forceful thud, gracelessly catching himself. Aethan cried out, pressing his hand to his ribs. Did he just break one? The ground beneath him shifted as he moved, sinking slowly. Aethan peered down to see black sand.

I'm beginning to hate sand.

Aethan pushed himself up, gripping his ribs as he took in the massive space. A new cavern, impossibly wide, the walls distant and unreachable. It felt like he had stepped into another world entirely.

Maybe this is the afterlife. Or maybe he had entered the trials in the Cavern of Lost Souls. *Wouldn't Von be thrilled by that? Unless I don't survive.*

He turned, peering up and expecting to find the hole he had come from only ten or so paces above him, but it was gone. No hole. No crack. The ceiling was lost in shadows, impossibly high. That fall should have done far more damage, if not killed him.

There has to be an exit somewhere. Aethan once more scanned the endless sand stretching in all directions. It rippled in flowing, gentle dunes beneath the glow of unseen light. Aethan exhaled and adjusted his grip on Stormshard.

The only thing that stood out in the endless expanse was a distant twisted archway of dark stone that reminded Aethan of the night sky. The exit. It had to be. He could barely see it across the softly rolling sand. Aethan moved, each step sinking deeper into the treacherous sand. It was slow going. The grains swallowing his boots with every movement, forcing him to work twice as hard just to move a single step.

Minutes passed—or maybe hours. It was impossible to tell in this place. His legs ached. His muscles burned with the strain of pulling himself through the endless sand. He tried to keep his eyes on the archway, but it never seemed to get any closer. Each time he looked up, it remained at the same impossible distance.

His breath grew ragged. Aethan stopped, pressing hands against his knees, sweat dripping from his brow. He needed to rest—just for a moment. Aethan fell to one knee, glaring at the distant archway as impatience took root in his heart. How could he possibly cross this space when his every motion seemed to make the distance greater? And the sand! It shifted beneath him unnaturally, swirling like a living thing.

Aethan tensed. Then, without warning, the ground rumbled beneath him. Surface sand bounced, shifting. He barely had time to react before he was sinking. The sand sucked him downward, dragging him into its grasp. He thrashed, fighting against it, but the more he struggled, the faster he sank.

Skeletal remains and lost weapons emerged as the sand shifted and revealed them hidden beneath the surface. Others had made it this far only to be swallowed up by the sand like Aethan would soon be. He gripped Stormshard, but the sword felt heavier, the weight of it pulling him down.

No. Not like this.

Aethan closed his eyes and took a breath to steady his nerves, stilling his body. He exhaled slowly. *Patience, Aethan. Think. There must be some way out of this.*

The sand continued to pull at him, but slower. Slower. Then it stilled when he was nearly waist deep.

Had his movement caused the sand to shift? If that was the case, how could he get across the expanse of the cavern without creating such a disturbance? If the sand was swallowing him because he struggled, then maybe—just maybe—stillness was the answer. Aethan took another deep breath and loosened his muscles. His racing pulse slowed, steadied.

Then, he felt a faint pulse from Stormshard.

The sword was vibrating gently in his grip. Aethan looked down at it, and by some instinct, he shifted his grip, easing the tip down into the sand slowly... slowly, letting it sink with him enough to use for leverage.

The pull of sand around his body weakened. Aethan took a careful breath and eased his weight against the sword.

Summoning all his patience, he shifted his weight forward, driving his free hand against the sand's surface with caution while keeping Stormshard in the other hand. Inch by painfully slow inch, Aethan dragged himself out, minimizing the impact on the sand.

With one final pull, he was free and back to his feet once more. Aethan allowed himself only a few seconds to recover. The archway was still there, still distant, but he now suspected that it was not unreachable.

Aethan kept Stormshard low, using it as a counterbalance as he walked. He didn't rush, didn't force his way forward. Instead, he traveled with the sand, keeping his steps light, shifting only with the hum he sensed in the ground beneath him. Progress was painfully slow.

But the exit drew closer.

Aethan didn't know how long it took him to cross the expanse at such a slow pace. By the time he reached the archway, hunger gnawed at his stomach.

Aethan paused for a moment, eating one of his fruits as he stood before the exit, attempting to peer beyond the opening. The void inside the archway shimmered like the night sky and he could see nothing but starlight.

What kind of magic runs this place? Aethan wondered. *And who controls it?*

He didn't want to entertain the notion that Von could have been right. Aethan looked back once more at the endless expanse of sand he had crossed. He could not see the other side.

Gathering his courage, Aethan took a steadying breath, then stepped through the archway.

Chapter 35

A Gentle Touch

Aslyn lay curled beneath the heavy blankets as the day passed her by without notice. Her body ached with the weight of sorrow and grief that sleep could not ease. Nothing could.

The world beyond her window progressed on without her—the movement of servants in the halls, the stomping of horse hooves in the courtyard, the distant call or thump as the palace prepared for tomorrow—but she remained motionless, unfeeling. It was easier this way. Easier to let the time slip past without her, to ignore the hollow ache in her chest and pretend that if she stayed still long enough, the pain might simply fade away. Or, if she was lucky, she would.

All the fight left her. The fire that had burned in her just the night before, the need to escape this place, was gone, replaced by emptiness.

So much death at the command of her brother.

Her mother.

Her father.

Aethan.

Aethan.

Just thinking about them broke her heart all over again, but there were no more tears to cry. Throughout the night she wept until sleep claimed her, only to wake and repeat the process. Aslyn had dried herself out in the night, spilling every drop until just before dawn.

Then she slept for hours, unable to motivate herself to get up, finding no reason to get out of bed or even open her eyes. What was the point? Dorin had what he wanted, her crown, and he had killed everyone she loved just to get it—including that sweet prince she had grown beside. Aslyn had nothing, and tomorrow, Marek would claim her as his wife in every possible way. She no longer cared.

Between her fits of sleep and wakefulness, Aslyn thought of Blackblade—of his blood oath. What good was it to her if he couldn't protect her heart from death as well? Did he even care that she was dead inside? Did he even *know*?

Servants came and went throughout the day, bringing her trays of food she left untouched. She couldn't eat. She wasn't sure she would ever eat again. Nothing in her life had ever hurt anywhere near as much as this.

During another bout of between wakefulness and slumber, Aslyn thought of Sybil. She still hadn't seen her friend. She hadn't apologized for her behavior. Would it even matter? Was Sybil getting along just fine without her? *Of course she is*, Aslyn thought dimly. *Everyone is. No one needs me.*

The door opened at some point later in the day. Heels clicked against the floor, approaching her bedchamber, approaching her bed. Aslyn didn't open her eyes.

"You truly are a pathetic creature," Lady Fia said, her words laced with disgust.

Aslyn couldn't disagree with her. She couldn't even muster anger at the words.

"Everyone suffers, princess," Lady Fia said. "It's a curse of being mortal." She grabbed the heavy comforter and yanked it back. Aslyn's eyes shot open at the sudden cold, but Lady Fia simply tsked as she looked her over. "Get up."

Aslyn drew in a deep breath and closed her eyes, burrowing her head deeper into the pillow.

The mattress sagged. "You were one of my favorites," Lady Fia said sadly. "Probably because you remind me of myself. Beautiful, proud, and so willing to turn yourself over to pleasure when it suits you." Her hand smoothed dark curls from

Aslyn's face, much as Aslyn's mother had once done when she was younger. The thought made her insides squeeze. "I thought you were stronger than this. So disappointing."

Aslyn hated every touch of Lady Fia's fingers, but she couldn't summon the energy to push her away.

She wasn't sure how it happened, but somehow Lady Fia coaxed her out of the bed and into the washroom, where she had a bath ready and waiting. The scent of roses hung in the air. With the help of servants, Aslyn was stripped of her ruined dress and helped into the clawed tub. They gently washed away dirt, soot, and dried tears, then worked the knots out of Aslyn's hair with scented soap and oils. Throughout the process, Lady Fia lingered nearby as if supervising the entire ordeal. Aslyn simply gave in to the efforts.

Once the bath ended, she was toweled off, lightly lathered in scented oil, and slipped into a nightdress that revealed much of her body beneath the sheer red garment. Aslyn didn't care. She would just crawl back into bed when this was done.

Lady Fia lightly brushed Aslyn's long hair, and with each stroke, steam rose from her head. By the time Lady Fia finished, Aslyn's hair was dry and fell in perfect, silky waves around her shoulders. When they were done with her, Aslyn felt as if she had been prepared with a specific purpose in mind.

"I promise I will be back for this." Marek's meaning had been clear. Was that what they prepared her for now? Was he back and eager to fulfill his promise?

I no longer care, Aslyn thought pitifully. It would be easier to give in than to fight back when no one would come for her and she had no hope of escape.

Lady Fia led Aslyn out of the bathing chambers, murmuring over her shoulder in some language Aslyn couldn't understand.

They entered the bedroom, and Lady Fia stepped toward the exit. Aslyn's gaze fell on the figure sitting on the edge of her bed, freshly shaved in nothing more than pants and a dress shirt that strained around his bulk. Marek's eyes devoured her in a way that made her skin crawl.

The door closed, sealing Aslyn in the room with Marek. Alone.

"The emperor has rewarded my victory with a taste of my bride on the eve of our wedding," Marek said.

Victory. Was he involved in the attack on Mordelic during the night? Did that mean the kingdom had fallen to the emperor?

Aslyn didn't shy away from his hungry gaze, nor did she consider running or fighting back. She simply stood there, resigned to her fate. Nothing would change the inevitable. She couldn't overpower him, nor escape him. The only weapon she had to stop him had been lost in Mordelic. Fighting would only make it worse. He had promised to break her if she resisted him, but there was nothing left to break. Aslyn was already broken.

For painfully long seconds, neither of them moved. He simply drank her in inch by inch with his eyes. Once he had his fill, Marek licked his lips and raked his teeth over them.

"Come here, Aslyn," he said softly, desire burning even in his words.

Some part of her, buried deep beneath impossible layers of sorrow, resisted and screamed at her to run for the door—or the balcony. But she knew he was faster than her. He would have her before she made it halfway to an exit. No, she would do this now, and when he left her, she would throw herself from the balcony in that crimson wedding gown.

Aslyn moved like a ghost toward the bed. Toward him. Once she was within reach, Marek's hands glided over her body—her breasts, down her hips, around to cup her backside. He pulled her between his legs, tighter against his body as he sat there, and his lips moved over the sheer fabric of the flimsy gown. Marek's fingers eased up the ridiculously short skirt of the gown, one hand pressing between her clenched thighs. He lifted his dark eyes to meet hers, desire hooding his gaze.

"Open up for me, or I will make you," he breathed, his voice rough with lust. "I think we would both rather have this done the easy way, don't you?"

A lump had lodged in Aslyn's throat. She couldn't speak if she wanted to—and she didn't want to. Marek was right.

Aslyn complied and he purred with praise.

She closed her eyes and allowed her mind to drift to happier times. To a time when she still held hope and fire and promise in her heart. To Aethan....

I will be with you soon, my love.

Bast hated everything about the imperial palace despite the wealth of shadows. He moved like a shadow through the halls, keeping close to the walls, every step carefully placed to avoid making any sounds. The palace was a labyrinth of corridors and grand chambers designed to confuse intruders—or, more likely, trap them. He despised it. There was no logic to the layout, no clean paths or easy escapes. Every turn brought another set of doors, another sweeping staircase, another gilded hallway that felt exactly like the last.

The palace was alive with movement. Servants hurried through the corridors, arms burdened with silks and flowers, making final preparations for the wedding. Black Guards stood watch at key junctions, their gazes sharp, though none suspected him yet. Bast timed his movements to avoid them, slipping through side passages and shadowed alcoves, trusting the chaotic energy of the upcoming ceremony to mask his presence.

Something deep within ached like a wound unable to heal. He didn't know why, but it reinforced his urgency.

He needed to find Aslyn. He didn't know where her room would be, but she had to be somewhere within these walls, likely higher up so she couldn't easily escape out a window. The emperor wouldn't risk her not being here on the eve of her wedding to Bloodstone.

As he crept past a long gallery lined with towering windows, Bast caught sight of the mountains beyond the palace grounds, a stark, unyielding range. Their peaks hid in a sea of gray clouds. His lip curled in distaste. So much open space, and yet the palace felt like a cage.

A sudden movement sent Bast ducking into a narrow alcove. Two ambassadors strode past, their voices low and unconcerned, yet urgent. Bast heard only a few scant bits of the conversation.

"... fires of blessing... harvest the stone through blood... ancient runes..."

None of it made any sense to him.

Bast held his breath, waiting for their footfalls to fade before moving again. He slipped through a half-open door, expecting another useless chamber. Instead, he stared at something far more interesting.

A passage. Hidden behind a false wall, the narrow stone corridor led downward, its steps vanishing into darkness.

A way out?

His pulse quickened as he took a step forward, noting the scent of damp stone and the cool draft curling up from below. He followed the passage. The air grew colder as he descended. The walls tightened around him, rough and uneven, as if carved in haste.

At the bottom, the tunnel opened into a narrow crevice in the mountainside. The wind howled low through the gap, bringing with it the scent of pine and wet stone. A narrow, treacherous trail snaked along the sheer cliff side, leading down toward the lower reaches of the southern mountains. One misstep could send him tumbling into the abyss below. This was an escape route, a way out of the imperial palace without detection. Dangerous, but their only option.

Satisfied, he turned back, retracing his steps through the passage. Now that he knew how to get out, he needed to find Aslyn.

Bast closed the hidden door behind him and marked it with his inverted shadow magic so he could find it again. Then he slipped back into the main halls, his mind focused on the task at hand. Somewhere in this cursed palace, she was waiting. He would find her and they would be long gone before the sun rose again.

When he reached the intersection with another hall, Bast marked it with shadows, leaving the trail behind him to follow for escape. The only question would be how much that path meandered.

"You broke her will," a woman said to her companion.

Bast ducked into the shadows, knife in hand just in case he needed to attack. The click of heels and stomp of boots together approached his junction.

Bast recognized the male voice.

"She was far too easy to break," Valen replied tersely. "It's disappointing, to be frank. But just in case she has one more trick up her sleeve and she is simply lulling us into complacency, we still have one more card to play."

The woman purred in delight. "Yes. He has been terribly resistant. I look forward to finally breaking him." They passed, and Bast recognized the woman as Lady Fia. Neither took notice of him lurking in the shadows. "I just left her chambers. She won't resist the Bloodstone boy tonight."

Bast's heart stopped and suddenly his palm burned, though whether it was in his head or whether Aslyn was in real danger he didn't know. His gaze darted up the hall they had come from. She just left Aslyn with Marek. Bast was close. If he could be quick enough, he could stop whatever Marek was forcing her to do. But he couldn't move until Valen and Lady Fia left the hall. He couldn't risk them spotting him even in the shadows.

"You gave her the oils?" Valen asked.

"Yes. All over. It required every last drop. Bloodstone had better perform."

Perform... Bast clenched his jaw, fist tightening around the knife in his hand.

Valen chuckled as they reached the end of the hall, and his words made Bast's skin crawl. "I don't think that will be an issue. He's been hungry for her since Stormvalor. Nothing short of his death will stop him tonight."

They entered an office at the end of the hall.

I will deliver that death, Bast thought with murderous intent.

Bast kept to the shadows along the walls, moving as swiftly as he dared in the direction they had come, marking each intersection until he reached what he could only assume to be the correct one.

At the end of the corridor stood a single Black Guard, stationed outside a heavy oak door. Aslyn's door. It had to be. He was running out of options.

Bast cursed under his breath. There was no chance of slipping by unnoticed. He needed a distraction to lure the guard away.

Drawing a slow breath, Bast reached for his magic, letting the shadows coil at his fingertips. With a flick of his wrist, the darkness slithered across the floor, unseen by the Black Guard, and it coalesced at the far end of the hallway. A priceless vase perched on a pedestal trembled, then toppled, shattering into a hundred gleaming shards.

The Black Guard's head snapped toward the noise. He hesitated for several long seconds and Bast worried he would have to fight the guard and risk drawing attention to his position. The guard finally turned and marched away, his boots thumping against the stone as he went to investigate. Bast released a breath of relief, but he didn't waste a single second.

The moment the guard turned his back and marched away, Bast slipped from the shadows and pressed himself against the door, fingers already testing the latch.

Unlocked.

Fools. They were so unconcerned with Aslyn trying to leave that they didn't bother considering someone else entering.

Bast slipped into the sitting room, easing the door closed quickly and quietly behind him. A quick sweep told him he was alone in this room, and his ears picked up on murmurs from the adjoined bedroom. Rage instantly flared in his veins and he moved like a wraith, an instrument of death eager for the kill.

The bedroom door remained open, and he once again laughed at the arrogance of these people. Bast cloaked himself in shadows and utter silence as he entered, and the sight immediately made him see red.

Marek stood at the foot of the bed, shirtless and stepping out of his pants. Then he crawled over Aslyn. She didn't move, didn't blink. Was the oil some kind of drug to make her complacent so Marek could have his way with her? A sheer red cloth bunched around her waist. It didn't even qualify as clothing.

A low rumble emitted from Marek's lips. Words, most likely, but Bast couldn't hear them through his fury.

Bast wasn't even aware of his own actions as the inferno in his veins and the shadows around him turned to violence. One second, Marek was crawling over Aslyn, clearly readying to have his way. The next second, Bast's shadows coiled around his throat and ripped him from the bed. Darkness collected in the room as if Morumbris himself visited the chamber. Marek choked and tried to form words as the shadows pinned him to the floor at Bast's feet.

Bast moved without thinking, sliding a knife into one hand, and in the other, the rock-hard length now exposed to open air with Marek pinned on his back. Bast sneered as he leaned close enough for Marek to see his steely eyes.

"I let you go last time," he growled. "This time I won't be so kind."

Marek fought to draw in deep breaths and attempted to speak, but Bast didn't give him the pleasure. He shoved a gag of shadows deep down Marek's throat. The man bucked and tried to break free, but it would do him no good.

Bast flashed the knife in Marek's face. "The poison on this blade works slowly," he explained, his voice utterly cold, the sound of death. "First, you experience heat. It gradually increases to pain like a simple wound. But it opens that pain slowly until your heartbeat increases. Your muscles seize. Your lungs fail. If you're lucky, you die. If you're unlucky..." Bast emitted a low, dangerous chuckle. "Well, let's just say your inability to get hard ever again will be the least of your worries."

Slowly, Bast touched the tip of the blade to Marek's flesh, careful not to cut him. Not yet. Soon. *Very* soon. Marek's entire body tensed in response.

"She will never belong to you," Bast promised darkly.

Marek's eyes bulged as the tip of the knife pierced deep into the flesh of his member. A scream stuffed deep in his throat as Bast slowly carved the blade along the length of his shaft. Marek's eyes rolled into his head at the pain. No, he wouldn't get the pleasure of passing out. Bast slapped him, forcing Marek's eyes open again.

"I'm not done with you, Bloodstone."

The giant of a man went utterly pale. Tears rolled down his temples, but still he couldn't make a sound. All he could do was flap his mouth like a fish out of water, gasping for air. Sweat beaded along his hairline and rolled down his temples. The drug worked already. Good.

Bast trembled with rage. He *burned* with it. The only cure came with a slow twist of his blade into what remained of Marek's precious family jewels, rupturing them, destroying them completely. Marek's back arched. His muscles tensed and twitched against the shadows binding him to the floor. The scream was blocked in his throat by the shadow gag, but his chorded neck muscles strained as his mouth opened in that silent scream. But the agony wasn't enough. Not by a long shot. Bast wanted to torture him slowly, to make him beg for death for days before giving him the sweet release.

Something pulsed against Bast's chest. He ignored it, yanking the knife out of what remained of Marek's mangled, destroyed family jewels. With malice in his steely eyes, Bast pulled out his black dagger and dragged the tip of the blade along Marek's biceps, severing the muscles, then along the muscles in his calf. The wounds would heal in time, but he wouldn't be able to stand or fight back until they were long gone.

Each time Bast struck, Marek grunted against the gag, unable to summon the strength for anything more. When he looked ready to pass out again, Bast slapped him several times to keep him alert. The scent of Marek's fear hung heavy in the air, mixed with the metallic tang of blood. The tip of the dagger carved a message in Marek's forehead.

RAPIST

Aslyn's whimper on the bed drew Bast from his haze of brutality as he finished the final cut. He blinked once, twice, admiring his handiwork.

Marek lost consciousness, and this time, Bast allowed it. He wiped the blood off his blades with Marek's discarded shirt, then rose to his feet slowly, turning toward her as he sheathed the knives.

Aslyn curled in a ball on the bed, trembling violently, exposed to him with the red gown completely around her waist. They didn't have much time. Marek hadn't made a sound, and the emperor would likely want them left alone, assuming Marek was having his way with the princess. But Bast wouldn't risk this opportunity. He had to get them out of here.

Bast pulled a rumpled blanket from the bed and wrapped it over Aslyn, careful not to touch her. "I'll only be a second," he promised.

Aslyn blinked, but her eyes didn't focus on him. Bast had never felt so shattered seeing her in such a state. Aslyn, the princess full of sass and fire. But the emperor had doused her flames.

Bast moved quickly to the bathroom, washing the blood off his hands. By the time he returned the room, Aslyn's gaze had focused...

On Marek's body.

Bast moved into her line of vision at the foot of the bed. "Aslyn, look at me."

It took painfully slow seconds, but her eyes lifted slowly—so heartbreakingly slowly—up his body until she saw his face. She blinked once. Twice.

"Did he hurt you?" Bast asked. If she said yes, Bast would kill him without hesitation.

Aslyn simply stared at him for painfully long seconds as if she couldn't connect reality to her own mind. Then she shook her head no, just once.

"We need to leave, but I need you to get dressed," he instructed slowly. "Wear something you can move in quickly. Can you do that for me?"

She didn't respond.

He didn't dare move closer. "Aslyn, can you go get dressed?"

She swallowed repeatedly, her lips parting, but no sound came out. Giving up, she simply nodded.

"I can help you, if need be, but I won't touch you unless you ask," he said.

Silver tears lined her amber eyes. Bast wanted to hold her, reassure her, but he meant what he said. He wouldn't touch her without permission. She was too fragile. He had seen this happen before and knew what could happen if he made the wrong move. It was the thing that led his stepfather into a fit of rage that killed his mother while Bast hid from his wrath.

I won't hide again.

Aslyn slipped off the bed, her legs unsteady. He held out his arms in case she needed him, but didn't make a move. As she padded to the walk-in closet, clutching the blanket tight around her body, her gaze locked on Marek. The bastard was still breathing. He deserved death, but Aslyn had been through enough. With luck, the poison would do the job for Bast.

The moment she disappeared, Bast grabbed the sheet from the bed and threw it over Marek. Then he set about gathering anything of value that they could use to pay their way anywhere but here.

Bast heard Aslyn weeping in the closet as she dressed. It made his heart ache for her. It made him wish he could torture Marek all over again.

When Aslyn emerged a few minutes later, Bast blinked in shock at her attire. Aslyn wore a sensible shirt and form-fitting pants, with boots suitable for hiking and not dancing. Leather training armor covered her chest. He hated himself for how much he warmed at the sight. The last thing she needed was another male objectifying her.

"Do you have a cloak?" he asked gently. "Something warm?"

She reached back and pulled a fur-lined cloak from a hanger. It was a fine piece meant to keep her warm in these cold halls, not ideal for hiking, but it would have to do for now.

"What happened to the knife I gave you?" he asked, moving toward the door and motioning for her to join him.

Aslyn's voice cracked as she spoke weakly. "Lost. In Mordelic."

Mordelic! How had she…? The realization dawned on him like the rising sun. That was why the oath had taken him. She had been elsewhere. But how did she get there and back so quickly?

Questions for later.

"We need to leave as quietly as possible," Bast said softly as they edged toward the exit. "But we have to get past your guard without raising any alarms. I need you for that."

Aslyn tensed from head to toe.

"I will protect you," he reassured her, but he wasn't sure if the words offered any comfort in her current mental state. "I will be behind the door. You will open it and lure him in. I will close the door and kill him before he can raise any alarm. He won't even touch you. I promise."

Aslyn swallowed, her amber eyes calculating something, then she nodded. Maybe her stunned visage would help make the call for help more real.

Bast slipped back behind the door and nodded to her, his black sword already drawn.

Aslyn licked her lips and opened the door. "We need your help," she said, her voice breaking over every word. "Please."

She stepped backward, not taking her eyes off the guard on the other side. Bast listened to the clink of armor as the guard moved slowly toward her. The moment he was clear of the door, Bast threw out his shadows in both directions. The door swung shut silently. Pulled by the encroaching shadows, the guard reeled backward into Bast's waiting blade. The weapon punched through a weak point in the back of the armor and out the other side. Instant death. It was probably a mercy, considering what this man had to have gone through to become a Black Guard.

The armor was so heavy it nearly pulled Bast down. He pushed the guard off the sword, away from the doorway, stumbling backward to catch his balance.

It was over in seconds.

Aslyn's eyes locked on the guard and Bast worried the death would be too much for her. Instead, that fire that drew him to her sparked in her eyes. Maybe she would be herself soon.

"Let's go," he whispered, dragging the door a crack. "Keep to the shadows and I can shield us from unwanted eyes."

Bast checked the hallway before slipping out and motioning for her to join him.

As he followed his hidden trail of shadows to the exit, Aslyn slid her hand into his, holding tight, as if he were the buoy holding her afloat.

Warmth spread through his chest.

This would work. They would make it.

CHAPTER 36

Shadows and Wraiths

Bast led Aslyn through the twisting corridors of the imperial palace, their footsteps silent against the marble floors. Shadows curled around them, a living thread of darkness that acted as a shield against unwanted eyes. He followed the trail of magic he had left leading from Aslyn's chambers to the secret passage. It was a whisper of power that even the emperor's hounds would struggle to trace.

Aslyn's hand was warm in his, her grip steady, but she hadn't spoken a word since they'd left her chambers. Not when they passed the grand hall where the emperor's banners hung in stiff, ominous silence alongside the crimson Bloodstone banners. Not when they ducked into alcoves to avoid patrolling guards pressed dangerously close to one another. When Bast occasionally glanced at her, searching for some flicker of emotion beyond the blank calm she wore like armor, nothing showed.

He worried about her more than he should. She had endured Marek's cruelty, survived whatever torment the emperor's pet had inflicted upon her, and she remained silent and utterly unreadable. Not so long ago, Bast would have made some sharp remark to get a reaction out of her, to test whether she would snap at him or smirk—or throw a shoe. Now? He wasn't sure he wanted to know what lay beneath that quiet.

They paused at an intersection in the halls and he glanced at her. "None of this is your fault, and you didn't deserve any of it," he said.

Aslyn flinched, tilting her face away so that her hair fell in her face.

It made his heart ache for her. Bast swallowed. He remembered the way his mother had hidden inward after trauma and abuse, how she needed that time to pull herself back together again. Perhaps Aslyn needed the same. "I'm here with you. I'm sorry I wasn't before."

Aslyn's grip on his hand slackened, and he feared she would drop it. A moment later, she held on tighter. Bast took it as a silent signal that she would be okay, as long as he could get her out of this place.

So, he kept moving. She followed without hesitation. Compliance and silence had never been her strongest qualities, and Bast found he quite disliked them.

He could sense the end of his trail. They were close. Just a few more turns, and they'd be safe.

Then Bast felt it.

A ripple through the shadows. A *wrongness* in them.

He slowed, instincts prickling the hair at the back of his neck. Aslyn must have sensed it too, because she stiffened beside him and her hand trembled.

A voice cut through the silence.

"Going somewhere, princess?"

Bast turned. His free hand shot to the dagger at his hip, ready to fight.

Lord Lund Bloodstone stood in the corridor behind them, crimson cloak pooling like spilled blood around his feet. His presence was a wall and his gaze was sharp. The flickering torchlight made the silver streaks in his dark hair gleam. The knowing smirk set Bast on edge. Bloodstone had caught them, and by the glint in his eye, he wasn't the least bit surprised. Had he been expecting Bast, or for Aslyn to attempt an escape?

Aslyn remained motionless beside Bast, but her grip on his hand tightened enough that it hurt his hand a little. Her amber eyes were locked on Marek's father in terror. Seeing that look in her eyes brought Bast's fury back to the surface. What had Marek's father already done to her?

Bast met Lord Bloodstone's gaze with a cool, unreadable expression of his own. "Didn't take you for the skulking in the dark type," he drawled. "Bit beneath you, isn't it?"

Lord Bloodstone chuckled lowly. "And yet, here we are." His eyes flicked to Aslyn. "Princess, I see you've taken to following bad influences."

She didn't respond. Didn't even flinch.

Bast's pulse quickened. Lord Bloodstone was known to play the long game, moving pieces across the board while others spilled their blood on it. If he had caught them, it wasn't by accident.

Which meant he had a reason for letting them stand there, unchallenged.

Bast flexed his hand slightly to encourage Aslyn to let go. For a moment she gripped him tighter, then she relented. Bast subtly slid a knife into her palm, then shifted his stance, placing himself between Lord Bloodstone and Aslyn. "You've mixed yourself up, Bloodstone," he said lightly. "The way I see it, *you* are the bad influence."

Bloodstone smiled, but there was no warmth in it. "The emperor does not appreciate uninvited guests, *Lord Khrahar*."

Fuck! If Lord Bloodstone knew who he was, Bast would be a fool to assume the emperor didn't as well. *Dorin*. It had to be him. That prick was the only one who knew who he was, and that he had masqueraded as Lord Zayne Khrahar in Stormvalor. Bast didn't deliver the Jewel of Arithia, and Dorin had done exactly as promised. He let the emperor know who he was, what he looked like.

Bast's grip on his dagger tightened. If he had to fight, he would, but Lord Bloodstone wasn't drawing his sword. He was waiting, and that unsettled Bast more than a bare blade ever could.

If he acted quick enough with his shadow magic, Bast could incapacitate Lord Bloodstone long enough for Aslyn to escape up the hall. With any luck, Bast would be right on her heels. The dagger would only be useful if Lord Bloodstone drew his weapon and attacked, and something told Bast that if he threw a knife at the man, he would fail in the assassination attempt.

Slowly, carefully, Bast drew the magic into himself, summoning shadows slowly enough that no one should notice. *Keep him talking*, Bast thought. Thankfully, Lord Bloodstone's ego made his lips loose.

"I know everything, princess," Lord Bloodstone said with a vicious smirk. "Your girl was such a good little spy. One of the few things my son did right was charming her into spilling all your secrets." His gaze shifted to Bast. "Blackblade. An assassin sworn by blood oath to a princess. How cliché. Admittedly, Kaiti was a little unclear about the details on *how* that happened."

Aslyn made a small sound, then spoke with far more force than Bast expected from her. "What have you done to her?"

"What have *I* done?" Lord Bloodstone chuckled. "Nothing at all. Marek was the one who won her over. A few charming words and empty promises, and she was eating out of his hand for *months*."

Months. How far back did the betrayal go? Did Kaiti help with the massacre in the royal suite? Bast recalled the girl's terror, and some of it was certainly real, but how much was an act? Maybe she hadn't realized how bad the fight would be until she saw what the Black Guard could do.

Bast didn't dare take his eyes from Lord Bloodstone, but he did edge Aslyn backward inch by inch. More. He needed more magic.

"Sadly, she wore out her usefulness to him." Lord Bloodstone shrugged as if none of it mattered much to him. But the implication was clear enough.

Those who were no longer useful to men like them were dead.

The magic inside of Bast hummed its seductive call as it grew, filling him with all he could hold.

"Aslyn, count to three in your head," Bast whispered, careful not to move his lips. "Then go. A right, then a left. Last door on the right. I'll catch up."

One...

"As delightful as this conversation has been," Lord Bloodstone said.

Two...

"I've grown bored with it."

Three!

Lord Bloodstone reached for his sword. At the same moment, Bast's shadows exploded out of him, directed into the space between them and Lord Bloodstone, thick and impenetrable. Bast heard Aslyn's boots against the floor as she fled.

With death in his eyes, Bast slipped his sword from the sheath on his back. A flutter of crimson swirled the shadows along the floor and Bast lunged into action. He angled his sword in a deadly strike toward what should have been Lord Bloodstone's neck.

A shock and vibration of clashing swords ran up his arm. How had the man known where the strike would fall in the dark?

Bast barely had time to register the shift in shadows before Lord Bloodstone moved.

The older man's blade lashed out with precision, forcing Bast to pivot fast, parrying just in time. Steel rang against steel, the sharp sound swallowed by the shadows curling thickly around them. Bast's magic poured from his body, spilling into the corridor like a living thing, suffocating the light. For anyone else, it would have been blindness. For him, it was an advantage.

Or should have been.

He felt it then—a wrongness slithering through the dark. The air grew heavy with something unnatural. A sharp, acrid scent burned in his nose, like sulfur smoldering nearby. His grip on his sword tightened.

Something moved beyond his control. A whispering hiss, barely human. The shadows churned, resisting him.

Bast twisted, catching Lord Bloodstone's next strike and forcing him back. The man was fast, but Bast had spent his life fighting in the dark. He should have had the upper hand. And yet, the shadows were wrong.

Shapes twisted in the gloom. Wraiths formed from the very magic he had unleashed. Not *his* creatures. Something else.

They tore away from his control, slipping past him with nightmarish shrieks, their inhuman voices grating against his ears. Not just formless darkness—these things had shape. Clawed hands stretched toward the woman retreating up the hallway.

Aslyn.

Bast snarled, cutting his blade through the space between them, slicing at the nearest wraith. His sword met only air. The creature reformed like smoke before racing past him.

Lord Bloodstone chuckled and the sound carried on the shadows with chilling effect.

"You've stopped nothing, Blackblade," Bloodstone said, voice calm even as he lunged again, forcing Bast to block. "Did you really think you were the only one who could shape the darkness to your will?"

Bast shoved him back, his mind racing. These weren't just random specters. Bloodstone was controlling them.

And they were all moving for Aslyn.

Bast dropped low, slashing toward Bloodstone's legs, but the man leaped back, sidestepping into the thick black haze. Bast barely caught the next blow, their swords locking. Bloodstone's strength was solid, unyielding.

"She's already broken, you know," Lord Bloodstone said, voice barely audible above the distant shrieks of the shadow wraiths on the hunt. "Used up and shattered by the very people she trusted."

Rage flashed through Bast, white-hot. "I delighted in neutering your useless spawn."

He twisted his blade, wrenching free and striking fast. Lord Bloodstone barely deflected in time, the force sending him skidding a step back.

"But you won't live to see what I have done to your bloodline," Bast growled. He could feel the seconds slipping from him.

He had to finish this. Now.

Lord Bloodstone howled with rage of his own, slashing at Bast's neck. He swiftly raised his sword to block. As their blades locked again, Bast ripped the dagger from his belt in one swift motion and slammed it into Lord Bloodstone's side. Then he twisted the jagged blade before ripping it out.

Warm blood splattered on his face. Lord Bloodstone gurgled, slumped, then fell dead at Bast's feet.

The familiar stomp of Black Guard boots approached.

Time's up. Bast took off after Aslyn, praying the shadow wraiths died with Lord Bloodstone.

When he rounded the corner, Bast skidded to a halt. The knife he had given her lay on the ground near a wall.

But Aslyn was gone.

Agony ripped at Bast's heart. *No...*

He cleaned his sword and dagger, returning them to their sheaths, then lifted his scarred palm to his chest, pressing against the Jewel of Arithia. *If ever the heir to your kingdom needed help, it's now*, he thought.

"Guide me," he commanded it, praying beyond hope that it would work.

The Jewel hummed in response against his skin. He followed its guidance through the palace corridors, ready to deliver death to any who got in his way.

CHAPTER 37

War and Peace

The cavern Aethan stepped into rippled with powerful magic, then vanished, replaced by a walled courtyard. He strode forward, his boots crunching over gravel. The tang of steel and dust hung heavy in the air, but beyond that, there was nothing remarkable about the place—just a wide courtyard flanked by shadowed alcoves and racks of weapons. He couldn't recall ever seeing this courtyard before. Not in Vorovesti or Novavito anywhere he knew.

The sky hung heavy with thick gray clouds, casting a dull, oppressive gloom over everything. He could not recall the last time he saw the sunshine.

As he strode deeper into the courtyard, eyes forward for signs of trouble, something cracked and crunched beneath his boot. He froze, peering down at the source of the crunch. His gaze caught on the skeletal remains—the arm—and his stomach clenched. When he looked up again, at least a dozen other skeletons lay scattered across the courtyard. The brittle bones were wrapped in the remnants of armor, rusted steel scattered among them. The sight sent a chill through him.

Others had stood here before him, facing whatever hid in the shadowy alcoves of the courtyard, and they had died. He gritted his teeth and wrapped a hand firmly around Stormshard's hilt.

Movement flickered at the edge of his vision. Aethan spun in time to see a group of warriors stepping from the alcoves, clad in all-black armor with their faces hidden behind visors. The Black Guards—the emperor's elite force. A dozen of them. Their weapons gleamed in the dismal light as they formed a loose half-circle, blocking his exit.

Aethan exhaled slowly and lifted Stormshard, assuming a defensive stance as he had been trained to do.

The silence before the fight was brief. No one moved. Aethan took the opportunity to size up each of the guards, probing for weak points in armor and stance.

The first guard lunged, a sharp thrust aimed at Aethan's ribs. The strike was brutal and deadly, testing his defenses. Aethan sidestepped smoothly, catching the blade with his own and deflecting it wide before pivoting into a counterstrike. His sword found a gap in the attacker's armor, and the guard lurched back with a choked gasp as dark blood seeped from the slice at his back. He staggered as if no longer in control of his legs, then fell to the ground. He wasn't dead. Not yet. But he wouldn't be able to stand again. Sometimes incapacitation was better than death when he didn't have time to land a finishing blow, just as he didn't now.

Before Aethan could resume his defenses, the remaining Black Guards descended upon him as one.

Steel clashed in a flurry of ringing blows. Aethan shifted and spun, his blade a blur as he wove between strikes. Stormshard seemed to move with a will of its own. When a strike came too fast for him to react, the sword adjusted for him, angling to deflect the blow. He parried high, dodged low, struck back with accurate, brutal efficiency. His opponents were skilled, their movements precise and highly coordinated, like a single entity determined to end his life. They pressed him relentlessly. Every strike vibrated up his arm and into his shoulder, meant to kill him. The sword pulsed in his grasp, demanding more speed from him, but he grew tired.

Aethan let his instincts take over, dancing around each attack to the best of his ability, flowing with Stormshard's adjustments. Several guards fell to fatal wounds, but the others did not relent.

A cut sliced across Aethan's upper arm—a shallow wound, but a reminder that he couldn't afford to misstep. Gritting his teeth, he drove his knee into an opponent's gut and used the momentum to slam the hilt of his sword into another's jaw. Something cracked beneath the impact, and the man crumpled.

Still, they came.

Aethan's breath grew heavy, muscles burning. By instinct, he shifted his grip, altering his stance as the next attack landed, deflected by his adjustment. He had taken down half of them, but the remaining fighters were adapting, altering to his movements. He needed to end this quickly.

Feinting a retreat, he let them press forward, luring them into overextending. At the last second, he twisted and struck. His blade cut through the air, a deadly arc that sent another man sprawling. He seized a fallen spear from the ground and flung it, impaling another through the eye. The man went down without a sound.

The dance continued in a flurry as the final four Black Guards closed in on each side of him. Aethan half crouched, his muscles coiled as their ring closed tight around him. He steadied his breath, counting each uniform step. Stormshard buzzed with wild life in his hand, as if sensing the end of the fight.

All four swords swing in unison, aimed at Aethan's neck. He tucked and rolled, slicing the calf of one guard, who then fell. As Aethan rolled back to his feet, he arched Stormshard up at an angle, slicing the neck of another. Blood sprayed from the wound, hitting his cheek as he twisted away from the final two guards.

As he moved cautiously back, keeping them both in his line of vision, the guards split toward either side of him. Aethan waited, practicing his even breathing despite exhaustion. At his feet, a short sword lay abandoned by someone who failed this fight before him.

The two guards moved as one, their boots hammering the ground as they closed in. Aethan crouched, snatching up the short sword and thrusting it behind him as he thrust Stormshard upward. Both blades found their marks, one through a guard's gut just below the armor, the other through the gap at the neck. Pain seared Aethan's back and he growled, fighting off the scream of agony until he knew the battle was over.

No one else moved. He released the short sword and the Black Guard stumbled a step, then toppled. He yanked Stormshard from the last guard as the man spit up blood, gurgling as he fell dead.

Aethan scanned the courtyard for further attacks, but nothing moved.

As suddenly as it had begun, the fight was over. His strength gave out, and he fell to his knees, gulping down air.

"Well fought." The rich female voice startled Aethan. It was the first voice he heard in days.

He looked around, holding Stormshard up for a fight, but saw no one else with him.

The voice came from everywhere... and nowhere. "You are what they claimed."

Aethan wiped the blood from his blade. "Who claimed?"

Nothing but silence greeted him.

Aethan glared around him, raising his voice. "What who claimed?"

The voice echoed around him. "But not all battles are won with a blade. Some paths require sacrifice in the name of balance."

Aethan's fingers tightened around his sword, and he staggered to his feet. "Show yourself!"

Once more, silence greeted him.

The courtyard around Aethan rippled and shifted. One moment, the cold stone and open sky of the courtyard stretched before him. The next moment, the air was still—unnaturally so. Darkness spread across the sky, devouring any traces of light.

Aethan blinked, his breaths quickening. The tattoo over his heart burned. All vanished into the ether, leaving only a single road stretching ahead of him. His boots felt heavier as he strode cautiously along the road.

After only a few steps, the road split into two paths. One was a war-torn landscape with smoke and blackness rising from the distance. The metallic tang of blood drifted along the air. Despite the darkness, Aethan could see the banners of the Vorovesti king snapping on the sharp breeze. His countrymen faced an insurmountable foe that would certainly swallow them whole in the final charge.

He moved toward the first path, drawn by the urgency, the need to defend his people, to preserve his kingdom. His fingers twitched around Stormshard's hilt. The path of war. He could almost taste it. The sharp edge of the blade, the fire of battle in his veins. It was the path of action, of strength, the path his training had taught him to embrace. To act decisively with strength, honor, and valor.

Yet Aethan hesitated as the second path called to him. Not with voice, but with need. With hope.

He peered along the second path. The sense of hope made little sense to him as he gazed at the desert and distant red mountains. Unlike the war path, this desert path blazed with sunlight, promising searing heat that could burn the unprepared alive.

Yet hope pulled him that direction.

It made no sense. How could a deadly desert offer more hope than defending his people in battle? *"We all have a path to walk, Aethan."* Sybil's voice called to him from the recesses of his mind.

Nothing moved in the desert save the waves of heat rippling off the sand.

Aethan stood at the crossroads. The distant cries of his dying countrymen and the thrum of battle violence tore at his heart.

Aethan exhaled slowly, grounding himself against the pain those cries created in his heart.

No, he thought, turning away from the desert path. *My people need me.*

He stepped away from the desert path, his pace increasing with each footfall as the pressure of the battle pulled at him. His tattoo burned like a hot iron against his skin and he gritted his teeth against the pain.

But just as he was about to step foot on the first path toward his kingdom, that unassailable tug of hope weighed down on him.

Once more, he peered down the desert path. Some voice in his mind warned him that if he turned from this path, all hope would be lost. Balance could never be restored to the five kingdoms.

"No," Aethan whimpered as the death cries of his countrymen called to him from the warpath. "I can help them." Once more, that path beckoned him.

"Stay the course," Sybil whispered in his mind.

"I can't. I'm not strong enough to turn my back on my people." What kind of terrible test was this?

"The only thing stronger than your sister is you." Lux Starkling's words rang in Aethan's mind.

Aethan turned toward the desert path once more as his father's voice drew him in that direction. Sybil believed Aethan was the key. He didn't understand how or why, but that sense of hope felt as familiar as his sister's hugs. Warm, welcoming... and vital.

With a last glance over his shoulder at the war path, Aethan stepped toward the desert.

The burning of the dragon tattoo vanished, transforming into a soothing balm for his aching heart.

And as only the path forward into the desert remained, Aethan could no longer recall why his heart ached.

CHAPTER 38

A Righteous, Mighty Wave

Aslyn repeated Blackblade's directions in her head the second she bolted, startled by the intensity of his shadow magic as it burst out of him. He would catch up. He *would* catch up, because Aslyn knew without a doubt that he was the only reason she found any strength to carry on. To hope. *He will catch up. He won't leave me again.*

The shrieks that came from the fight in the other hall were unnatural. They froze her blood and slowed her steps momentarily. She heard them before. In Stormvalor.

The wraithlike monsters rounded the corner, all wispy shadows, sharp claws, and even sharper teeth. The sight only paused her for a fraction of a second before she pivoted and ran as fast as her legs could carry her. Could she even outrun nightmare creatures?

They swarmed her in moments. Aslyn tried to fight back, swinging the knife Blackblade slid into her palm with desperate slashes, but the blade passed through nothing at all. Dark shadows swirled around her, grasping her in a tight hold. Ice cold pain shot up her arm from where one of the creatures grabbed her wrist. Her fingers numbed and the knife fell from her palm. Aslyn struggled, but the more she moved, the harder the shadows squeezed her. She opened her mouth to scream, but darkness poured into her, silencing her cry.

When she could see again, Aslyn opened her eyes to a gruesome tiled mosaic beneath her. Her heart stuttered.

The throne room. How had she gotten here?

"I'm starting to think you are more trouble than you're worth," Valen said coldly.

Aslyn pushed herself off the floor, glaring at the emperor on his black throne. In a moment of defiance, she spit on the tiled face of the first emperor, Narcisse.

Her amber eyes swept the throne room, searching the shadows for Blackblade but she couldn't see him or sense him. How much time passed from the hallway to here? Was Blackblade even alive? Hope of escape once more evaporated.

They were not alone in the throne room. At his side, so close she should have just been on the throne with him, sat Sybil. Something about her was different. Her golden skin was paler, but her hair had a new luster to it, and her eyes burned a fierce shade of blue they hadn't had before. Aslyn swore if she looked closer enough she could see pools of silver light in Sybil's eyes, twinkling like stars.

"Be a dear and stay quiet for once," Valen said.

An invisible gag kept all sound from escaping Aslyn's throat almost instantly. All of her sword training had proven utterly useless. Never mind that she had no sword to wield. If she did, she would take her chances trying to strike down the emperor, even if it meant her instant death.

There were no Black Guards. No Lady Fia.

A muffled grunt to her right drew Aslyn's gaze to Lux Starkling, beaten, bound, and bleeding. Someone had tied his arms up on either side of him with thick, knotted ropes that cut into his wrists as it held him on his knees. He was shirtless, revealing a tattoo on his chest just like Aethan's, and his back was slashed to bleeding ribbons. What was he doing there? And what were they doing to him?

"Now, where were we?" Valen mused, but malice glowed in his depthless black eyes. "Ah. A confession."

Aslyn's gaze darted back to Sybil, who did a fantastic job looking at everything *except* her father. Their eyes met briefly, and in that instant, clarity shone in Sybil's eyes. Clarity and agony.

"How do we unlock the runes, Lux?" Valen asked sharply.

Lux lifted his weary head, and hatred burned in his blue eyes. He curled his lips in disgust and clenched his jaw tight, snarling at the emperor.

Snap!

Aslyn winced as Lux screamed when an invisible whip of air sliced deeper into his back. Where was Blackblade? Had Lord Bloodstone killed him? *Stop looking for him. He's dead.*

"I know what your father did to Olivya," Lux growled through his panting breaths.

"Do you?" Valen smirked. "How delightful it would be were that true. But something tells me you have no clue what happened to your wife. Not really."

Lux bared his teeth as if ready to take a bite out of Valen's neck, his own bulging as he strained against the bindings holding his arms out.

"Now, I asked you a question, Lux, and you have not answered," Valen continued, ignoring Lux's obvious hate and rage. "If you prefer, I can continue to experiment on your daughter to get answers for myself."

Continue?

That caught Lux's attention. He tugged at his ropes, howling in rage. "Your father killed my wife. Why? What happened to Olivya's necklace?"

"Why?" Valen scoffed. "For power, obviously. And Sybil has far more than your wife. I wonder just how much she is hiding from me."

"Stop!" Lux's demand fell on deaf ears.

Valen ignored him as he reached over and unbuttoned the flap of the dress that covered Sybil's neck.

Aslyn gasped at the scars on the other woman's chest, but her gasp made no sound.

Valen traced a finger along one of the runes like a lover. Sybil stiffened and tears sprang to her eyes. "Shall I ask again, or experiment again?"

"I told you... I don't know," Lux said through his pain, teeth gritted.

Valen sighed heavily, then reached into his boot and pulled out a knife. "Let's find out, shall we?"

Sybil tried to pull away, but Valen grabbed the back of her neck, his grip unrelenting.

In a stark moment of clarity, Aslyn realized she was not bound. Valen thought so little of her he hadn't bothered restraining her.

As Valen pressed the tip of his knife to Sybil's runes, Aslyn sprang to her feet and rushed up the dais steps. Her hand wrapped around Valen's throat as the other reached for the knife.

Too slow, though. She was too slow for him.

The knife sliced down her cheek, deep and agonizing. Aslyn cried out but still reached for the knife as she squeezed his throat.

"Stop!" Lux screamed.

But Aslyn realized too late that he wasn't shouting the command at her.

Sybil threw herself at Valen, screaming like a wild woman and knocking Aslyn to the floor. She tumbled down the steps. By the time she reached the bottom, Valen had Sybil's beautiful hair in his fist, her back arched over his lap and the knife poised at her throat.

"Settle down, darling," Valen said in an affectionate tone that in no way matched his actions. "Save something for later."

"Light and dark. Amber and sapphire." Sybil's words were soft, but Aslyn heard each one clearly. "The stormveil has been pierced." She closed her eyes. "He shall rise like the tides, born again of the storm, and in his wake, justice will roll down like water, and righteousness will follow like a mighty wave." Her eyes snapped open, and Aslyn swore she saw starlight in them. "Kill me and secure your fate."

Valen's breathing became labored, his already pale skin whitening even more. "Lies."

Sybil didn't flinch, her starlight eyes fixed on him and he stared down at her, transfixed. "Look into my eyes. See the truth."

Painfully long moments passed where no one moved. No one seemed to breathe.

In a flash, Valen shoved Sybil off his lap and snapped his upward palm closed.

Aslyn cried out silently as she heard the crack and snap of bones. Tears flooded her vision as she turned her attention to Lux Starkling's slumped form. His eyes remained open, chin against his chest, staring lifelessly at the floor.

J ust when Sybil thought her heart couldn't break any more, Valen forced her to watch as he tortured her father in a desperate attempt for answers about the runes in their dragon tattoos. But they had no answers. The marks simply were and always had been for every natural-born Starkling for hundreds of years. That answer hadn't been enough for Valen. Nothing was ever enough for him.

When Valen used her as a manipulation tactic against her father, Sybil's entire body trembled, recalling how he had carved her skin before. The cuts had only just healed, leaving scars behind, and she had no doubt he would try again and again until he found the answers he sought or accepted that they were nothing. Could she survive that long?

Watching the space around Valen warp with forbidden magic had curdled everything inside of Sybil.

Everything happened so fast after that. Aslyn attacked Valen. Sybil sense him preparing a magical strike that would either kill or seriously injure Aslyn, and Sybil had snapped. All the pain and betrayal and fury surged to the surface in a flurry of rage.

As Valen held her hostage in his lap, pulling on her hair, Sybil sensed something surging through her veins. It pulsed and warmed and then she *Saw*. Words spilled from her lips without conscious thought, as if some other power spoke through her. Sybil had no awareness of the words, only that they were spoken through her.

Hearing her father's neck snap had ripped her back into the present. Sybil couldn't breathe, couldn't think, couldn't move even as Valen discarded her like a useless weapon. Her eyes remained focused on her father slumped against the rank holding him up, at his lifeless gaze aimed at the floor.

Everything.

That was what she had told Valen she lost. But she hadn't. Not yet. Not until today.

Sybil had lost everything. Her mother. Her kingdom. Her brother. Her father. The empire had stolen everything from her.

The Jewel of Arithia guided Bast through the halls of the imperial palace. He didn't even question where it led him, trusting that it would steer him the correct way. Meanwhile, he killed any who crossed his path. Servants. Black Guards. Unfortunate merchants. Everybody between him and Aslyn was an enemy and he wouldn't waste his time differentiating innocent from guilty. As far as he was concerned, anyone walking these halls willingly was guilty of supporting the emperor.

The wrath pulsing through Bast's body didn't burn with hot anger. It was cold, detached. He would tear every stone in this palace to the ground to find Aslyn if that was what he had to do. Nothing would stop him.

Instead of leaving a trail of shadows in his wake to retrace his steps later, Bast left a trail of bodies. Knives flew in all directions on tendrils of shadows. The magic flowed through him like a tempest and he was the eye of the storm. Shadows crushed bones, snapped necks, crumpled armor so tight it killed instantly. Any who evaded his knives and slipped past his deadly shadows were swiftly cut down by Bast's black sword, the gray stone in the pommel pulsing with life.

He was wrath. He was death.

Bast paused at the throne room doors. The carvings on the doors glowed with magical light, highlighting Emperor Narcisse as he climbed to the peak of a mountain of bodies—human, elf, and dragon—hoisting his flag in victory. Some of the bodies still lived, bloodied and reaching up as if begging for mercy beneath the mound of the dead. At the base of the mountain of bodies, Black Guards moved ever so slightly, killing survivors.

But as Bast watched the mural, those movements stopped. Nothing in the carved mural moved. All froze as if waiting to see what Bast would do.

He snarled and stepped forward, wrapped in pure darkness from the shadows he had collected along the way.

Then he was on the other side of the door where a single Black Guard instantly died to his shadows, falling to the ground without a sound.

Before Aslyn could even gather her thoughts, Valen's vicious chuckle pierced her shock.

"After weeks hunting you down, you foolishly come right to me." He tapped his fingers against the arm of the throne. "I feel you out there," he growled. "These shadows are mine."

Shadows? Aslyn blinked back her tears, scooting away from the dais as she searched the shadows of the throne room for Blackblade. It had to be him Valen spoke to. She knew of no one else able to use shadow magic like him.

"Stolen power." Blackblade's deep voice echoed from one corner of the room.

Valen extracted the darkness from that corner to the dais with him. "No one has ever dared penetrate my home and lived."

"There's a first time for everything." This time the voice echoed from another corner.

Valen once more collected the darkness. It settled around him like a cloak of dark power.

Aslyn tensed as a thin wisp of shadows caressed her ankles. She watched as it retreated to the darkness near the throne, and the intent was clear. Subtly, she shifted toward that darkness.

"How glorious it will be to consume your raw power," Valen crooned. "I can sense it already, enticing, and so... delicious."

Chills rolled down Aslyn's arms. Consuming power... Was he actually... consuming magic like one would drink wine? Her gaze darted to Sybil. They couldn't leave her, but as their eyes met, Sybil gave a small shake of her head. *Leave me*, it said. *Run*. But Aslyn couldn't leave her there in his hands. She was all that remained of the Starkling line. The vision Sybil spoke of required Aethan. With him dead, there was no reason for Sybil to remain here.

The room exploded with shadows like a bomb, breaking pillars and shattering windows. Aslyn hurried to her feet and rushed toward where the shadows had directed her, praying her instincts were right and Blackblade was sending her a signal.

But she skidded to a halt as the darkness parted and she saw Blackblade behind Valen, his dagger piercing the emperor's heart. He snarled and twisted the blade, then ripped it out.

Valen didn't scream. But he also didn't slump in death. He simply... laughed.

Blackblade stumbled back in shock. It wore off quickly as he drew his sword and prepared for a fight.

Valen crouched over Sybil at his feet. He murmured something, then starlight exploded from Sybil's body. And to Aslyn's horror, as Sybil weakened and paled, inching toward death, Valen rolled his neck. The wound in his chest stitched shut before their eyes.

Blackblade skidded to Aslyn's side, snatching her hand and jerking her toward the exit. The doors to the throne room flew open at a tug of shadows. Aslyn jerked back, calling to Sybil, crying for her friend as Blackblade tightened his grip and pulled. She raced alongside him, watching Sybil slowly die over her shoulder.

Bast moved the moment Valen staggered, his grip tightening around Aslyn's wrist as he pulled her toward the massive doors at the end of the imperial throne room. But she resisted, crying for Sybil and slowing their escape. The air crackled with raw power behind them, but the emperor had yet to fully recover. If they were fast enough—if they could just get out before—

The doors slammed shut.

Shadow wraiths appeared around Sybil, and she vanished into darkness.

A surge of dark energy exploded through the chamber, throwing them both forward. Bast twisted midair, curling around Aslyn protectively and taking the brunt of the blast. Shadows slammed into him. Cold, slicing agony lashed across his back and arms. The impact drove him to his knees, his breath ripped from his lungs.

"Aslyn, stay back!" he rasped, shoving himself up. She shook her head, eyes wide, stunned but uninjured.

Bast climbed to his feet, stepping away from her. Fighting the emperor had never been part of the plan, and he wasn't even sure he *could* beat him. Not if a dagger to the heart hadn't worked.

Valen's laughter echoed, low and dark, as he straightened. The tails of his black coat became ribbons of darkness. It spilled from his hands. His eyes—once simply a cold black of imperial command—burned with abyssal darkness.

"Abomination," Bast breathed.

"You think to flee?" Valen sneered. "You, who *crawl* through my shadows like vermin?"

Bast didn't answer. Words were useless. *Keep yourself between him and Aslyn*, he thought.

He assumed a combat stance—sword in one hand and dagger in the other—ready to fight despite the pain burning in his body. The surrounding shadows stirred in response, whispering their hunger. But hunger for Valen's blood or his, he could no longer be sure.

Valen struck first. His sword materialized in his hand, a blade not of steel, but of pure hardened darkness. He attacked in a vicious arc, black energy coiling along the blade. Bast barely dodged and parried, rolling aside as the strike shattered the stone where he had stood. He came up with a sweep of his sword, narrowly deflecting the follow-up strike meant to cleave him in two.

Shadows lashed out, Valen's and Bast's colliding midair in a chaotic dance of darkness. As their shadows fought, the two men moved in a dance of blades. The throne room filled with the sharp ring of battle, each strike met with deadly precision. The gray stone in the sword pulsed brighter and brighter with each strike and parry, as if the impact brought the weapon to life in a way it never had before.

Valen's fingers curled, and the ground beneath Bast's feet convulsed. Jagged stone shot upward, clamping around his legs with crushing force. The trapped earth lost its color, becoming ashen and lifeless, as if something consumed all its vitality. Dark, forbidden, dangerous magic that even Bast didn't dare touch. He struggled against the clamps around his legs, shadows writhing around him, but the stone held firm.

Valen's grin widened, triumphant as he circled his kill.

"You don't even understand the weapon in your hand," Valen said.

Bast heard something similar before. The ambassador who attacked him at the inn spoke of the sword as well. He didn't have time to contemplate it, but there was no denying some form of magic pulsed in the weapon.

The stone tightened around Bast's legs, unyielding and ice cold. Valen's magic drained the very life from the ground, and Bast knew he had only moments before the emperor capitalized on his advantage. He summoned the surrounding shadows, forcing them to coil at his feet. With a sharp inhale, he willed them into the cracks of the stone, expanding them like roots through weakened earth. The rock splintered with a deafening crack. The terrible mosaic of Emperor Narcisse slaying his enemies broke, making the art unrecognizable. With one final wrench, Bast tore free, his boots scraping the ground.

As he stumbled forward, Valen's sword arced toward him, a killing stroke aimed for his exposed side. But before the blow could land, a clash of steel rang through the air. Aslyn had found the fallen Black Guard's sword and thrown herself between them, deflecting the strike with sheer desperation. Her arms trembled under the force, but she held firm, eyes blazing with determination. Seeing that light glowing in her eyes renewed Bast's strength.

Something powerful coiled around the two of them the moment she came to his defense. A formidable magic he could neither see nor understand. Yet Bast felt it like a flash of light tethering them. Then something snapped into place and fresh power surged through him.

Bast launched himself forward, blades flashing, meeting Valen's next attack head-on, forcing his steps back.

Valen was fast, his movements fueled by magic and fury. But Bast was faster. He wove between attacks, his knives slicing through the tendrils of darkness reaching for him, then using them to hasten his own attacks. He shifted like a wraith, his shadows shifting with him, striking where Valen's guard faltered.

Aslyn matched his pace, her strikes weaving seamlessly with his. Where Bast's blades carved through shadows, Aslyn's sword met steel, deflecting Valen's counters with precise, instinctive movements. He fought her once in Stormvalor, but this was different. Like something wild drove her onward with more skill than Bast knew she possessed. When she sparred with Starkling in Stormvalor, it had been a good match, but this... It was as if she and Bast had trained for this moment, their battle rhythm perfectly in sync. It was glorious, and she glowed in a way he had never seen before. Damn him if he didn't love it.

When Bast feinted left, Aslyn struck right; when Valen lashed out at her, Bast was already there, parrying the blow. Together, they pressed the attack, a relentless storm of steel and shadow.

Still, Valen did not falter. The emperor's strength was impossible. Every parry sent jolts through Bast's arms. The force behind every blow numbed his grip a little more each time. His breath came fast and sharp, but he did not give ground.

Valen's magic surged, the very air twisting.

A wave of black fire roared toward him. Bast barely had time to raise his arms and create a shield of shadows before it struck. Pain ripped through his nerves, shadows searing into his skin despite the shield. He stumbled.

"Aslyn—" he gasped, forcing himself to move, to stay between her and the storm of darkness.

Valen grinned. "You cannot protect her forever, Blackblade."

Bast's eyes met Aslyn's, and something passed between them that went beyond the need to help each other, or to survive. In fact, Bast couldn't put it into words, yet he knew what Aslyn would do next.

Bast spat blood and growled in response. "Who says she needs my protection?"

In a fit of desperation to save them both, Aslyn gripped the Black Guard sword tighter. Bast's worry for her eclipsed his pain as she lifted the weapon. Desperation, a *need* to help her, pulled at his bones until he swore he sensed a pull between the two of them. Seven Gods save him. She had never been more beautiful!

A brilliant light coiled up her arm, around him, and flared along her sword's length, illuminating the darkness like the sun piercing through the abyss.

Bast's hood slipped back, and he didn't dare allow even a second to pull it back up.

Valen's eyes bulged when he saw Bast. "Impossible!" Then the rage in his eyes turned feral. Bast could *feel* the magic surging in Valen like a colossal tidal wave aimed straight at him, determined to annihilate him.

Aslyn moved, her fear and anger visceral in Bast's own chest. With a cry, she swung, the blade cutting through Valen's shadowed form. The force of it sent him reeling, his magic unraveling as he staggered back, a raw, furious snarl tearing from his lips.

Before Valen could recover, Aslyn struck again with a battle cry so fierce it filled Bast with all new respect for this warrior princess. It ignited feelings long since dead in his chest as surely as fuel to a flame—feelings he never thought he would feel again. Then light exploded through the throne room like a righteous, mighty wave of power. Bast shielded his eyes from the blinding light. Aslyn's familiar hand slipped into his and she whispered the single command urgently.

"Run."

And he did, stumbling through the blinding light, trusting her to guide him as she had trusted him in the darkness.

CHAPTER 39

Reflections of Vanity

Aethan stepped out of the desert in a blink, entering a vast hall. His footsteps were soft against the smooth floor. He paused, taking in his new surroundings. Had he actually passed from one cavern to another, or was it an illusion created by the magic permeating this place? The walls seemed to stretch endlessly, reflecting the same opulent golden hues in repeating patterns. Polished stone walls and ceilings arched high above him. The floor beneath his feet was smooth, like marble, and there was no dust, no sign of age.

But it wasn't the walls that captured his attention.

It was the mirrors.

Everywhere he looked, large and small, ornate and simple, there were mirrors. Hundreds of them, maybe thousands, stretched across the room in an infinite maze of reflections. Each one displayed the chamber in its own way. Each replicated him in different ways. The reflections were perfect, unblemished, and in each one, Aethan saw himself not as he was, but as something more powerful, more regal, more invincible.

At first, nothing moved. Aethan stood there, his heartbeat steady but quickening as his eyes darted to each reflection. They mirrored him exactly: his pale blond hair, his sky-blue eyes, the gleam of Stormshard at his side. But then something shifted, a subtle change in the reflections.

He took a cautious step forward, and the mirrors shimmered.

Stormshard, hummed faintly at his side, its presence a steady reminder that he wasn't alone. Amid these mirrors, he felt a strange pull. It was as if each reflection beckoned him, calling him toward an image of himself that seemed more desirable than the last.

Each mirror showed him a different side, a different ideal, all pieces of his deepest desires on display—strength, honor, valor, glory... Aslyn. The allure of each reflection became stronger with every step he took through the room. Some part of him knew that if he just reached out, that version of him could manifest for real.

But then something shifted. In the far corner of the hall, a mirror seemed to glow with a softer inviting light. Aethan approached it cautiously, his fingers curling around the hilt of Stormshard, as if the sword too were uncertain of what lay ahead.

He turned only to see another mirror. The Aethan in this one was taller, more regal, draped in fine silks, adorned with battle-scarred armor, and wearing a gold and silver crown upon his head. His gaze was commanding, his presence overwhelming. He looked like a king, a conqueror. His armor gleamed with gold, and the light seemed to bend around him, flattering him in ways that made his chest swell with pride. He stood atop a mountain, surrounded by banners flying high in the wind, the cheers of countless followers ringing in his ears.

This is what I deserve, the thought echoed in his mind, unbidden. *This is what I was born for.*

Aethan gripped Stormshard's hilt tighter, the weight of the sword grounding him in reality.

His heart hammered in his chest. Power was a heavy burden. This reflection was an illusion.

Aethan recoiled, moving away from the reflection, but more mirrors came to life. A version where he had never been scarred by loss, one where he stood victorious on a battlefield with enemies at his feet and his queen at his side, and one where his face bore the deep lines of wisdom earned through years of hardship and study.

Are these reflections what I could be? he thought. For a moment, he felt the desire to reach for the image. But something deep inside urged him to move on.

When he turned away, an older, wiser Aethan Starkling stared back at him from another mirror, the weight of time settling into his features. His eyes held the quiet power of someone who had lived through the hardest battles, who had earned their place through suffering and sacrifice. He wore a crown of silver, his expression commanding and full of wisdom.

This is the man who leads with honor, Aethan thought, feeling the tug of that reflection. The man in the mirror was not just a warrior—he was a legend, a hero sung about in stories. *Perhaps this is the version of me that's destined to be, the man who overthrows the emperor and saves Aslyn's crown and kingdom.*

He couldn't help but stare, tempted toward this version of him, yearning for that future with Aslyn. But Novavito crowns were golden, not silver. This couldn't be his future with her. And if his future was not with her, he didn't want it, so he turned away.

The reflections became a chorus of voices. Each one seemed to promise him something more than he had now. Something better.

His hands trembled and doubt clouded his mind. The weight of all his choices pressed down on him, each vision a siren's call, each promise more tempting than the last. Sometimes he stood beside Aslyn, sometimes she stood beside him, and sometimes he stood alone.

Aethan stepped back, shaking his head, suddenly feeling unsettled.

When he turned a corner, Aethan's eyes fell on a flawless version of himself. The gods themselves seemed to have sculpted every detail. His armor was crafted from the finest metals, etched with symbols of the gods, each one representing a different power he had mastered. His hair shone golden, blazing like the sun. A brilliant, glowing sapphire light gleamed in his eyes, and he exuded an aura of absolute control, emanating a mix of power and charm. Aethan could *feel* the weight of respect from those around him, the silent admiration. He was more than a warrior—he was a leader of nations.

This Aethan was unassailable. Unbeatable. Every flaw, every imperfection, gone. He was everything he had ever dreamed of being and more.

For a moment, Aethan stood frozen, staring at the flawless image of himself. The mirror promised everything—power, respect, untold strength. He lifted a hand, noticing the golden crown he wore.

Aslyn...

Why did he wear her crown?

Stormshard vibrated with discomfort against his side. Aethan's heart skipped a beat, and he felt as if he had been snapped out of a spell.

The reflection before him was perfect, yes, but it felt... *wrong*. He could see it in the way the light danced off the armor, the way his eyes gleamed with too much certainty. This version of himself was a dream—a hollow, false promise of who he could be. And deep down, Aethan knew that the man he saw before him wasn't the man he truly was. He was a vision, a lie crafted to tempt him into abandoning everything that had shaped him into who he was. A lie tempting him to do what? Steal her throne? Where was Aslyn in all of this?

Stormshard buzzed again, its hum louder this time, as if urging him to reject the image. Aethan's breath caught in his throat. The sword seemed to burn with clarity now, its energy pushing against the false allure of perfection. Aethan stepped away from the mirror, his grip tightening around the hilt.

With one last glance at the perfect reflection, Aethan turned away. The temptation had been great. He had felt it deep in his bones. At that moment, Aethan realized he had to accept himself as he was—not as the image the mirrors offered. It was a harsh truth, but it was his truth.

He knew the path that had led him here, the promises he had made, the responsibility to his friends and the cause he believed in. He had made choices. He had to see them through. His path. His future. No reflection would dictate his choices.

Stormshard buzzed once more, this time with satisfaction as Aethan walked away, keeping his head down as he wandered through the maze of mirrors.

A familiar scent brushed his senses. Jasmine and roses. He paused, breath catching in his throat. Slowly, his eyes lifted from the floor as a new reflection appeared before him. But it wasn't another version of himself. No, this one was entirely different. The one thing he wanted above everything else.

Aslyn.

His heart lurched. She was more beautiful than he remembered, her silken hair falling in waves around her shoulders, her amber eyes shining with warmth and love. She smiled at him and Aethan nearly fell to his knees. Something about her presence, the way the light wrapped around her, felt so right. Like a piece of him that had been missing, waiting to be found.

"Aethan," she said, her voice a melody that seemed to echo in his very soul. "I knew you would come for me."

He swallowed, stepping forward instinctively, his chest tightening. The temptation to pull her into his arms was unbearable. Every step he took drew him closer to something he longed for. A life with *her*.

"I've missed you, my beautiful Stormvalor Champion," Aslyn said, her eyes never leaving his. "You've fought so hard. You've carried my burden for too long. You don't have to walk this path anymore. Let's go home and start planning the future we promised each other."

Her words were like a balm on his aching soul, soothing the painful parts of him that longed for her. He remembered their stolen moments together—their conversations in Stormvalor; the feel of her body against his; the way her laughter had made everything seem lighter.

He wanted that. He wanted *her*. It was the only thing he was certain about.

Aslyn stepped closer, her gaze soft, almost pleading. Her hand moved gently over her belly, her fingers tracing the curve in a slow, deliberate motion. Aethan's breath caught in his throat. His entire body froze. Her hand lingered over her swollen belly, and for the briefest moment, his world tilted.

"You and I can build that life we planned with our child, Aethan," she whispered, her voice filled with a quiet, undeniable certainty. "We can raise our family and be happy together at last. Just take my hand."

His mind raced. *Our child.* The weight of her words pressed down on him, filling him with a longing that made his chest ache. He could see it. A life with her. A life free of betrayal and murder. A life of warmth, of family, of love.

The images filled his mind like memories. Holding their child. The warmth of their home. Her glowing smile as they spent a lifetime together, raising their family.

He could *feel* it, the joy of simply *being* with her, of being the man he had always dreamed of becoming with her.

Aslyn reached out to him, her eyes steady and full of love. "Come to me, Aethan. You've given so much. Let me give you this. Let me give you peace."

His body moved on its own, reaching toward her, drawn to her in a way that he could not control. Every part of him screamed for him to take the step forward, to embrace this life, to escape the pain, the responsibility, the endless fight. She was right, wasn't she? Maybe he didn't have to fight anymore. All he needed was her.

Just as his fingers brushed against hers, something in the back of his mind screamed at him to stop, buzzing in his bones like a sharp warning. He froze, an abrupt breath escaping his lips.

This wasn't real.

It couldn't be.

Aslyn—his Aslyn—would want him to fight at her side for her crown. She would tell him to stay strong, to continue fighting, to become the king he was meant to be. He was Aethan, the leader. The one who promised his love, his life, to her cause. The one who led his friends through the Stormvalor battle. The one who faced his own death to save others. This was the path he'd chosen. He had made sacrifices that cost him so much. He couldn't take the simple path out now. There would be no shortcut to this future.

As much as the idea of family, of peace, called to him, he could not abandon everything he had fought for—everything *she* needed him to fight for. Seven gods willing, the peace and family would come after he was done.

The vision of Aslyn flickered for a moment, as the surrounding air grew hazy. His fingers twitched, withdrawing away from her, the pull of his own will battling the temptation.

"I'm sorry," he whispered to her, his voice cracking. "I can't."

Aslyn's smile faded, replaced by sorrow that broke his heart. Her hand dropped from her belly, and she stepped back. "Don't leave me alone with this child," she pleaded, her voice cracking.

Aethan's soul splintered at her desperate plea. But was she truly carrying his child? "I won't," he whispered. "I will find my way back to you."

"I'm right here," she cried. "Look at me."

Aethan shook his head and turned away.

"Please," Aslyn begged. "My king without a crown."

Aethan covered his ears and screamed in agony, falling to his knees. "No!"

"Aethan!" Aslyn cried for his attention.

In a surge of desperation, Aethan climbed to his feet and, with a fierce battle cry, he swung Stormshard through the air. The blade shattered the illusion mirror containing Aslyn's image. The mirrors all cracked, then shattered, raining down all around the vast chamber. Aethan heaved deep breaths, fighting for control of his emotions as tears streamed down his cheeks. By the time he regained control of himself and lifted his gaze from the broken mirrors littering the floor, a glittering golden door waited in front of him.

No more...

CHAPTER 40

Escape

The throne room of the imperial palace had grown thick with magic. Sybil was dragged into darkness at the back of the room, far from the dangers of the fight and out of sight to Aslyn and her companion. But Sybil still saw. And she trembled, watching shadows fight pure darkness—watching the shadow assassin fight the emperor in a way no one had ever done. No Black Guards entered the throne room, and Sybil couldn't help but wonder where they had all gone.

Every movement was like a twisting dance of shadow, and with each passing moment Sybil felt that magic pressing down on her will, stamping out any desire to fight back. No one had joined the emperor in the fight because he *willed* it so. No guard would come to his aid. No ambassadors. Not even Lady Fia. Valen somehow used sheer force of will to keep others away so he could fight this battle himself. The arrogance of it nearly made Sybil break into hysterical laughter.

Then light. Pure, radiant, blinding light.

Light and darkness.

When the light finally faded, Sybil slowly sat upright, watching Valen's pure terror. He lay on his back, face tilted to the side, eyes closed.

But his chest still rose and fell.

Whatever had just happened, it was the first time Sybil had ever heard of anyone besting the emperor. He would not forget it when he woke. He would tear the five kingdoms apart looking for Aslyn and her shadow guard.

The magic had broken the rack holding Sybil's father. She rose on shaking legs and hurried across the throne room to where he lay. Sybil fell to her knees at his side, leaning over him as tears spilled down her cheeks. Had she been wrong about everything? Had she misunderstood her *Sight*? For the empire to fall, for her father's dreams to become real, for her brother to rise, Sybil had to come here. That was what she *Saw*. That was what she thought.

But now, as she pulled her father's head into her lap and closed his eyes, she doubted her assertion. Her father had died believing in her. The guilt burrowed into her, devouring her as she stroked her father's cheek.

I'm sorry, father, Sybil thought as her tears dripped from her chin onto his cheeks. She tenderly brushed his hair from his face.

Sybil released a wail of grief, pulling her father closer, curling over him, weeping. It was her fault. If she hadn't forgotten, hadn't given in to Valen, her father wouldn't have died. *I am so, so sorry*.

She would never escape Valen. The only way out would be his destruction.

And it was coming. Sybil saw it in her visions rising against him like an ancient, unstoppable force. Sybil would ensure he didn't expect his demise.

That was the reason she was here. To be Valen's undoing. She had allowed herself to forget, to get consumed by him, and it had cost her everything.

But now, Sybil remembered.

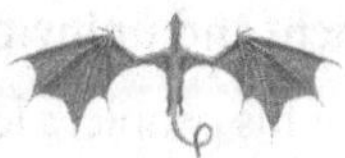

The scent of damp stone filled the passage, thick and cloying, as Prince Gannon led the last of the refugees deeper into the underground corridors. The walls pressed close, ancient, rough-hewn, and uneven, and the air held the stale weight of centuries. A torch flickered in his grip, its weak light casting jagged shadows over the weary faces trailing behind him.

The king had prepared for war, for a fight they both knew would come. But when the emperor reached their gates, they had underestimated his cleverness. They were ill-prepared for the emperor's forces despite it all.

He had failed everyone.

With every faltering step, the thought coiled around his mind like a serpent, hissing its accusations. The palace was lost. The city was lost. His father—gods, his father—was dead. Yet when his kingdom needed him the most, here he was, trudging through the dark, fleeing like a beaten dog with the remnants of a people who no longer belonged to him. He was no prince. He was no king. He was a coward.

A hand brushed his arm.

"We need to keep moving," Iskra murmured, her voice low but firm. Even here, surrounded by despair, she carried herself with an unshaken resolve, her eyes scanning the path ahead. Her unwavering presence was the only solid thing in his crumbling world.

Gannon nodded but said nothing. His throat was tight and words felt too heavy to force out. Not that he had the words to share. In a thousand years, Mordelic had not fallen to enemy forces. His ancestors held the throne proudly, unswervingly. *Until I came along...*

Behind them, the group shuffled forward, a mass of frightened nobles, wounded guards, and palace servants who had dared to follow a doomed prince into the unknown. Gannon glanced back at them, his gaze lingering on their hollow faces—at the way mothers clutched their children close, the way the men kept glancing behind them as if expecting death to come sprinting down the passage.

Wouldn't they be safer without me?

The thought struck hard, sudden, and uninvited. He had always been raised to believe that a prince was a shield for his people, a leader they could trust. But he had been no shield, and he had allowed his people, his kingdom, to fall into the hands of a tyrant. His one consolation was Lux Starkling's lie, claiming Gannon had burned in the courtyard fire. Was Lux still alive, or had Gannon failed him, as well?

If he left—if he simply vanished into the darkness—would these people have a better chance?

His fingers tightened around the torch, knuckles going white.

"You're thinking something foolish."

Gannon turned sharply. Iskra was watching him, her gaze like a blade cutting through the gloom.

He swallowed hard. "And if I am?"

"Then stop." Her voice carried no warmth, only certainty. "These people need you, Gannon. Whether you believe it or not, you are their king."

He looked away, jaw clenched. No. He was not their king. But arguing with her would be pointless. She likely would construct an argument to sway him and, right now, he just wanted to let this grief swallow him.

"We need a plan, Gannon," Iskra said urgently.

He gave no response. A plan? Right now, his plan was to put one foot in front of the other and dare the earth to consume him.

King Orrin's dead body, his lifeless gaze, flashed into Gannon's mind, consuming him. He gritted his teeth so hard they made audible noise.

Iskra once more laid a hand on his arm, urging him to stop, just for a moment.

But he couldn't stop. He would walk and walk until his boots wore out, until his feet bled, with only his failure as his companion.

She pulled more insistently. "My king!"

At that, Gannon froze. Every muscle in his body locked up and his sea-green eyes burned into Iskra. "I am no—"

"You are!" She straightened, and even with her hair disheveled and her dress dirty, she looked regal. More regal than he felt.

"Trystain—"

"Is a tyrant," she snapped.

He flinched. Trystain, his friend. His usurper. King killer. Gannon's throat tightened.

Behind them, Gannon heard the whimper of children and the shuffling of dozens of feet. How many followed him?

"He can put that crown on his head and claim the kingdom, but he is not the king. You are."

The lump in Gannon's throat grew. How could he explain it to her—to everyone? Trystain hadn't just stolen his crown. The emperor had placed it on his head through Lady Fia. Gannon was no king. Trystain had been his friend. Only he and Aethan were closer than he and Trystain. The betrayal ripped out his heart, hollowing him.

He didn't have it in him to argue with Iskra. He barely had the energy to continue walking.

"What do you suggest?" he asked, giving up the fight.

"We need an army," she said. "If we can make it to Arithia, we can reconnect with Aethan and Cavis, and ally with the princess. Then we can return and retake your—"

"Aethan is dead!" Gannon snapped. Iskra flinched and several others behind them whimpered at his outburst. But they needed to understand the situation they were in. "Executed in Arithia for treason. As for the princess, she has been missing ever since Stormvalor. If rumors are to be believed, she is in Umbr with Emperor Valen. No one is coming to our aid, Iskra. If you want to go searching for Cavis, be my guest. I won't keep you away from your betrothed. But know that if you remain with me, you must accept that we are alone. Completely alone."

His chest heaved with angry breaths. Tears brimmed Iskra's eyes and she shook her head, her lips fluttering for words, but nothing came out.

Behind them, guards gripped their weapons—not intending to use them, but for fear that they may have no choice. Sniffles and moans of sorrow whispered through the group.

They had to keep moving. He had to get these people somewhere safe.

Then he could disappear for good, a stain on Vorovesti history. The coward prince who vanished instead of fighting.

He lifted the torch higher and stomped forward.

"Let's go," he snapped.

Aslyn and Blackblade moved in complete silence through the palace. So much had happened in the past two days. Her world had changed. It overwhelmed her, and she couldn't snap back from the numbness in her soul. The only thing tethering her to any feeling were the roiling emotions rolling off Blackblade, palpable and devastating.

When they passed the doors to the artifact room, Aslyn stopped and entered the space. Blackblade released her hand as she stepped toward the armor of Queen Loralai. Aslyn eyed the armor but left it. She did not, however, leave the fine elfish sword. Aslyn dropped her Black Guard weapon in favor of the lighter and more balanced Shieldmaiden sword. Once it was secured to her belt, Aslyn turned to leave, startled to find Blackblade standing in front of King Quade's armor, his eyes distant. The tattered green cape slid through Blackblade's fingertips, then he brushed the golden rose clasp holding the cloak in place.

Aslyn didn't know what came next, but she knew she wouldn't survive it without him. It made that ache in her heart tear open again as she thought about just how much she needed him—how he deceived her and saved her.

"Let's go," Aslyn said softly, sliding her hand back into his.

Blackblade broke from his trance, blinking at Aslyn as if trying to remember who she was and where they were. It only lasted a few seconds, and when it passed, he returned to his usual stoney façade that did nothing to hinder the tempest of emotions she sensed inside of him.

They hurried from the artifact room, following a trail only he could sense, to the secret passage. No Black Guards crossed their paths—none living, anyway. Their dead bodies littered the palace floors. He had killed them all to get to her. Without a scratch. She marveled, staring at him sidelong as he guided their way.

They reached the corridor where Blackblade had fought off Lord Bloodstone. The man's body remained in the hall. Blackblade paused long enough to search him for anything of use, stripping off a couple daggers, discarding the sword, pocketing a purse of coins. The whole endeavor only took him a few seconds, then they were moving again.

Sybil. She vanished in that throne room. Valen somehow teleported her elsewhere to keep them from stealing her away. His own personal fountain of power. Just thinking about that made Aslyn's stomach twist with disgust.

She still couldn't understand how Valen had survived a knife to the heart, or the power he wielded so effortlessly.

"We have to go back for Sybil," she whispered, barely able to utter the words.

"If we do, we are all doomed," Blackblade said coldly, but Aslyn sensed his sorrow and regret. "It's her or all of us, because we won't defeat him like that again, and he won't let us take her from his side."

Aslyn knew it was true, but it only made all of her pain and loss worse. So much worse...

Because Sybil still breathed, and Aslyn couldn't raise a finger to help her.

I will be back for you, Aslyn thought. *I promise.*

Blackblade led the way through a narrow passage and out onto a very unstable and treacherous looking cliffside path. Aslyn hesitated at the doorway, staring into the abyss below. One wrong step and they would plummet to their death.

After a few steps, Blackblade stopped, looking back. His hood had fallen and his dark hair whipped in the breeze. For a moment he waited, worried, but Aslyn couldn't make her feet move. How much more could she suffer in a day?

With a small sigh, he retreated those few steps and reached his hand out to her, waiting for her to accept. Just as he had said he would do. He had only touched her twice without permission, both times to save her life.

Aslyn swallowed, then slid her hand into his and it was like grounding herself. It was the dangerous cliff or the wrathful emperor. She would take her chances.

As Blackblade guided her along the narrow path, Aslyn looked back at the doorway.

She left Sybil. What kind of nightmare had Aslyn abandoned her friend to? Regret churned in her stomach, and she nearly turned back. But she didn't know where Sybil was sent, or if she was even still in the palace. Aslyn couldn't go back.

Overhead, storm clouds gathered, spreading across the entire landscape as far as Aslyn could see. Thunder rumbled through the mountains.

"We need to move quickly, Aslyn," Blackblade said. "If it rains on this pass, we're doomed to slip and fall to our deaths." He pointed further down the pass. "It evens out down that way. If we can reach that part of the pass, we should be safe, but we can't stop moving." His eyes darted up to the sky as thunder boomed loud and hard enough to make her ears ring. The earth shook.

With a pulse of fear and a gentle tug at her hand, Blackblade led Aslyn along the cliffside path. The wind howled through the jagged peaks of the Umbr Mountains, tearing at Aslyn's cloak as she clung to Blackblade's hand. Both of them were bloodied from the fight. The narrow path beneath their feet was little more than a crumbling ledge, slick with moisture from the gathering storm. Far below, the dark valley stretched endlessly, a void that threatened to consume them with a single misstep.

The sky above them churned with restless clouds, deep gray streaked with flashes of light. The air was heavy with the scent of rain and the sharp bite of stone.

Blackblade moved ahead of her, his grip firm, his balance unwavering despite the treacherous terrain. He moved with a balance and grace Aslyn couldn't help but envy as her own feet stumbled and shifted uncertainly. Shadows clung to him even here, flickering at the edges of his form like living things. He didn't speak, but neither did he let go. That, more than anything, steadied Aslyn.

She exhaled slowly, forcing her focus onto each step on the rough-hewn rock beneath her boots. The wind tugged at her, testing her footing, but she would not fall. Not with Blackblade catching each slip of her feet with his shadows to steady her.

Another growl of thunder rolled through the peaks, louder and more ominous. Soon, the skies would open, and the path would become even more dangerous.

Aslyn glanced at Blackblade, his face carved in shadow and sharp angles, his steely eyes scanning the way ahead. He tightened his grip, a silent reassurance.

As they rounded the bend Blackblade indicated would lead them to the safety of the mountain pass, an endless light show joined the thunder in the clouds. Flashes strobed continually.

A storm was coming.

Chapter 41

And the Skies Answered

Gannon shielded his eyes from the bright afternoon light as he led the people out of the tunnels beneath the city and away from Mordelic. The sky was dismal and overcast, but somewhere beyond that, the sun still shined brighter than their torches in the tunnels.

Iskra raised a hand over her eyes like a shield as they adjusted. She said nothing since his outburst hours ago aside from a few reassurances to those in their party that all would be well.

Their hungry, dirty group of nobles, guards, and servants carried on without complaint, but Gannon heard all of their stomachs rumbling and he had no idea how to feed so many. He hadn't been trained for this kind of survival.

When they crested a hill, the group stopped beneath the shade of a small grouping of trees, collapsing to rest after hours of endless walking. They were hardly safe, but even Gannon needed time to breathe and assess the situation. His calves burned like they did after his morning run, and his feet were ready to rest.

All of them turned back, one-by-one, to stare toward Mordelic in the distance. They had come several miles through the night, so the city itself wasn't visible at this distance. Nevertheless, they looked.

Guards assumed their natural roles, circling the perimeter to ensure the people remained safe. But even the guards needed a chance to rest. Gannon admired their fortitude as he watched the senior most guard take natural command of the situation, assigning their meager group of guards to jobs. Scouts, hunters, foragers, guards. It wasn't much, perhaps a dozen guards in total versus three times as many citizens. How many of those citizens knew how to fight?

"It isn't farewell forever," Gannon said, unsure why he felt the need to speak the words. "It's simply a goodbye for now. We will return, revenge, and restore."

Every eye turned to him as he spoke.

One-by-one, they kneeled, swore fealty, and named him their king. While he appreciated their dedication and accepted their words, Gannon was no king. Not until he tore Trystain from his place and restored Vorovesti to its rightful order. Just like he promised these people.

They'd barely made camp when the sky began to die. Gannon could think of no other way to describe it as he stood on that hilltop, the wind tugging at his tattered coat, watching the heavens turn against them.

From the direction of the Umbr Mountains, a spiraling mass of darkness uncoiled like a leviathan in the clouds. It spread with slow, terrible grace. What daylight remained drained away until everything fell into darkness, drained of color, of warmth, of hope. Behind him, his people whispered prayers or stood frozen, eyes lifted toward the sky they no longer trusted. Children cried. A few people kneeled and prayed to the lost gods.

Gannon didn't speak. This felt like a prophecy fulfilled, like the fall of thrones wasn't the worst thing that could happen to the world, and perhaps it wasn't.

Then came the light—a sudden lance of brilliance that pierced the heart of the darkness. It burst upward and rippled outward, pushing the darkness back with a soundless wave of golden radiance. The world brightened—not fully, not truly, but enough to breathe again. Enough to *hope*.

No one spoke for several long minutes, dumbfounded by the display.

Until the earth thundered beneath them and a storm began.

It didn't come from one direction, but from *everywhere*. Thick gray clouds that bloomed to life before their eyes. Lightning scattered across the sky like cracks in shattered glass above them. Gannon stumbled back as thunder crashed so loud it seemed to split the earth. Trees swayed. Stones shifted. The ground *moaned*. It was as if the gods had heard the people's prayers—and answered them with wrath.

"Gods help us," Gannon muttered.

The trip north had taken weeks, and Roric did his best to put on a brave face in front of the two men escorting him, but he missed Lord Aethan. Every night as he closed his eyes beneath the endless night sky, Roric prayed to the lost gods to protect Lord Aethan and guide him to the glory he deserved—the glory that had been stripped away from him.

When they at last reached Lemheller Gap, the city was lively with excitement. Weylen had a hard time finding rooms for them at an inn with a nice enough stable for their horses. The city was cramped, buildings awkwardly squashed together and rising several stories, as if people continued building another floor every few years... and not always with what looked like the safest of construction. Roric hoped they wouldn't need to stay long.

They had one mission. Help Aslyn in whatever way she needed—escape, vengeance. It didn't matter. Roric would carry out Lord Aethan's orders.

All the way north, Weylen had sharpened his weapons every night and several times vowed to end Marek Bloodstone himself. The look in his eyes worried Roric. It worried Kern, too, but he said nothing about it.

Weylen marched over to them after checking in with the innkeeper, his face grim. "We're out of time already."

Kern frowned. "What is it?"

Weylen stepped close to them and lowered his voice. "The princess is marrying Bloodstone. Tomorrow."

Ice shot down Roric's spine. She wouldn't...

"At the imperial palace," Weylen finished, nodding toward the distant castle high in the mountains.

Kern cursed under his breath.

"There's no way she agreed to this marriage willingly," Weylen growled.

Yes, that had to be it. They were forcing her into it somehow. Roric couldn't imagine any other reason Aslyn would agree. She loved Lord Aethan.

Roric shifted the saddle bags with their dwindling supplies on his shoulder as he marched away from the stables with the other two.

That was when the sky started to darken unnaturally and *twist*. The horses stomped and whinnied in their stalls, their agitation growing with each second that passed.

Roric stared up and up, heart quickening. "Kern?" he called, but Kern and Weylen were already staring straight up at the strange storm of darkness.

Over the imperial palace, the clouds swirled into something *wrong*—like a whirlpool in the sky, spinning wider and wider, swallowing all light. Roric felt it in his stomach, the way you felt a fall just before it happened. Darkness fell and the birds went silent. *Everything* was silent. No one said a word as they were plunged into the darkest of nights only a little past midday.

Then the screaming started as panic took over the streets of Lemheller Gap.

"Get inside," Kern said, still staring up at the darkness. "Get inside!"

The trio broke into a sprint for the back door of the inn. Terror clenched Roric's heart in a way he never knew possible. This was the end of the world.

Then, like the world exhaling, a shaft of light burst upward into the heart of the darkness. It was blinding—pure—and it raced across the sky, chasing that darkness away. Roric shielded his eyes with his arm and squinted against it, gasping. For a breath, he felt something like *relief*. Maybe it was over.

But the quiet that followed wasn't peace. It was a *pause*.

Gray clouds sprang to life from nothing, followed by a flicker—then another—and then a thousand bolts of lightning forked across the sky at once, crackling in every direction as far as they could see. The ground shook beneath Roric's boots. The mountains groaned around them, and somewhere, a boulder cracked apart like an eggshell and tumbled from the mountains.

Roric dropped to his knees and prayed to the Seven Gods for mercy, then gazed up at Kern, wide-eyed. "Is this... the end of the world?"

Neither Kern nor Weylen answered. They looked utterly dumbfounded.

It was as the squires had whispered in Stormvalor.

The day the skies answered.

The Queen's Vow proved to be one of the finest remaining ships in the Arithian fleet. Cavis hadn't asked permission when he commandeered it for King Dorin's "mission". It was a fast ship, and they made good time, reaching the river bay half a day south of Mount Fjaroe in just a few days, where they docked to resupply before setting out again.

All day, the sea had been calm—eerily calm—for hours. The kind of stillness sailors didn't trust. Cavis stood at the prow, squinting toward the horizon while the wind coiled low against the sails. Somewhere behind him, Von joked with Cormic about their luck at avoiding storms, that it must be a good omen.

But Cavis didn't laugh. Something felt *wrong*.

Then he saw it.

A darkness bled from the northeast—from the mountains where the emperor reigned—and it was moving. Fast. Not a fog. Not even weather. But something worse. It stretched like ink in water, a spiraling whirl of darkness that consumed the sky faster than natural clouds ever could.

"Cormic," he called, his voice low laced with worry.

Cormic turned. Then froze, as did everyone else aboard the ship.

Day dimmed into a false night, and the ocean turned black as oil, reflecting *nothing* back at them. Cavis's heart beat like war drums in his ears. He gripped the rail hard enough to blanch his knuckles. Cormic and Von joined him, along with a handful of soldiers and sailors.

"The Nameless End," Von breathed, and the words made Cavis shudder.

And then the world cracked open and bled golden fire. The shadows recoiled. The darkness vanished.

No one spoke as the strange show ended. No one *moved*.

The world groaned, making Cavis's heart seize. That couldn't be good.

Lightning stitched itself across the sky in every direction. Cavis spun around toward where it had originated. To the south. The mast hummed. The ship moaned. Thunder hit like a hammer to the chest, and the ocean pitched suddenly, violently beneath them, rolling in vicious waves that had the sailors scrambling to keep the ship upright.

Cavis threw his arm around the rigging and shouted, "Hold fast!"

Cormic joined him, grinning like he was on some grand adventure and not about to be swallowed by the ocean waves. Saltwater crashed and sprayed over the deck.

And Von laughed, arms raised toward the stormy sky, leaning against a mast and only grabbing hold to steady his feet.

"I told you!" Von shouted above the storm, pure delight in his raised voice, laughing like a madman the whole time. "*I told you!*"

But it couldn't really be true. If it was...

Aethan survived. Cavis joined Von's laughter somewhat apprehensively, as if he didn't dare to hope—to pray—that Von was right.

That dangerous hope filled Cavis's lungs, and before he knew what he was doing, he called back to the ship's captain.

"Turn the ship south!"

If there was a chance Aethan survived, he would need them.

And Cavis would be there.

The view from the throne room of Novavito stretched wide—peaks upon peaks layered in mist and glory. Dorin had once loved that view, had thought it made him *look* like a king from so high up. Today, it made him feel small.

He adjusted the crown on his dark waves as he stared out the open space.

Umbogo strolled up behind Dorin, standing so close to Dorin's back that he could feel the warmth from Umbogo's body, smell that strange scent of earth and stone he had become familiar with.

"He won't kill you if you fail," Umbogo reassured him for the dozenth time since Lady Fia's warning. "He needs you."

"Does he?" Dorin couldn't help the doubt clawing at his mind. How many kings and queens had fallen to the whims of the imperial throne?

Umbogo stepped around Dorin, turning him to face Umbogo directly. His dark eyes pierced Dorin's soul. What did he see when he looked at Dorin? A king or an imposter? Depending on the day, Dorin felt like either. Today, he was not a king.

Umbogo's fingers grazed Dorin's neck, palm cupping his face as his thumb stroked Dorin's cheek. "What did I promise you?"

Dorin's eyes fluttered, pressing ever so slightly into the touch. "A long and powerful reign."

Umbogo edged closer. "And what did you promise me, my king?"

Dorin licked his lips, heart hammering. "Faith and trust."

"You know what these promises mean," Umbogo said gently. "I will continue to hold my end of the promise. But you must hold yours."

Their breaths mingled for a deliciously enticing moment before their lips met in a slow, intimate kiss. Dorin's heart had broken him when Ned married Dalma—when Ned refused another stolen night together because he and his wife had to focus on their marriage, on creating an heir. Ned had been his everything. The rejection created a bitter hole in Dorin that nothing could fill.

But Umbogo saw his true pain while everyone else seemed blind to it. And he saw Dorin's true *potential*. The stableman everyone thought Dorin loved was nothing to him but a deflection, because if his sister, his parents, had discovered who he truly desired, they would have kept the two apart. And Dorin would have moved heaven and earth for Umbogo.

When the kiss ended, still holding one another, Dorin opened his eyes...

... to darkness.

For a moment, all Dorin could see was Umbogo's face. He stepped back carefully, turning toward the towering open arches of the throne room and gazed out.

From far across the northern edge of the world, the horizon *darkened*.

Not clouds. Not dusk. A swirling black vortex rising, spreading from a distance. Dorin walked slowly to the window's edge. Umbogo trailed him, also staring at the strange darkness.

It spread unnaturally, swallowing light with intention. Dorin pressed a hand to the arching stone frame. "What is that?" he whispered.

But before Umbogo could answer, light burst—sharp, radiant, unearthly—like a blade piercing the heavens. It flared across the horizon in slow-moving waves, peeling the blackness back like a veil.

Umbogo murmured something under his breath.

For a moment, the world felt steady again, though neither of them spoke. Neither of them *moved*.

Then the palace shook. Dorin lost his balance and pitched forward, nearly tumbling off the edge of the palace into the waterfalls below until Umbogo wrapped an arm around him and hauled him back away from the edge—from his doom. They stumbled back away from the edge deeper into the throne room.

Then lightning came.

Not a single storm—*all storms*, everywhere, at once. Bolts cracked and scattered across the sky in all directions, coming from the south, away from the darkness and light. Thunder rolled through the mountains like an avalanche, once more shaking the high halls of Arithia's palace. One of the banners above the throne snapped from its post and fell like a torn wing.

Dorin stood frozen, heart racing. Was that an ill omen? "Bo?" he asked, his voice shaking, unable to look away from the storm.

"No..." Umbogo breathed the word more than he spoke it, his dark eyes widening in shock... then terror. "It can't be..."

"What?" Dorin demanded. "It can't be what?"

"We killed him," Umbogo said, as if pleading to the gods, fearing their wrath. "He *died*."

Terror seized Dorin as the storm brewed and shook the world. Then betrayal. Despite all Dorin had given him, done for him, Umbogo still kept secrets. What did Umbogo not tell him?

The sky was the color of old bruises when Trystain stepped onto the palace balcony with Fia. The air smelled strange—ozone and ash—and even the banners on the spires hung still, as though the wind itself had paused in dread.

He didn't notice the dark at first. He noticed the silence, like the city of Mordelic—the *world*—held its breath.

Darkness crept in, swallowing all light. It didn't come from above, but from the horizon, sweeping in tendrils like a great black tide spilling over the edges of the world. Trystain felt a hollowness in his chest as he watched, waited, as if all hope had been consumed by that darkness.

It spun in spirals, massive and swirling like the sky itself had cracked open to reveal a mouth behind it. The light fled. The city dimmed. People in the streets stopped and prayed.

Then the screams began. First from the southern part of Mordelic, sweeping up and over the entire city like the terror of a million people all calling out for mercy together. From the palace balcony, Trystain watched as citizens near the palace ran north, like they could outrun this creeping death. But he knew there would be no outrunning it.

Fia sauntered up beside him, eyes turned upward, not the least bit bothered by this terrifying display. If anything, she looked... delighted. A smile of satisfaction crept across her luscious lips, and she sighed.

"Finally."

Trystain frowned, but before he could question her, a column of pure golden light, fierce and blinding, shot into the heart of darkness. It rippled out like waves in water, pressing the darkness back and restoring something close to day. Trystain blinked hard until his vision adjusted to the sudden light.

Beside him, beautiful and fearsome and full of fury, Fia gripped the stone balustrade so tight her hands turned red. Then the stone melted beneath her grip and, for the first time, he truly feared her as rage burned like fire in her eyes. Those glorious lips curled into a feral snarl and the wrath poured off her like it could light the world on fire.

"What...?" It was all he could manage, stunned and terrified.

Fia drew in a deep breath, and when she released it, he swore he saw smoke rolling from her lungs. Trystain edged cautiously back from her. One step. Then another.

Her head snapped around to him, and her eyes burned like flame—actual, molten flame.

What are you? He thought in horror, stumbling another step back.

She swayed toward him, her red dress flickering with sparks. He blinked, thinking it had to be his imagination, until she drew close enough that it *singed* his overcoat.

The world trembled, saving him from her burning touch as she stumbled away from him as the world rocked. Then lightning *screamed* across the sky, everywhere all at once. Fia froze like someone had suddenly encased her in ice. The fire in her eyes winked out in an instant, widening in... terror.

What could scare her?

Trystain dared to turn his gaze away from her toward the storm. It was *everywhere*! Bolts snapped and shattered and laced the heavens. Thunder slammed the city like a giant's fist. The palace windows rattled. People screamed. Somewhere, bells rang as if sending a warning call.

Trystain turned to Fia, the fear in her eyes and the knowledge he knew she kept from him.

"What is happening?"

Her eyes shimmered, not only with fear but with tears. "He's coming."

"Who?"

"The beginning. The ending." She swallowed, and he noticed her trembling. "The retribution."

CHAPTER 42

Through the Veil

Aethan stumbled through the golden doorway, not even caring as it slammed shut behind him. He fell to his knees and curled over himself in agony, burying his face in his hands as he wept. Regret pooled in his stomach. He turned his back on Aslyn. He walked away from her. Even though he knew it wasn't real, that it wasn't her, Aethan couldn't hold back the regret. He turned his back on Aslyn and his child.

What nightmare was he fighting his way through? Aethan didn't even know if he was alive or dead, where he was, what was real, or if he could ever hope to find a way out of this place. If there was any way out. *I lived and died with strength, honor, and valor. Why am I being punished?*

Aethan kneeled on the cold, uneven ground, his breath ragged as he rasped for air. His limbs ached with exhaustion and the wounds in his arm, gut, and back burned with fierce intensity. But more than the exterior pain was a gnawing emptiness in his chest.

What did I do wrong to deserve such torture? If this is a test of the lost gods, I want no part.

The weight of the silence pressed down on him, suffocating him in a way that had nothing to do with the physical world. It was as though the very air around him conspired to keep him from moving, from finding an escape. He closed his eyes, but the darkness behind his lids felt deeper, more oppressive than the darkness around him.

How long have I been here? His mind screamed for an answer, but there was nothing. Only the cold. The silence. His heartbeat. *Why does my heart still beat?* Each thud seemed to echo louder in the void, as though the world itself might collapse with each beat. *Is this...* His thought trailed off. *Is this what death feels like?*

The sound of a low, distant rumble sent a shockwave through him. It was not quite a quake, but something powerful, something ancient. His heart skipped in his chest, and before he could process the sensation, the ground shook beneath him with greater force. Aethan braced himself instinctively as his situation snapped into focus.

From the shadows, a gleaming pair of large golden eyes fixed on him.

Aethan surged to his feet. He scrambled backward, heart pounding, instinctively reaching for the sword at his side. He hit jagged stone, making the wound in his back scream in agony. As he gripped the hilt, the sword shuddered.

Aethan scanned his surroundings, probing for an escape. The cave of stalagmites and stalactites closed tightly around him. He could barely move. The air of the cave grew thick and hot.

A growl, low and predatory, rumbled from deep within the darkness. Aethan's breath hitched as the shape loomed closer. It was huge. Impossibly huge. As it breathed in, dangerous light filled its massive chest.

Aethan's heart stopped as he identified the sapphire scales backlit by deadly breath brewing within it.

A dragon.

The sheer size of it crushed the air from his lungs as terror clawed at him. Aethan had only seen dragons in paintings. No dragon had been spotted since the War of Two Crowns over a thousand years ago. Yet there was no denying the deadly beast before him was a blue dragon.

Its claws scraped against the rocky floor, sending sparks flying. Its long, sinuous body twisted in the cramped space.

The cavern was too small for a dragon, let alone a dragon *and* a human.

If I'm not dead yet, I will be soon, he thought.

The dragon's jaws snapped at him with a speed he couldn't even follow. It was only blind, dumb luck that had him falling to the side, out of the dragon's deadly path. Survival instincts kicked in and Aethan pushed to his feet as the dragon slowly adjusted to find him in the small cave. Its hot, foul breath made the already warm cave unbearable. Sweat rolled down his temples.

A dragon. He swallowed as fear took root in his bones.

A growl of hunger rolled out of the beast. Aethan clutched his ears against the sound as it hammered into his skull.

He had to find a way out of here before the dragon made him dinner.

He scrambled around the wall, trembling, trying to keep away from the dragon's searching jaws and swishing tail as he sought for the exit. Darkness plunged in the cave once more as the light from the dragon's chest died away. But he could still hear it breathing, still feel its heat. Aethan's heart beat so hard and loud he was certain the beast could hear it as well.

Aethan slipped on something piled on the floor, and he fell forward. The sound rang loudly in his ears and he winced, holding his breath for a moment as he waited for the inevitable jaws of doom to close around him. It didn't come.

As he pushed himself up again, he felt the source of his fall. Bones. A pile of bones, likely the remains of the dragon's meals. A heap of lost souls who managed to get this far into the cavern only to become dragon fodder.

Aethan pulled Stormshard from the sheath, knowing he would have to fight his way out. When was the last time anyone fought a dragon and survived? His odds were not good. Aethan took a steadying breath to calm his racing heart.

The dragon's rumble made the bones beneath him bounce and shift. Aethan shifted his feet, digging his boots in to find stable ground. Light from the dragon's chest once more glowed, and he braced himself for the breath of death.

Too late, Aethan realized the dragon's open mouth was only inches from his skin. He thrust Stormshard up, hoping to impale the beast through the roof of its mouth. The sword pulled away, sending him staggering backward.

Aethan cursed and tried again, but the sword resisted. Fear once more took hold as he realized he had no way to fight the dragon if the sword would not permit him to swing.

The dragon sniffed at him, and he felt his hair ruffle from the force of its breath.

This is it, Aethan thought, limbs shaking. His sword refused to aid him and there would be no escaping the dragon's hungry attack this time. Not this close.

The dragon's body rose as it shifted, the tail slapping the wall and sending stalactites crumbling to the ground. Aethan ducked, covering himself with his arms.

As the dust settled, he heard a rattle. Aethan dared to peek. His eyes locked onto the heavy chains that bound the dragon's legs to the floor. Thick, iron links embedded into the rock itself, securing the creature in place. It was hungry—starving.

No wonder it wanted him for dinner. Cautiously, he peeled his arms back to find the dragon licking its dagger-like teeth. Its mouth alone was as large as his entire body.

Calm it. The thought hit him with a sudden clarity, though it felt out of place. Yet what choice did he have? He couldn't overpower it. He couldn't kill it.

"Hundreds of years ago," Aethan began as he slowly edged toward the chains, sword in hand. His voice quaked. The dragon watched him with one molten gold eye. "Humans and dragons were allies."

It blinked at him, snarling. He paused, holding his breath as he waited for the inevitable. But it didn't attack.

"We forged bonds with dragons as a gift from the gods," Aethan continued. For some reason, his voice held the dragon at bay... for the moment. That bolstered his confidence somewhat, and he gained poise with each word, each step. He edged close to the chains, gripping Stormshard in a white-knuckled fist and trying not to shake too violently. "But one by one, dragons were killed in the war against Emperor Narcisse, or they vanished when their riders perished." The chain was close. He would be within striking distance in a few more steps.

Aethan didn't know why the dragon was chained, nor why it couldn't break free. He didn't much care to question it. Freedom and mercy could be the only thing that saved him. And if the dragon knew a way out, he could follow.

The dragon's head turned toward him again, once more sniffing at him. Aethan paused as he waited to see what it would do. Nothing. He took another cautious step.

"The last dragon vanished with Justis, the God of War," Aethan said, his voice gentle, soothing. "Some believe the dragon still lives in the Isles of Storm, but none have ever returned after piercing the stormveil."

It lowered its head, studying him more closely. Studying the tattoo showing through his open shirt.

Aethan shuffled another step. "They say that the dragon guards great power. A power that could destroy the empire. A power that could restore balance to the world in the hands of Justis' chosen champion." Another step. "The Cavern of Lost Souls serves as ethereal home to the spirits of fallen great warriors." Another. "Mythos says that only he of indomitable spirit and unwavering heart untainted by hubris can unlock the dormant magic."

"And is that you?" a male voice asked in Aethan's mind. The dragon reared its head back, the light within glowing bright.

Aethan took a deep breath, his fingers still gripping Stormshard, but now with a different intent. *"That's not for me to decide,"* he replied in his mind.

He could feel the power within the sword. While the dragon pulled back, he dove toward the chains that bound the creature. He heard the growl of frustration in its voice—a sound that was almost human in its torment.

With a mighty heave, Aethan struck the chain with Stormshard, sending sparks flying. The dragon roared, the sound splitting his skull with pain. Instead of attacking, it paused, its head lowering as it regarded him. The air between them was charged, the chains rattling as if the creature, too, felt the shift.

For a moment, they both froze, regarding one another with caution. Neither attacked. Then the dragon turned its gaze away at the chain.

Emboldened, Aethan heaved at the chain again, and the sapphire stones on the cross guard glowed. Pure power raced down the blade with that strike, shattering the link tethering the dragon in place.

Aethan's breath was ragged.

The dragon inhaled deeply and heat filled the cavern. Aethan braced himself for the breath of death. He dipped his head away as blazing blue flame streamed over his shoulder, singeing his skin and burning the shoulder of his shirt. He gritted his teeth and screamed in pain.

When the heat at last ceased, Aethan dared to look up, afraid to see the damage to his shoulder. Nerves had burned away, numbing some of the pain.

The dragon stretched its neck as much as it could toward the stalactites on the ceiling. Gripping Stormshard like the only thing anchoring him to life, Aethan peered over his shoulder and gaped.

The dragon's breath had melted the stone, creating a doorway. The passage through the doorway rippled with blue magic like the door in the Stormvalor arena dungeons. Glancing back at the dragon as it drew in another deep breath, Aethan turned slowly toward the strange magical gateway. Perhaps this was his way out, or the way home.

The dragon breathed again, and the stalactites melted from the ceiling. The earth above them rumbled dangerously. Rock fell or dripped like liquid stone into the cavern. If Aethan lingered, it would crush him.

Hoping to escape before that happened, Aethan darted through the shimmering veil of magic even as the cavern roof gave way.

The air on the other side was heavy with energy unlike anything he had ever felt. A haze of vibrant, pulsating colors, bleeding into one another, warped and twisted the world around him. The very fabric of the air hummed with raw, untamed power, an ancient force beyond comprehension.

Pain coursed through Aethan's body, like a thousand knives being driven into his flesh all at once. Aethan opened his mouth to scream, but no sound came out. His muscles shrieked. His bones groaned in agony. But the worst of it was the magic tearing into his soul, ripping him apart. It wasn't just physical pain. No, Aethan was certain the very essence of his being was unraveling.

Aethan's vision blurred as the magic attacked him, each pulse of power spinning around him, through him, sending waves of excruciating heat through his chest, like molten iron flooding his veins. His limbs locked, back arched, and for a moment, Aethan thought he might be consumed by the energy surrounding him. Breathing became a battle. Aethan's heartbeat spiked, then slowed, up and down until he was certain one more rise or fall would be his last.

The sky above, if it could be called that, churned with swirling clouds of color and crackling lightning. The air was alive with a thousand whispers, voices lost in time, speaking of things Aethan couldn't comprehend. Every whisper, every sound, every flash of lightning cut straight through him like a blade to his soul. His lungs. His mind. His muscles. His bones. His heart.

When he could take no more, Aethan dropped to his knees, trying desperately to hold on to his consciousness as the magic ripped him apart and put him back together again, breaking him, rearranging him. The pain—the *torture*—was unbearable. His body couldn't withstand the overwhelming tide of energy, the sheer power that surged through him, against him.

His vision wavered as the ground beneath him pulsed, then shifted with a life of its own, threatening to consume him.

Aethan was no longer certain if he breathed, or if his heart beat. He could no longer see anything but power and light. He could no longer feel anything but burning agony. The magic tore through his flesh, through his thoughts, dragging him closer to the edge of oblivion.

"Give in or give up." A voice, deep and ancient, boomed in his mind, shaking the very foundation of his existence. It was a voice that carried the weight of centuries, the power of storms, the fury of nature itself.

Aethan's heart thudded again in his chest as he surrendered to the power.

The thump of his heartbeat grew weaker. The power peeled his skin away, layer by layer, unraveling him at the seams. It was too much. The world tilted. Rock and earth rained down on him. His vision faded into eternal darkness.

A single word pulsed through him, shocking him back to life. The pain intensified, but now it was *different*. A spark had been ignited within him, a beacon in the center of the storm.

"Stormborn."

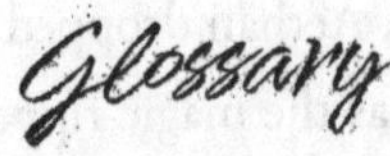

NOVAVITO

Aslyn Kiernan *(Arithia)* – Crown Princess

Cavis Dysart *(Arithia)* – Stormvalor competitor & noble

Cormic Dysart *(Arithia)* – Stormvalor competitor & noble

Dorin Kiernan *(Arithia)* – prince

Elisio *(Arithia)* – Aslyn's former guard/lover

Giata Kiernan *(Arithia)* – queen

Javon Nadier *(Arithia)* – king's advisor/banker

Kaiti *(Arithia)* – Aslyn's maid

Novin Kiernan *(Arithia)* – king

Shino *(Arithia)* – Captain of the Royal Guard

Umbogo *(Citadel)* – emperor's ambassador

VOROVESTI

Aethan Starkling *(Mordelic)* – king's nephew & Stormvalor competitor

Borin *(Mordelic)* – Stormvalor competitor

Calvin *(Mordelic)* – Stormvalor competitor

Gannon *(Mordelic)* – Crown Prince

Iskra Pridell *(Mordelic)* – noble

Lux Starkling *(Stormvalor)* – Lord of Stormvalor

Olivya Starkling *(Stormvalor)* – princess/married to Lux

Orrin *(Mordelic)* – king

Roric al'Mar *(Stormvalor)* – Aethan's squire

Sybil Starkling *(Mordelic)* – king's niece; Aethan's sister

Trystain Cyrus *(Mordelic)* – noble & Stormvalor competitor

Zambuul *(Citadel)* – emperor's ambassador

ELPISIO

Gorim *(Elysia)* – Stormvalor competitor

Qin *(Bleakburn)* – Stormvalor competitor

Von Huntsman *(Elysia)* – Stormvalor competitor

Yun *(Elysia)* – Stormvalor competitor

OSHON

Henric *(Lago)* – Stormvalor competitor

Kern *(Lago)* – Stormvalor competitor

Ryker *(Lago)* – Stormvalor competitor

Weylen *(Lago)* – Stormvalor competitor

UMBR

Emperor Narcisse Strong *(Mordelic)* – First Ruler of the Five Kingdoms of Divica

Emperor Oxon *(Umbr)* – previous ruler of the Five Kingdoms of Divica

Emperor Valen *(Umbr)* – ruler of the Five Kingdoms of Divica

Bryse *(Lemheller Gap)* – Stormvalor competitor

Fia *(Umbr)* – emperor's chief advisor

Lady Bloodstone *(Lemheller Gap)* – noble; Marek's mother

Lund Bloodstone *(Lemheller Gap)* – noble; emperor's military advisor; Marek's father

Marek Bloodstone *(Lemheller Gap)* – noble; Stormvalor competitor

Porrige *(Port Verix)* – innkeeper of Loam and Fiddle

HISTORICAL NAMES & LOCATIONS

Kieta the Strong *(Mordelic)* – noble turned legendary warrior; first dragon rider

Lemhaldruun – former metropolis during the War of Two Crowns; now lost

Loralai a'Malik *(Kruos)* – Kruos elf princess; married to Quade Martnarving

Malik *(Kruos)* – Kruos elf king

Malikai *(Kruos)* – Kruos elf Crown Prince

Quade Martnarving *(Arithia)* – king of Novavito during the War of Two Crowns

Sil *(Kruos)* – Kruos Shieldmaiden

Solfia *(Goka-atun)* – Tiberis's wife; hails from Sarak across the ocean

Tiberis Strong *(Mordelic)* – king of Vorovesti during the War of Two Crowns; Narcisse's younger brother

Vanna Strong *(Mordelic)* – queen of Vorovesti during the War of Two Crowns; Tiberis's second wife from Mordelic

Acknowledgements

Aethan Starkling is the very first character I ever created. While I had some clue all those years ago where his path might lead him, I don't think either of us fully understood where he was headed at the time. He will always hold a very special place in my heart, as all firsts do. But Aethan isn't the only one I created all those years ago. Several others joined his cast not long after I dreamed him up. Bast came next. He had a different name at the time (Dayen), but after writing my historical fiction where one of the main characters was (historically) named Dayan, I thought that might be too confusing for my loyal readers. So Dayen became Bast, but the heart of his character is much the same. Next came Sybil and Lux (both of whom also had different names at the time) to help flesh out Aethan's family background. Aslyn and her brother Dorin were next, a balance of light and dark.

And, of course, the First Emperor Narcisse. What's a hero without a villain? Though his story goes further back in the world, his roots remain the same. If you want to learn more about Narcisse and his brother Tiberis, I recommend reading the prequel novellas, *War of Two Crowns*. And more dragon action is coming... I promise!

The Stormborn army is growing! I am so blessed to have so many amazing people in my life to help make these books possible. Grifynn, who listens to me ramble even if he doesn't much care to read the books mom writes. Ty, my crazy beautiful child. You make the best assistant and sounding board. I truly value everything you bring to the table as I continue on this journey. Tazz, you stole my heart and helped me find my soul. I adore you more than you realize. Thank you for your patience with the mess of book boxes in our house, but mostly, thank you for giving me the time and space to pursue this crazy dream. To my parents, sister, and other family members who continue to encourage me and support me, whether with kind words or by spreading the word about my books, thank you for believing in me.

To Chloe, Jennifer, Kory, Ashley, Sylvia, and Kevin, you are the best beta readers I could ask for! I appreciate your enthusiasm for this series, your candid comments, your brilliant insights, but mostly, for the time you set aside to help me make this the best series it can possibly be. Your heart and soul are in this book just as surely as my own. Roxanne, your editorial insights and dedication to finding all the mistakes I was sure didn't exist, I couldn't have done this without you. To my ARCs, who are too many to list, I can't thank you enough for your earnest enthusiasm for this series! It bolsters my confidence to read your beautiful reviews.

And let's all take a moment to appreciate the growing team of artists who have brought these characters to life. Kateryna, who stunning cover art brought me to tears when I laid eyes on fully rendered art, I am so happy I chose you! The award you won for your *Stormvalor* art is so well deserved! Therena, who breathed first life into the visual renderings of Aethan, Aslyn, and Bast, I adore everything you do, and how you go above and beyond by joining the ARC team and leaving such a glowing review for *Stormvalor*. I sincerely hope you love *Stormveil* just as much! TL Combs, you took my somewhat messy notes about Sybil and Valen and created something truly beautiful. Mu'sab, I appreciate your patience as I asked for more and more alterations on the dragon. I fear I gave you an impossible task and you rose to the occasion. And Jan... Wow! I sent you the art I had from Aslyn, Bast, and Valen, told you about the battle, and you created a piece that stopped my heart when I first saw it! I appreciate you all.

And don't think I've forgotten about the bulk of the Stormborn army... you. Each and every one of you reading this series are so amazing for taking a chance on me. I will do my best not to let you down! Thank you, thank you, thank you!

About Starr Z. Davies

STARR Z. DAVIES is an award-winning author of over 20 tales that span dystopian realms, epic fantasies, and echoes of forgotten histories. Dubbed the "Character Assassin," she weaves stories where heroes are tested by fire—both emotional and physical.

From her woodland home in northern Wisconsin, she crafts worlds while surrounded by her greatest allies: a supportive husband, two imaginative children, and a curious menagerie of robotic pets. When not conjuring new adventures, she dabbles in home enchantments, swims like a siren, battles through video game quests, and devours books like ancient tomes of power.

If you want to become friends with Starr, dark chocolate, Doctor Who, Parks & Rec, The Office, and the MCU are all fantastic ways into her heart. That or a love for fantasy books by indie authors.

Learn more about Starr and her books.

Keep up with Starr by signing up for her newsletter.